Her dreams are WILD!

Her imagination is MAGICAL!

And her whiskers are always a MESS!

Welcome to . . .

THE BIG ADVENTURES OF BABYMOUSE

HEY! THAT'S ME!

OOOH! THIS BOOK LOOKS GOOD. I CAN'T WAIT TO READ IT!

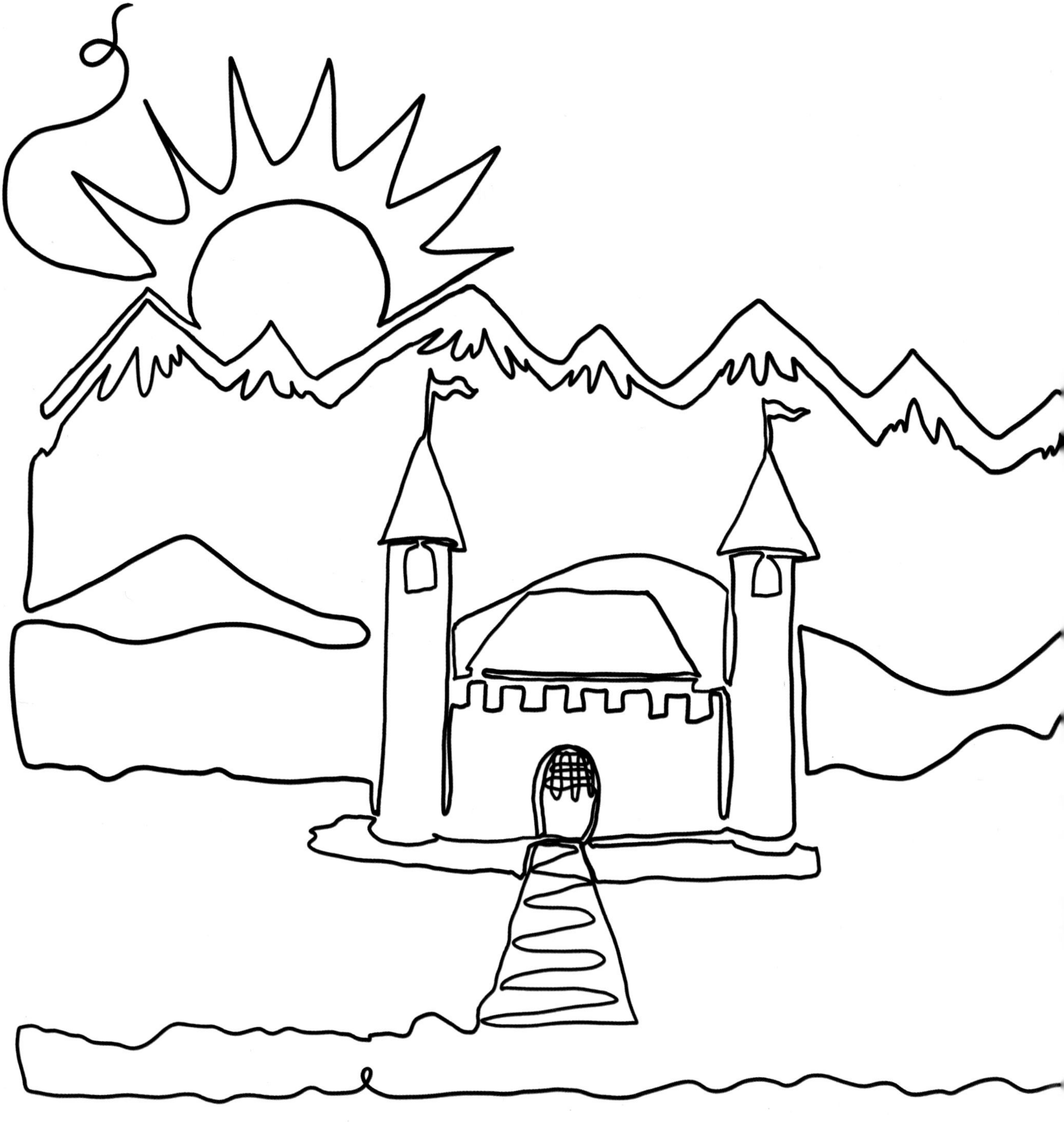

THE BIG ADVENTURES OF BABYMOUSE

ONCE UPON A MESSY WHISKER

JENNIFER L. HOLM & MATTHEW HOLM

Random House New York

Copyright © 2022 by Jennifer L. Holm and Matthew Holm

All rights reserved. Published in the United States by Random House Children's Books, a division of Penguin Random House LLC, New York.

Random House and the colophon are registered trademarks of Penguin Random House LLC.

Visit us on the Web! **rhcbooks.com**

Educators and librarians, for a variety of teaching tools, visit us at **RHTeachersLibrarians.com**

Library of Congress Cataloging-in-Publication Data is available upon request.
ISBN 978-0-593-43090-3 (trade) — ISBN 978-0-593-43091-0 (lib. bdg.)
ISBN 978-0-593-43093-4 (trade pbk.) — ISBN 978-0-593-43092-7 (ebook)

MANUFACTURED IN CHINA

10 9 8 7 6 5 4 3 2 1

First Edition

For Teri Lesesne

PART ONE

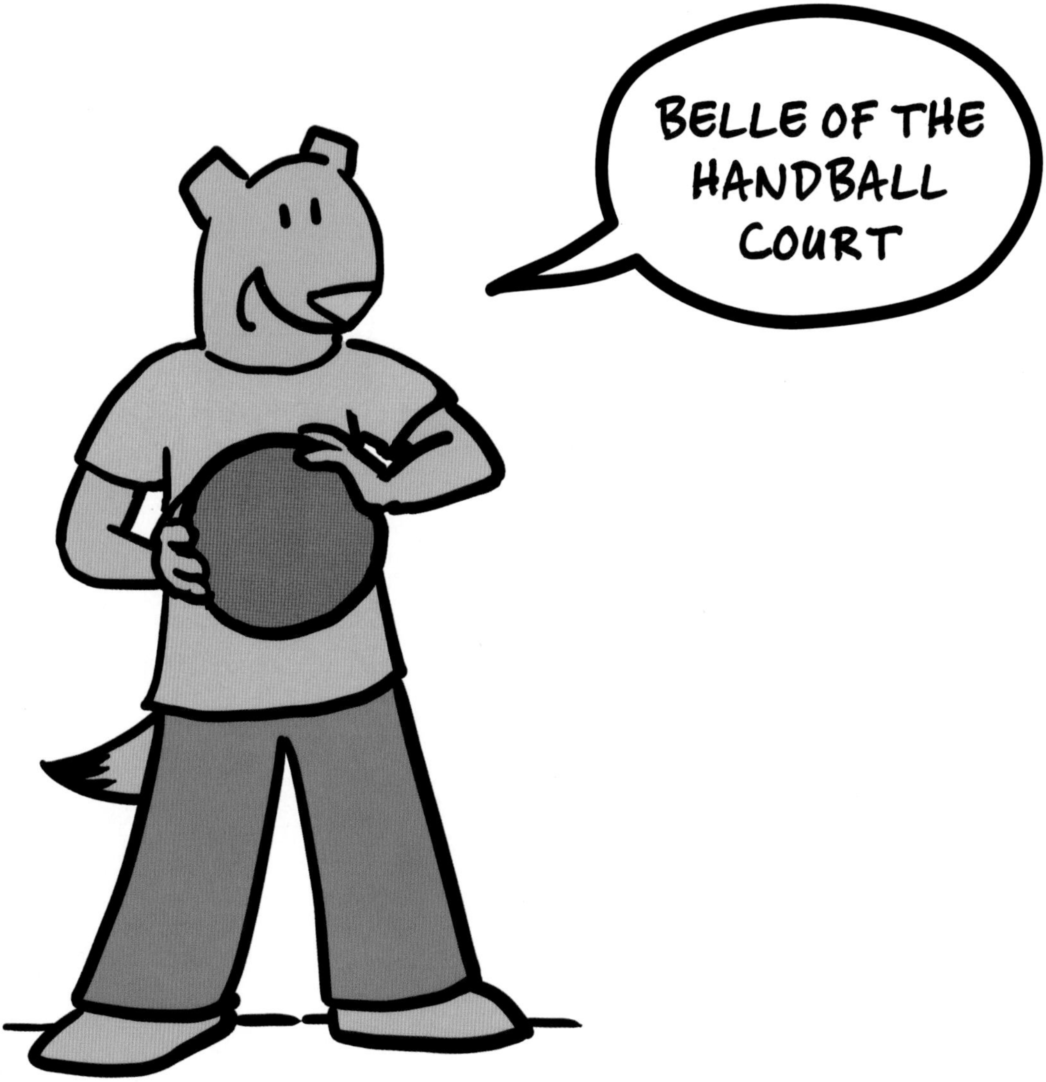
BELLE OF THE HANDBALL COURT

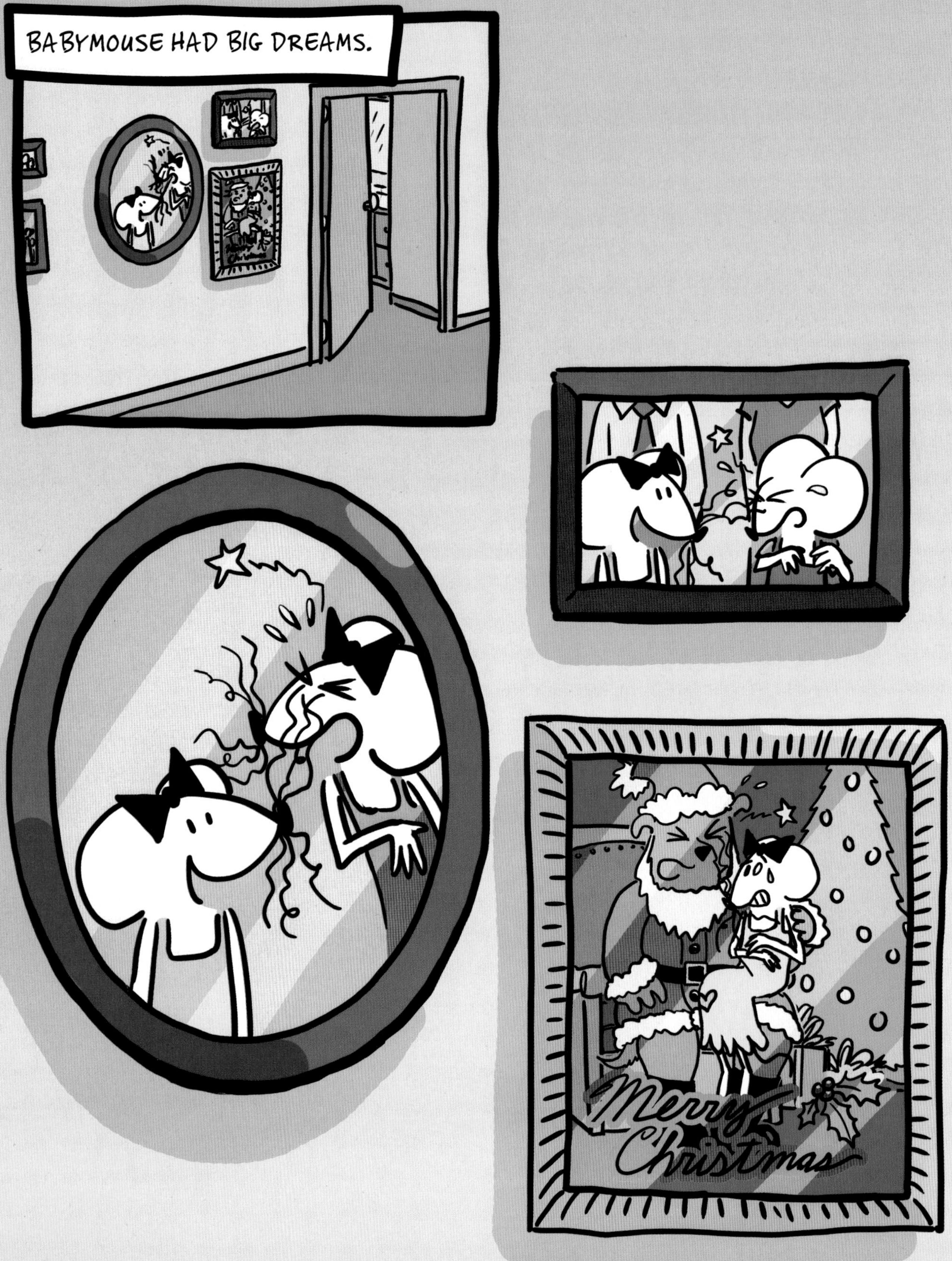
BABYMOUSE HAD BIG DREAMS.
Merry Christmas

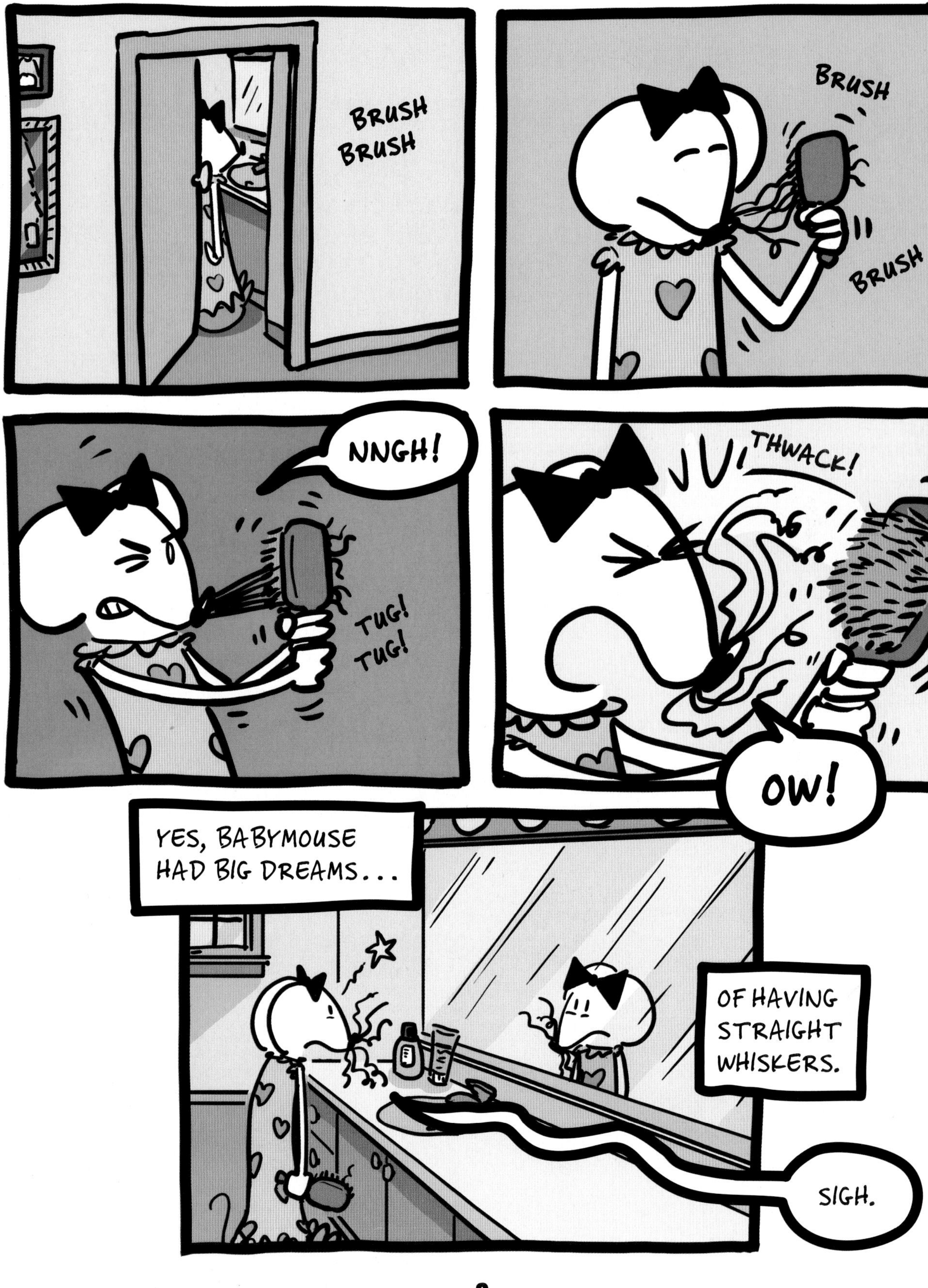
BRUSH
BRUSH
BRUSH
BRUSH
NNGH!
TUG!
TUG!
THWACK!
OW!
YES, BABYMOUSE HAD BIG DREAMS...
OF HAVING STRAIGHT WHISKERS.
SIGH.

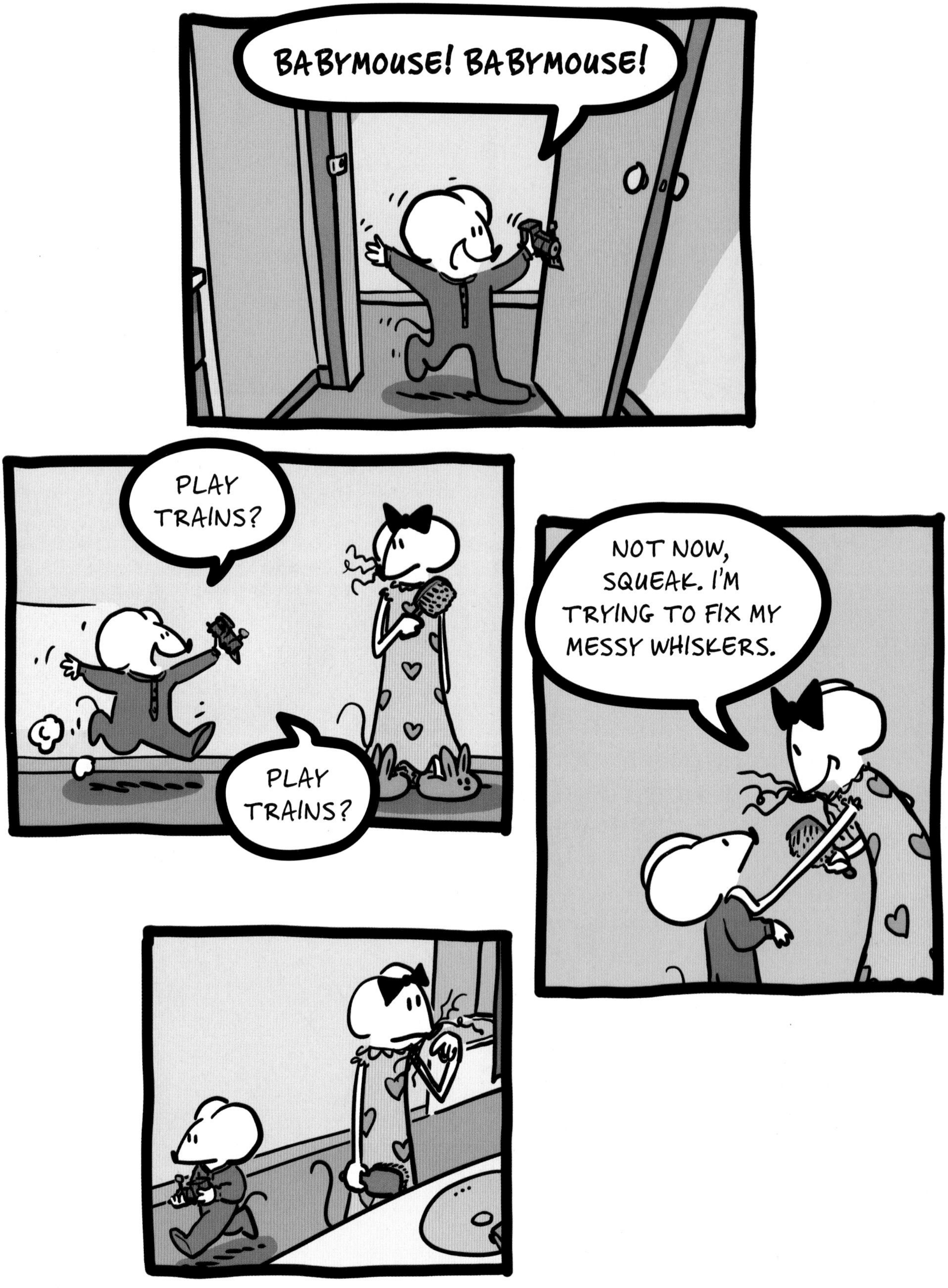
BABYMOUSE! BABYMOUSE!
PLAY TRAINS?
PLAY TRAINS?
NOT NOW, SQUEAK. I'M TRYING TO FIX MY MESSY WHISKERS.

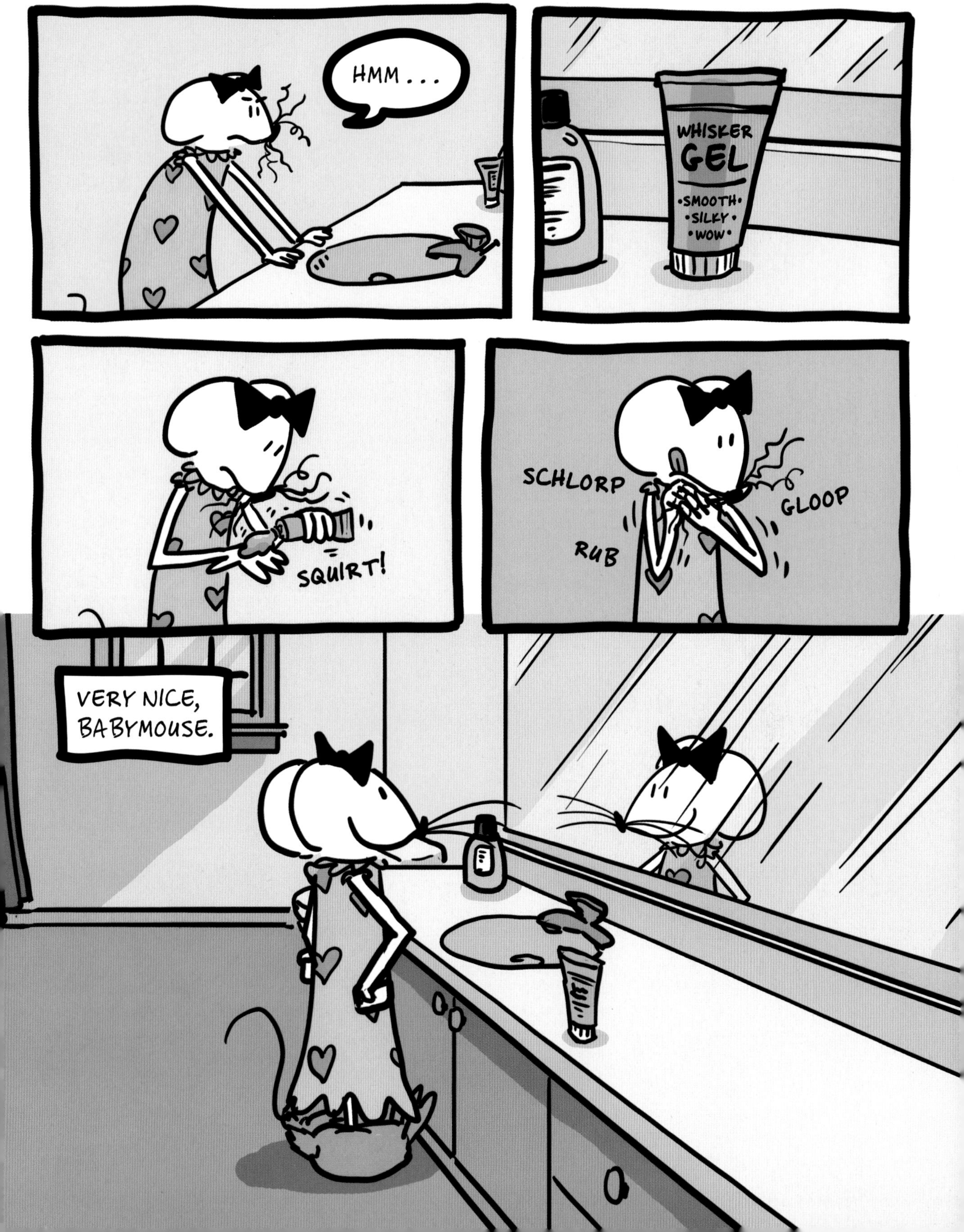
HMM . . .
WHISKER GEL
•SMOOTH•
•SILKY•
•WOW•
SQUIRT!
SCHLORP
GLOOP
RUB
VERY NICE, BABYMOUSE.

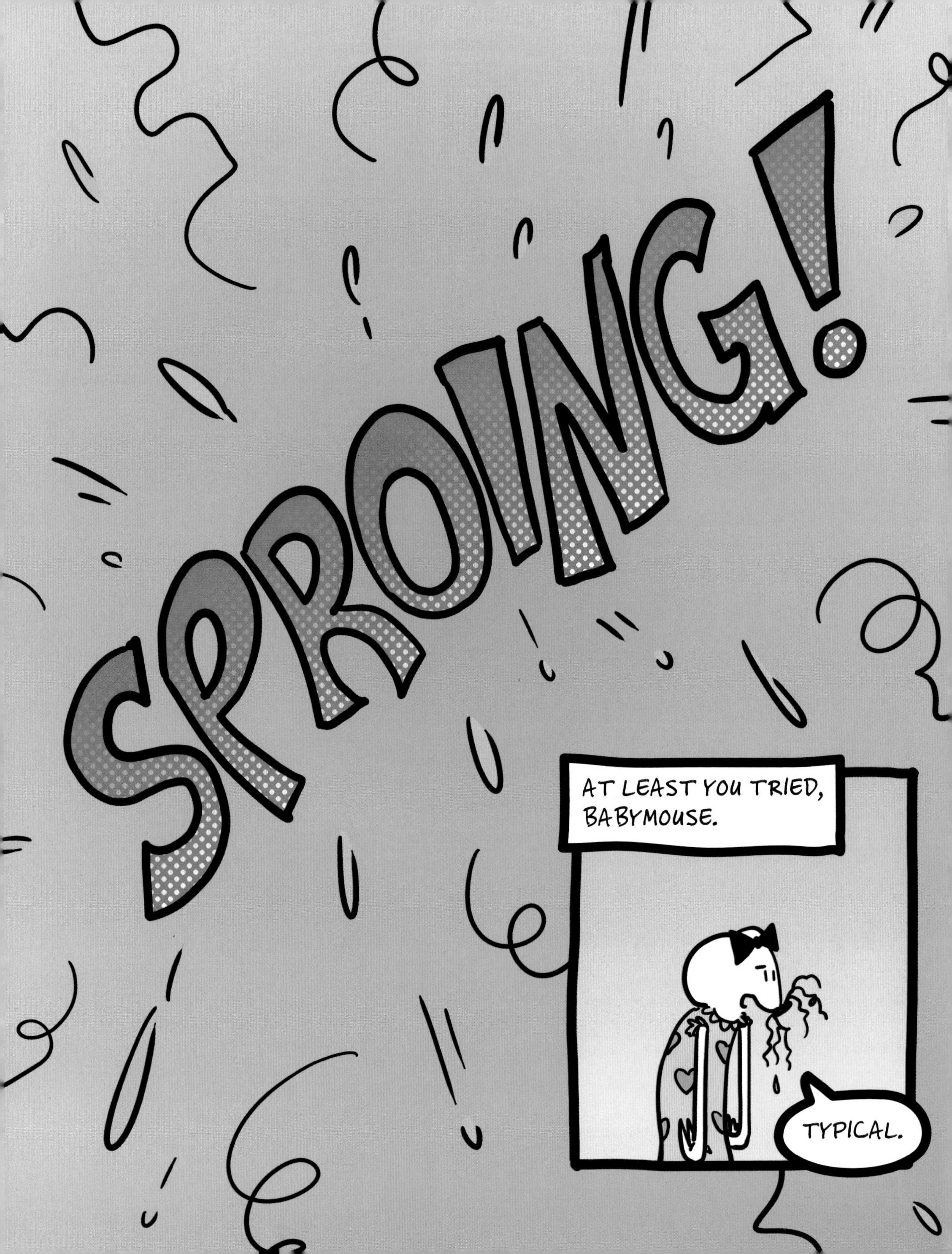
SPROING!
AT LEAST YOU TRIED, BABYMOUSE.
TYPICAL.

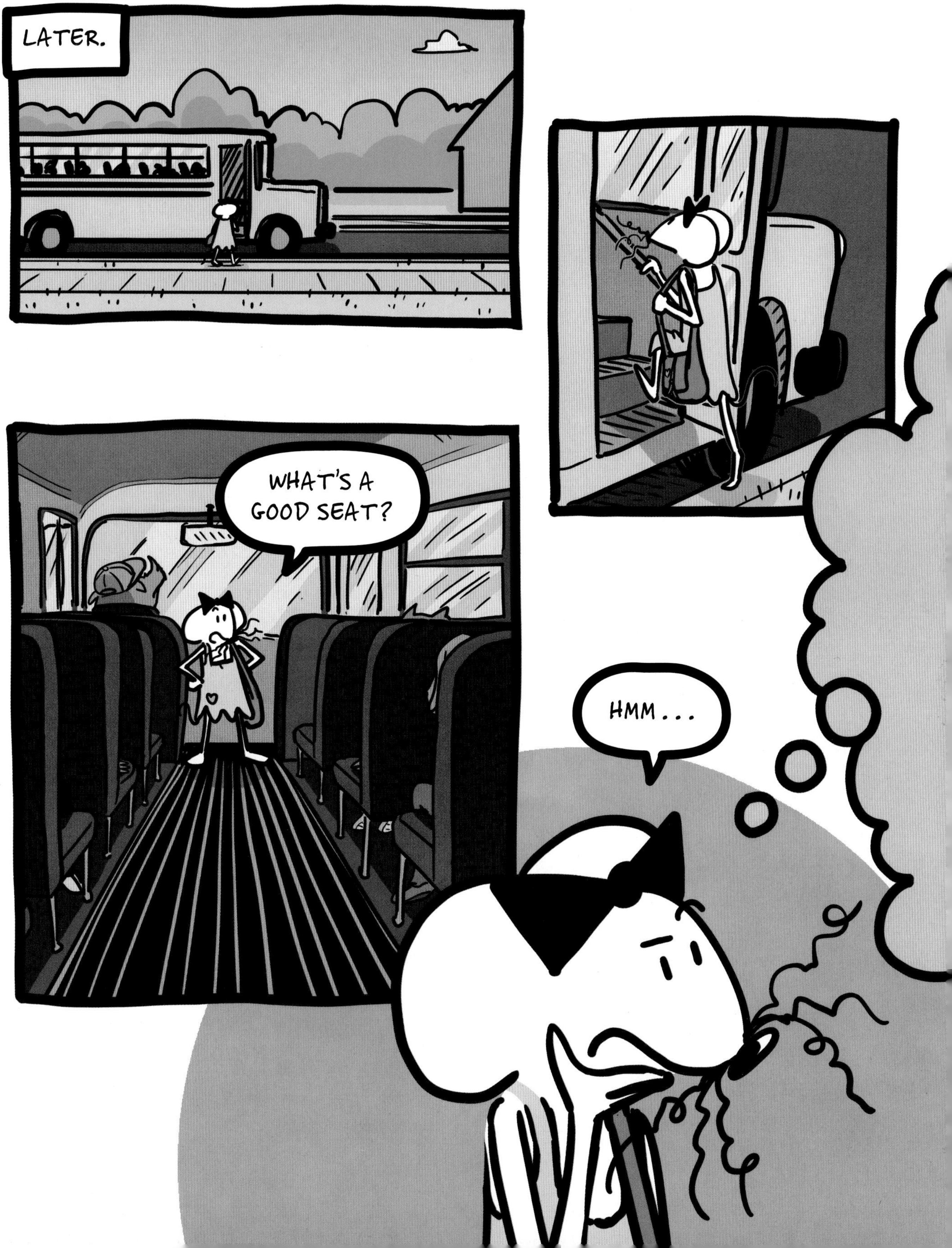
LATER.
WHAT'S A GOOD SEAT?
HMM . . .

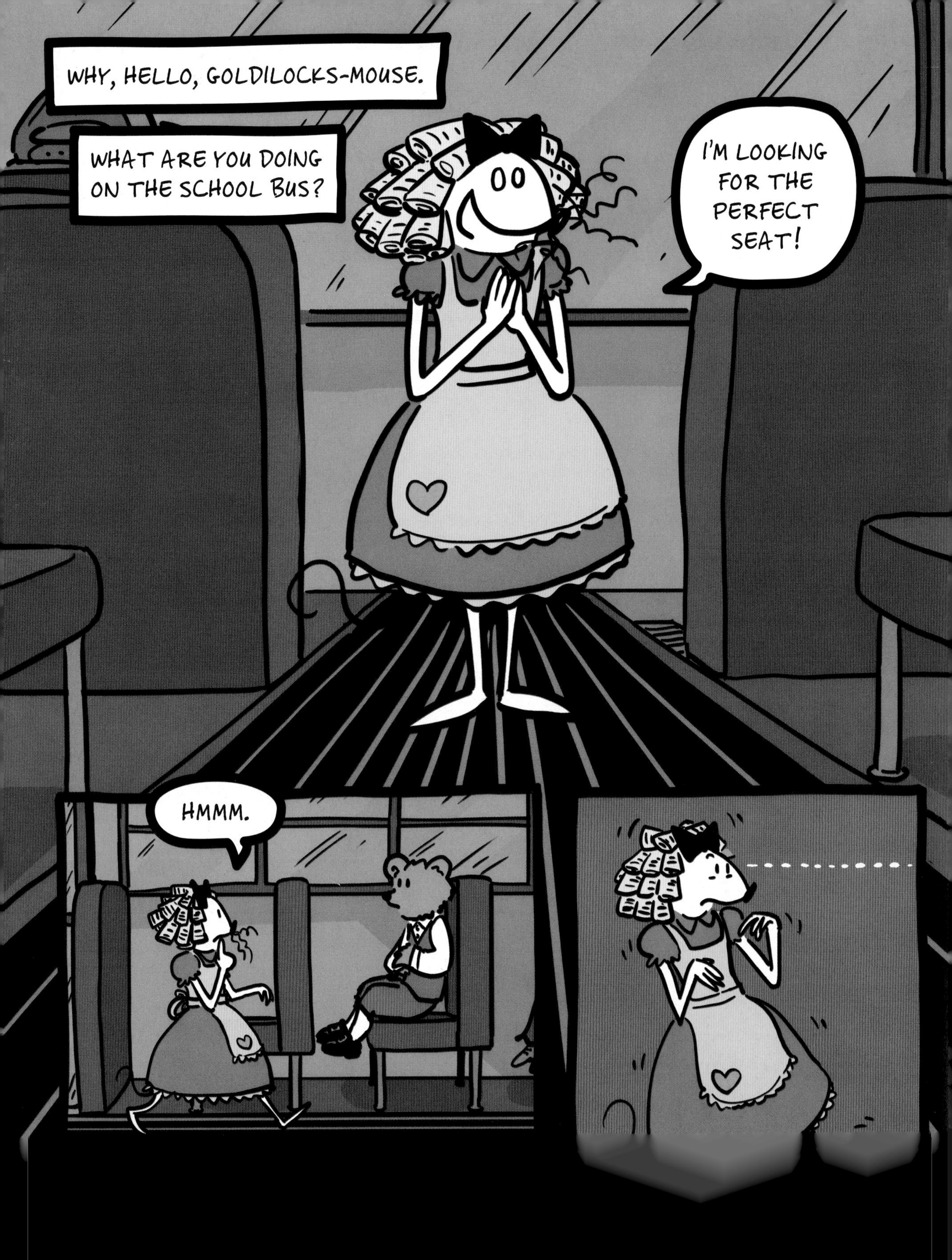

WHY, HELLO, GOLDILOCKS-MOUSE.
WHAT ARE YOU DOING ON THE SCHOOL BUS?
I'M LOOKING FOR THE PERFECT SEAT!
HMMM.

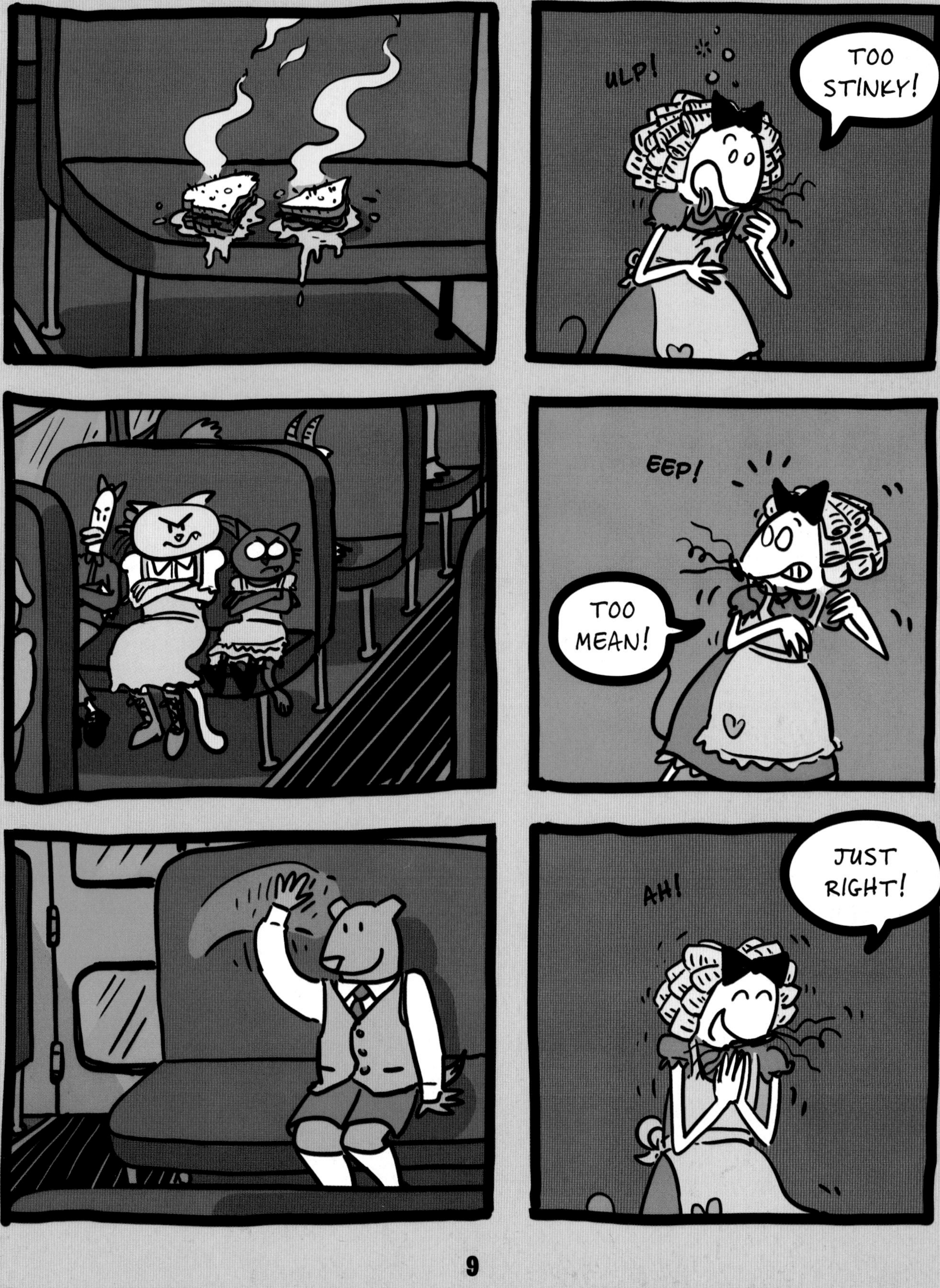
ULP!
TOO STINKY!
EEP!
TOO MEAN!
AH!
JUST RIGHT!

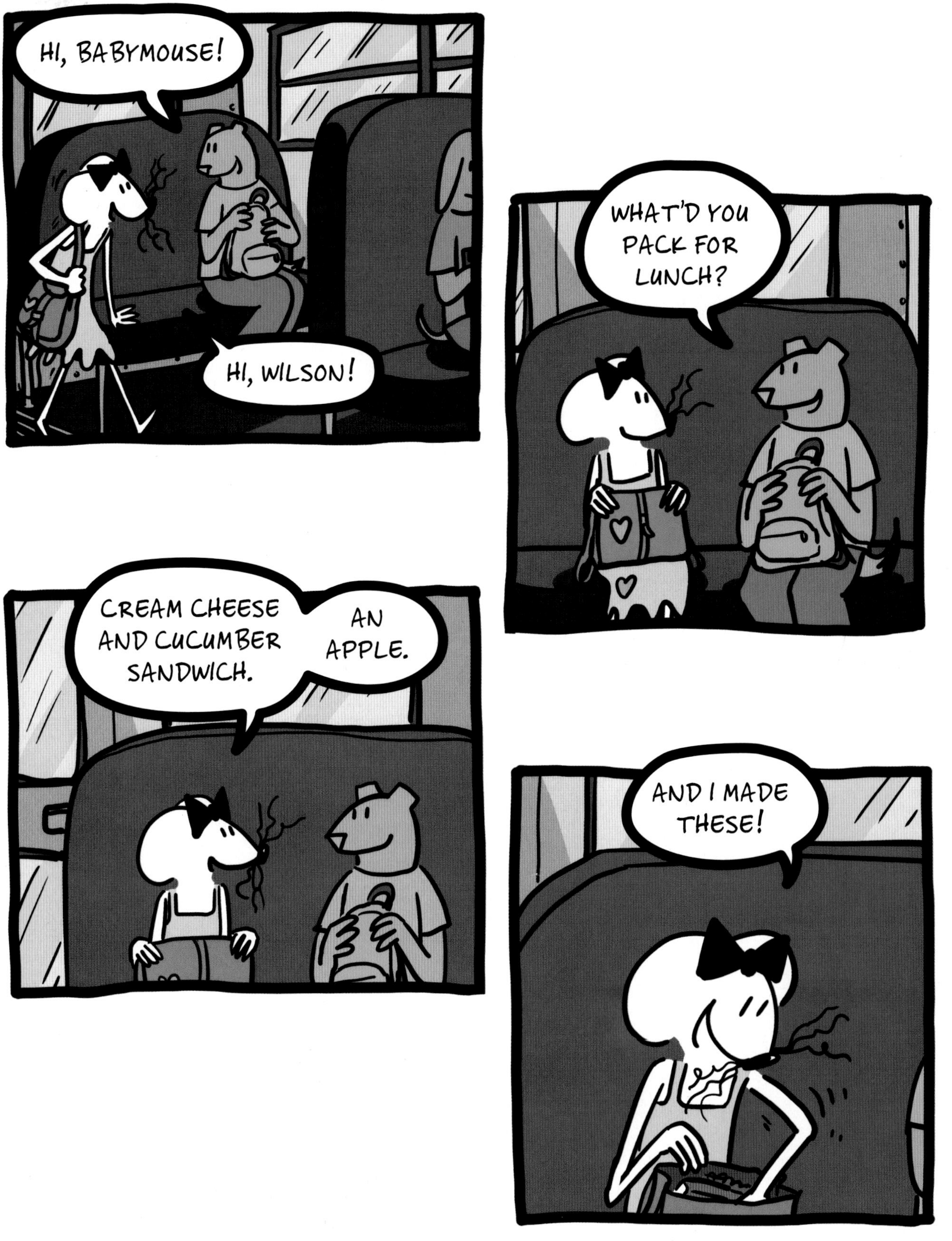
HI, BABYMOUSE!
HI, WILSON!
WHAT'D YOU PACK FOR LUNCH?
CREAM CHEESE AND CUCUMBER SANDWICH.
AN APPLE.
AND I MADE THESE!

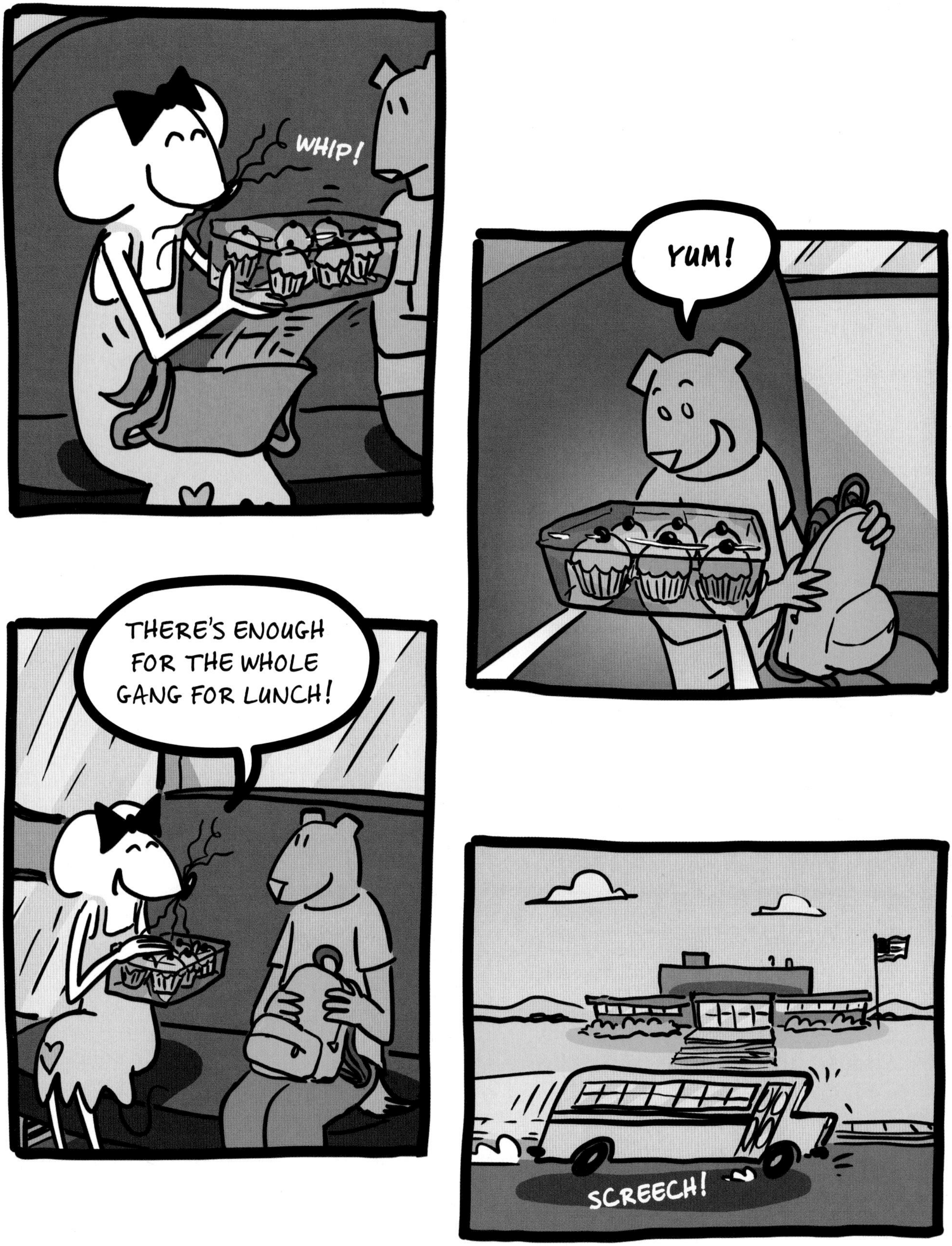
WHIP!
YUM!
THERE'S ENOUGH FOR THE WHOLE GANG FOR LUNCH!
SCREECH!

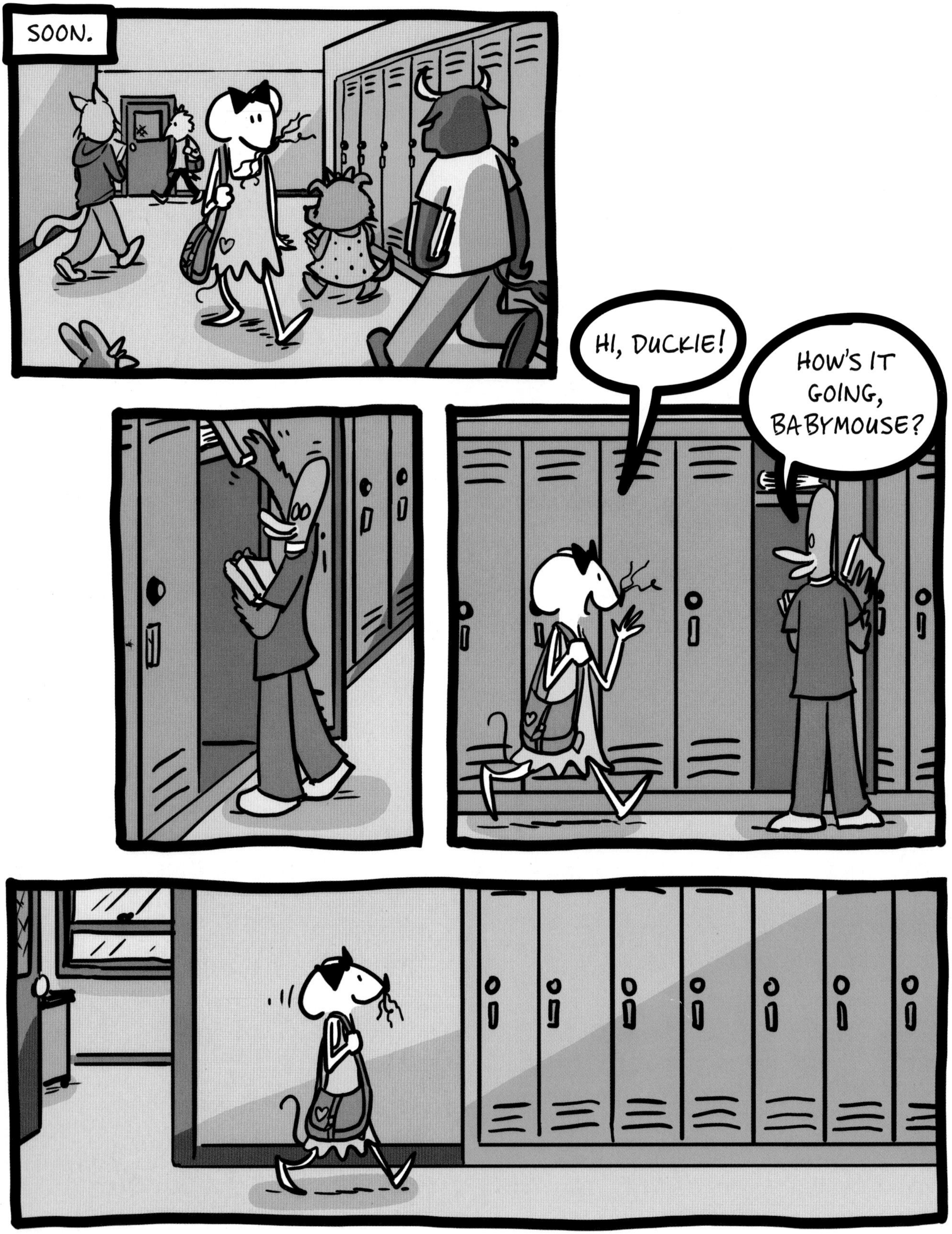
SOON.
HI, DUCKIE!
HOW'S IT GOING, BABYMOUSE?

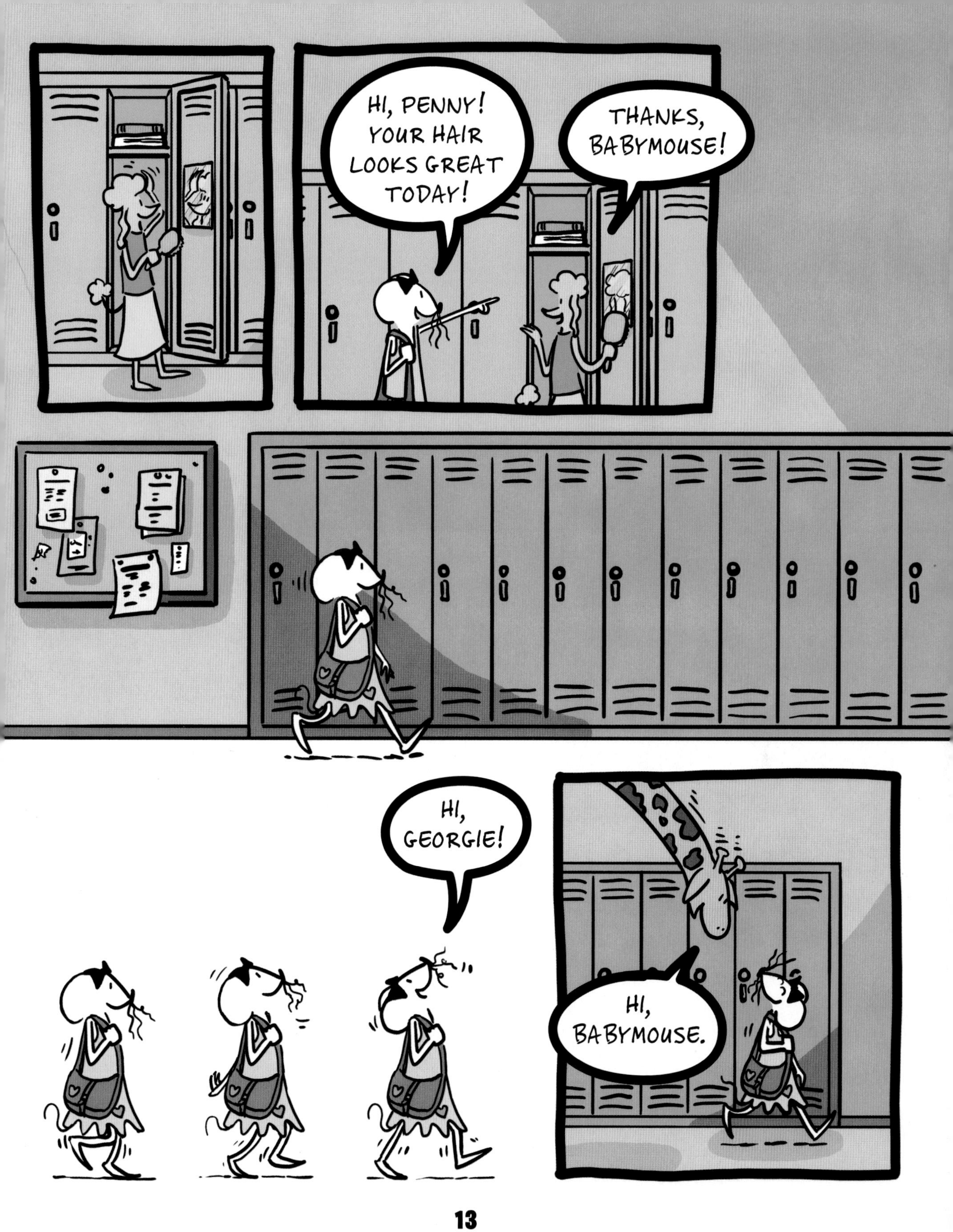
HI, PENNY! YOUR HAIR LOOKS GREAT TODAY!
THANKS, BABYMOUSE!
HI, GEORGIE!
HI, BABYMOUSE.

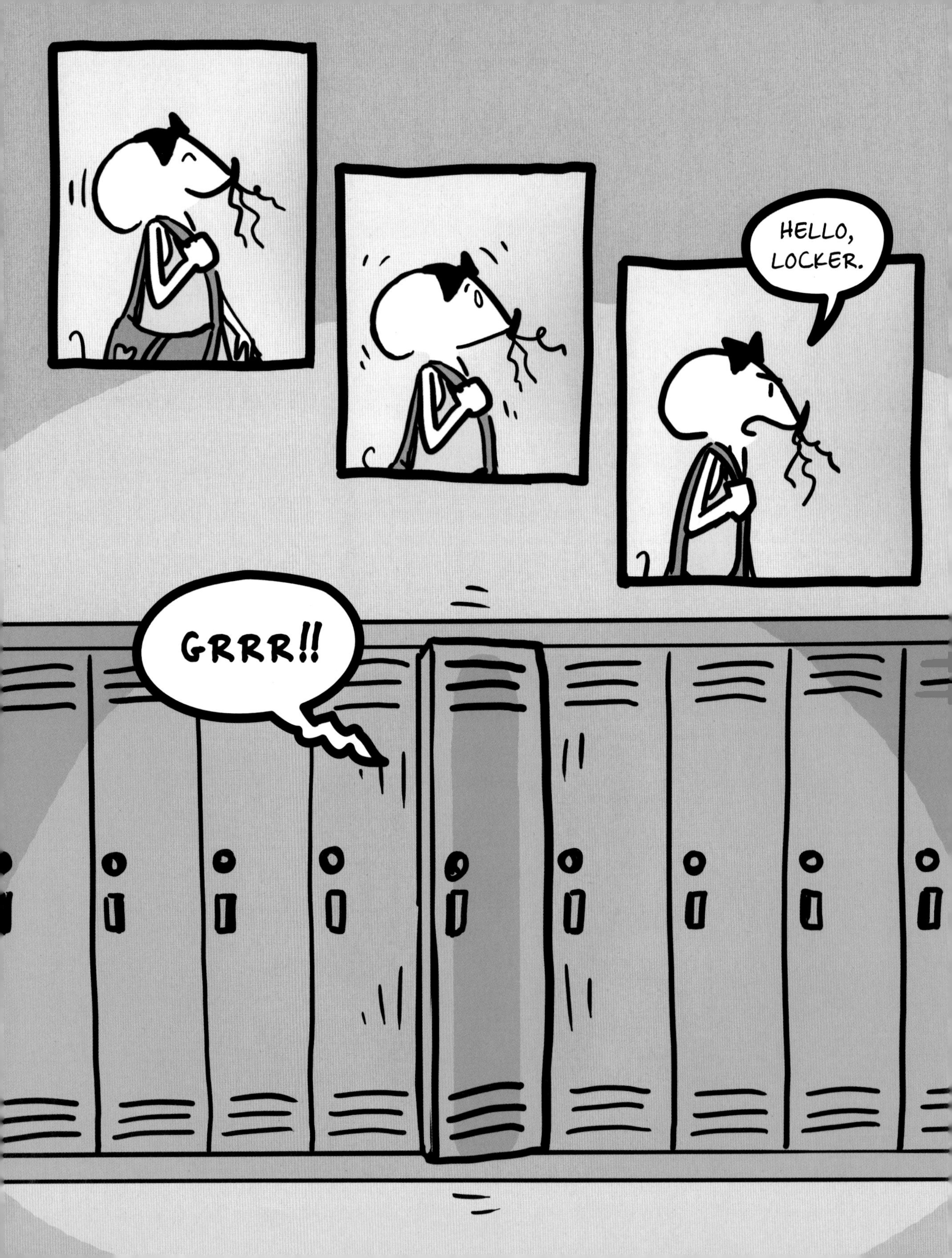
HELLO, LOCKER.
GRRR!!

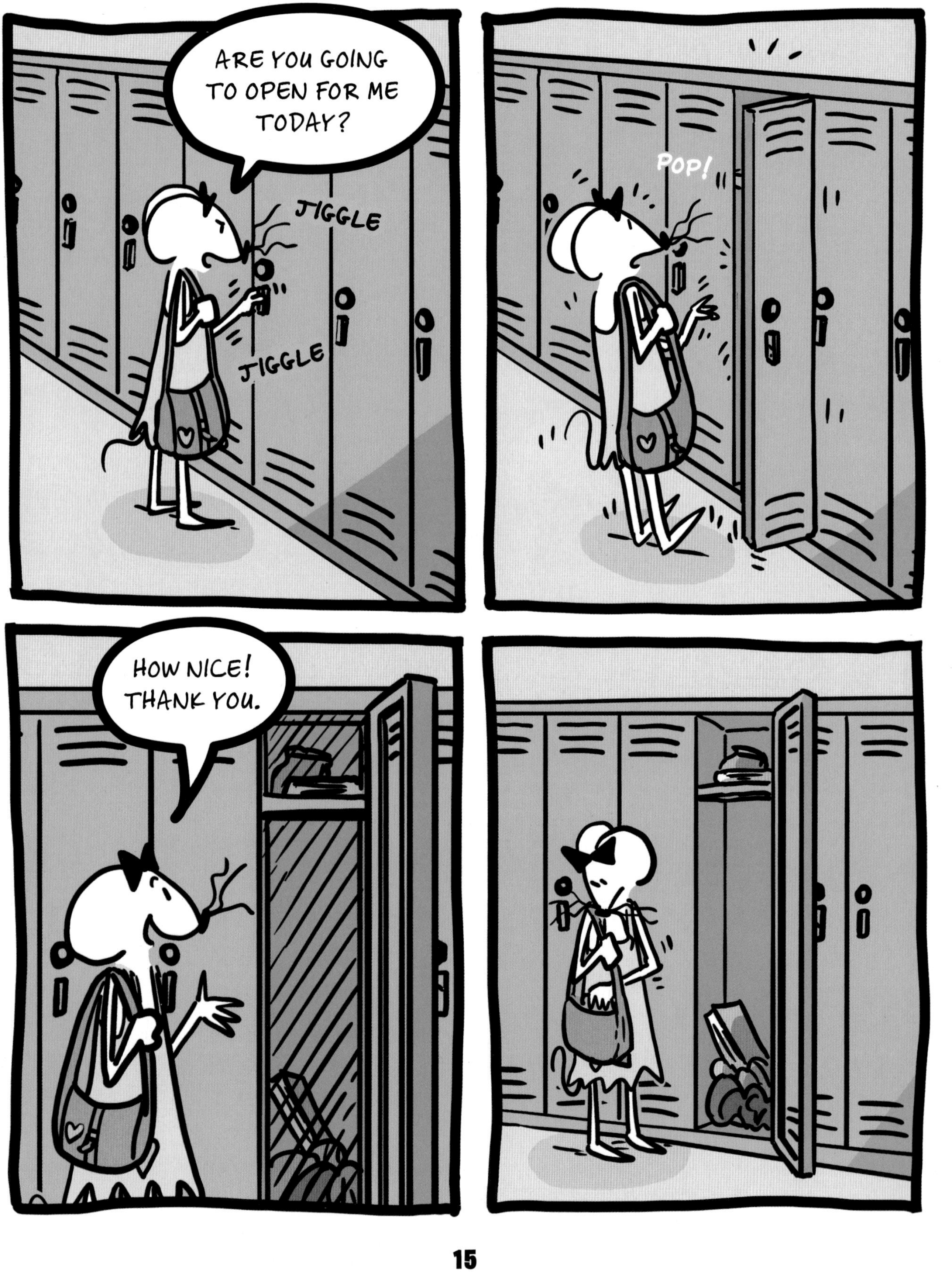
ARE YOU GOING TO OPEN FOR ME TODAY?
JIGGLE
JIGGLE
POP!
HOW NICE! THANK YOU.

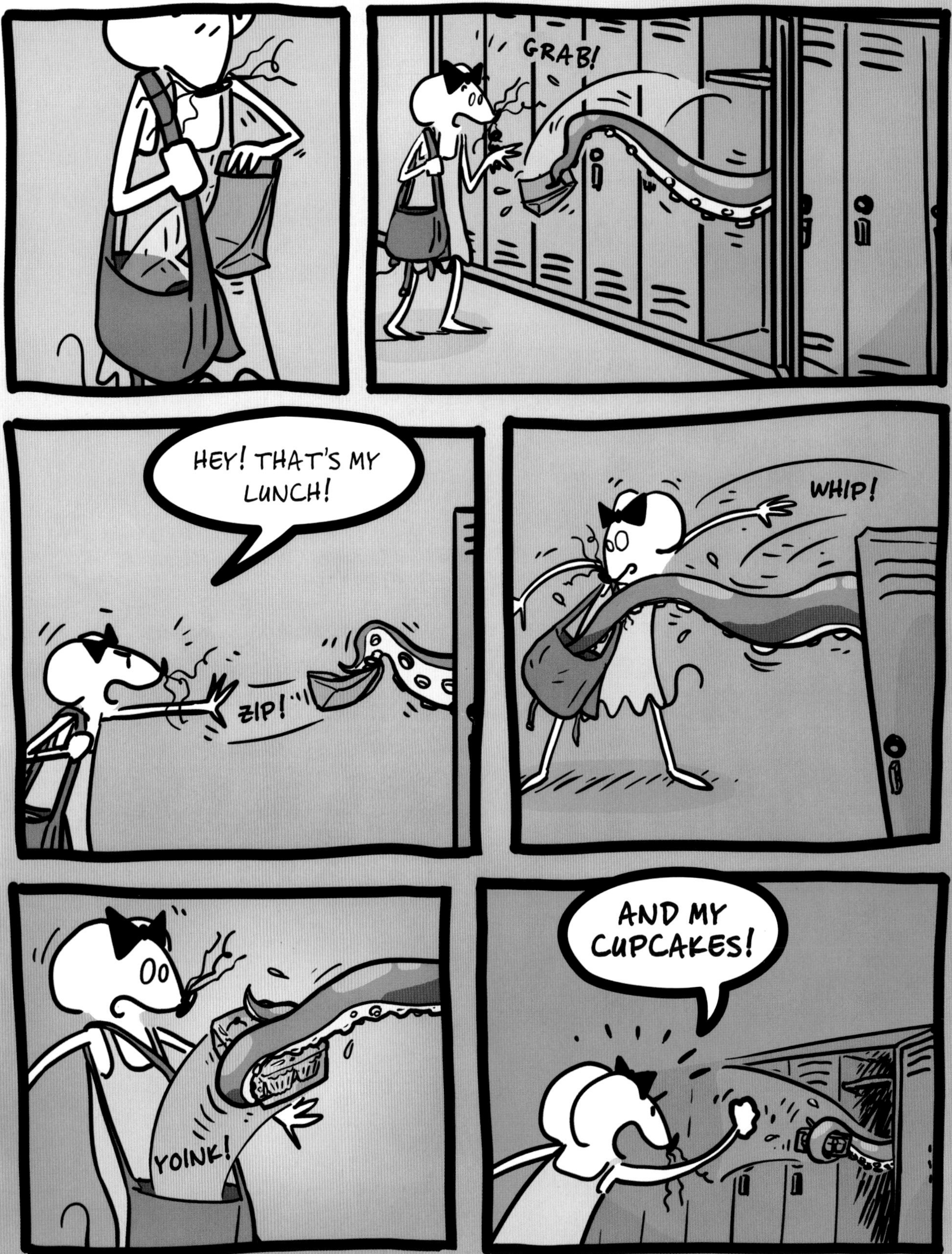
GRAB!
HEY! THAT'S MY LUNCH!
ZIP!
WHIP!
YOINK!
AND MY CUPCAKES!

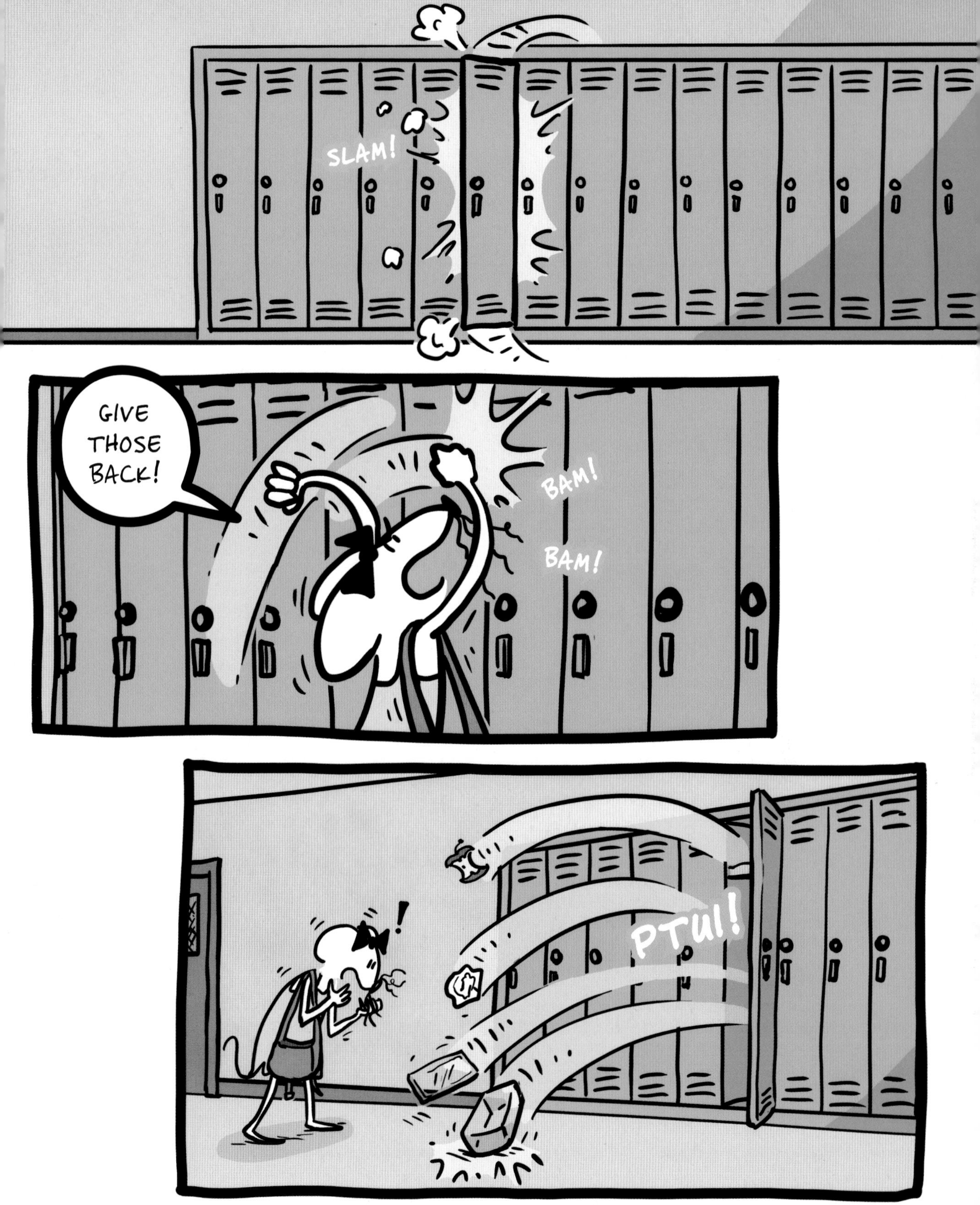
SLAM!
GIVE THOSE BACK!
BAM!
BAM!
!
PTUI!

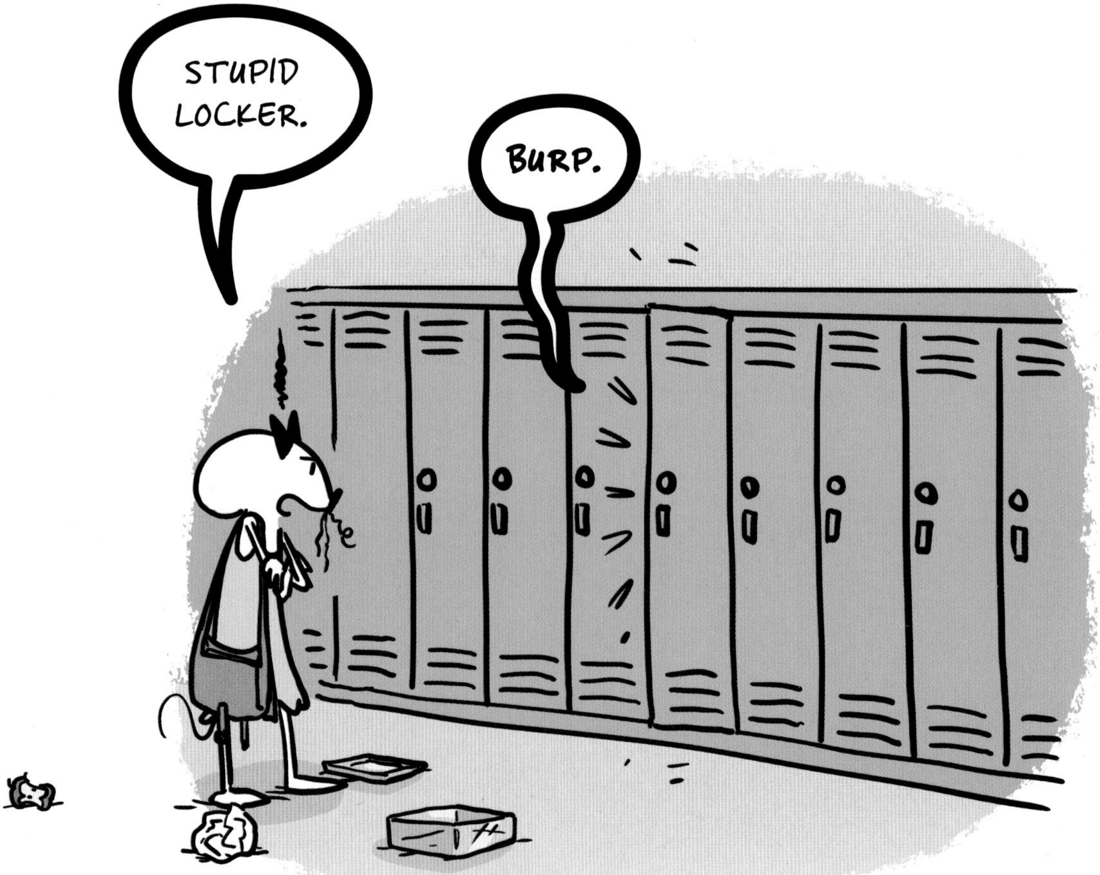
STUPID LOCKER.
BURP.

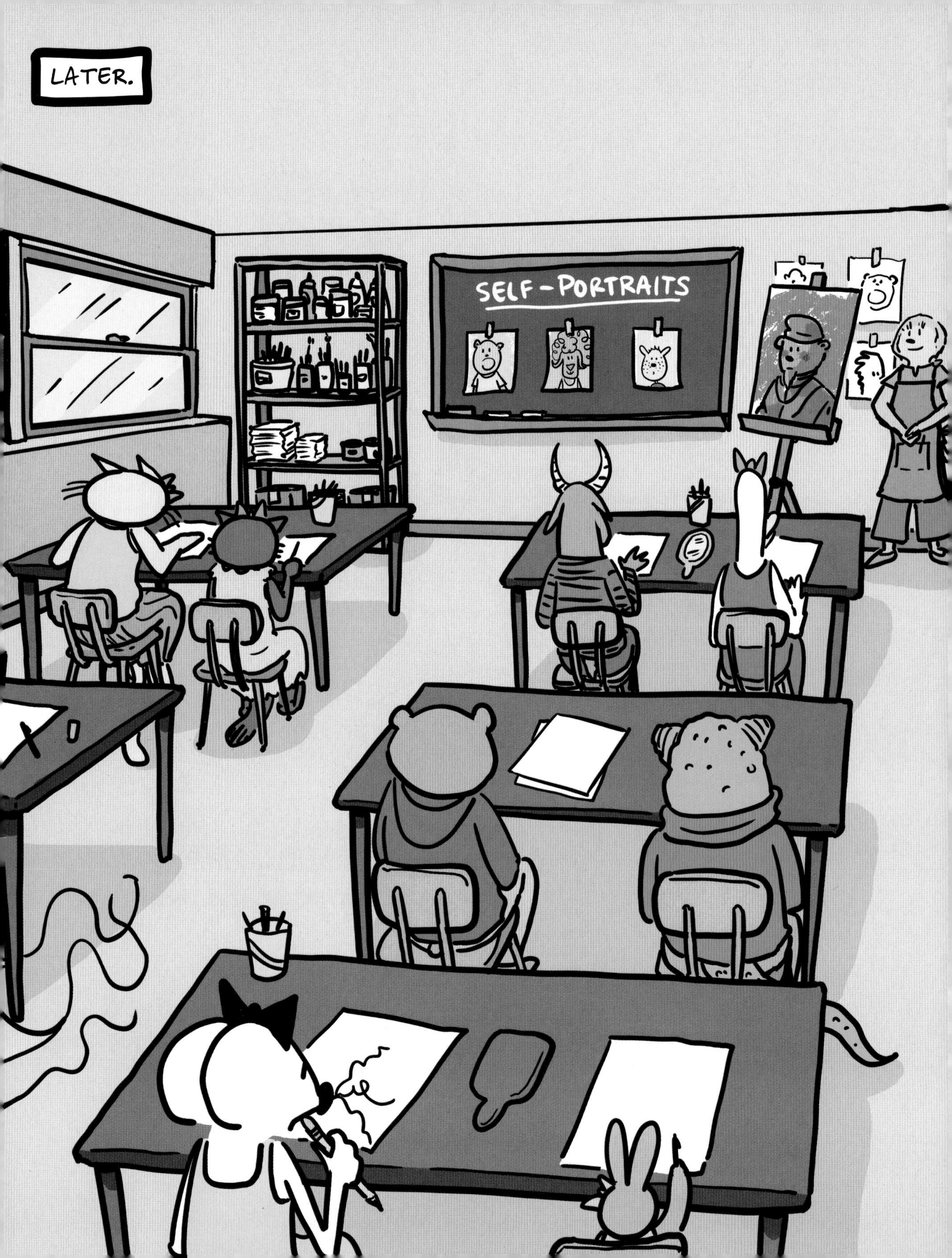
LATER.
SELF-PORTRAITS

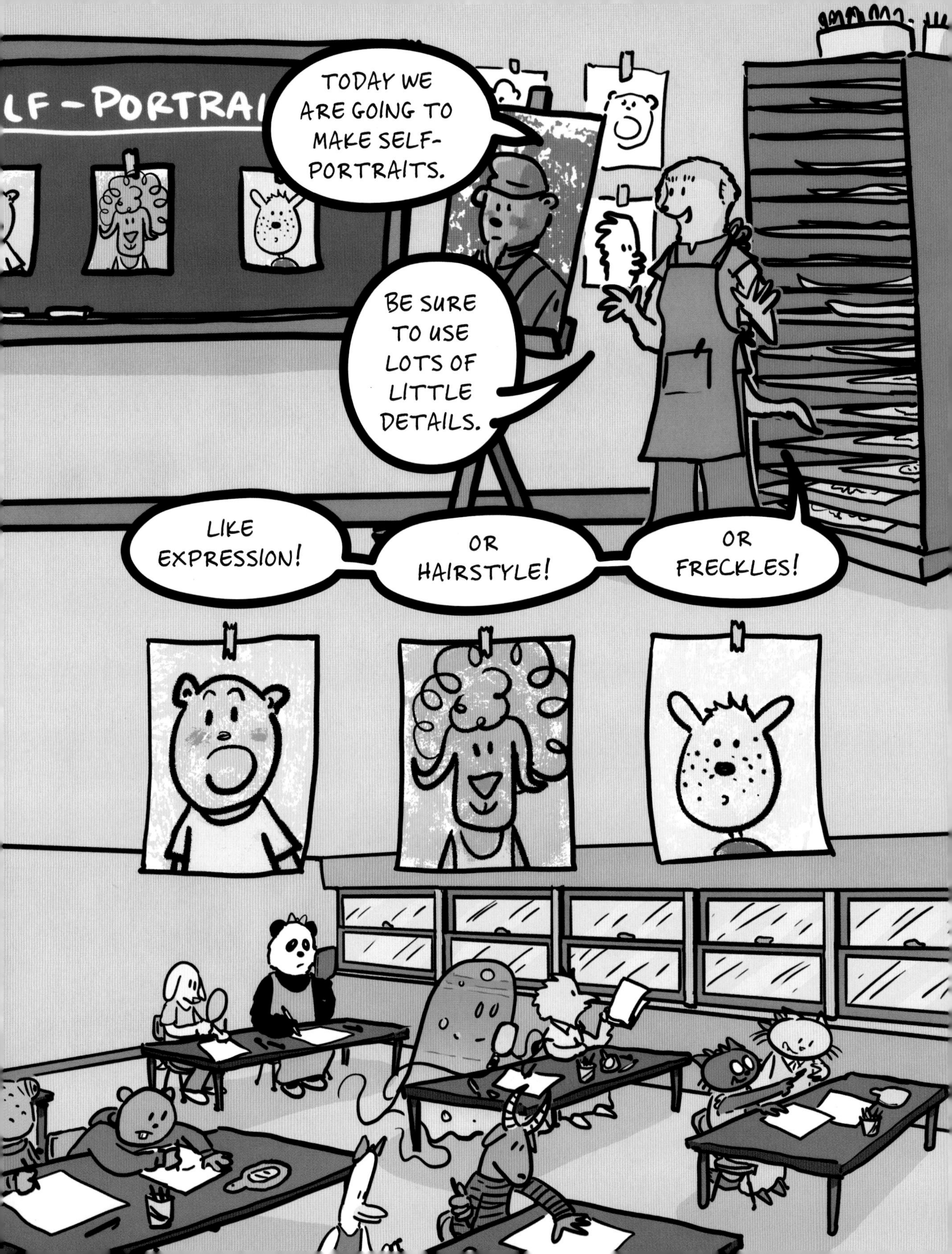
LF-PORTRAI
TODAY WE ARE GOING TO MAKE SELF-PORTRAITS.
BE SURE TO USE LOTS OF LITTLE DETAILS.
LIKE EXPRESSION!
OR HAIRSTYLE!
OR FRECKLES!

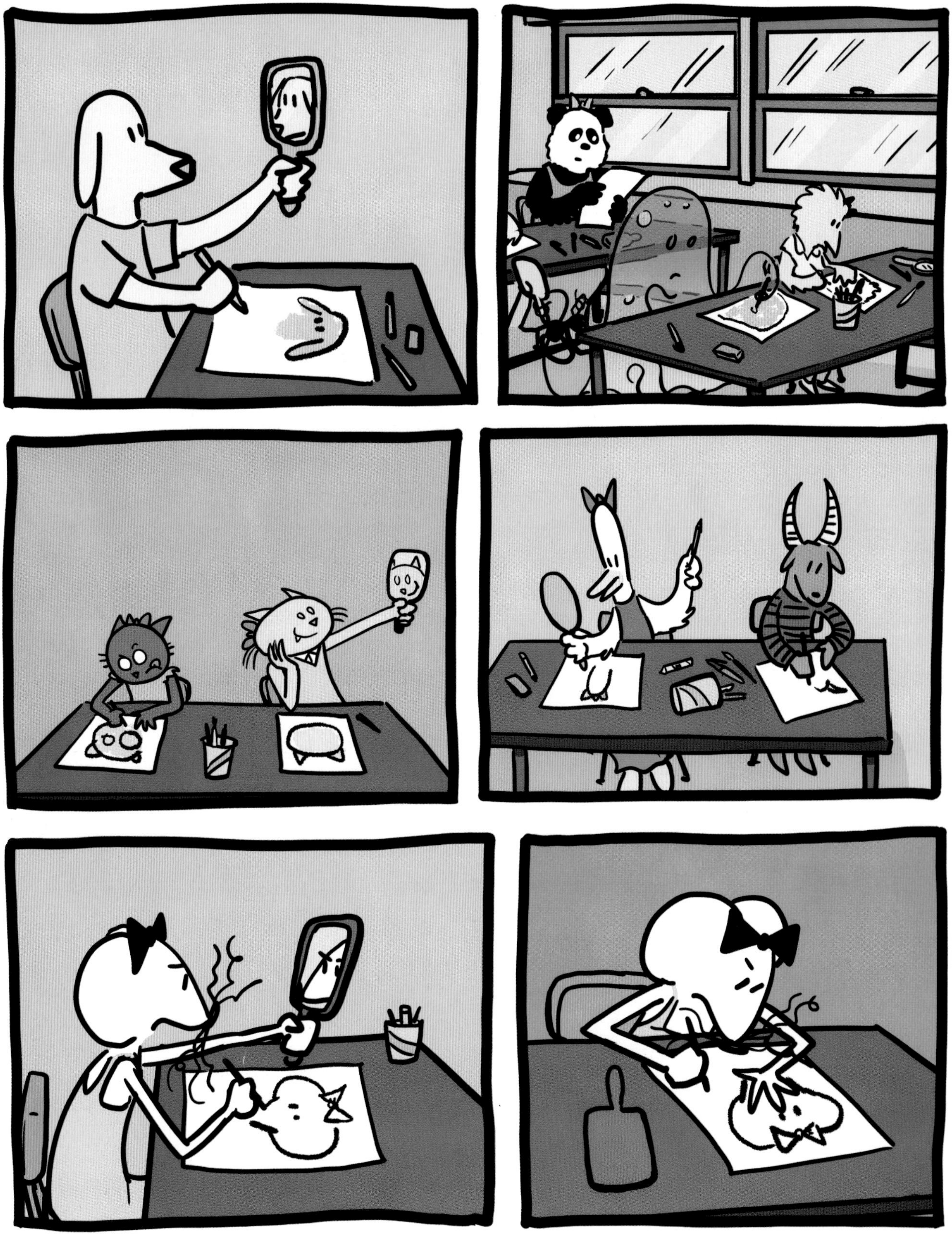

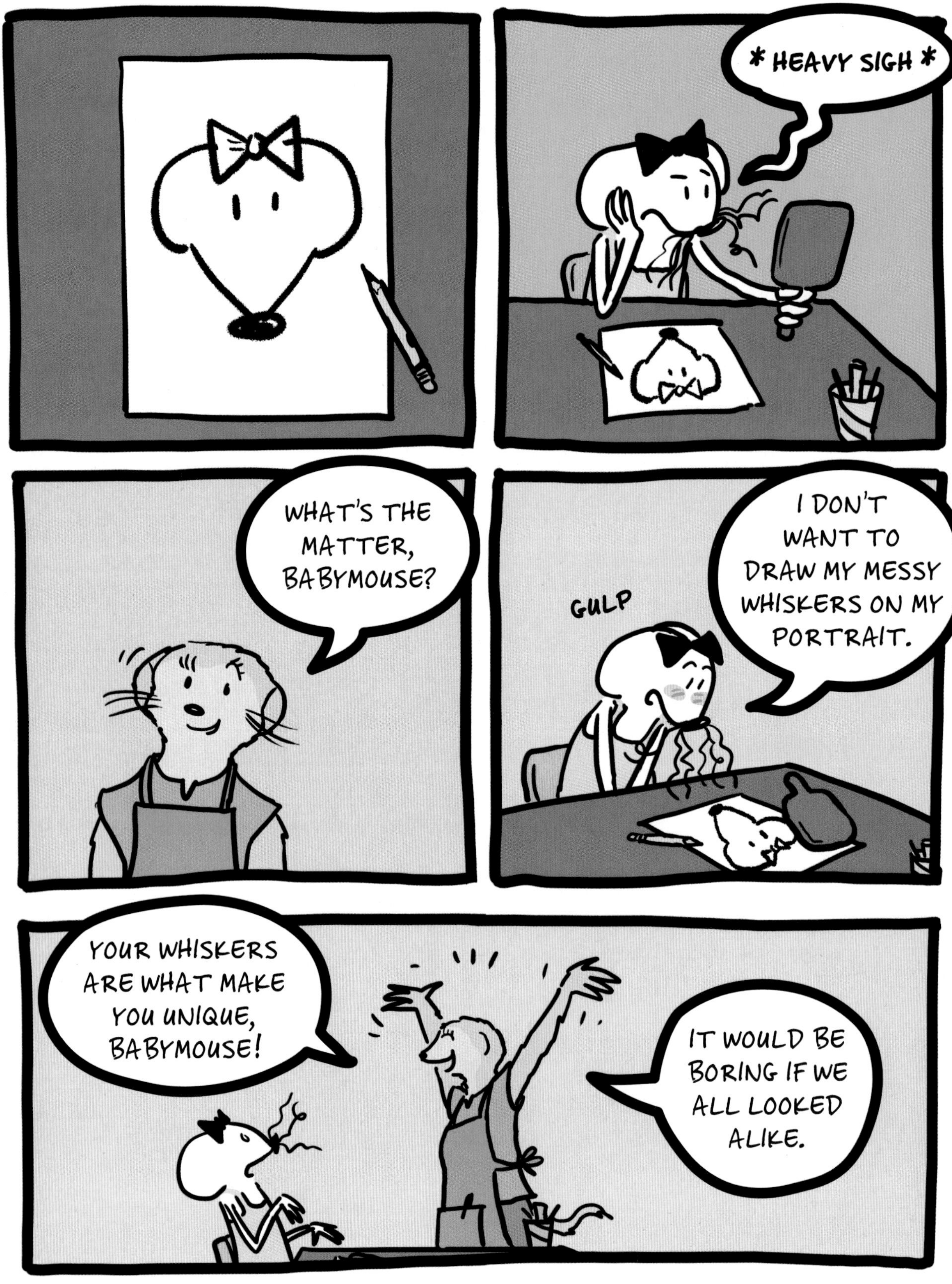
* HEAVY SIGH *
WHAT'S THE MATTER, BABYMOUSE?
GULP
I DON'T WANT TO DRAW MY MESSY WHISKERS ON MY PORTRAIT.
YOUR WHISKERS ARE WHAT MAKE YOU UNIQUE, BABYMOUSE!
IT WOULD BE BORING IF WE ALL LOOKED ALIKE.

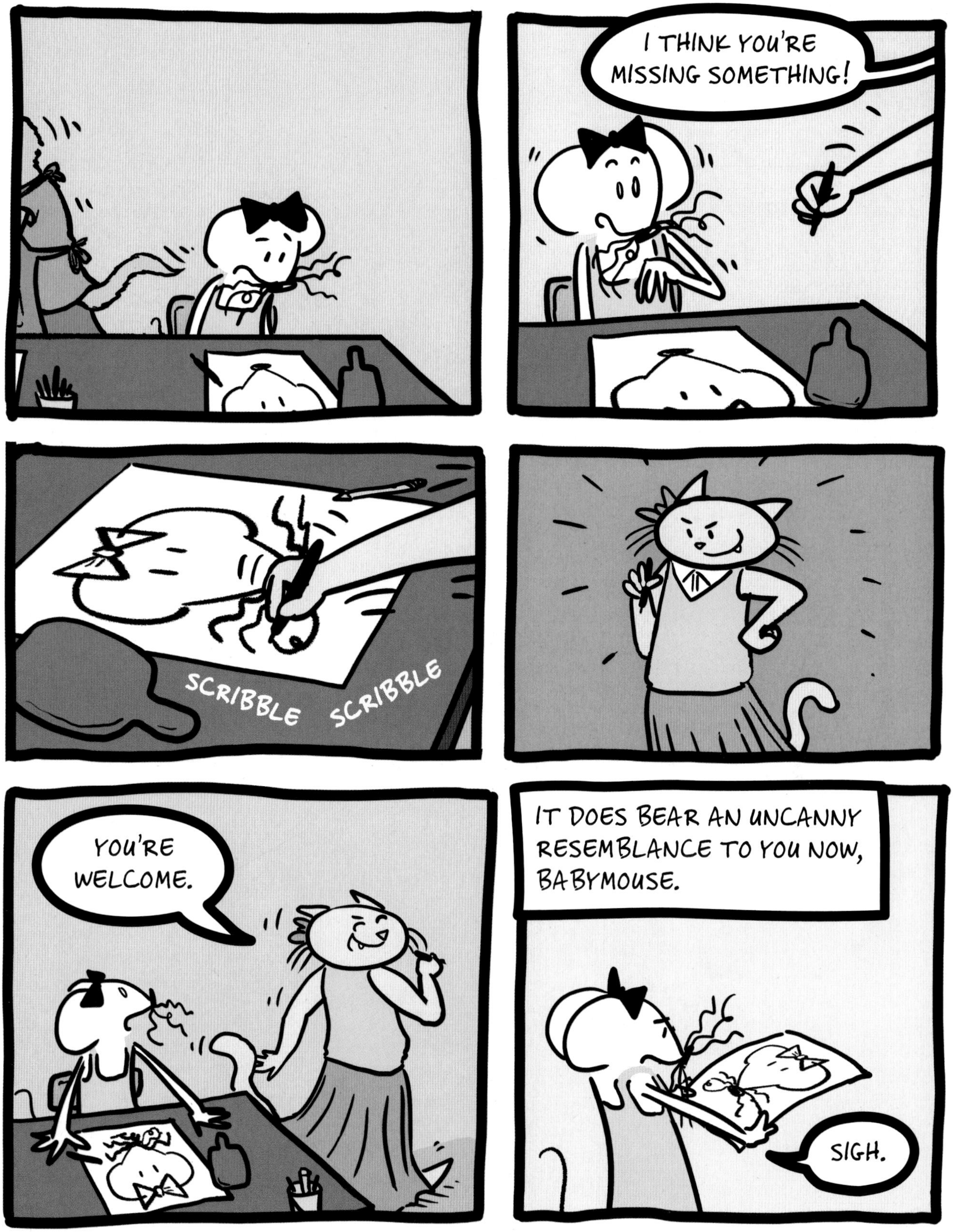
I THINK YOU'RE MISSING SOMETHING!
SCRIBBLE SCRIBBLE
YOU'RE WELCOME.
IT DOES BEAR AN UNCANNY RESEMBLANCE TO YOU NOW, BABYMOUSE.
SIGH.

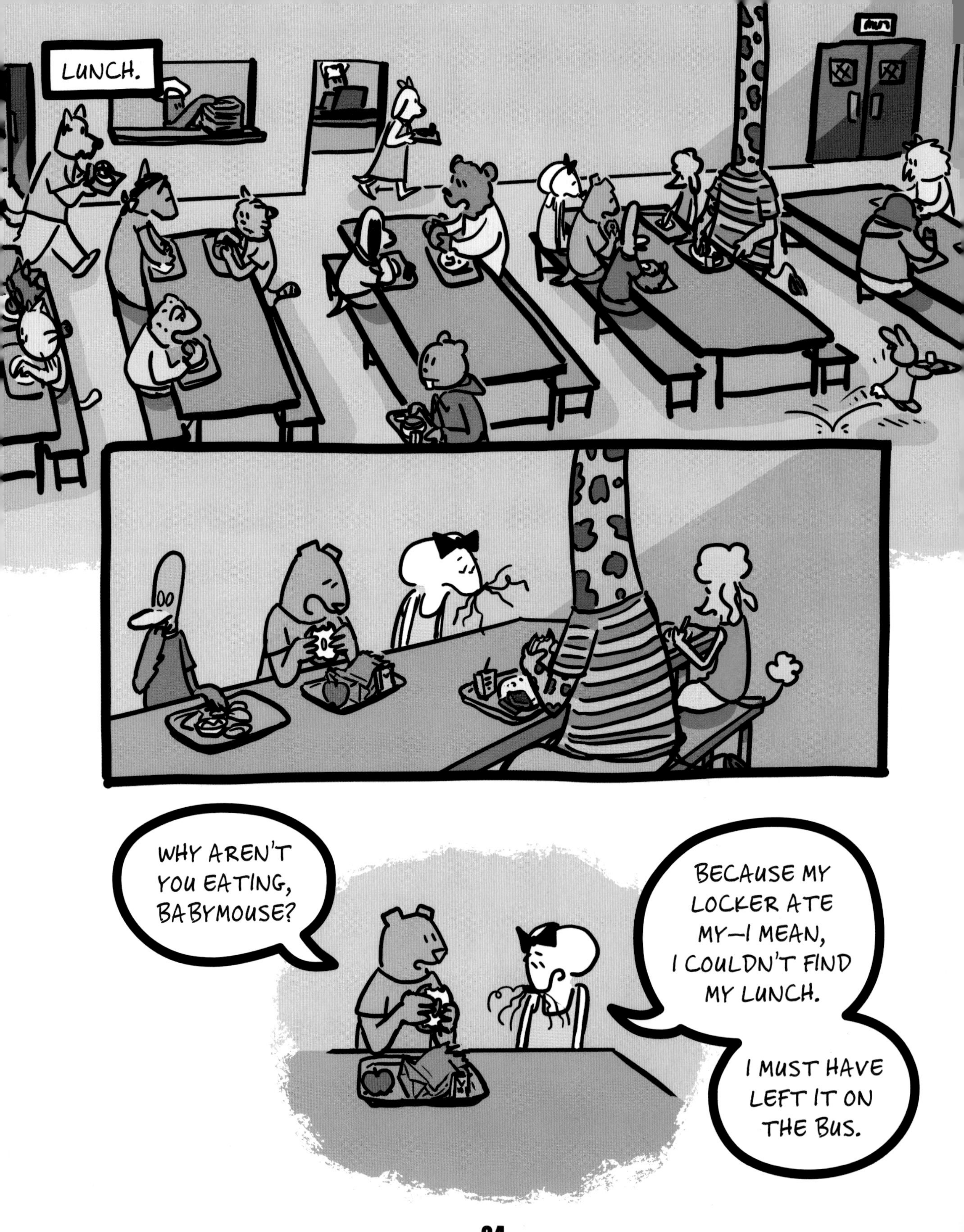
LUNCH.
WHY AREN'T YOU EATING, BABYMOUSE?
BECAUSE MY LOCKER ATE MY—I MEAN, I COULDN'T FIND MY LUNCH.
I MUST HAVE LEFT IT ON THE BUS.

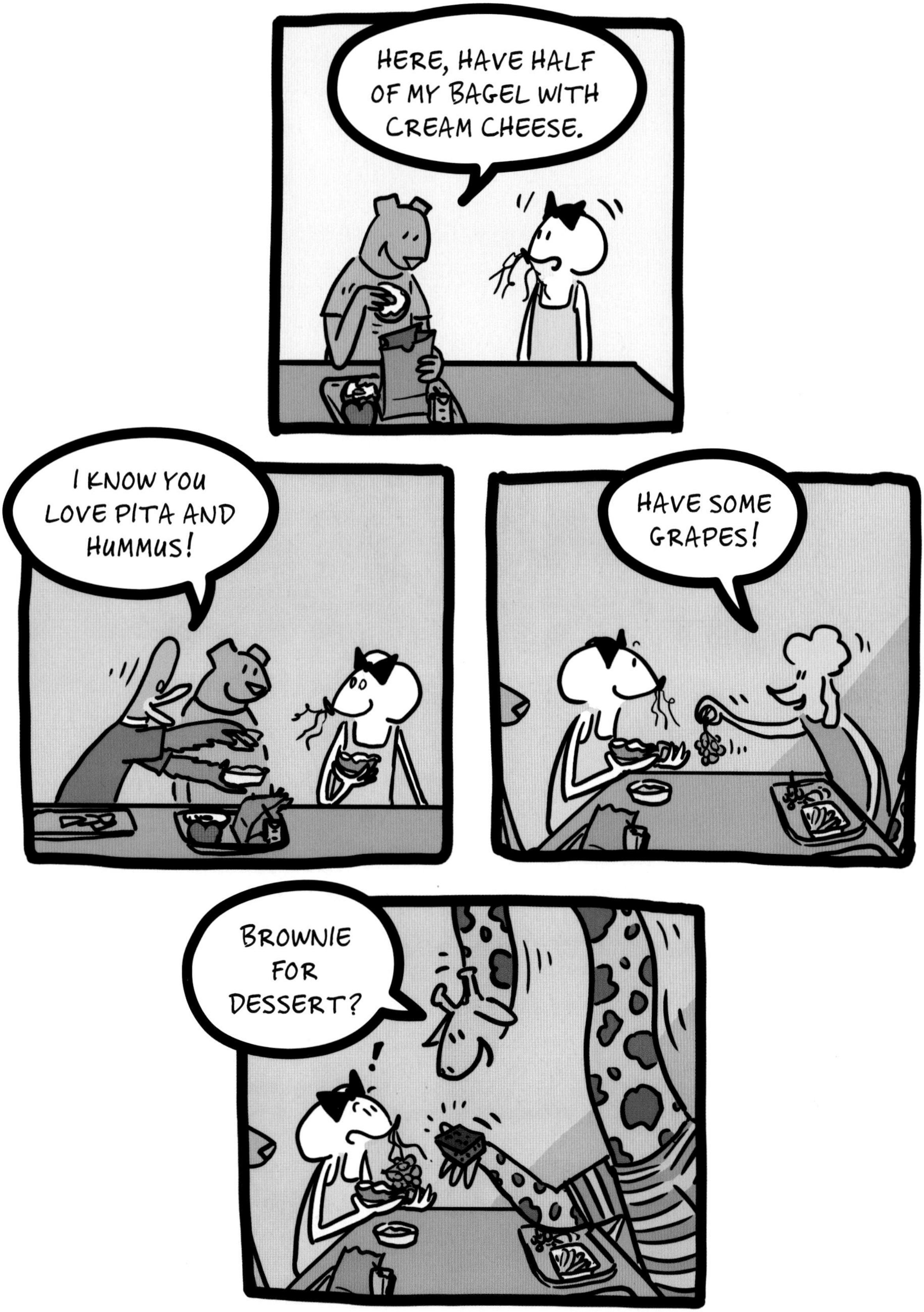
HERE, HAVE HALF OF MY BAGEL WITH CREAM CHEESE.
I KNOW YOU LOVE PITA AND HUMMUS!
HAVE SOME GRAPES!
BROWNIE FOR DESSERT?
!

THANKS!
ANY CHANCE YOU WOULD LIKE TO SHARE THAT BROWNIE WITH ME, BABYMOUSE?
I AM YOUR FAVORITE NARRATOR.

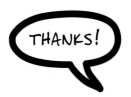

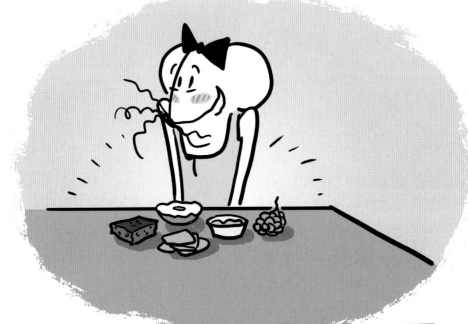

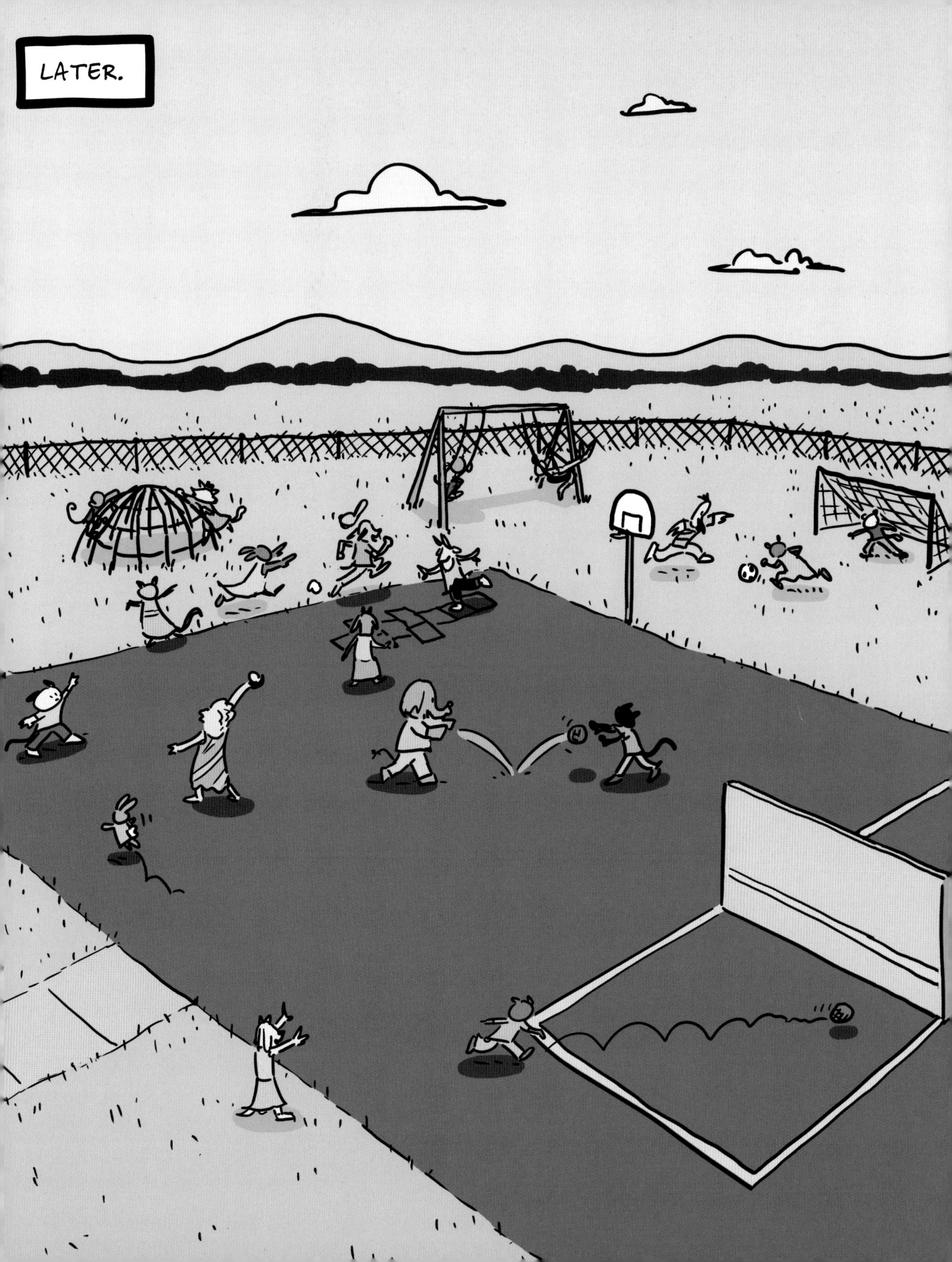
LATER.

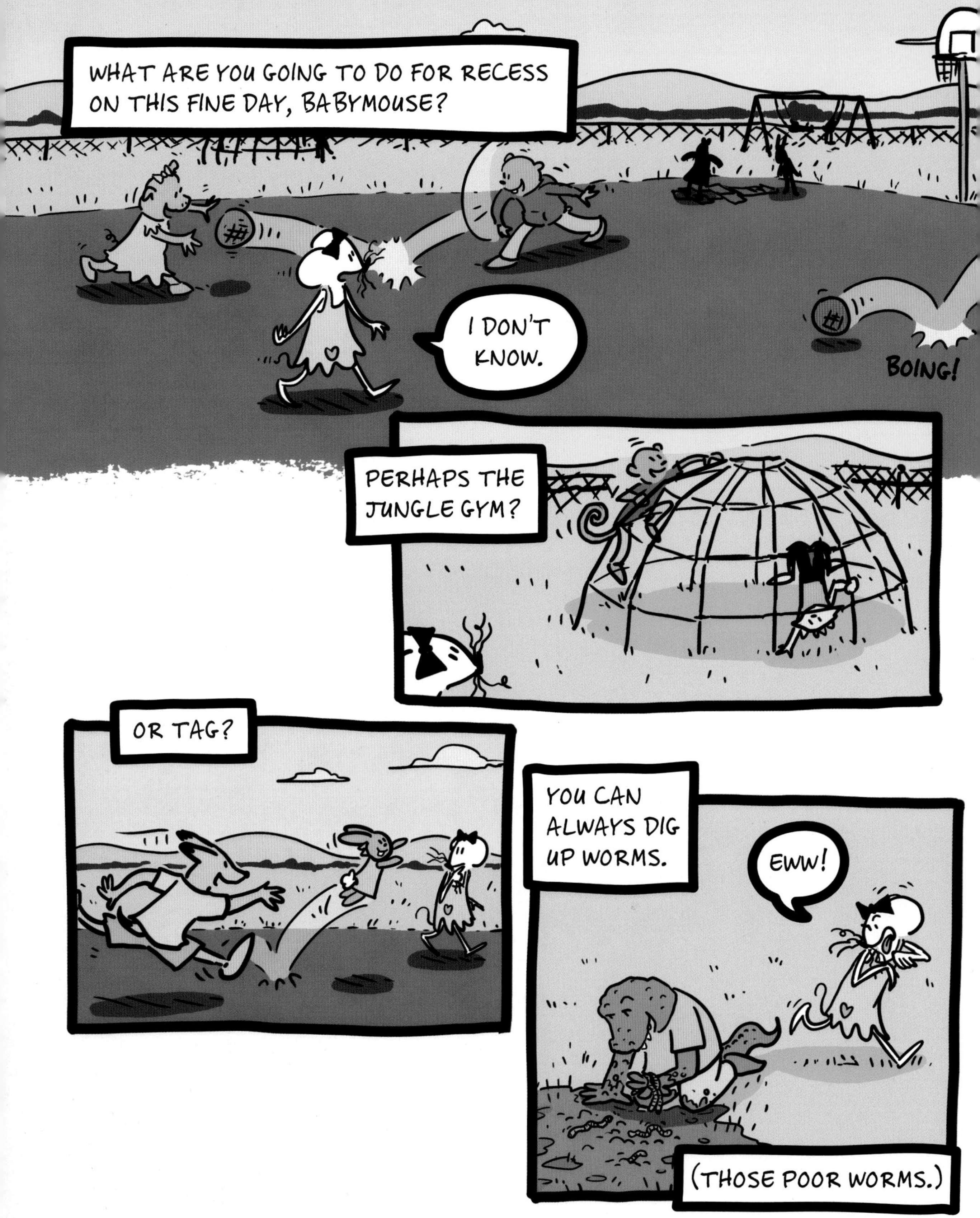

WHAT ARE YOU GOING TO DO FOR RECESS ON THIS FINE DAY, BABYMOUSE?
I DON'T KNOW.
BOING!
PERHAPS THE JUNGLE GYM?
OR TAG?
YOU CAN ALWAYS DIG UP WORMS.
EWW!
(THOSE POOR WORMS.)

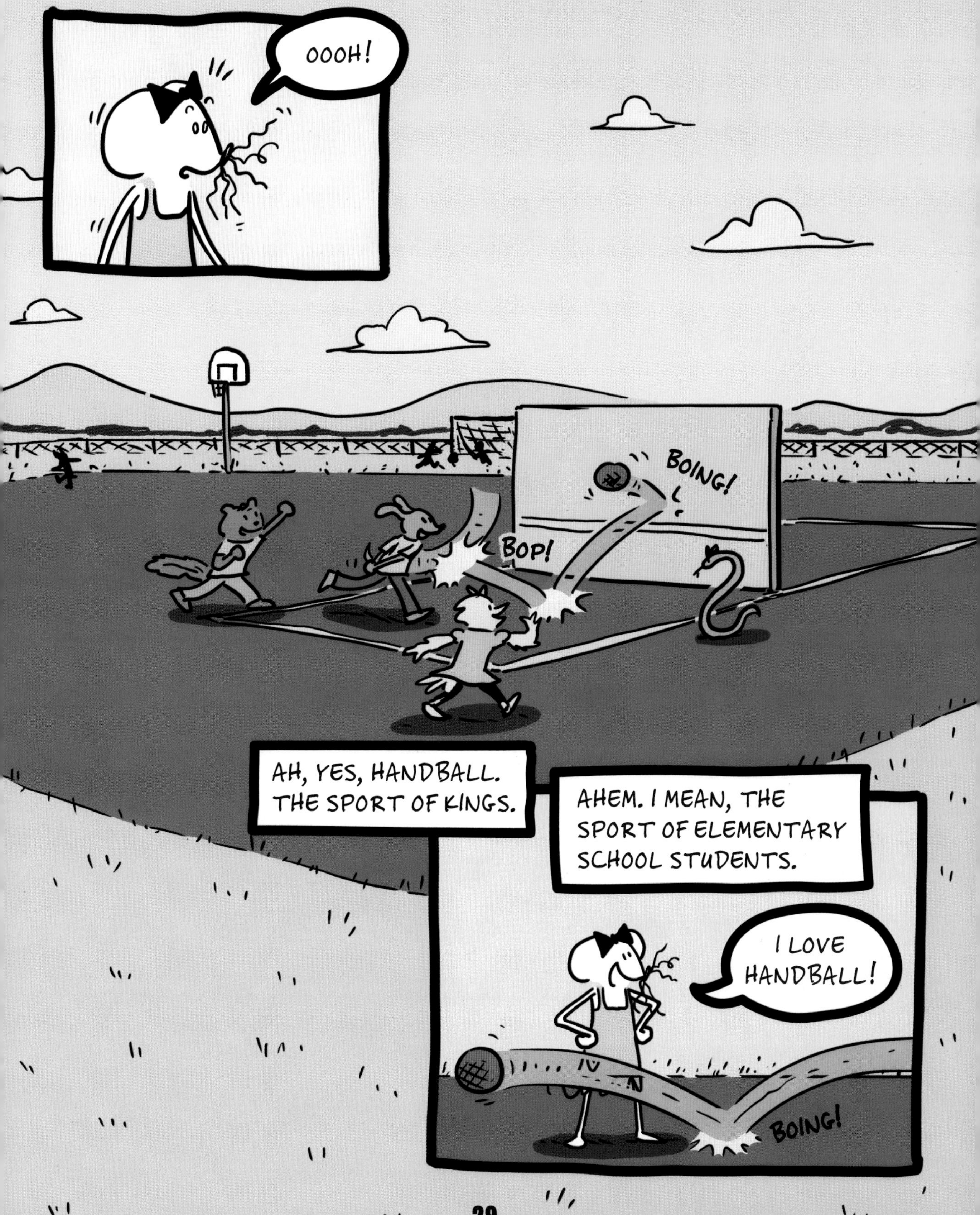
OOOH!
BOING!
BOP!
AH, YES, HANDBALL. THE SPORT OF KINGS.
AHEM. I MEAN, THE SPORT OF ELEMENTARY SCHOOL STUDENTS.
I LOVE HANDBALL!
BOING!

WHY HANDBALL IS SUPERIOR!

YOU DON'T NEED A FIELD!

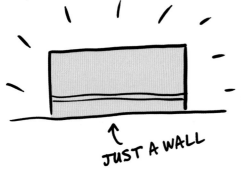

↑
JUST A WALL

YOU DON'T HAVE TO BE TALL!

NO FAIR!

SORRY, BABYMOUSE.

YOU DON'T HAVE TO PICK A TEAM!

I PICK ANYONE **BUT** BABYMOUSE.

YOU DON'T NEED A LOT OF EQUIPMENT!

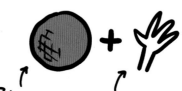

BASIC BALL   HAND

OOH! I HAVE **TWO** HANDS!

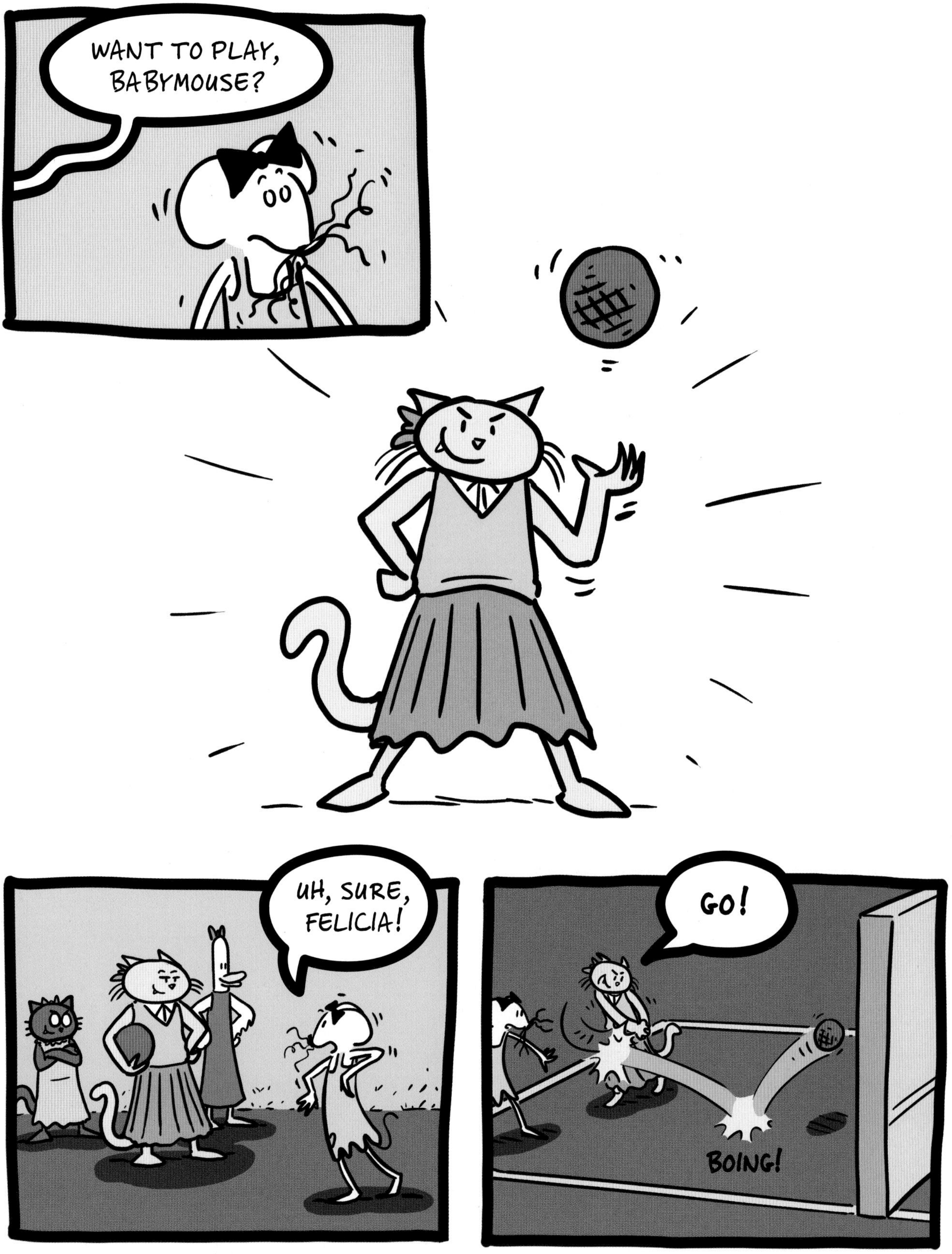
WANT TO PLAY, BABYMOUSE?
UH, SURE, FELICIA!
GO!
BOING!

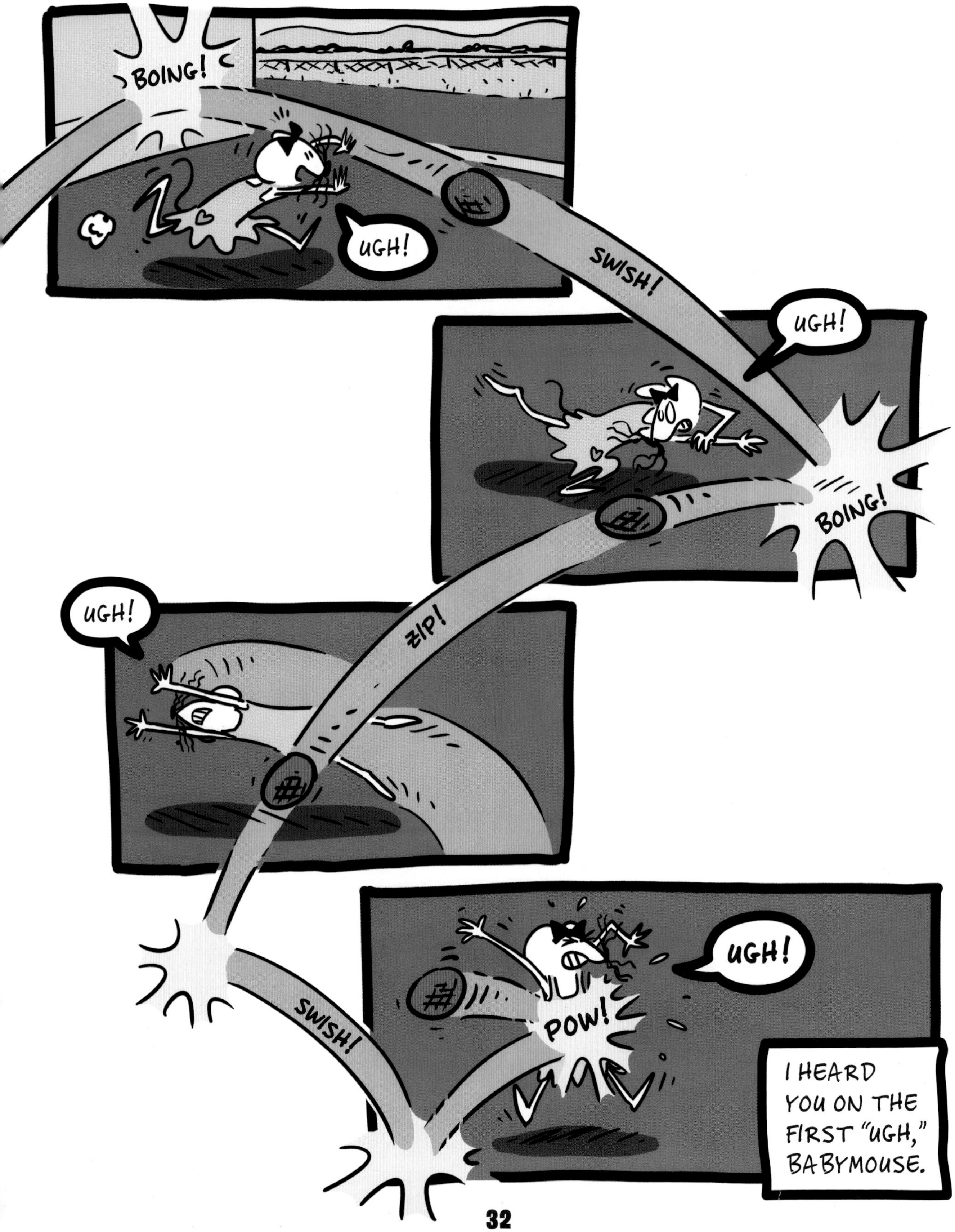
BOING!
UGH!
SWISH!
UGH!
BOING!
UGH!
ZIP!
SWISH!
UGH!
POW!
I HEARD YOU ON THE FIRST "UGH," BABYMOUSE.

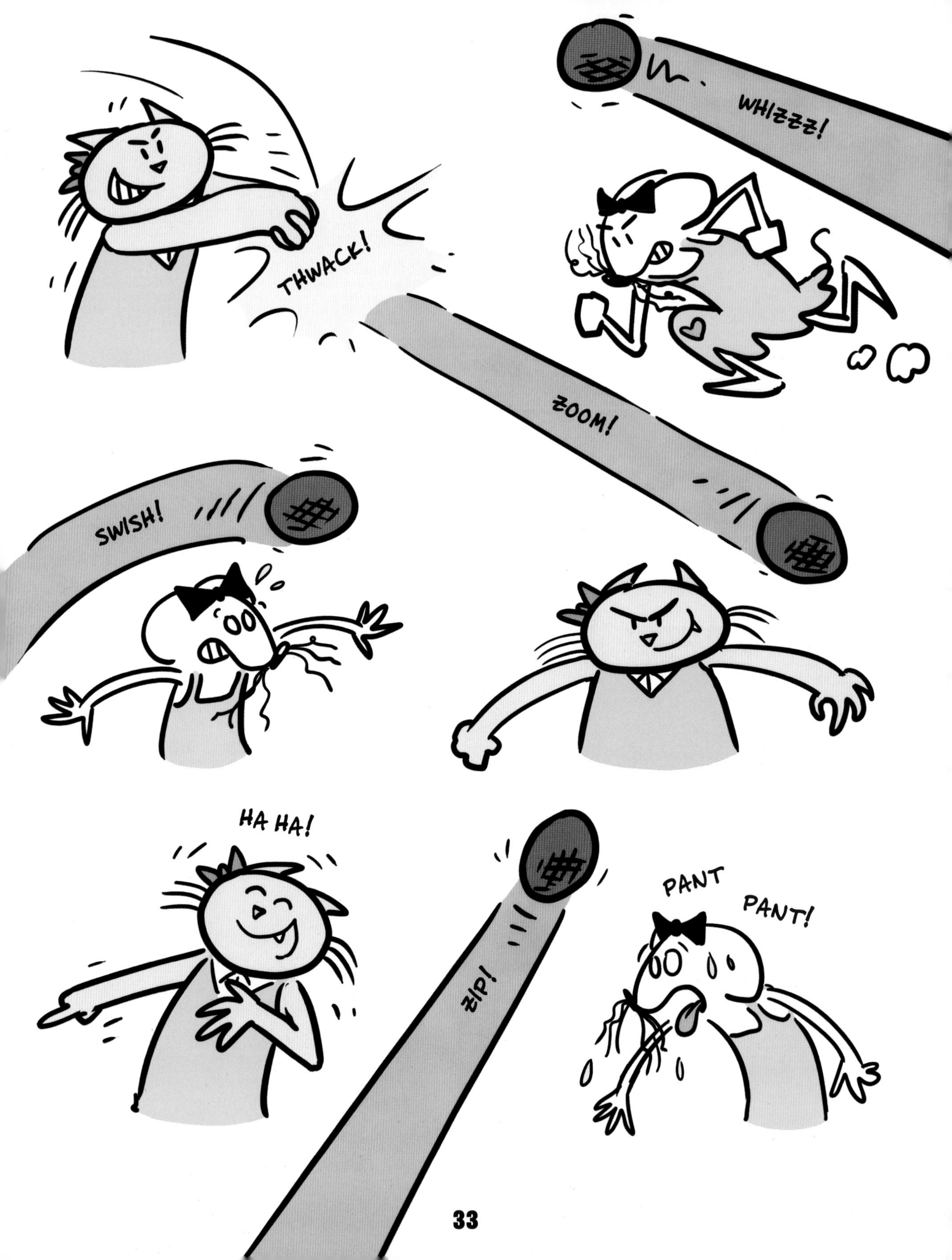
THWACK!
WHIZZZZ!
ZOOM!
SWISH!
HA HA!
ZIP!
PANT
PANT!

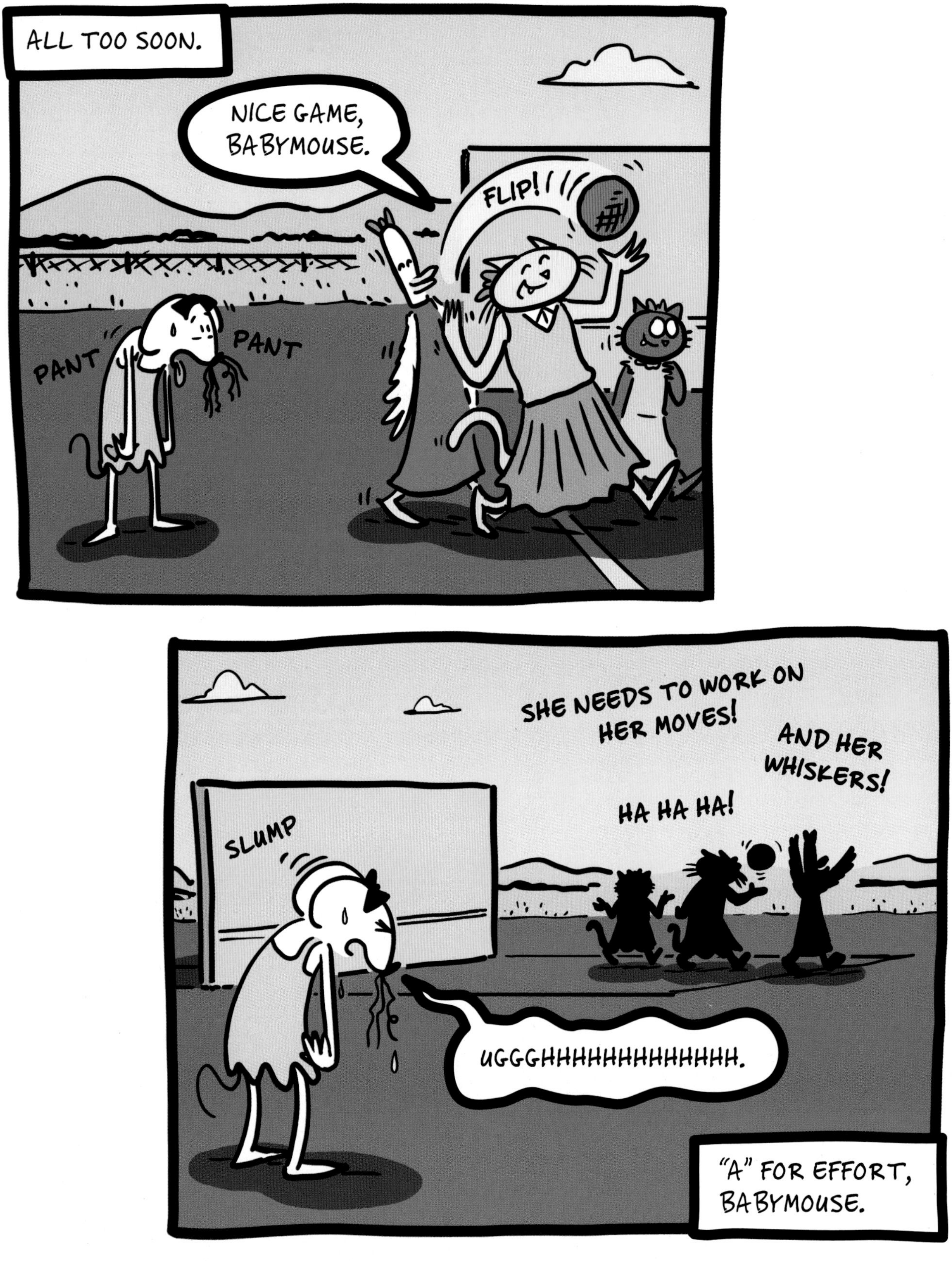

ALL TOO SOON.
NICE GAME, BABYMOUSE.
FLIP!
PANT
PANT
SHE NEEDS TO WORK ON HER MOVES!
AND HER WHISKERS!
HA HA HA!
SLUMP
UGGGHHHHHHHHHHHHH.
"A" FOR EFFORT, BABYMOUSE.

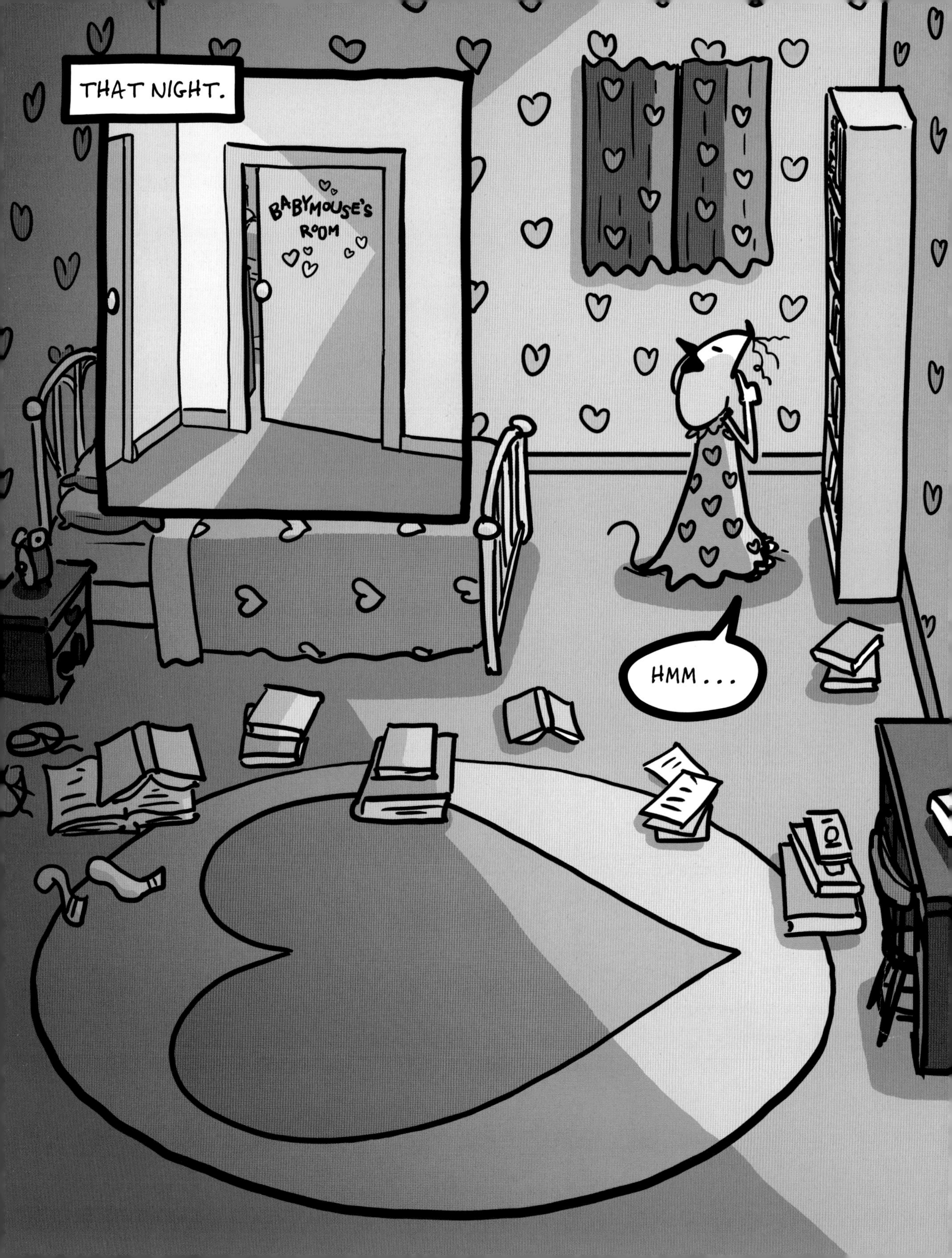
THAT NIGHT.
BABYMOUSE'S ROOM
HMM . . .

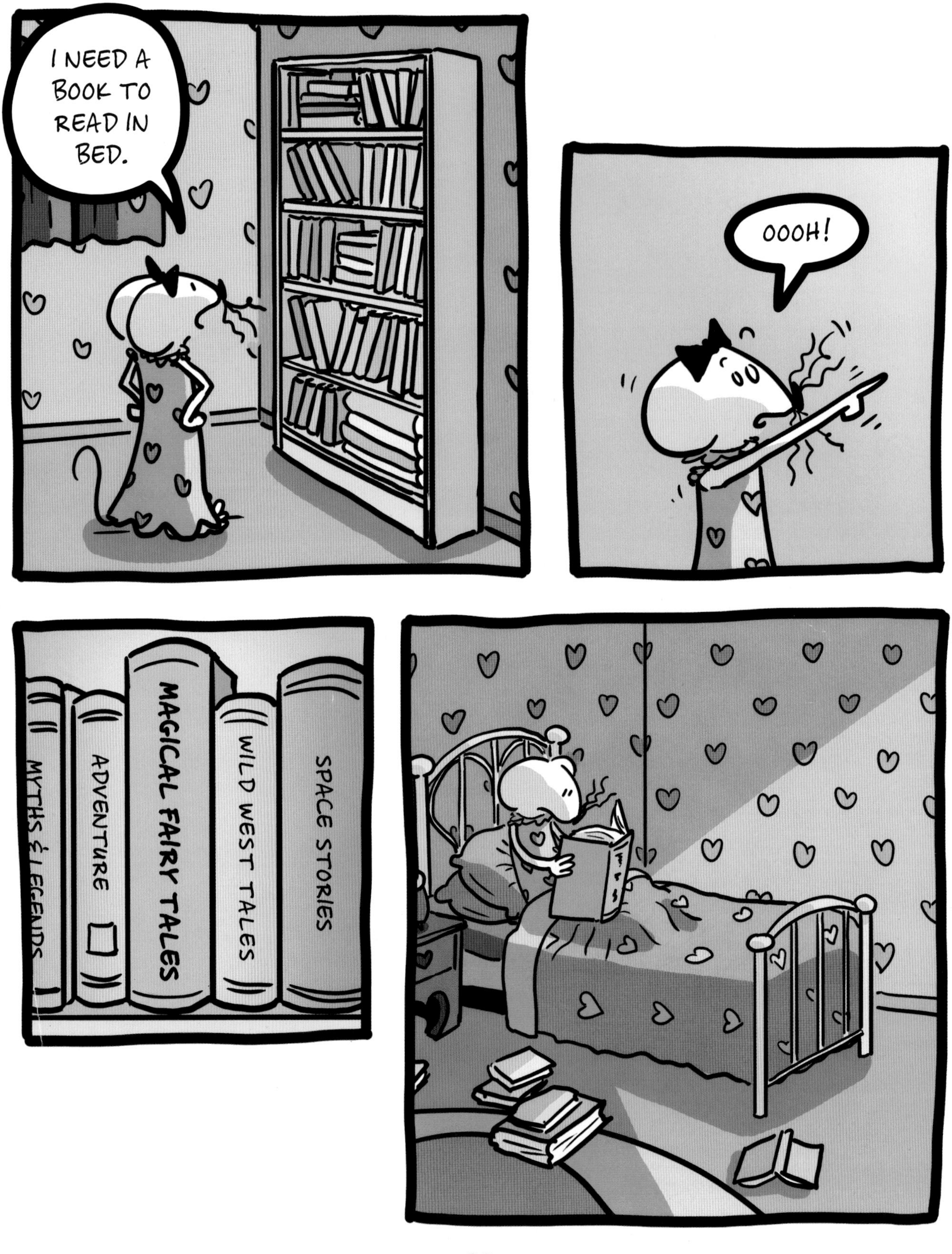
I NEED A BOOK TO READ IN BED.
OOOH!
MYTHS & LEGENDS
ADVENTURE
MAGICAL FAIRY TALES
WILD WEST TALES
SPACE STORIES

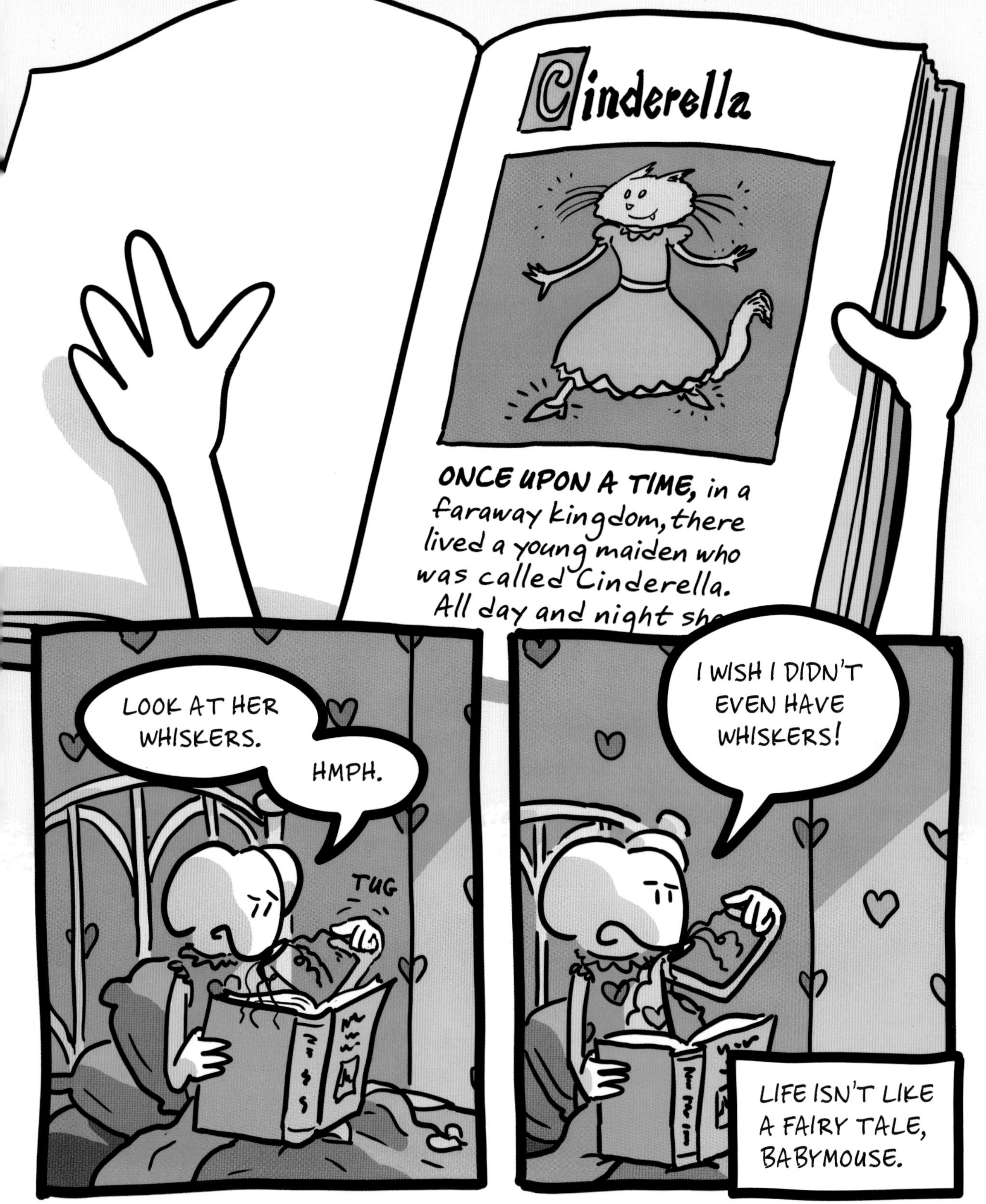
Cinderella
ONCE UPON A TIME, in a faraway kingdom, there lived a young maiden who was called Cinderella. All day and night she
LOOK AT HER WHISKERS.
HMPH.
TUG
I WISH I DIDN'T EVEN HAVE WHISKERS!
LIFE ISN'T LIKE A FAIRY TALE, BABYMOUSE.

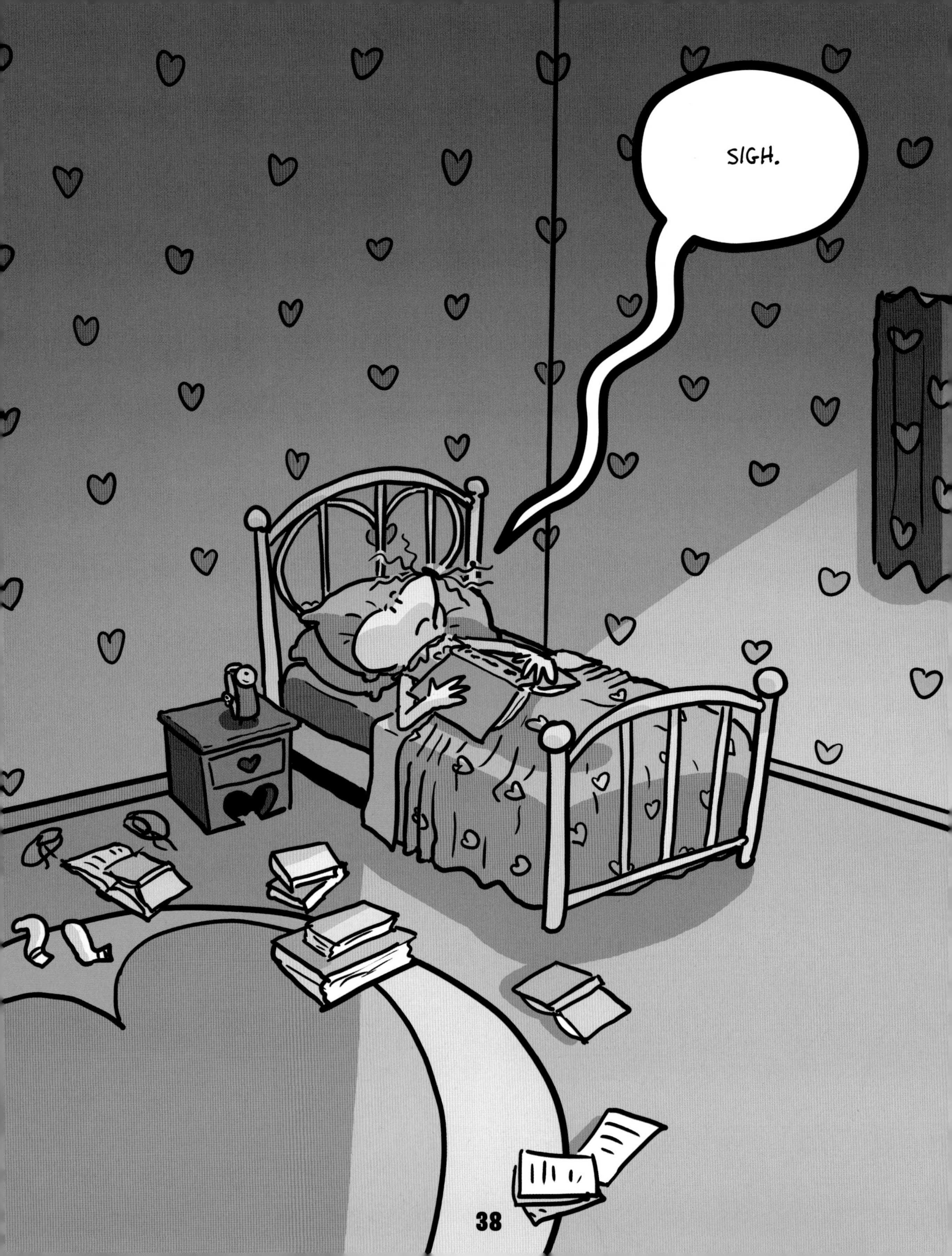
SIGH.

PART TWO

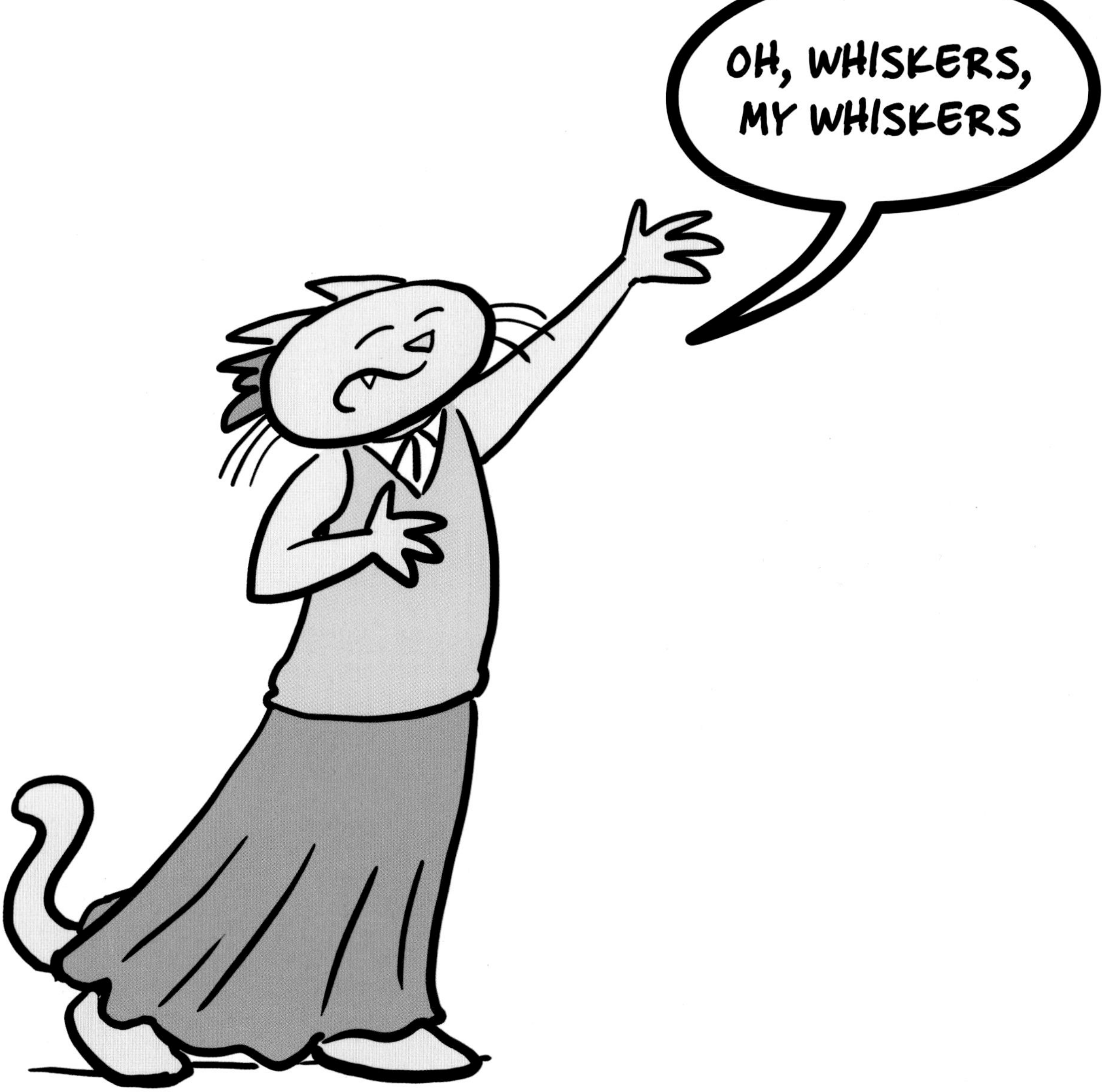
OH, WHISKERS, MY WHISKERS

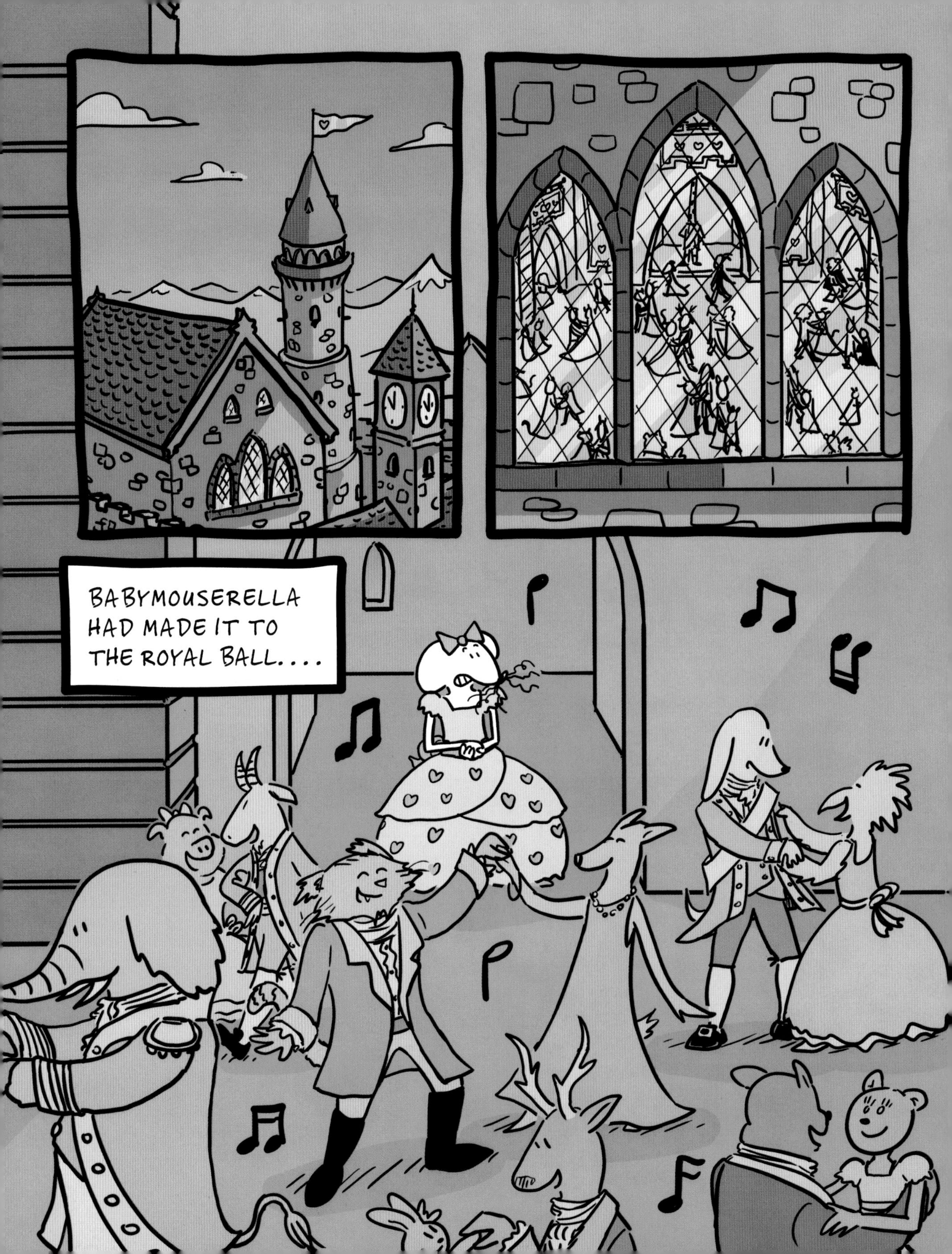
BABYMOUSERELLA HAD MADE IT TO THE ROYAL BALL....

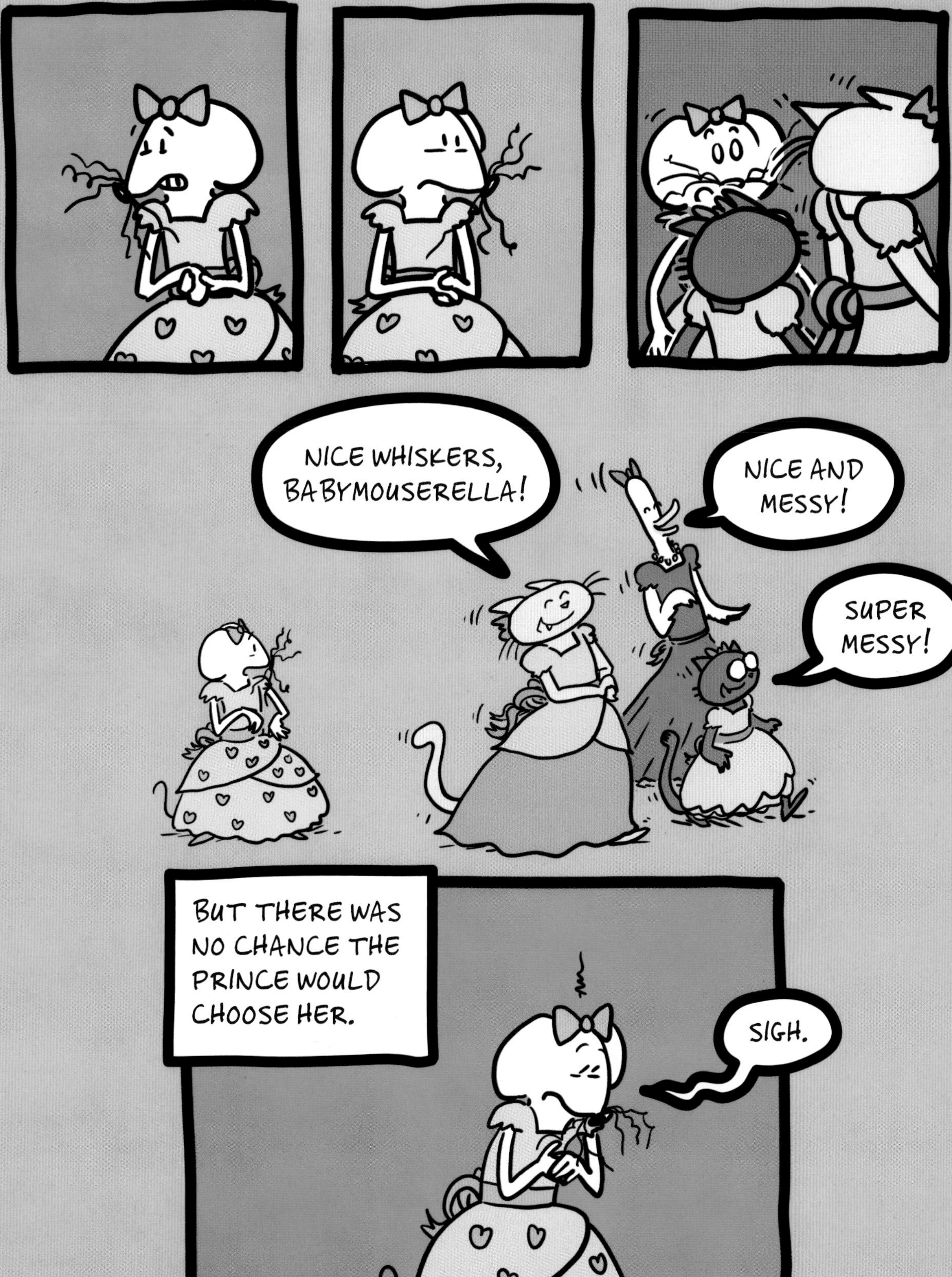
NICE WHISKERS, BABYMOUSERELLA!
NICE AND MESSY!
SUPER MESSY!
BUT THERE WAS NO CHANCE THE PRINCE WOULD CHOOSE HER.
SIGH.

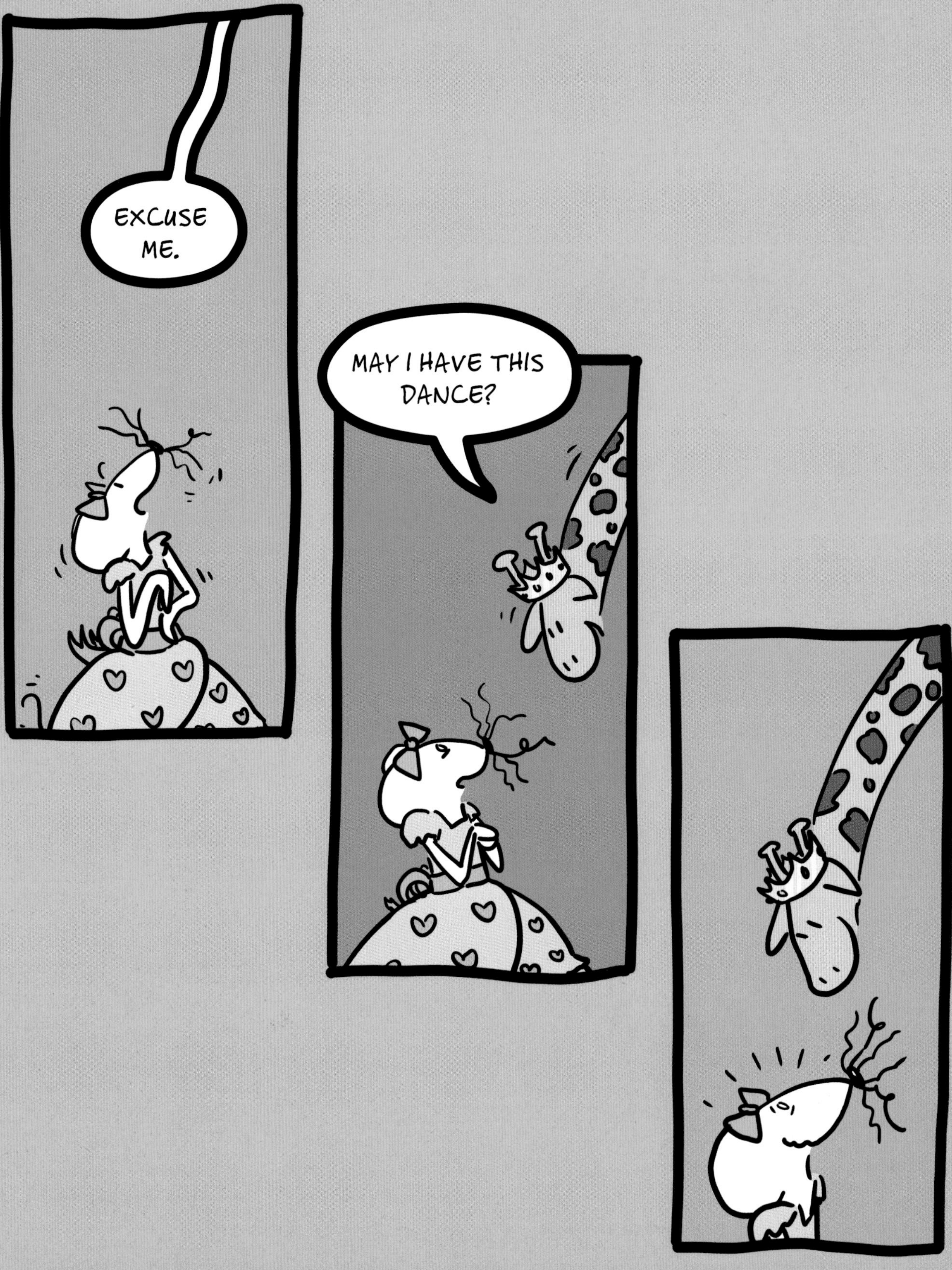
EXCUSE ME.
MAY I HAVE THIS DANCE?

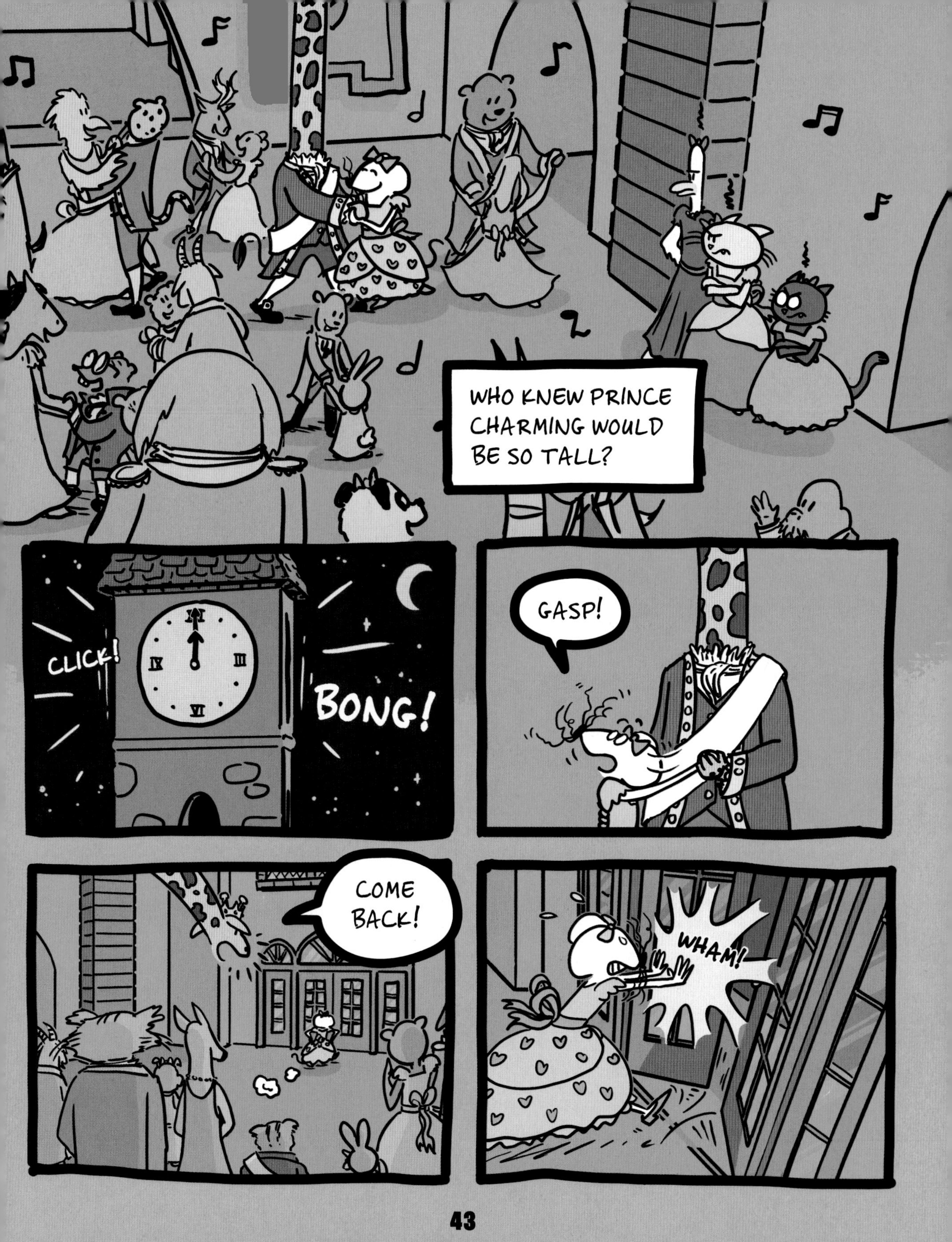

WHO KNEW PRINCE CHARMING WOULD BE SO TALL?
CLICK!
BONG!
GASP!
COME BACK!
WHAM!

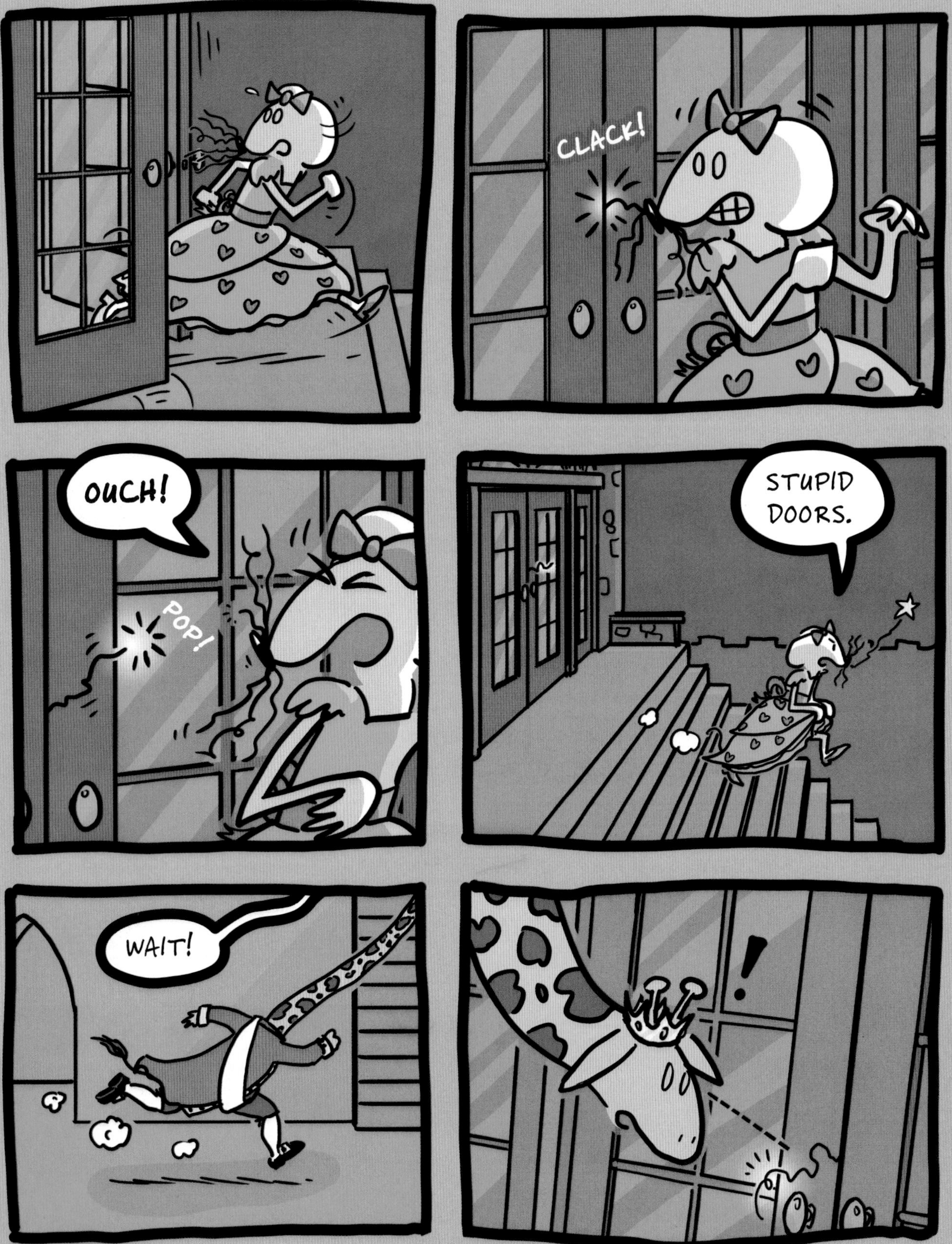
CLACK!
OUCH!
POP!
STUPID DOORS.
WAIT!
!

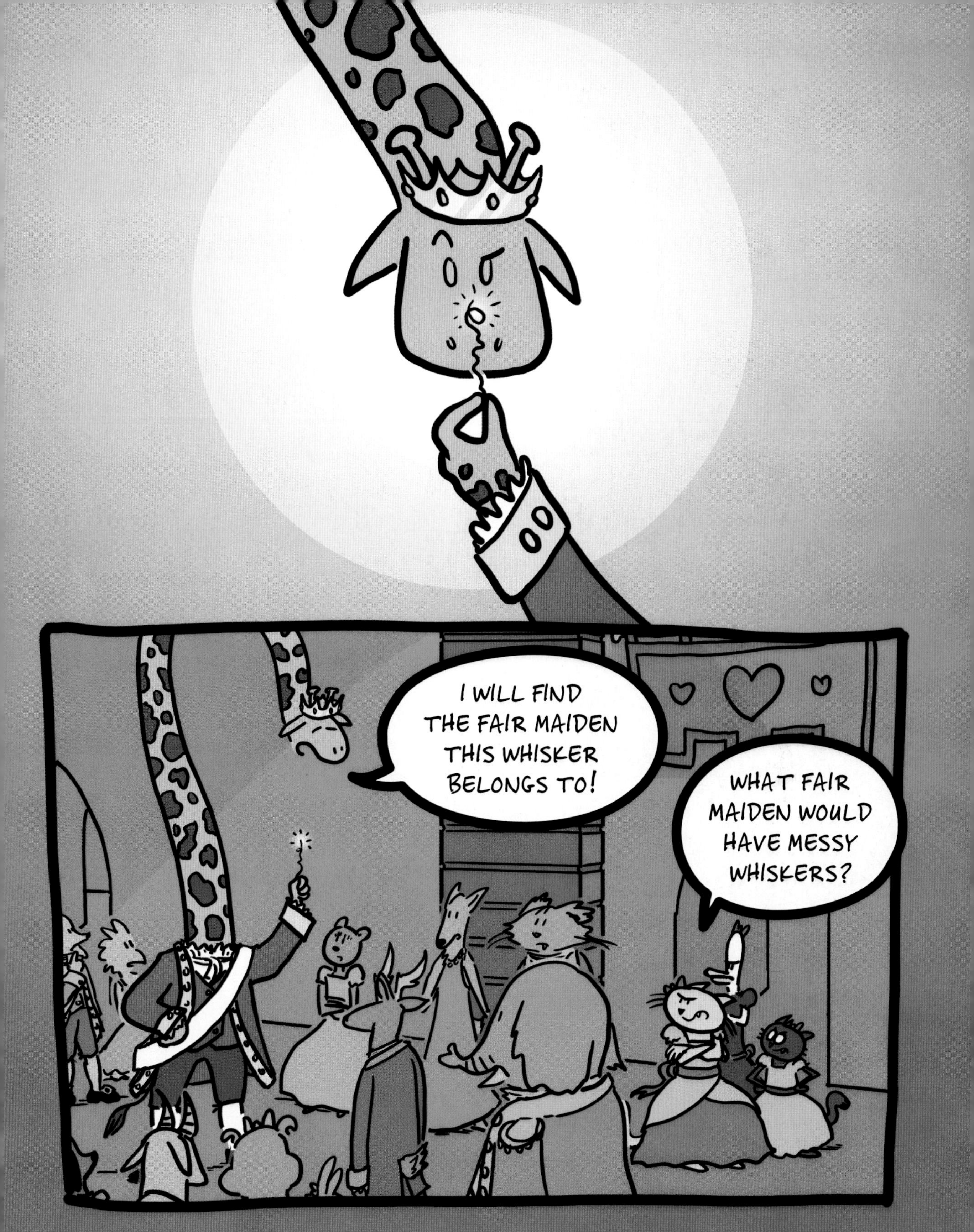
I WILL FIND THE FAIR MAIDEN THIS WHISKER BELONGS TO!
WHAT FAIR MAIDEN WOULD HAVE MESSY WHISKERS?

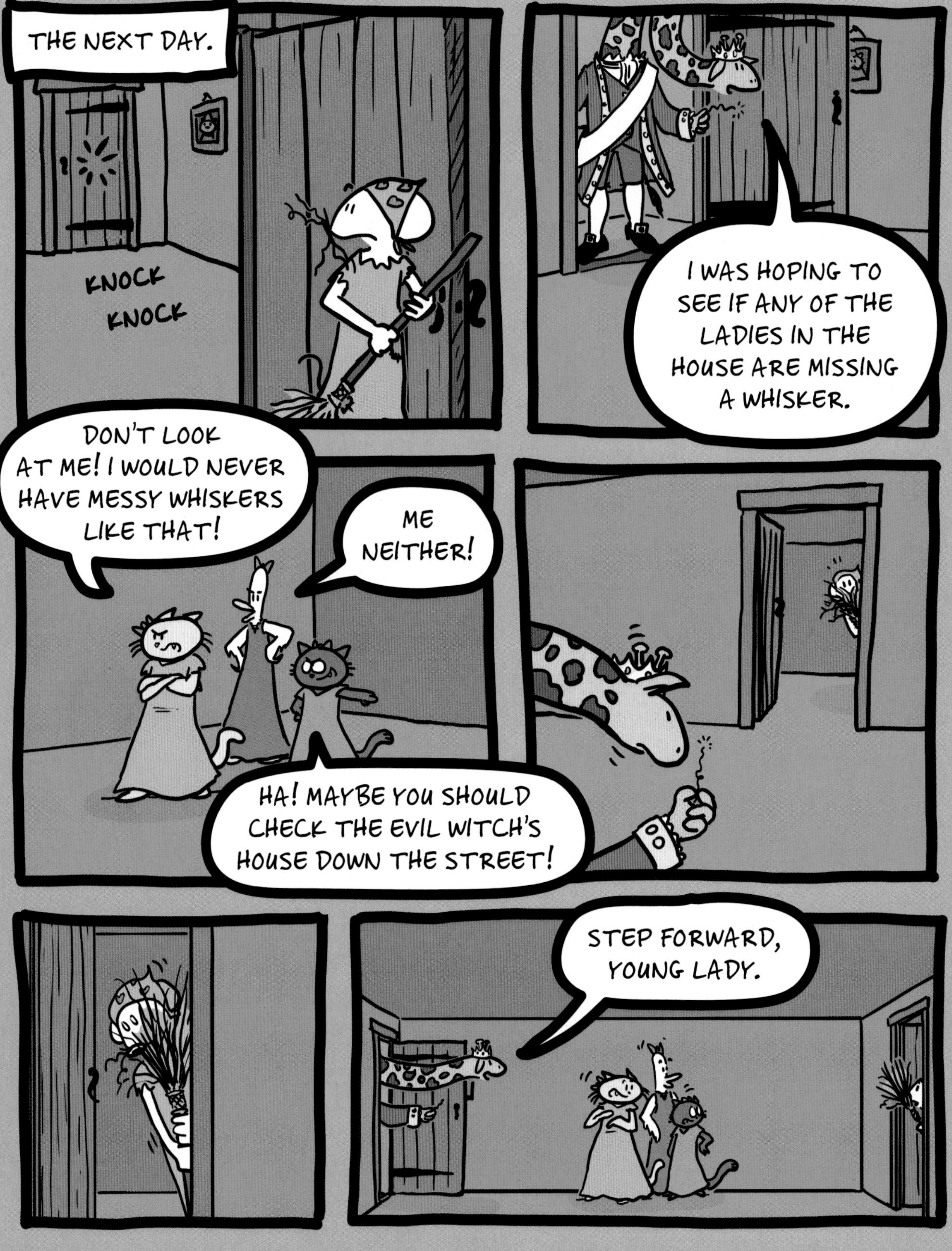
THE NEXT DAY.
KNOCK KNOCK
I WAS HOPING TO SEE IF ANY OF THE LADIES IN THE HOUSE ARE MISSING A WHISKER.
DON'T LOOK AT ME! I WOULD NEVER HAVE MESSY WHISKERS LIKE THAT!
ME NEITHER!
HA! MAYBE YOU SHOULD CHECK THE EVIL WITCH'S HOUSE DOWN THE STREET!
STEP FORWARD, YOUNG LADY.

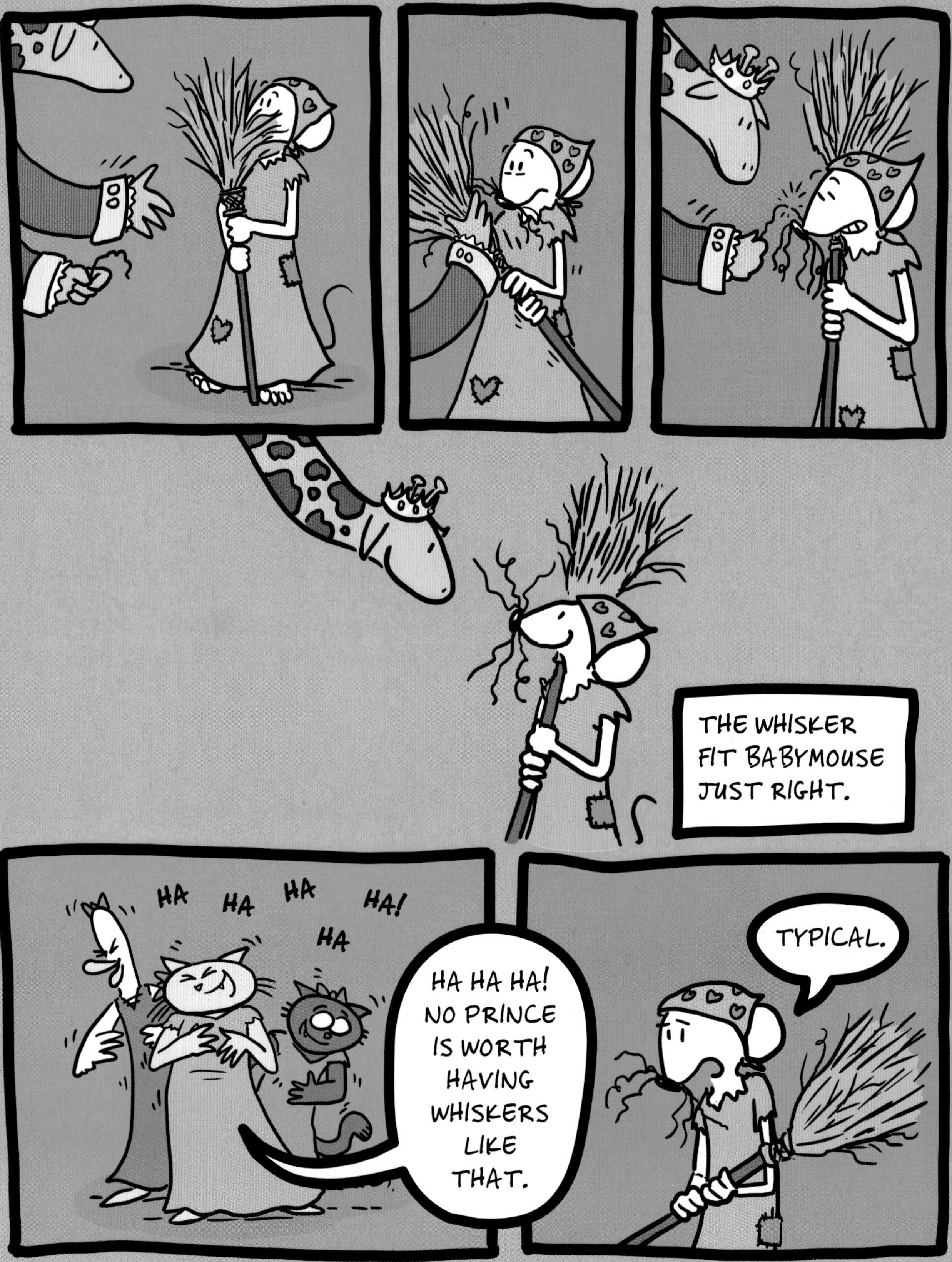
THE WHISKER FIT BABYMOUSE JUST RIGHT.
HA HA HA HA! HA
HA HA HA! NO PRINCE IS WORTH HAVING WHISKERS LIKE THAT.
TYPICAL.

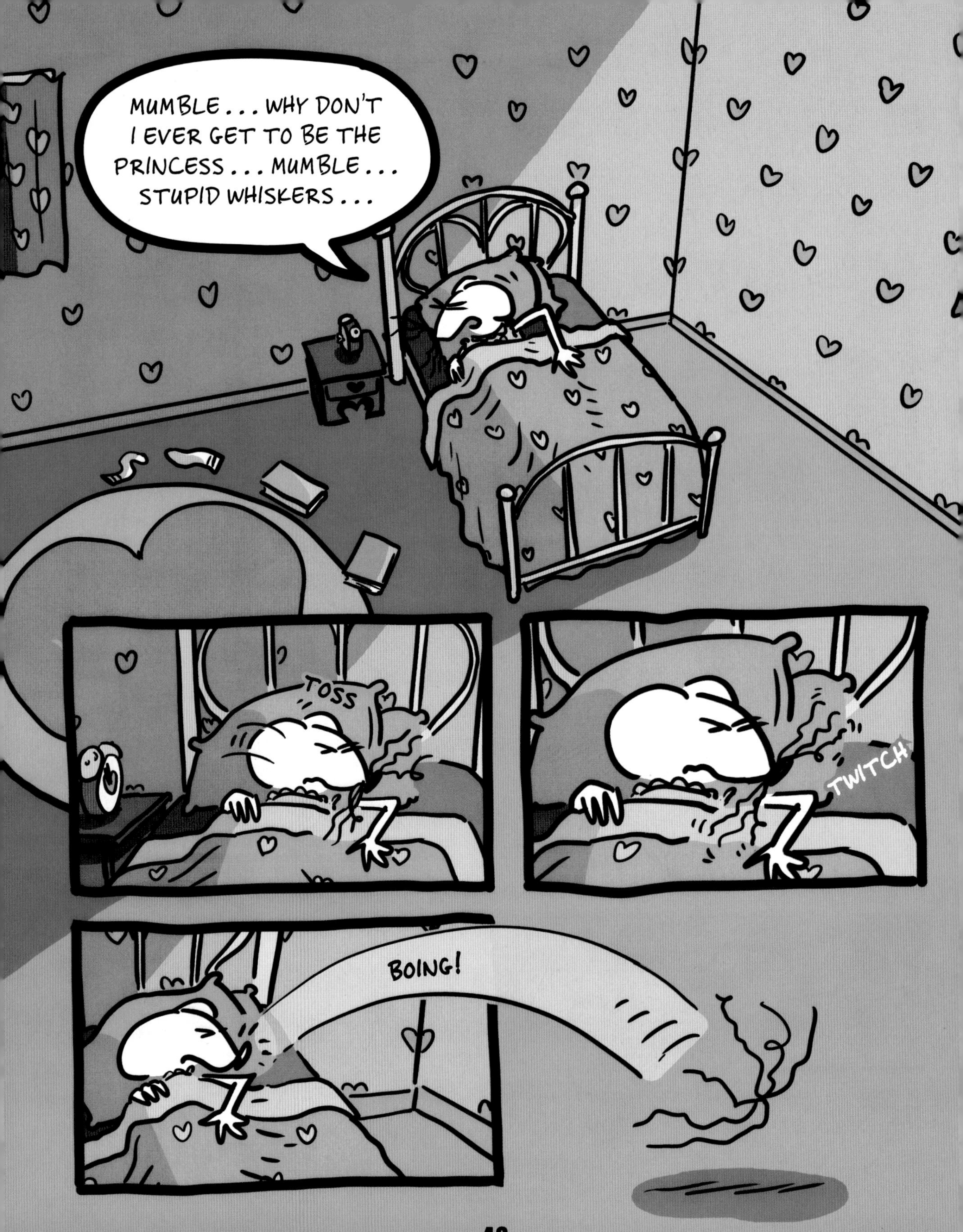
MUMBLE . . . WHY DON'T I EVER GET TO BE THE PRINCESS . . . MUMBLE . . . STUPID WHISKERS . . .
TOSS
TWITCH
BOING!

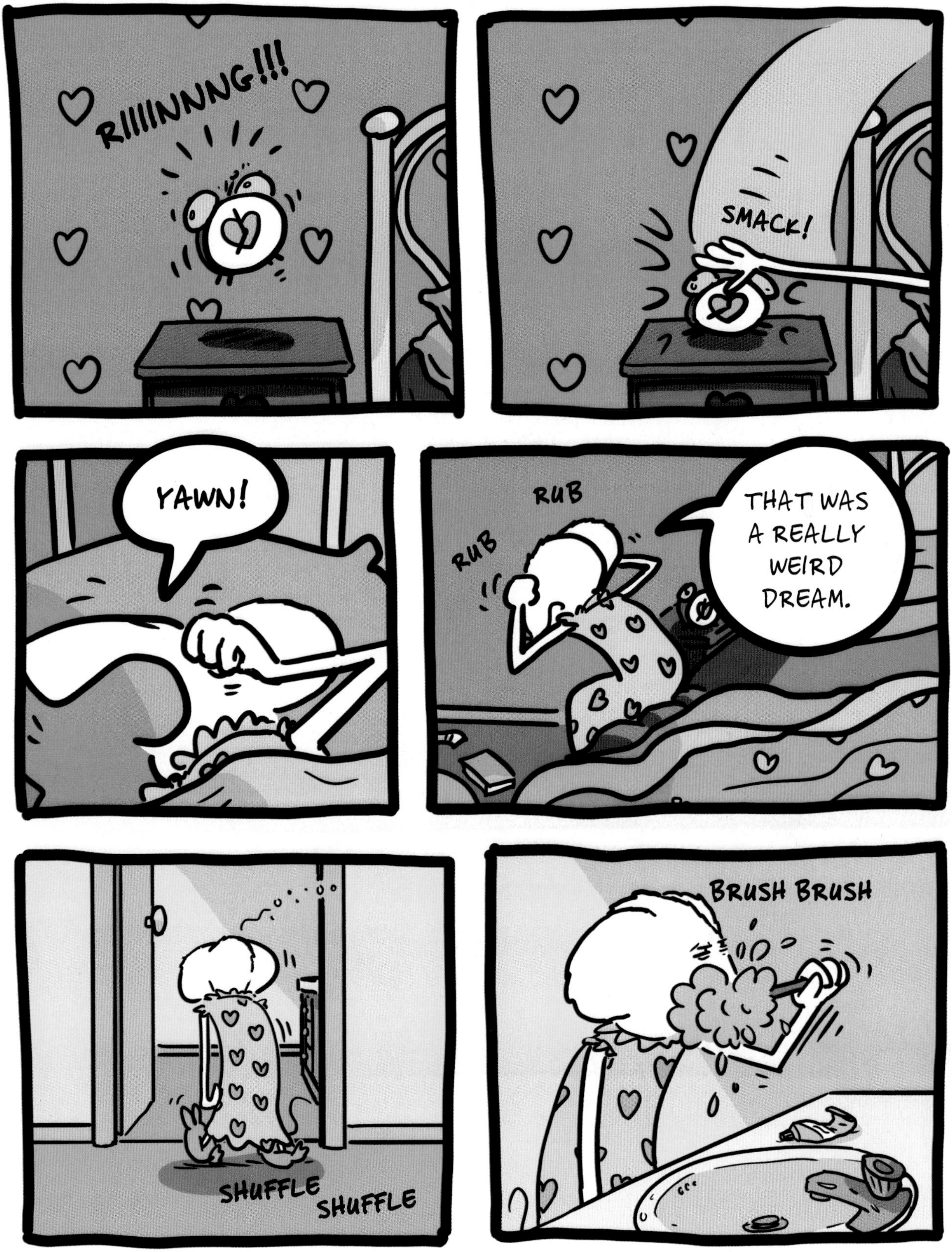
RIIIINNNG!!!
SMACK!
YAWN!
RUB
RUB
THAT WAS A REALLY WEIRD DREAM.
SHUFFLE
SHUFFLE
BRUSH BRUSH

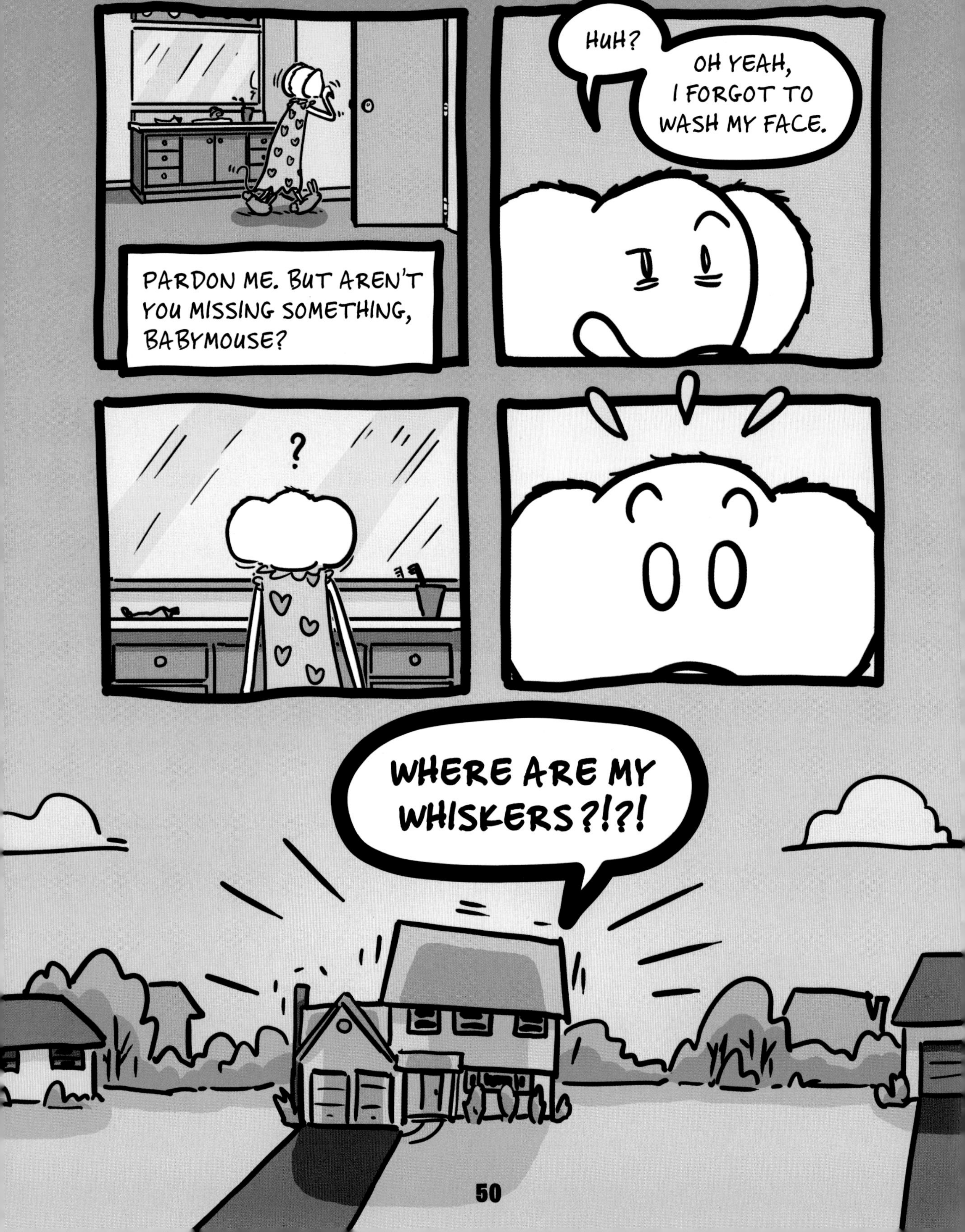
PARDON ME. BUT AREN'T YOU MISSING SOMETHING, BABYMOUSE?
HUH?
OH YEAH, I FORGOT TO WASH MY FACE.
?
WHERE ARE MY WHISKERS?!?!

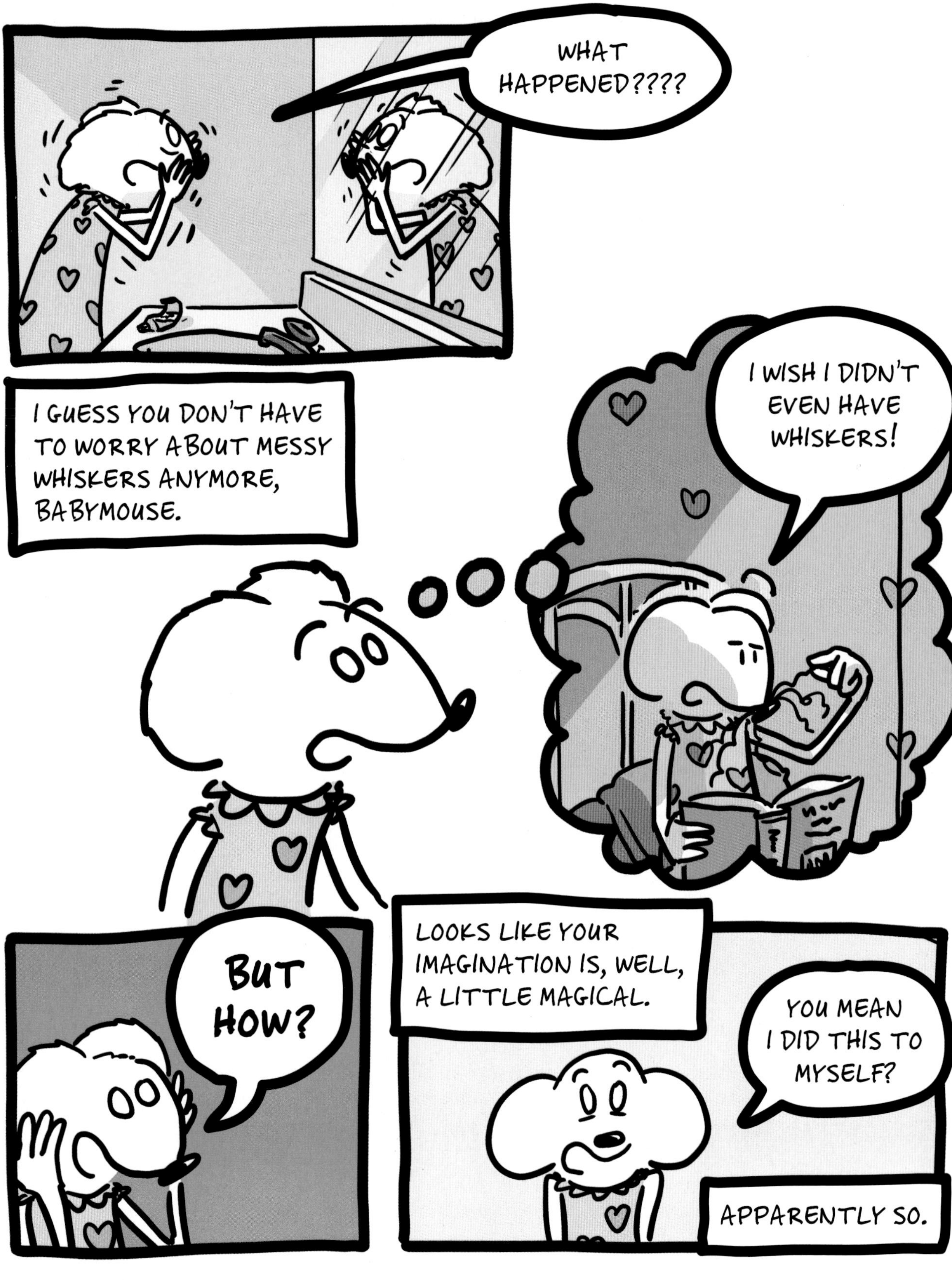
WHAT HAPPENED????
I GUESS YOU DON'T HAVE TO WORRY ABOUT MESSY WHISKERS ANYMORE, BABYMOUSE.
I WISH I DIDN'T EVEN HAVE WHISKERS!
BUT HOW?
LOOKS LIKE YOUR IMAGINATION IS, WELL, A LITTLE MAGICAL.
YOU MEAN I DID THIS TO MYSELF?
APPARENTLY SO.

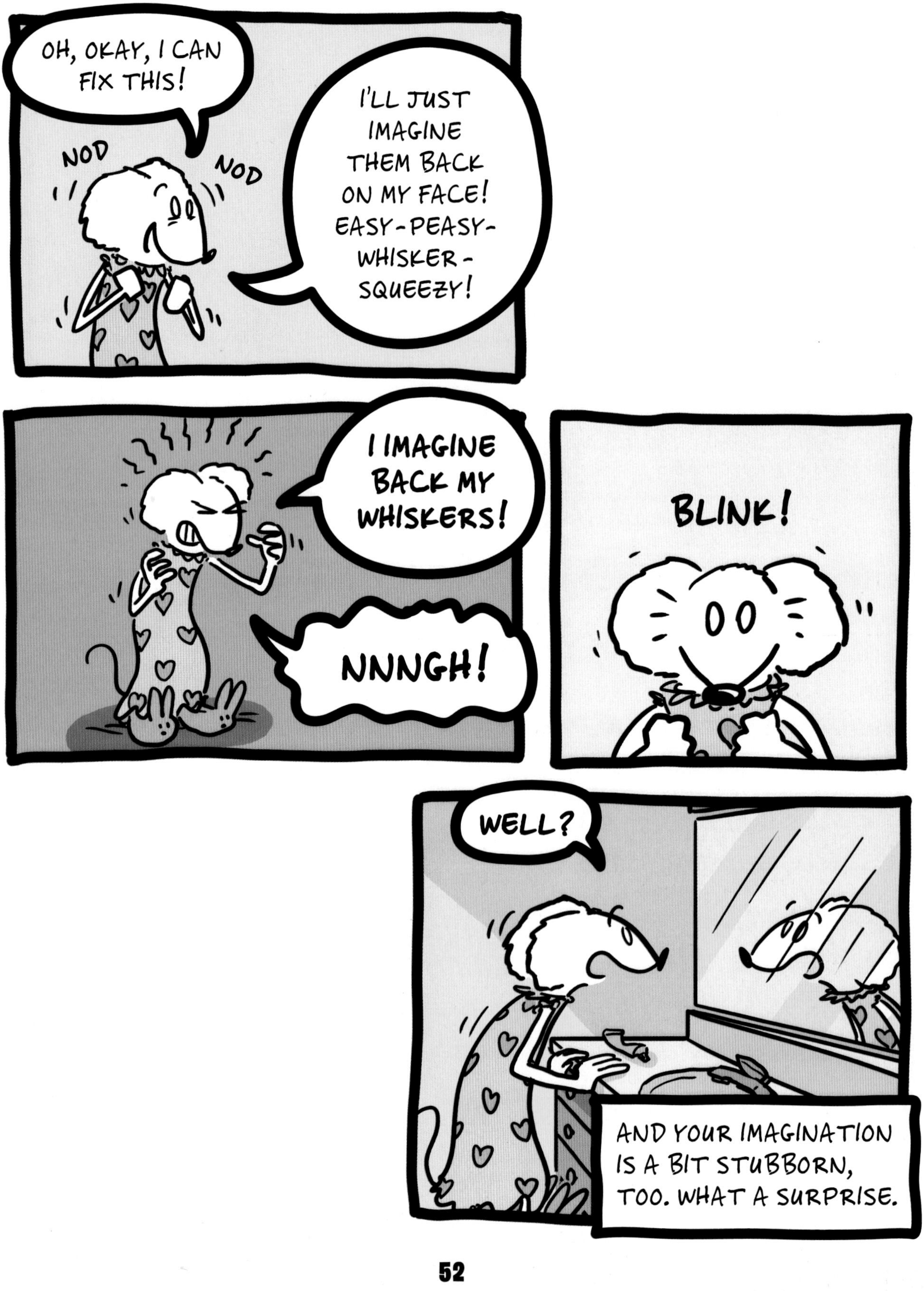
OH, OKAY, I CAN FIX THIS!
NOD
NOD
I'LL JUST IMAGINE THEM BACK ON MY FACE! EASY-PEASY-WHISKER-SQUEEZY!
I IMAGINE BACK MY WHISKERS!
NNNGH!
BLINK!
WELL?
AND YOUR IMAGINATION IS A BIT STUBBORN, TOO. WHAT A SURPRISE.

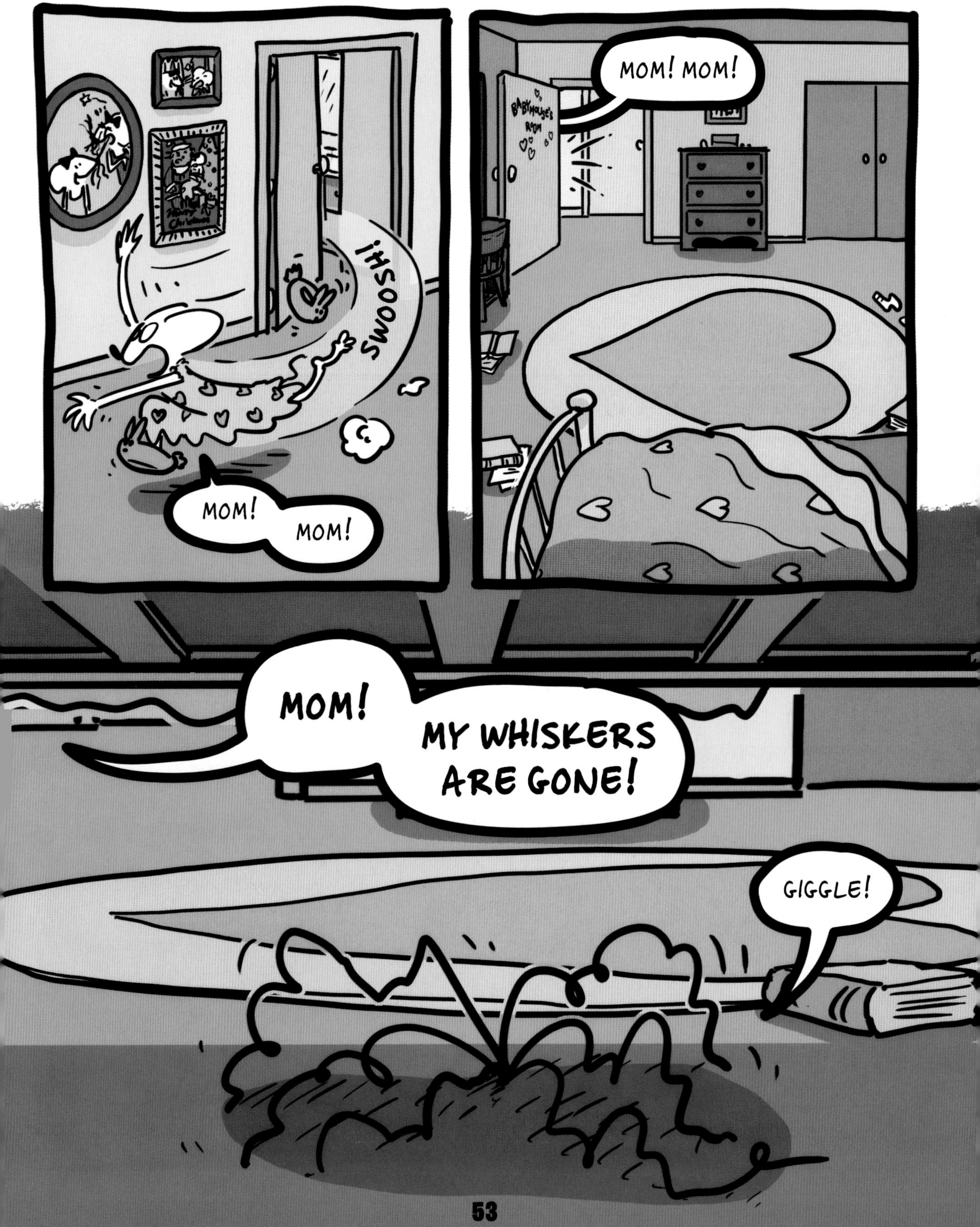
SWOOSH!
MOM!
MOM!
MOM! MOM!
BABYMOUSE'S ROOM
MOM!
MY WHISKERS ARE GONE!
GIGGLE!

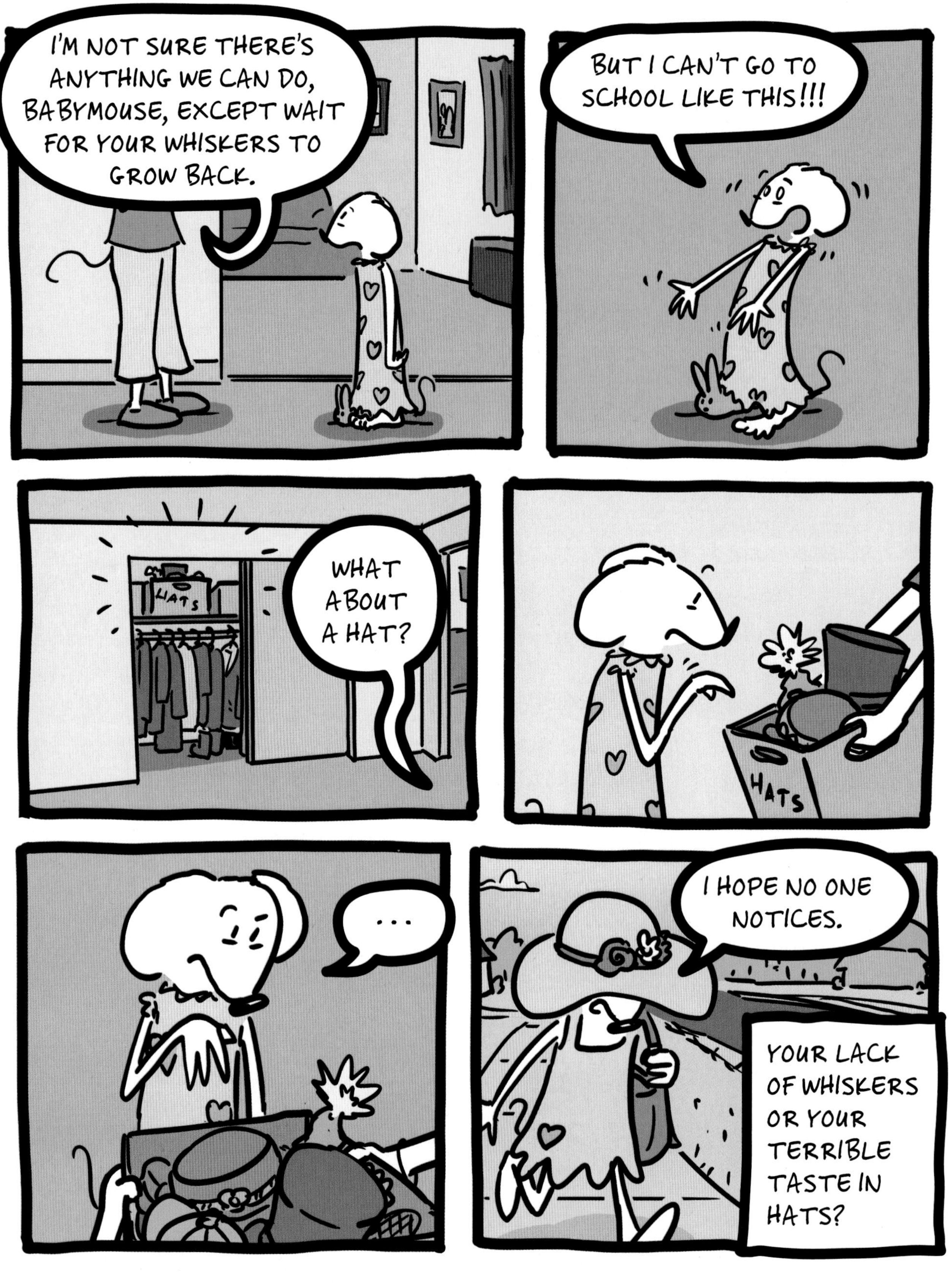

I'M NOT SURE THERE'S ANYTHING WE CAN DO, BABYMOUSE, EXCEPT WAIT FOR YOUR WHISKERS TO GROW BACK.
BUT I CAN'T GO TO SCHOOL LIKE THIS!!!
HATS
WHAT ABOUT A HAT?
HATS
...
I HOPE NO ONE NOTICES.
YOUR LACK OF WHISKERS OR YOUR TERRIBLE TASTE IN HATS?

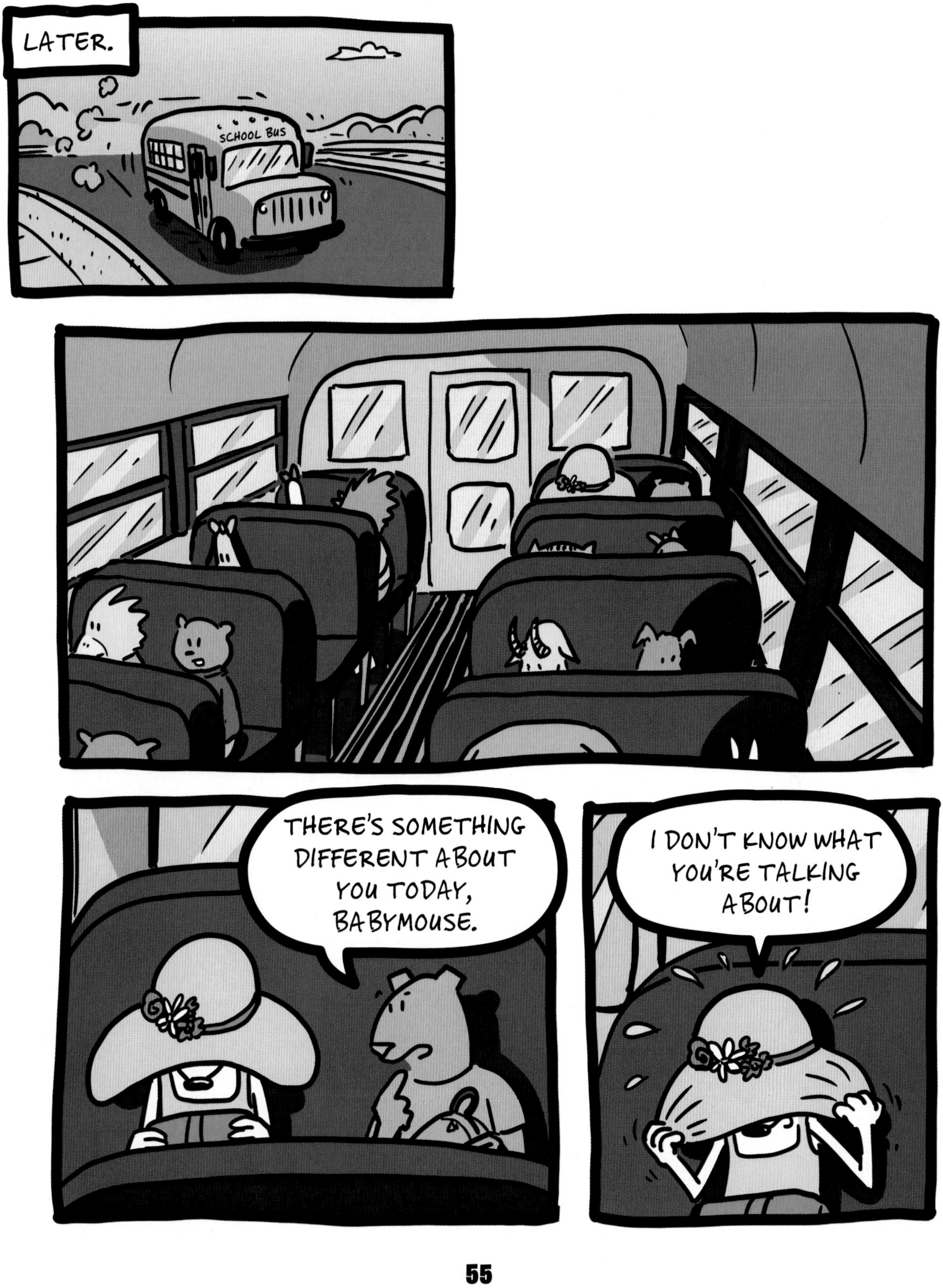
LATER.
SCHOOL BUS
THERE'S SOMETHING DIFFERENT ABOUT YOU TODAY, BABYMOUSE.
I DON'T KNOW WHAT YOU'RE TALKING ABOUT!

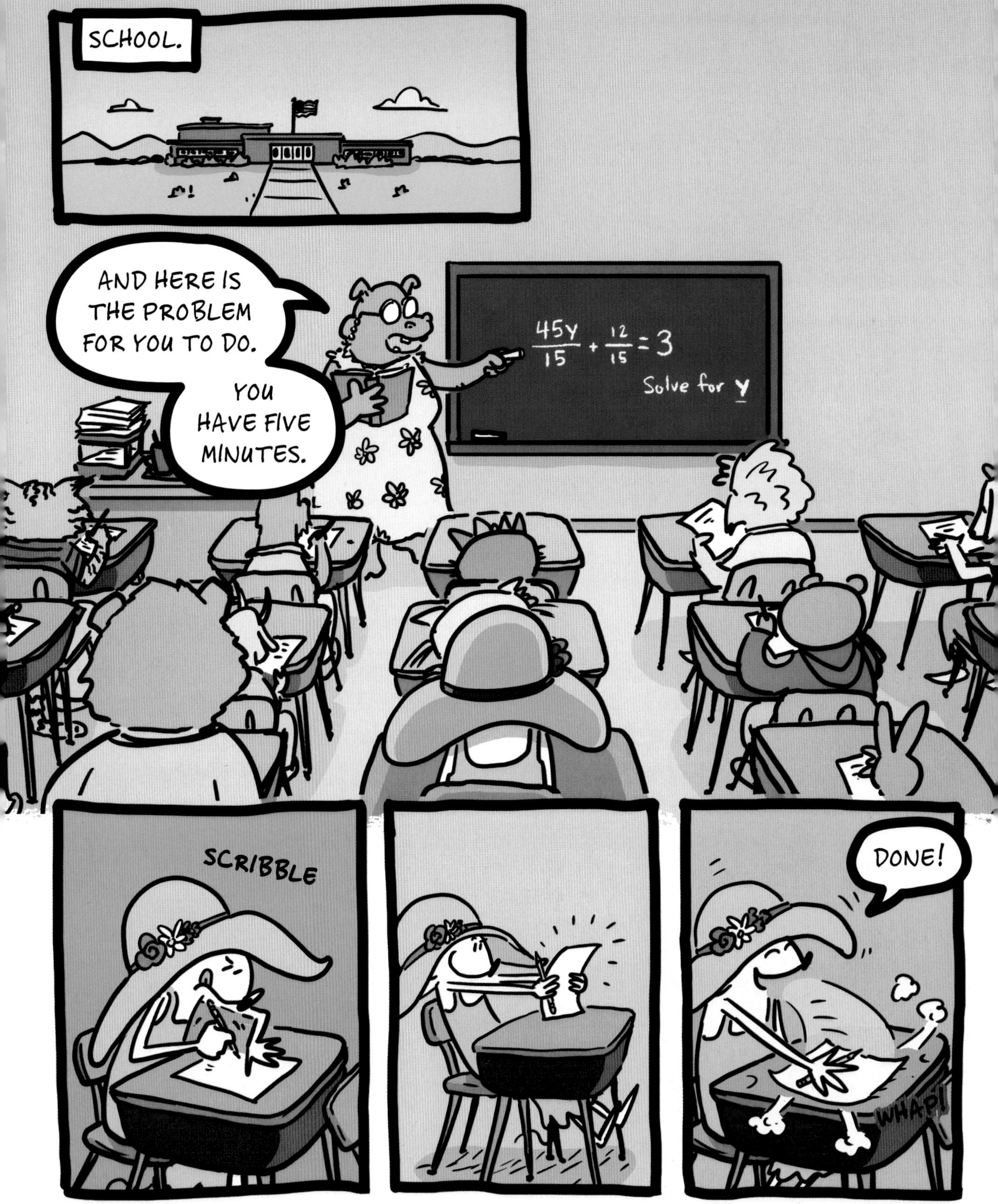
SCHOOL.
AND HERE IS THE PROBLEM FOR YOU TO DO.
YOU HAVE FIVE MINUTES.
45y/15 + 12/15 = 3
Solve for y
SCRIBBLE
DONE!
WHAP!

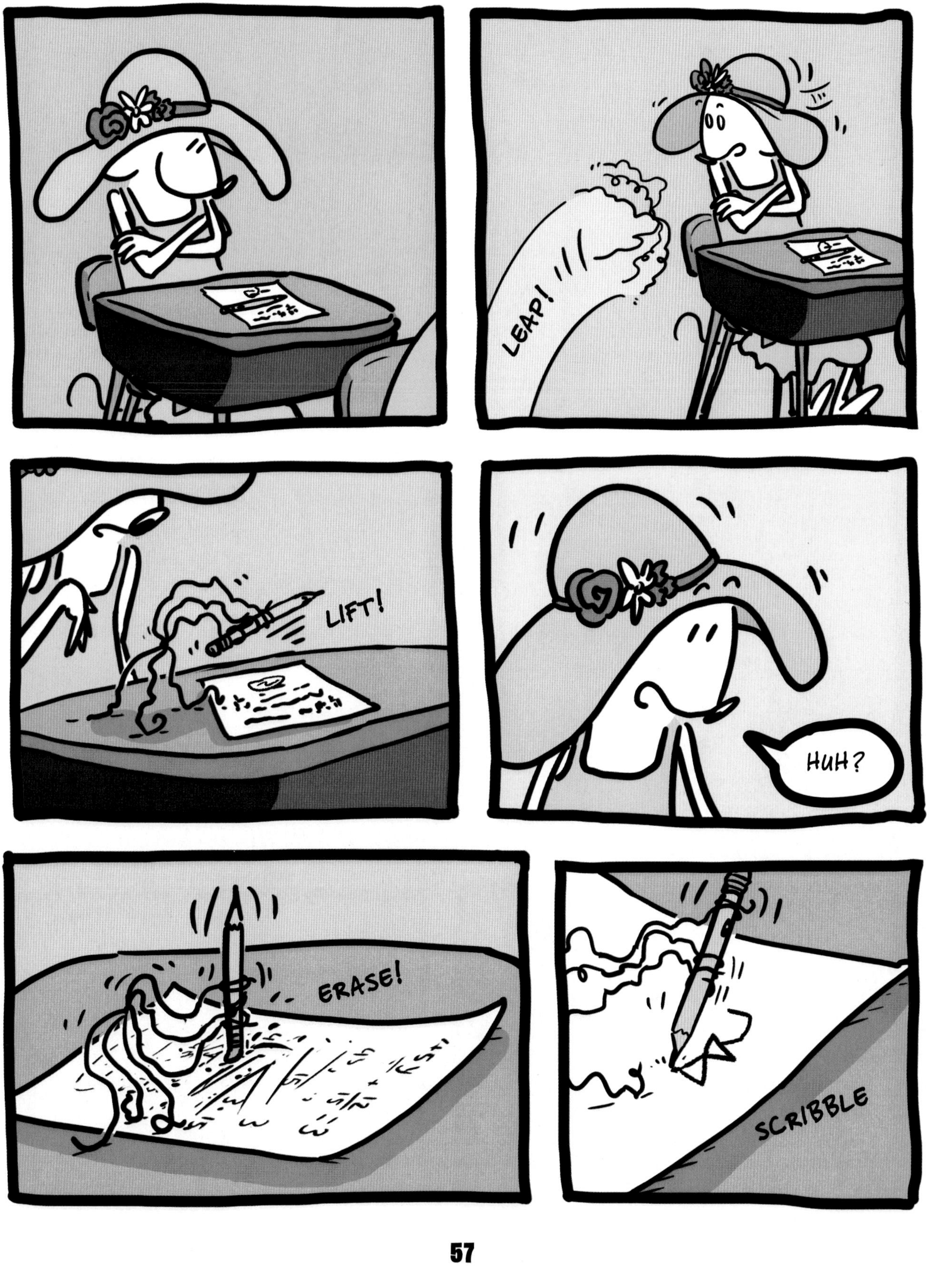
LEAP!
LIFT!
HUH?
ERASE!
SCRIBBLE

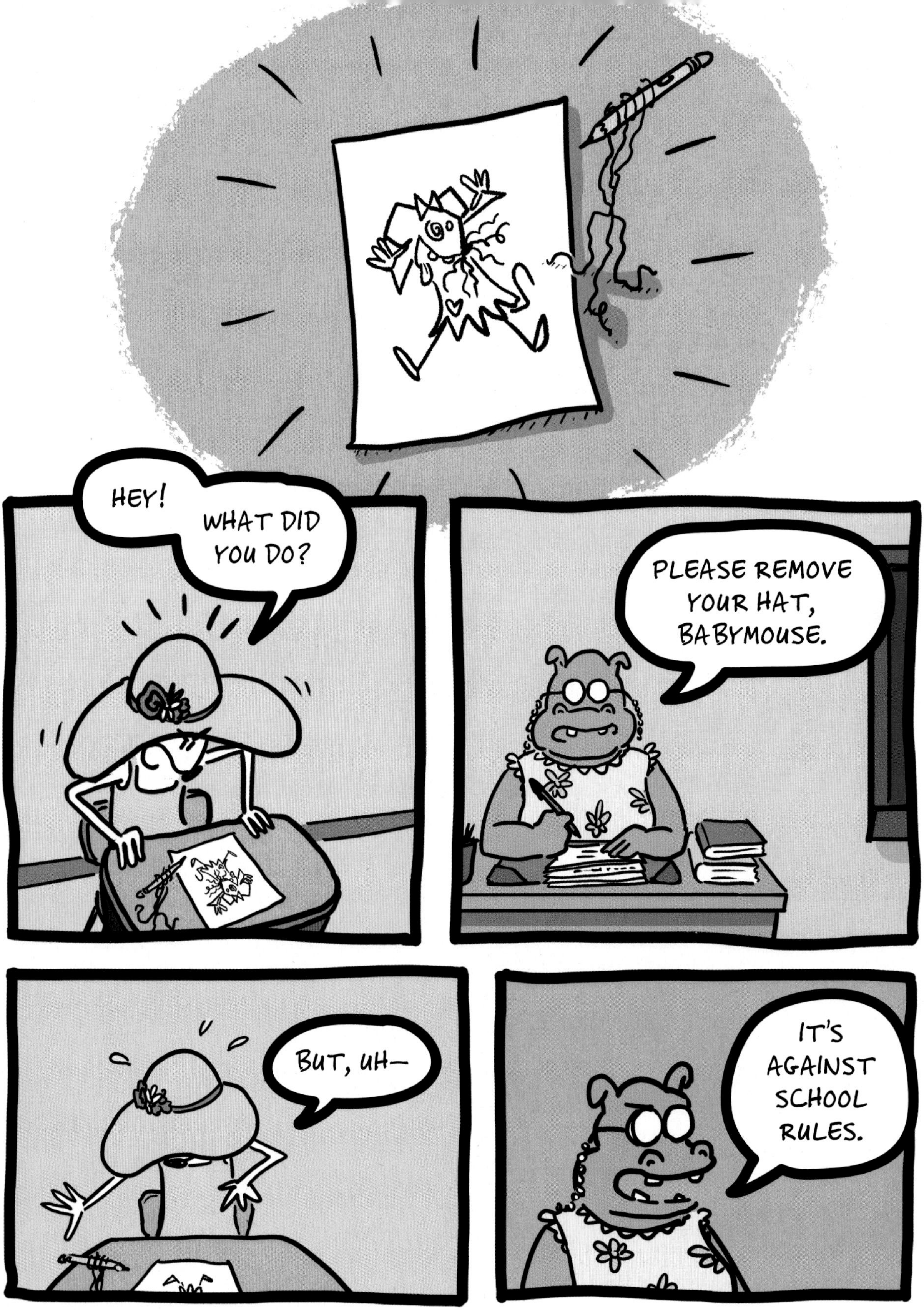
HEY!
WHAT DID YOU DO?
PLEASE REMOVE YOUR HAT, BABYMOUSE.
BUT, UH—
IT'S AGAINST SCHOOL RULES.

HA HA HA HA HA HA HA HA HA!!

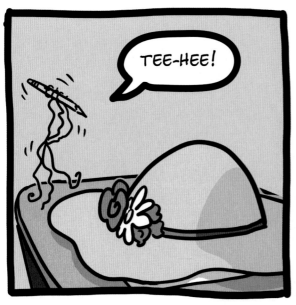

TEE-HEE!

HA   HA   HA   HA!
          HA

SIGH.

SNICKER!

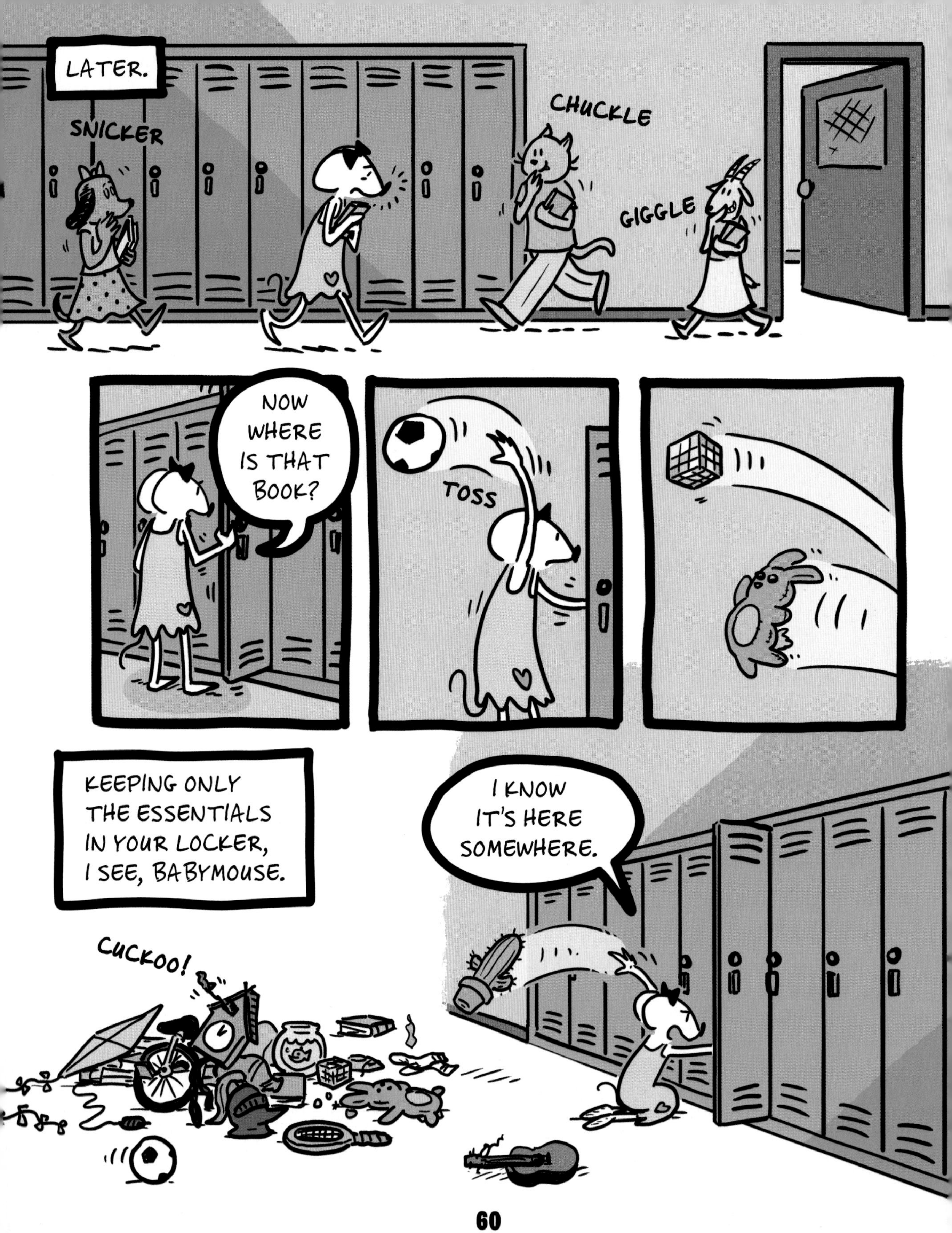
LATER.
SNICKER
CHUCKLE
GIGGLE
NOW WHERE IS THAT BOOK?
TOSS
KEEPING ONLY THE ESSENTIALS IN YOUR LOCKER, I SEE, BABYMOUSE.
I KNOW IT'S HERE SOMEWHERE.
CUCKOO!

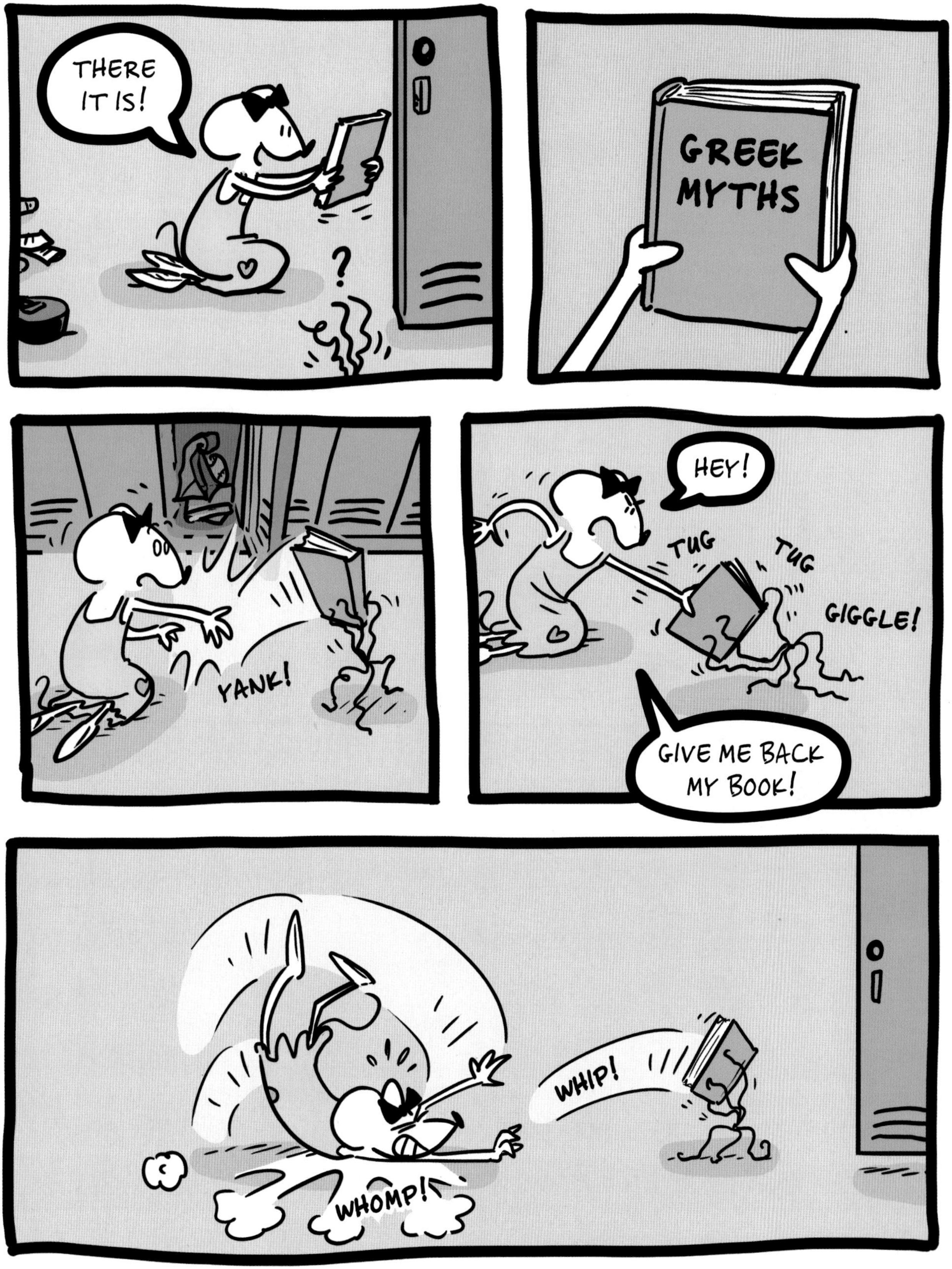
THERE IT IS!
?
GREEK MYTHS
YANK!
HEY!
TUG
TUG
GIGGLE!
GIVE ME BACK MY BOOK!
WHIP!
WHOMP!

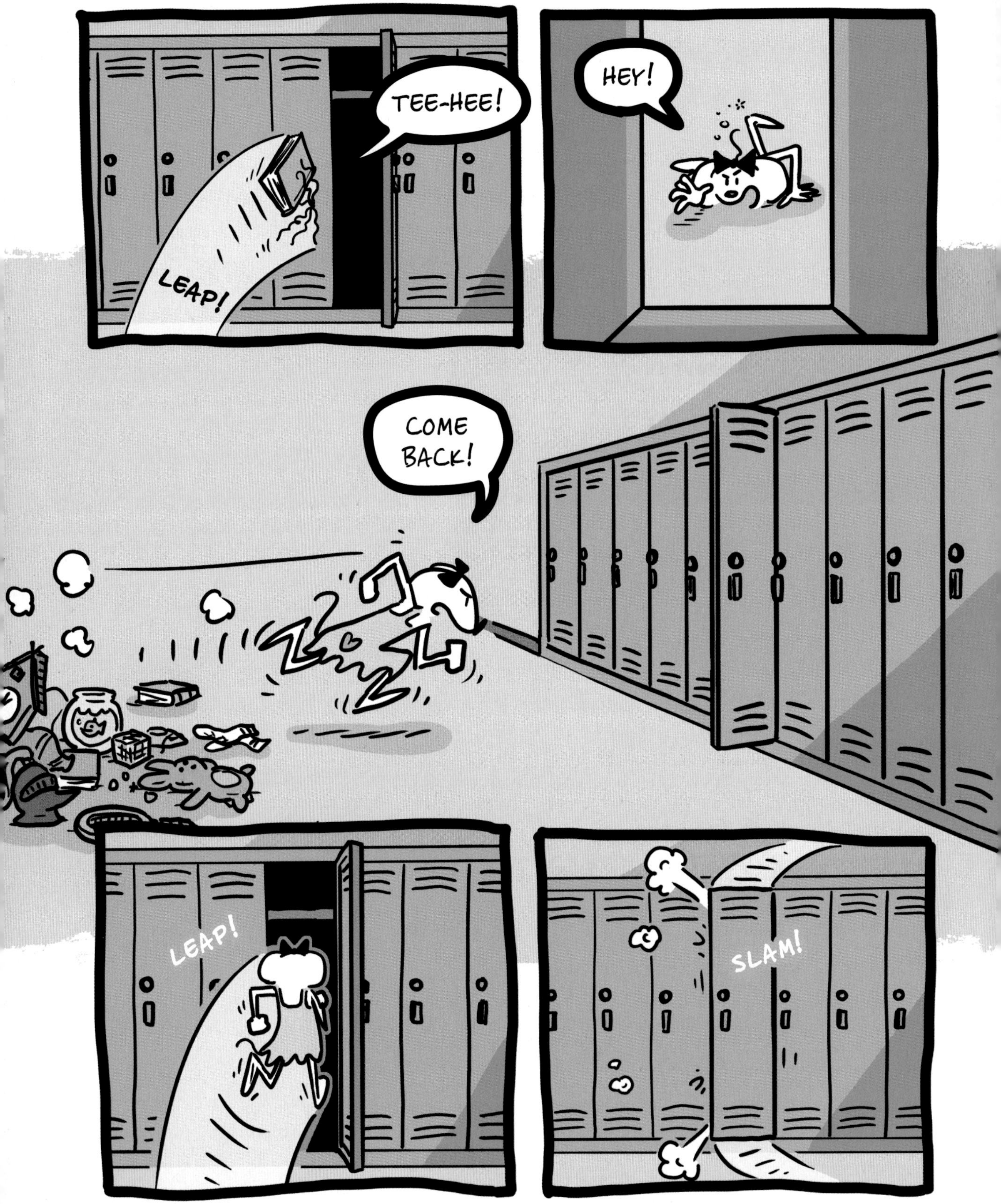
TEE-HEE!
LEAP!
HEY!
COME BACK!
LEAP!
SLAM!

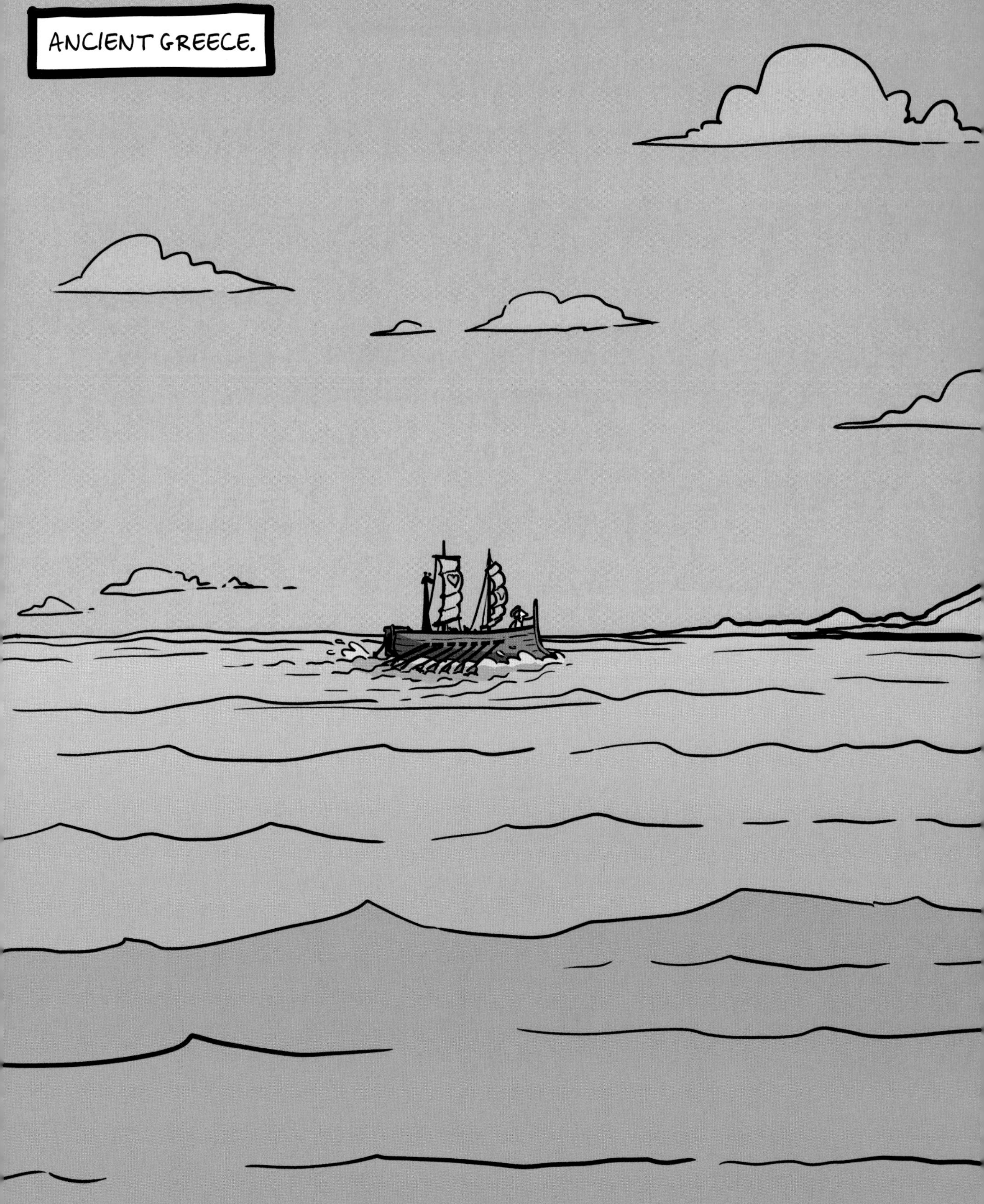
ANCIENT GREECE.

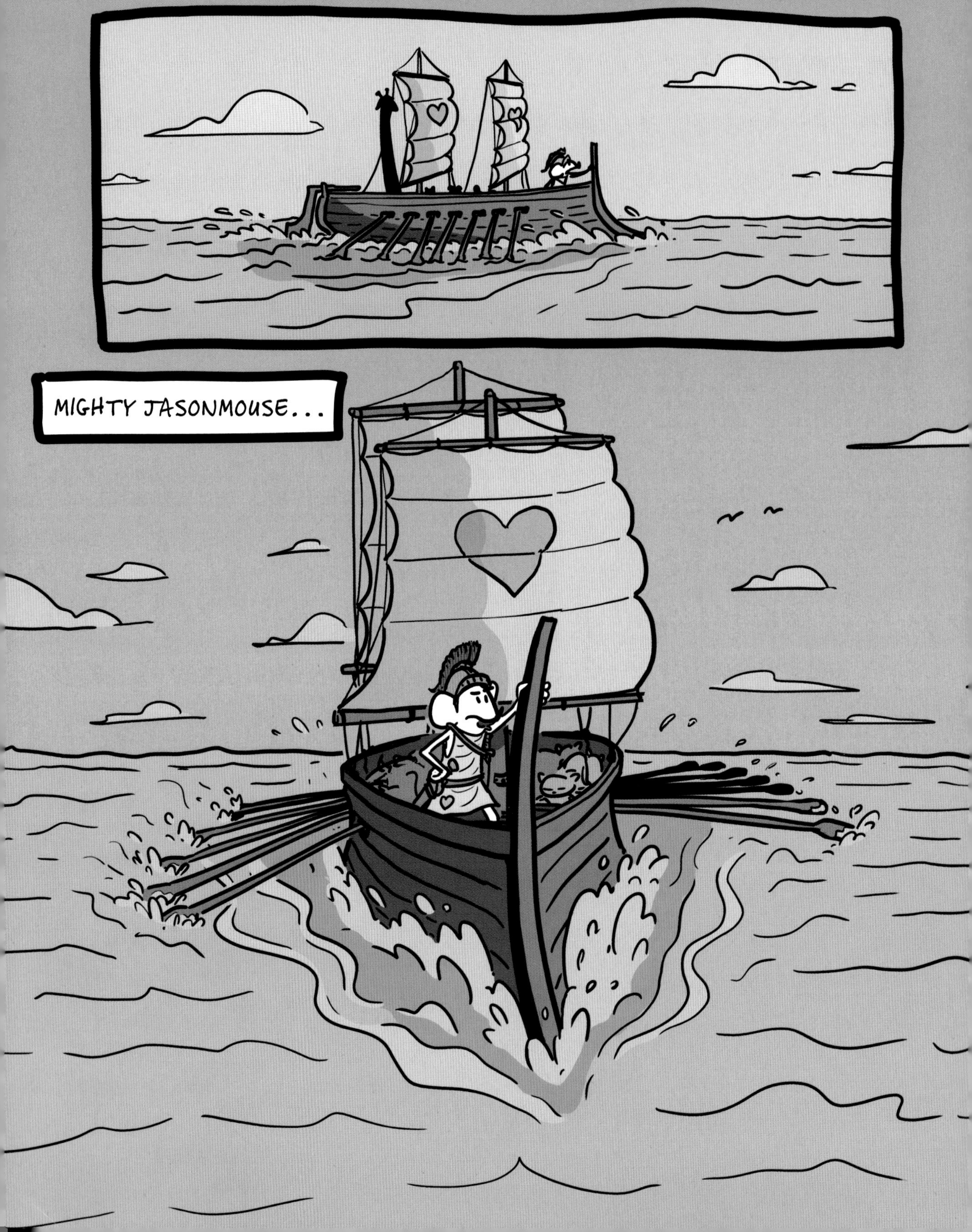
MIGHTY JASONMOUSE...

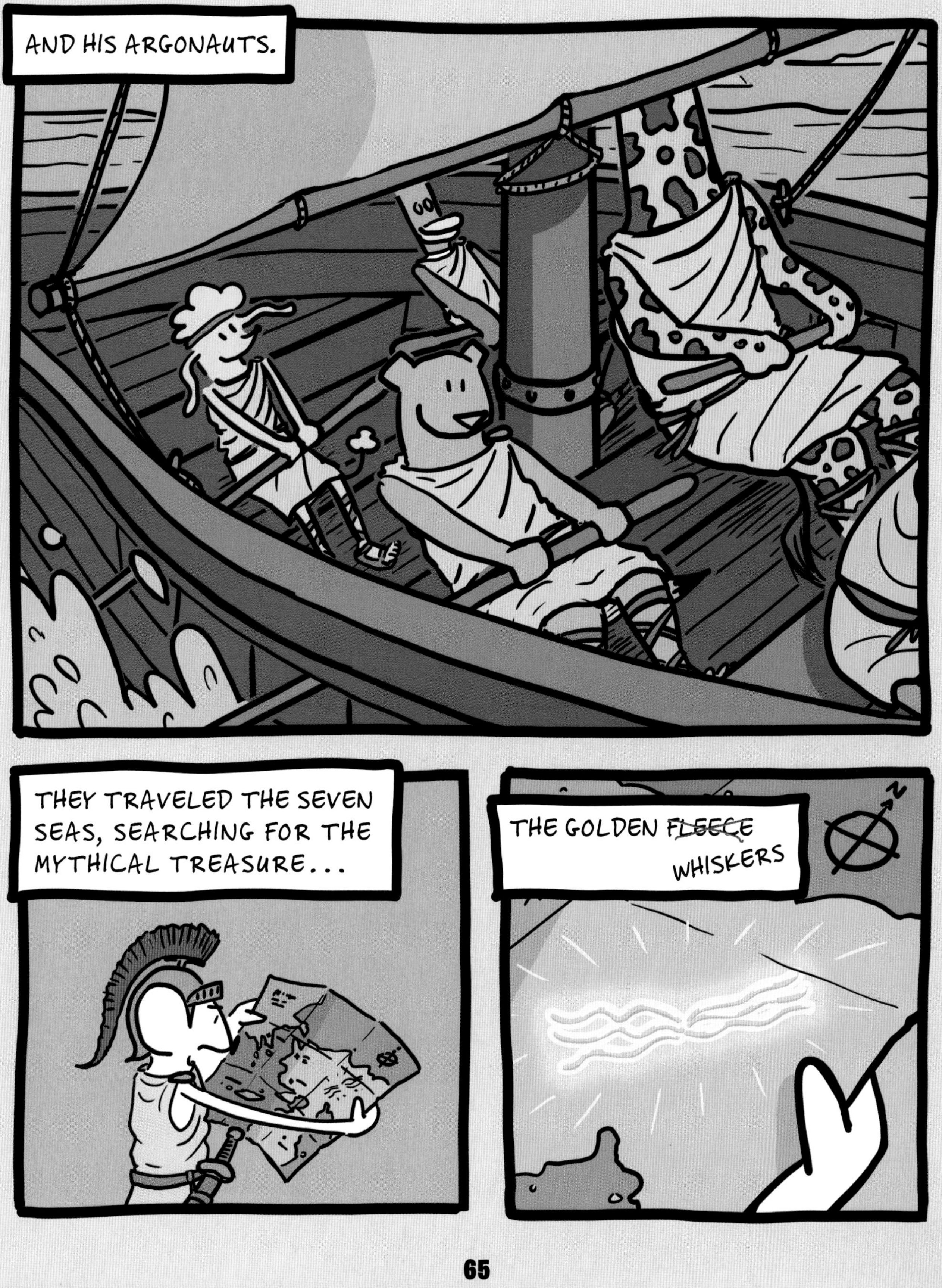
AND HIS ARGONAUTS.
THEY TRAVELED THE SEVEN SEAS, SEARCHING FOR THE MYTHICAL TREASURE...
THE GOLDEN ~~FLEECE~~ WHISKERS

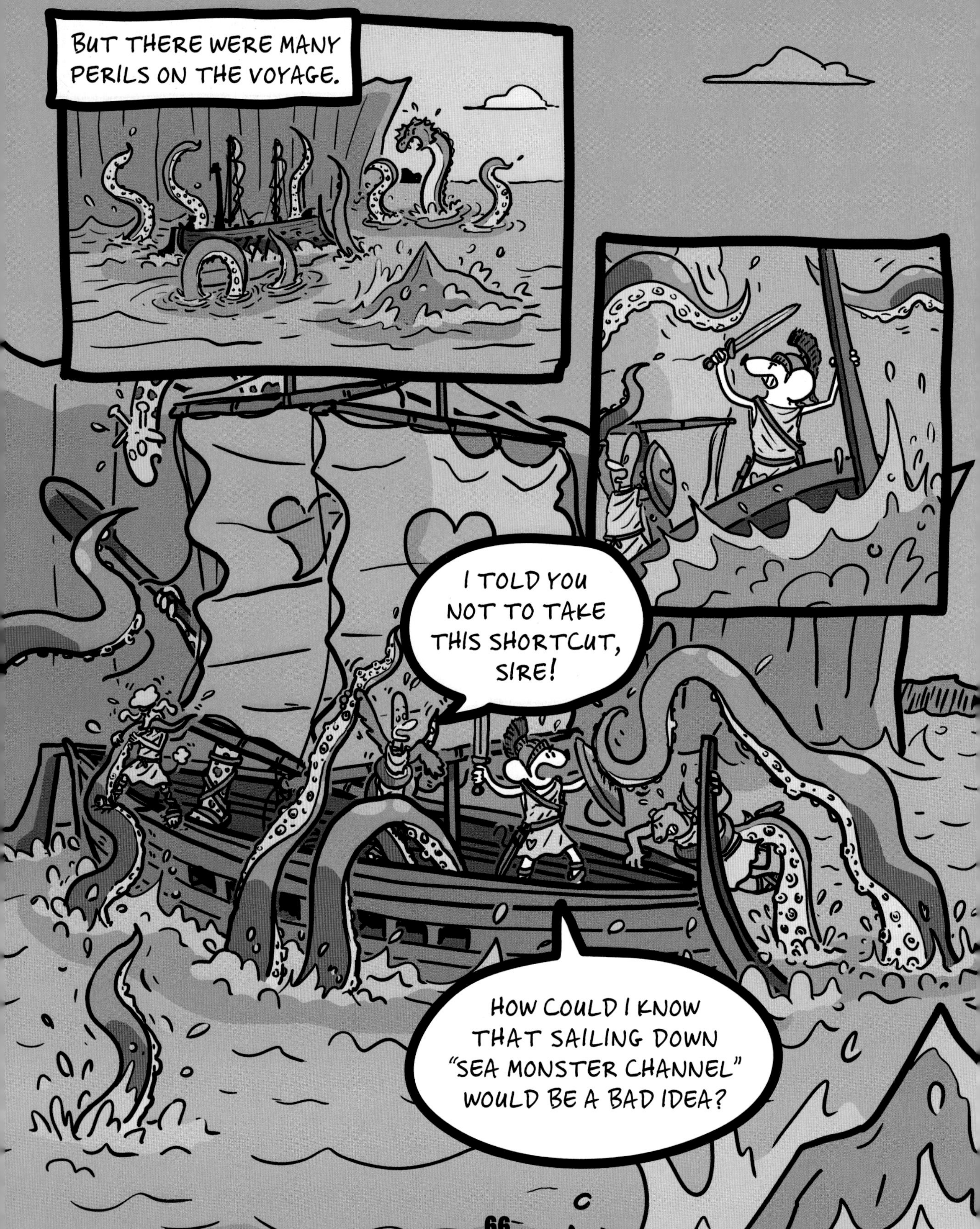
BUT THERE WERE MANY PERILS ON THE VOYAGE.
I TOLD YOU NOT TO TAKE THIS SHORTCUT, SIRE!
HOW COULD I KNOW THAT SAILING DOWN "SEA MONSTER CHANNEL" WOULD BE A BAD IDEA?

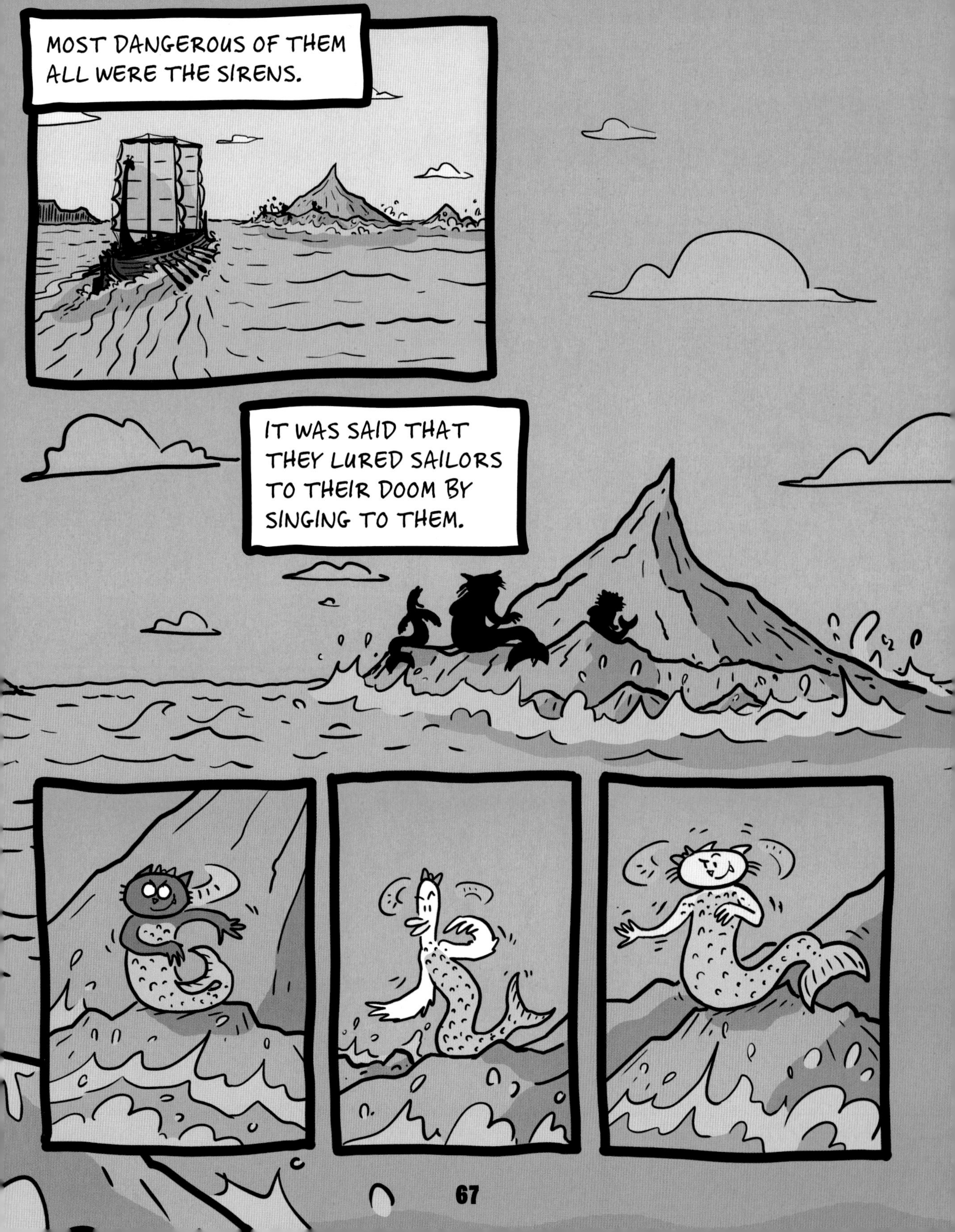
MOST DANGEROUS OF THEM ALL WERE THE SIRENS.
IT WAS SAID THAT THEY LURED SAILORS TO THEIR DOOM BY SINGING TO THEM.

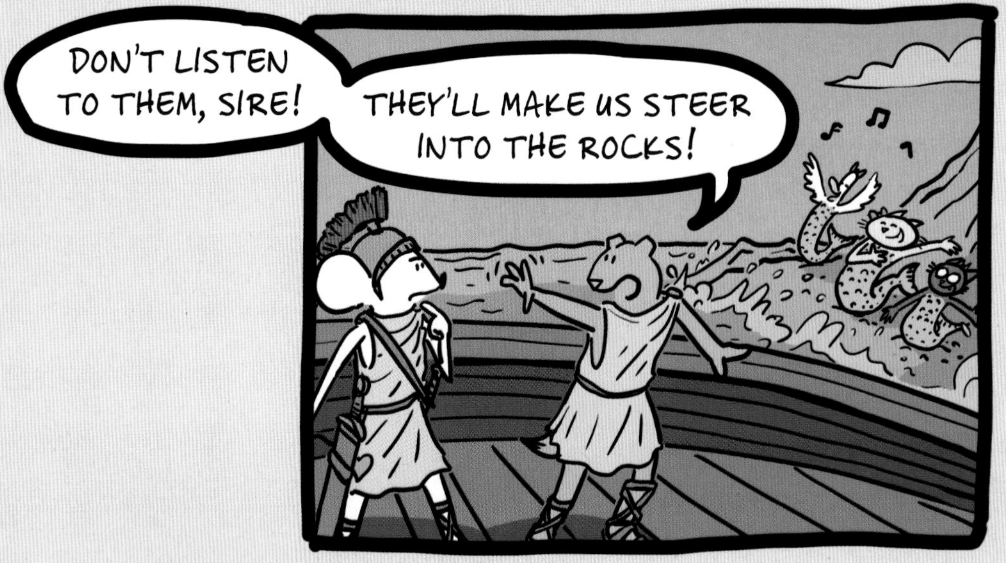
DON'T LISTEN TO THEM, SIRE!
THEY'LL MAKE US STEER INTO THE ROCKS!

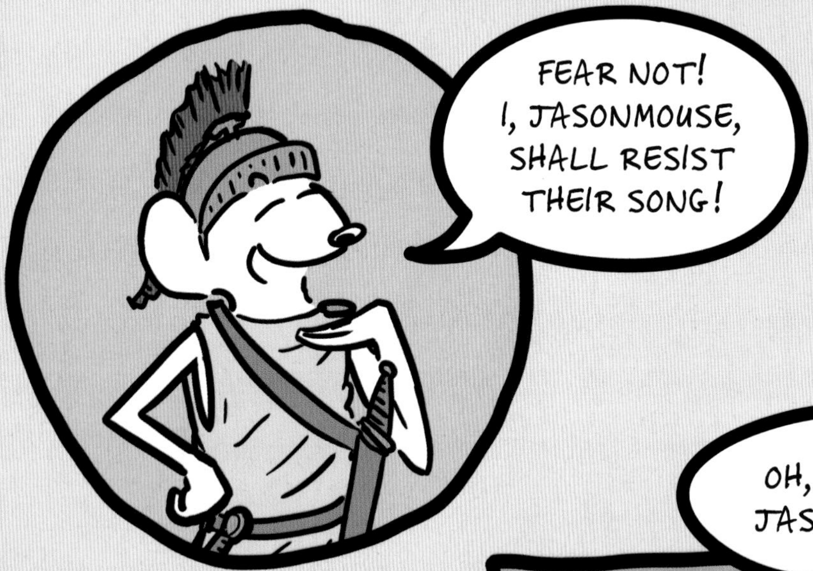
FEAR NOT! I, JASONMOUSE, SHALL RESIST THEIR SONG!

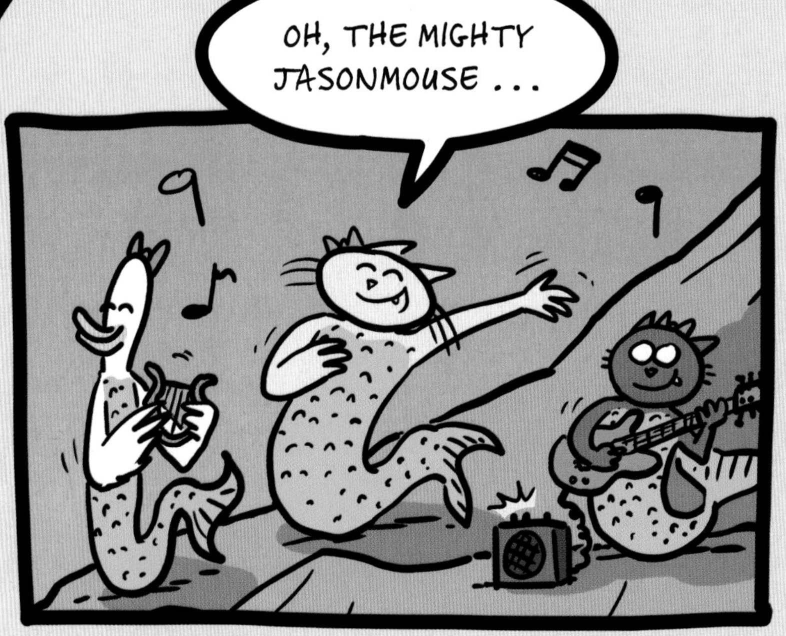
OH, THE MIGHTY JASONMOUSE . . .

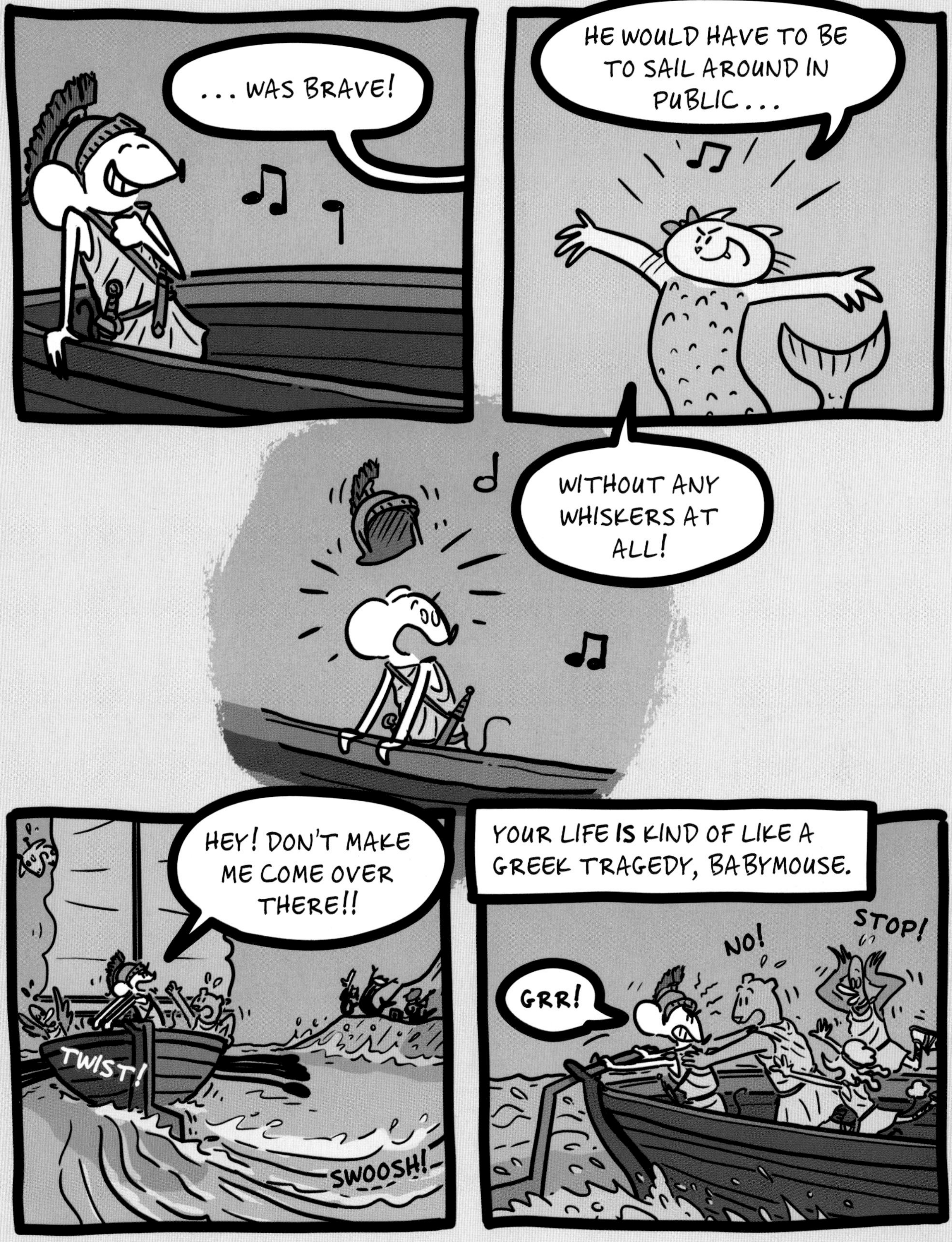
. . . WAS BRAVE!
HE WOULD HAVE TO BE TO SAIL AROUND IN PUBLIC . . .
WITHOUT ANY WHISKERS AT ALL!
HEY! DON'T MAKE ME COME OVER THERE!!
TWIST!
SWOOSH!
YOUR LIFE IS KIND OF LIKE A GREEK TRAGEDY, BABYMOUSE.
NO!
STOP!
GRR!

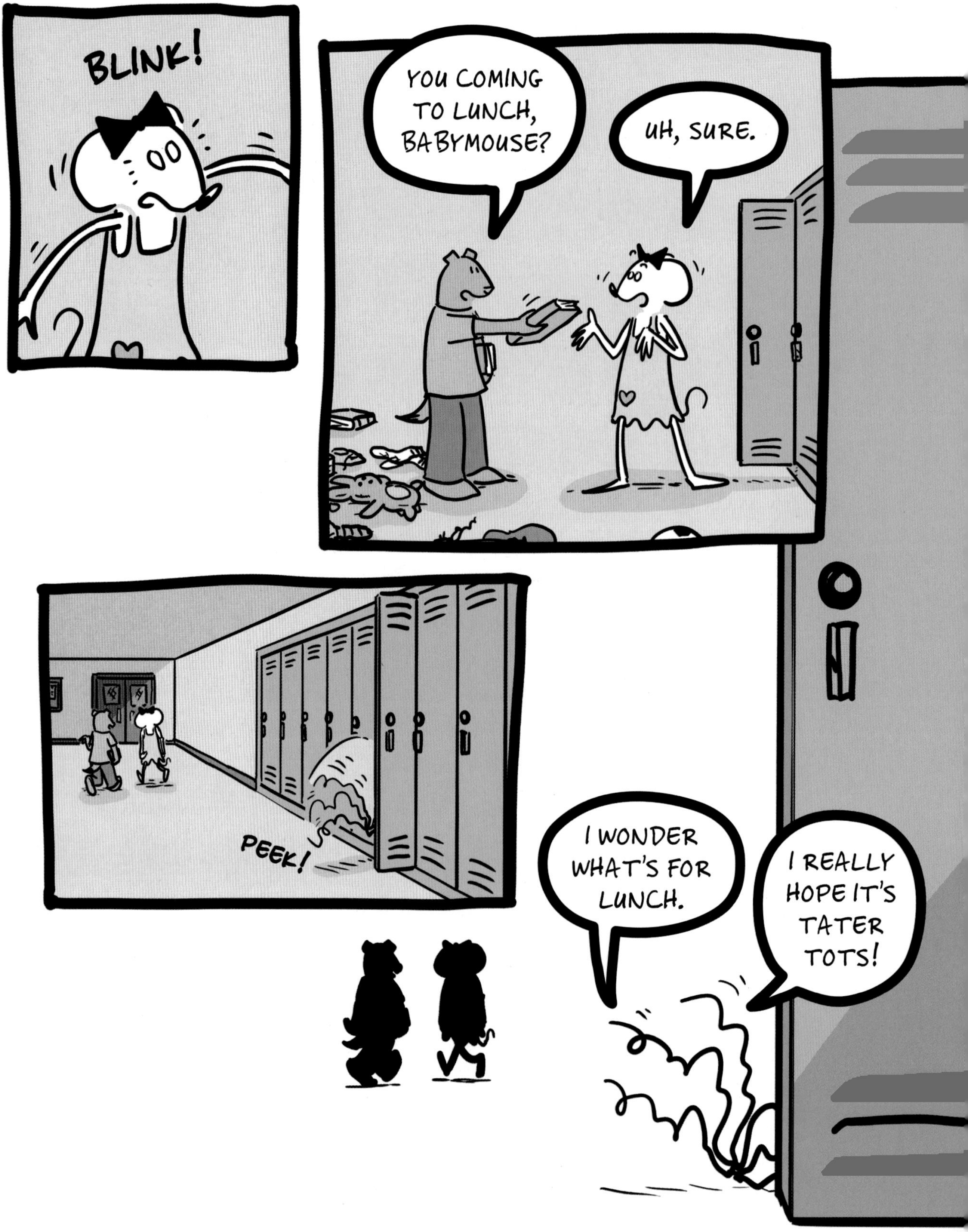
BLINK!
YOU COMING TO LUNCH, BABYMOUSE?
UH, SURE.
PEEK!
I WONDER WHAT'S FOR LUNCH.
I REALLY HOPE IT'S TATER TOTS!

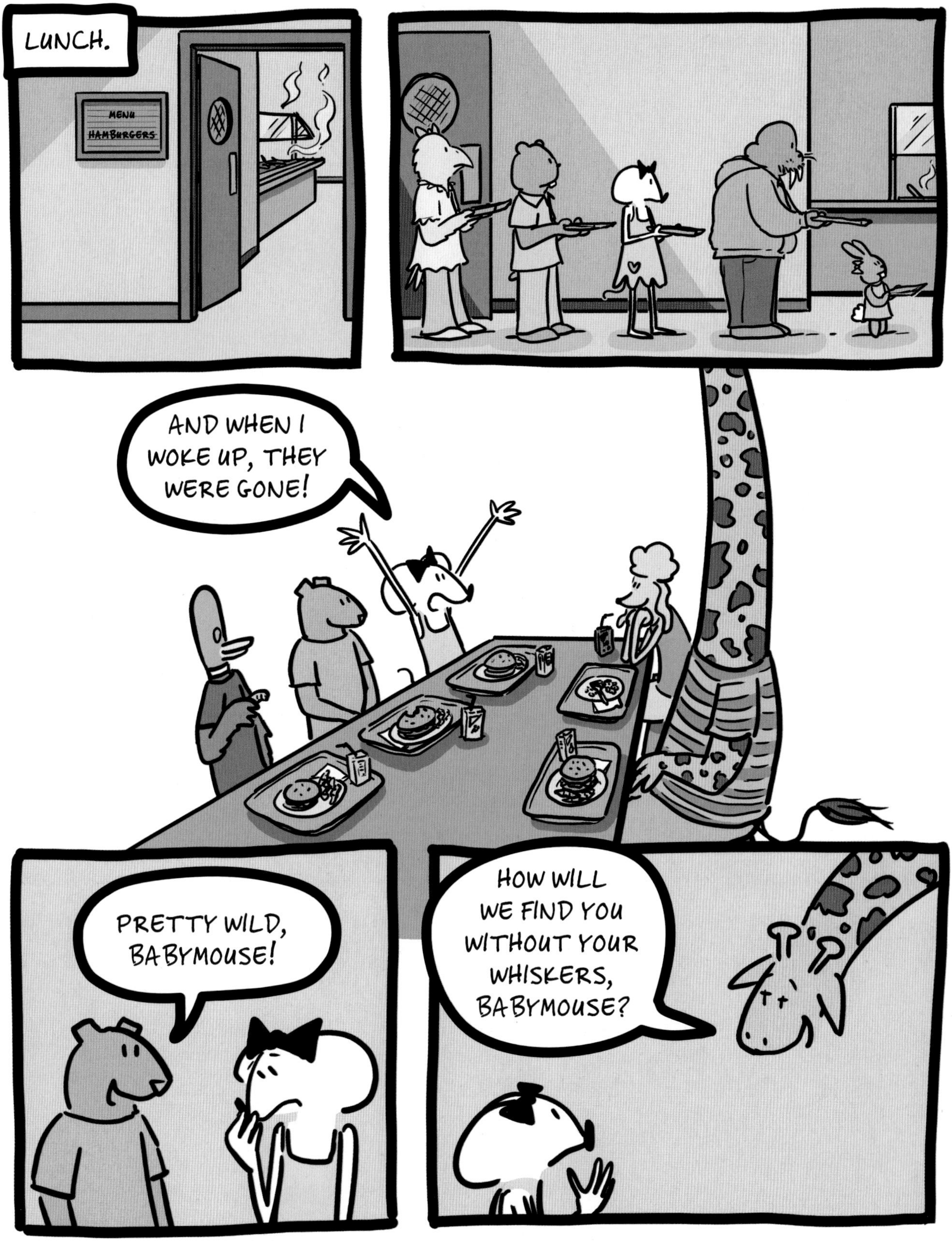
LUNCH.
MENU
HAMBURGERS
AND WHEN I WOKE UP, THEY WERE GONE!
PRETTY WILD, BABYMOUSE!
HOW WILL WE FIND YOU WITHOUT YOUR WHISKERS, BABYMOUSE?

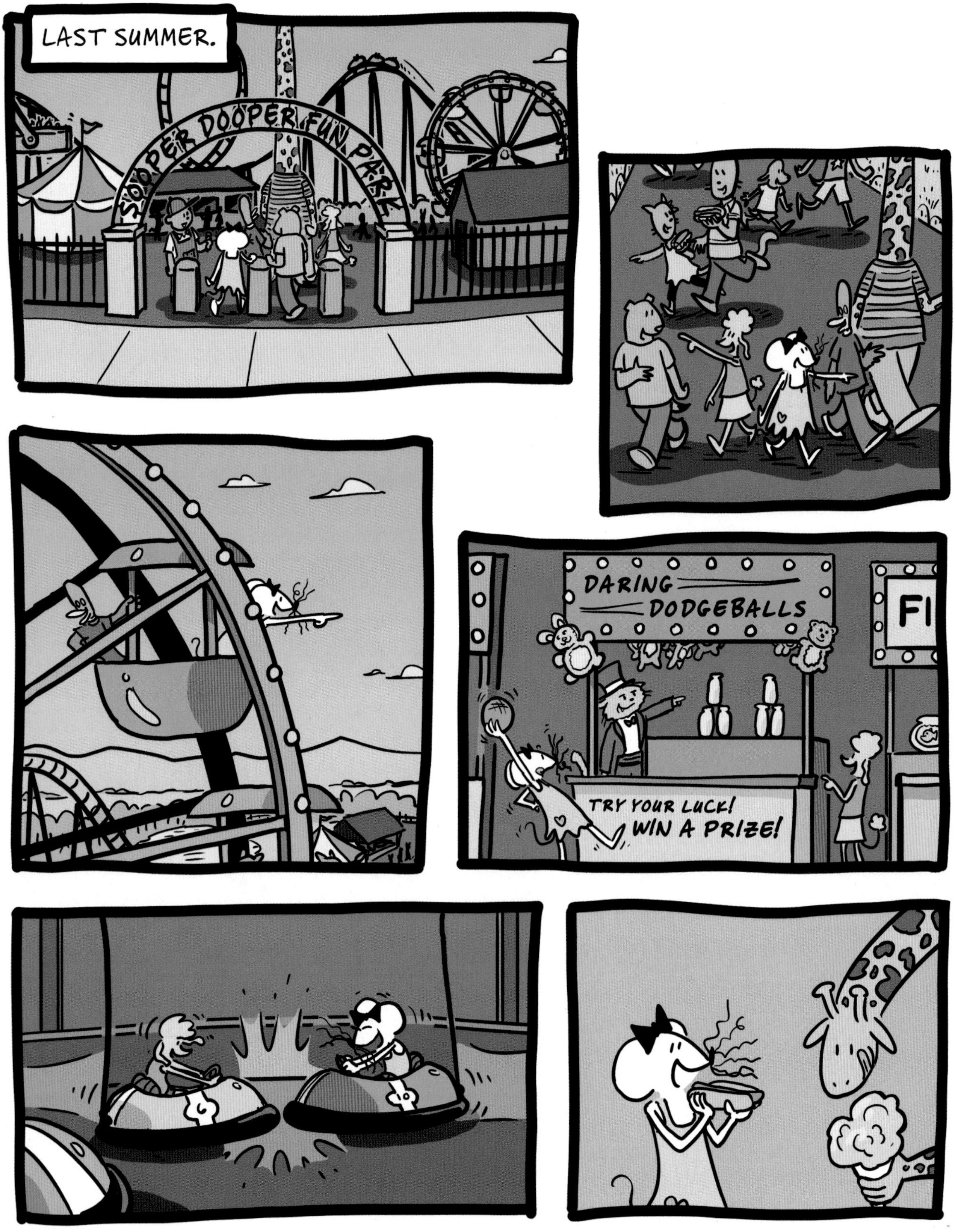

LAST SUMMER.
SOOPER DOOPER FUN PARK
DARING DODGEBALLS
FI
TRY YOUR LUCK! WIN A PRIZE!

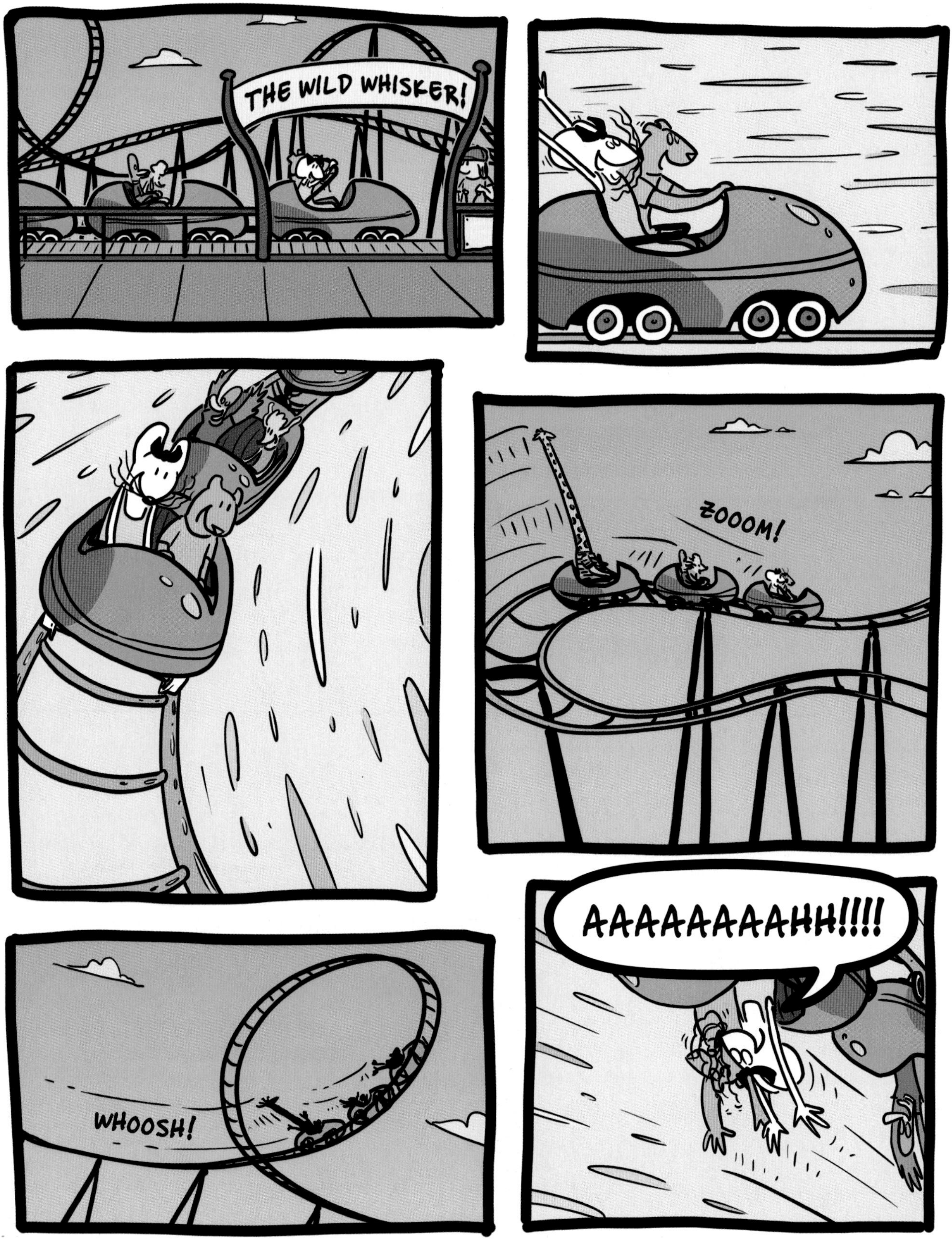
THE WILD WHISKER!
ZOOOM!
WHOOSH!
AAAAAAAAAHH!!!!

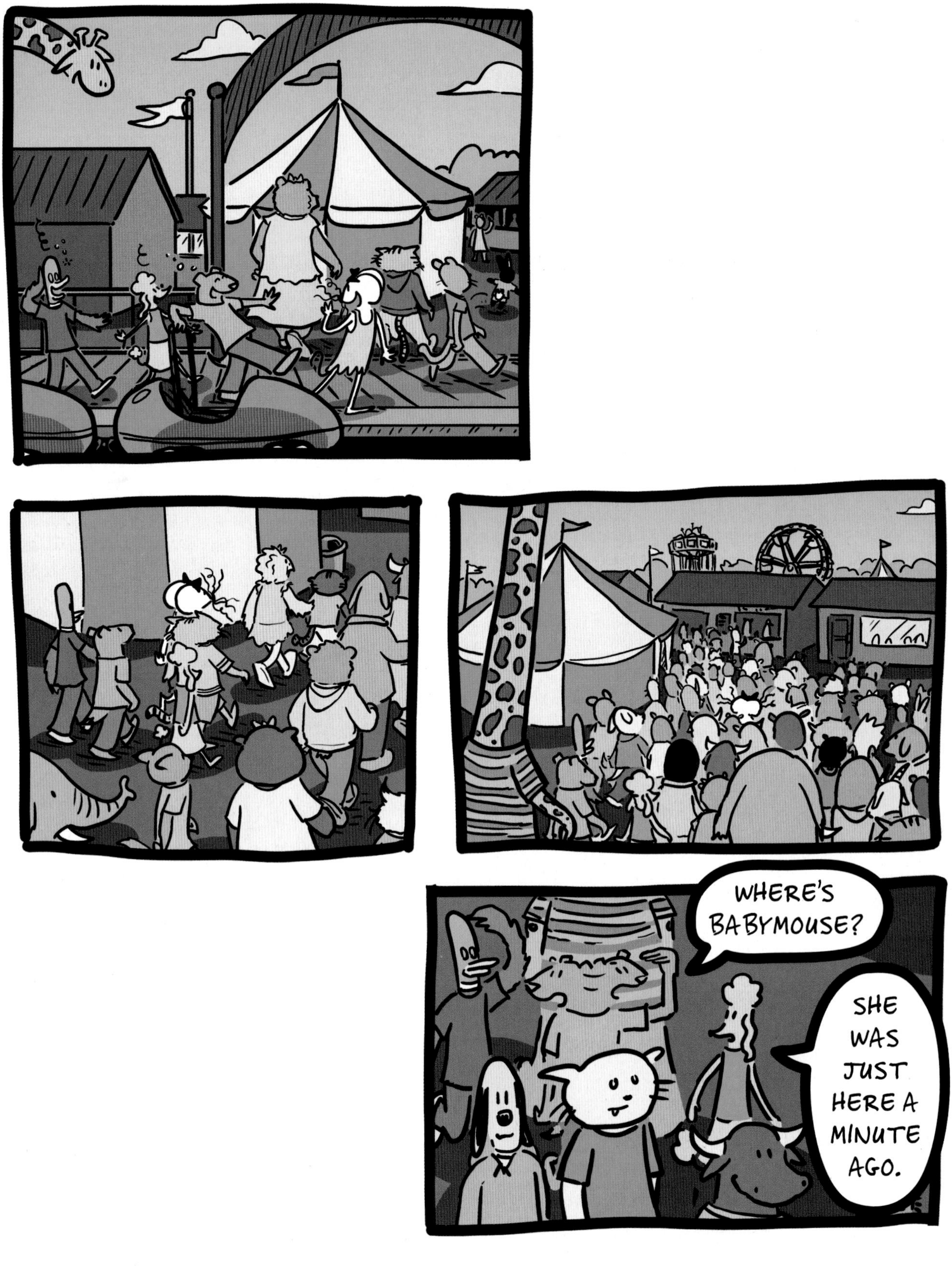
WHERE'S BABYMOUSE?
SHE WAS JUST HERE A MINUTE AGO.

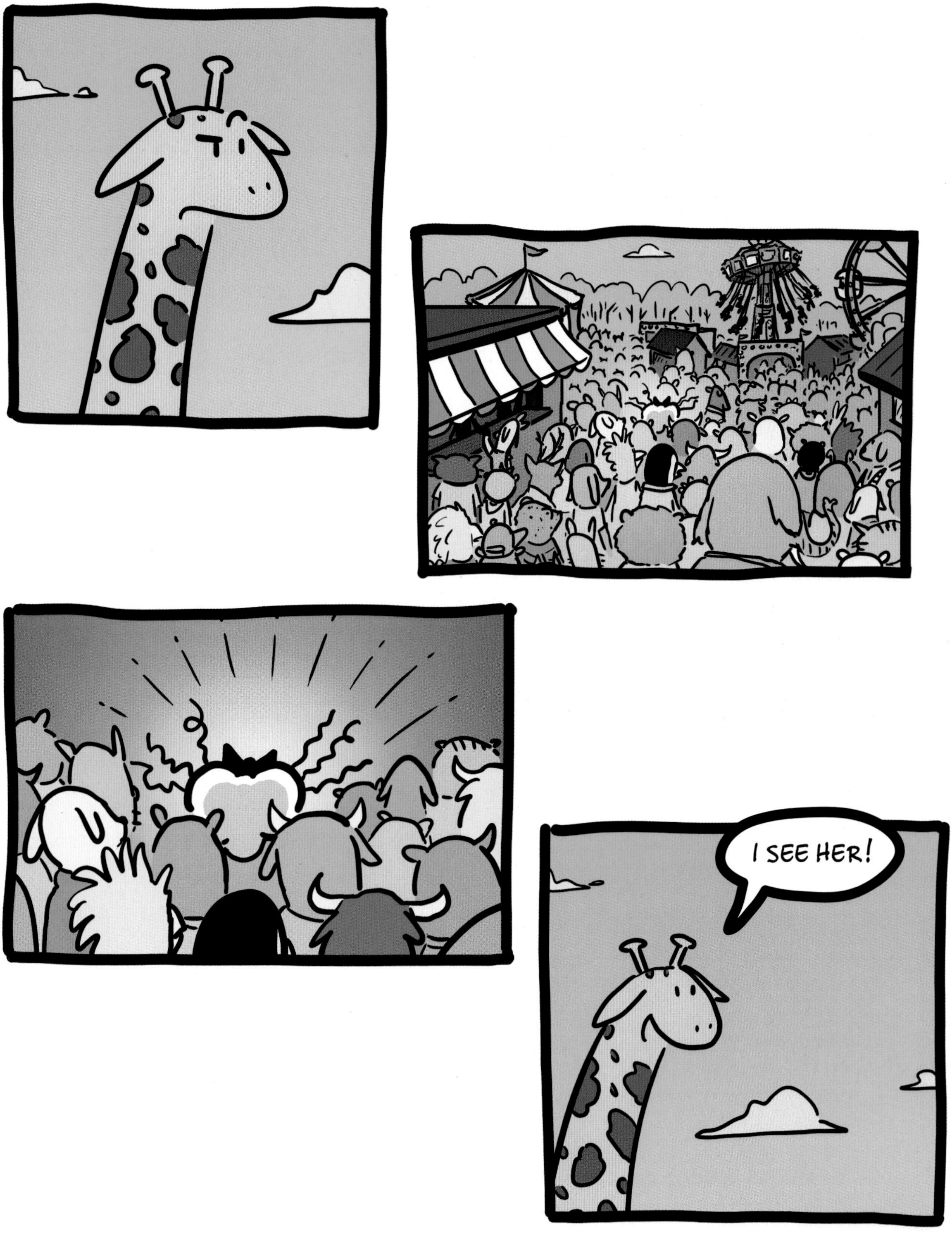
I SEE HER!

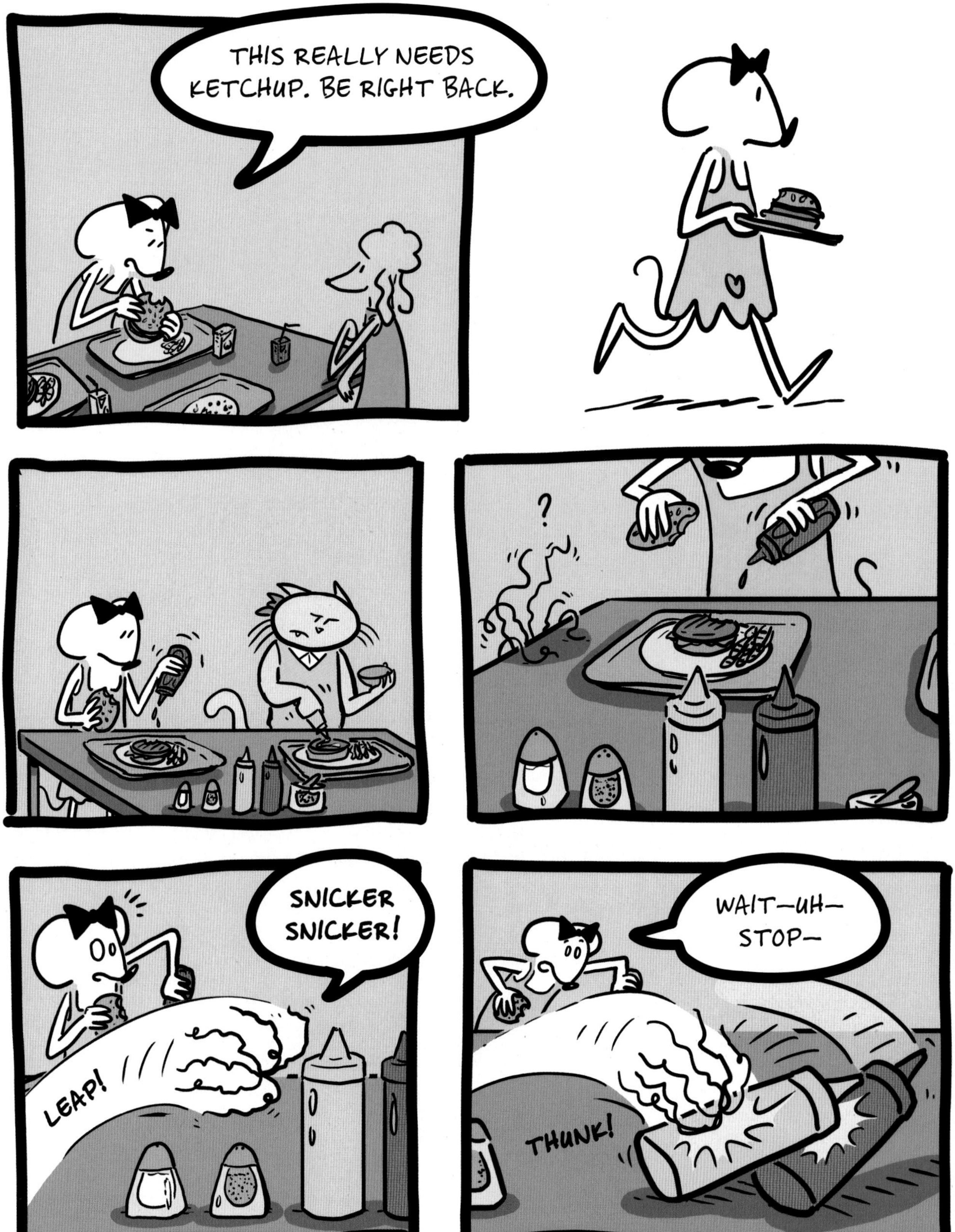
THIS REALLY NEEDS KETCHUP. BE RIGHT BACK.
?
SNICKER SNICKER!
LEAP!
WAIT—UH— STOP—
THUNK!

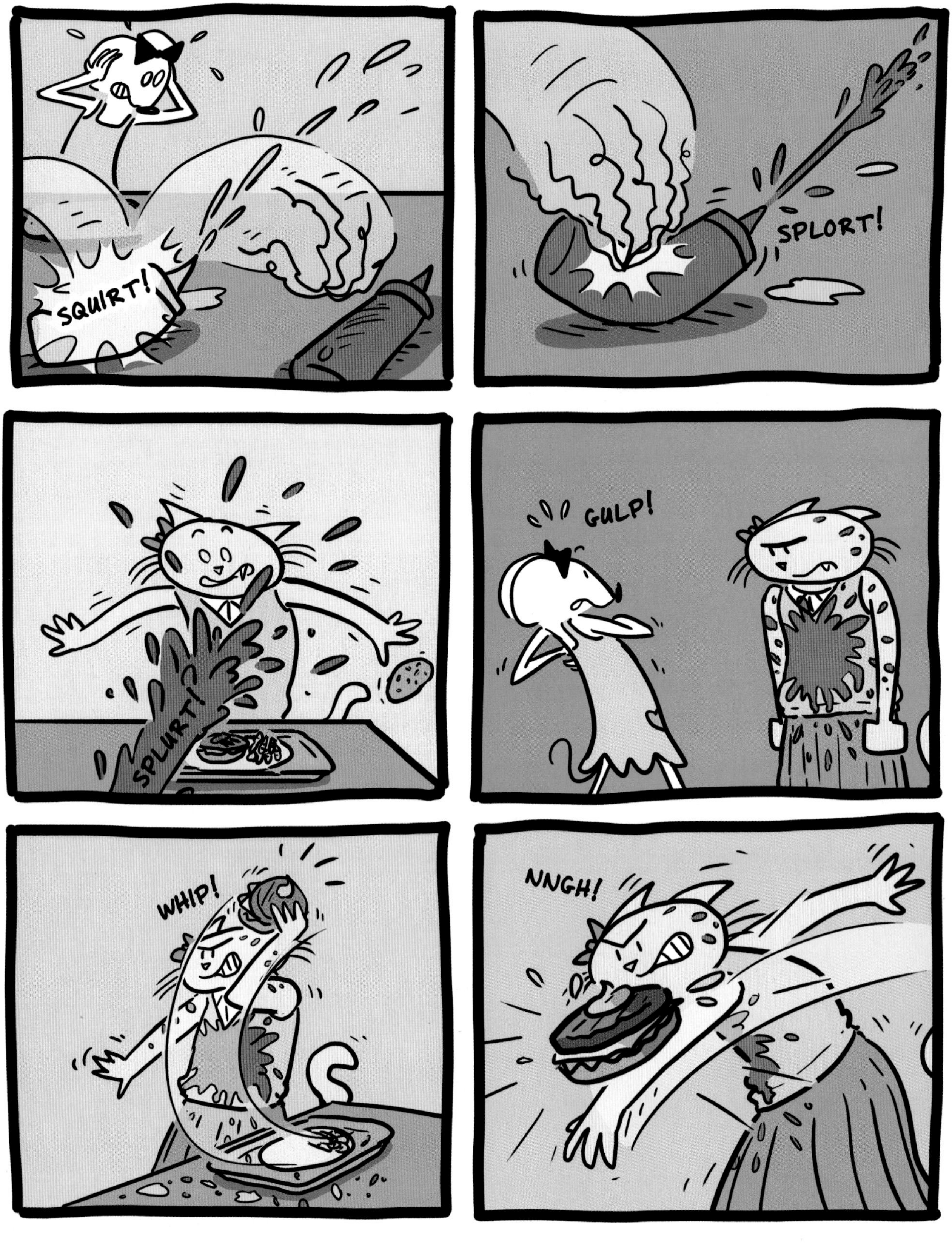
SQUIRT!
SPLORT!
SPLURT!
GULP!
WHIP!
NNGH!

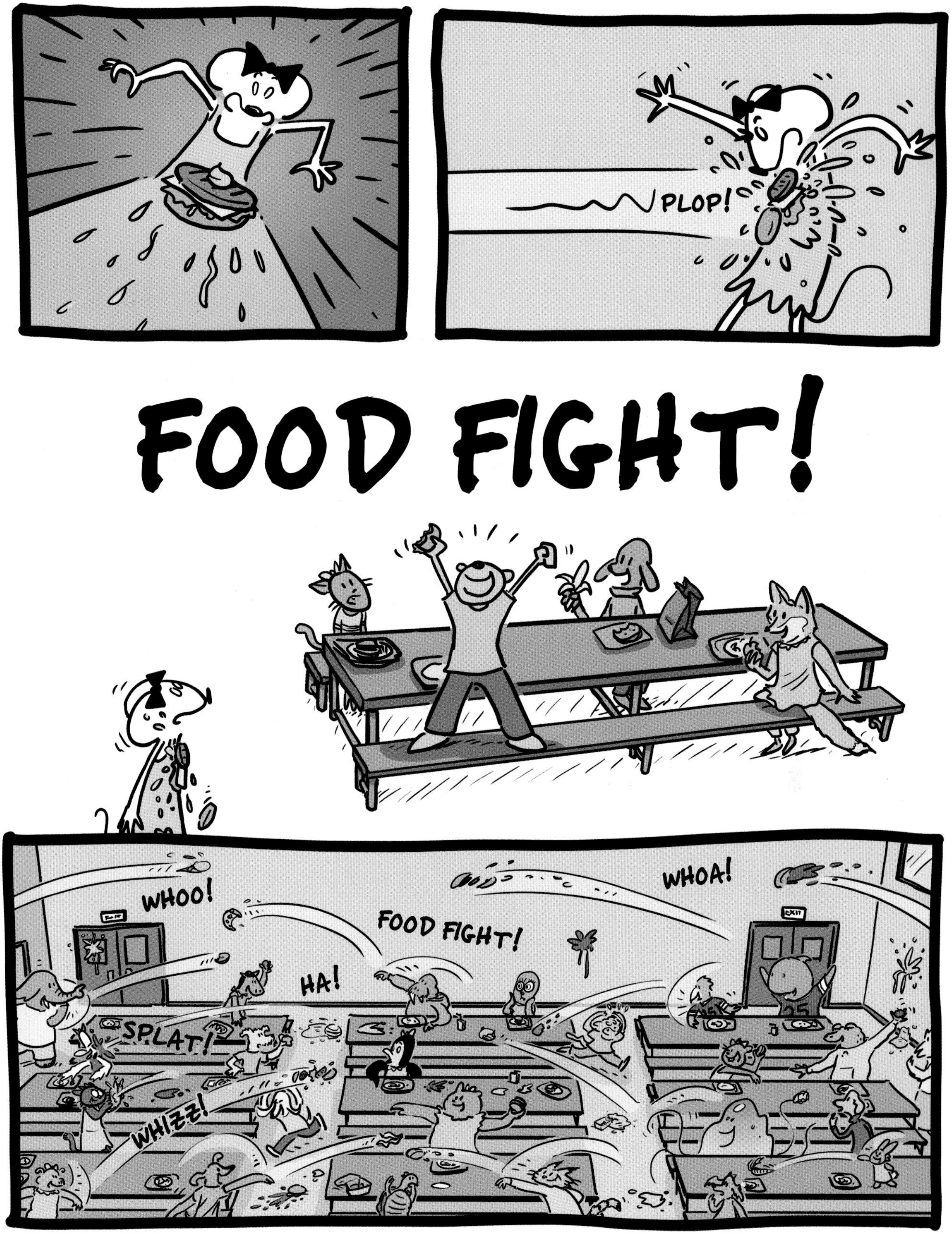
PLOP!
FOOD FIGHT!
WHOO!
FOOD FIGHT!
WHOA!
HA!
SPLAT!
WHIZZ!

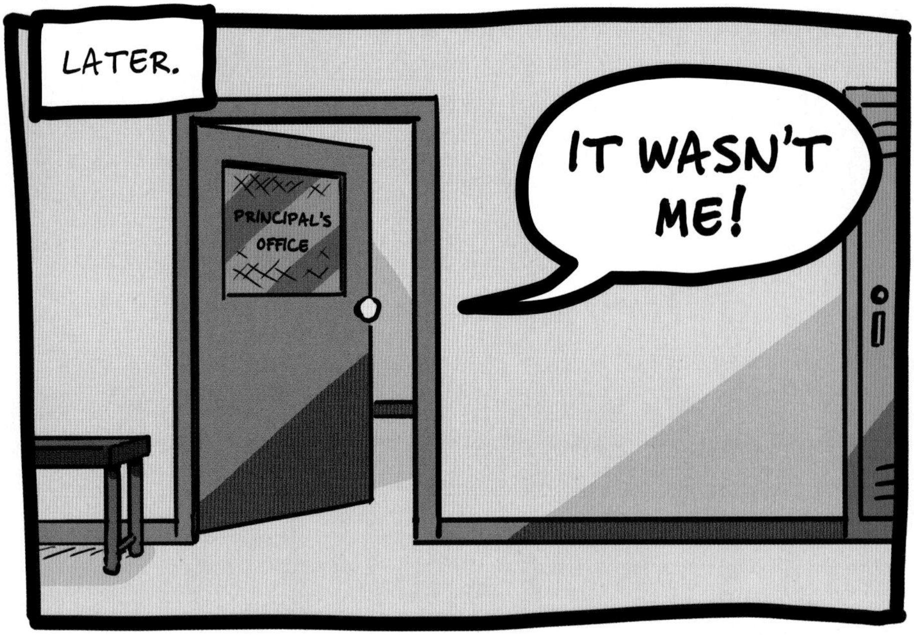
LATER.
PRINCIPAL'S OFFICE
IT WASN'T ME!

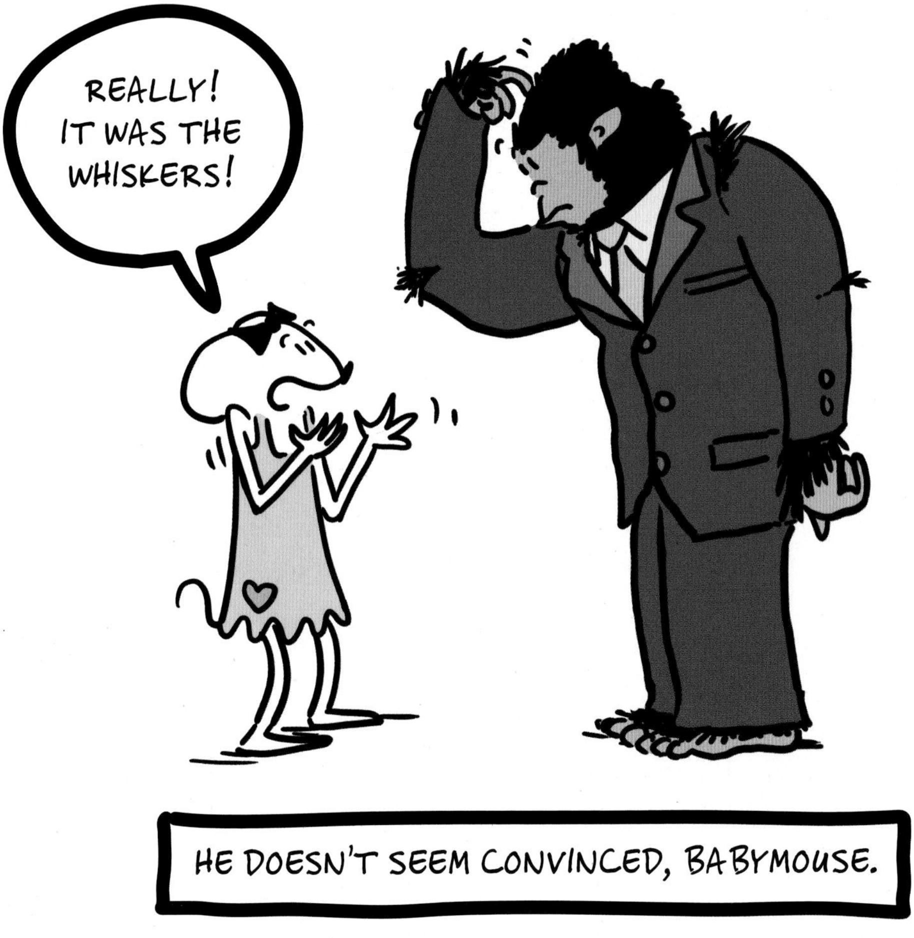
REALLY! IT WAS THE WHISKERS!
HE DOESN'T SEEM CONVINCED, BABYMOUSE.

THAT NIGHT.

BABYMOUSE'S ROOM

WHY ARE YOU SO SAD, BABYMOUSE? I THOUGHT YOU HATED YOUR WHISKERS?

I FEEL NAKED WITHOUT THEM!

SNIFF

THE THREE LITTLE KITTENS

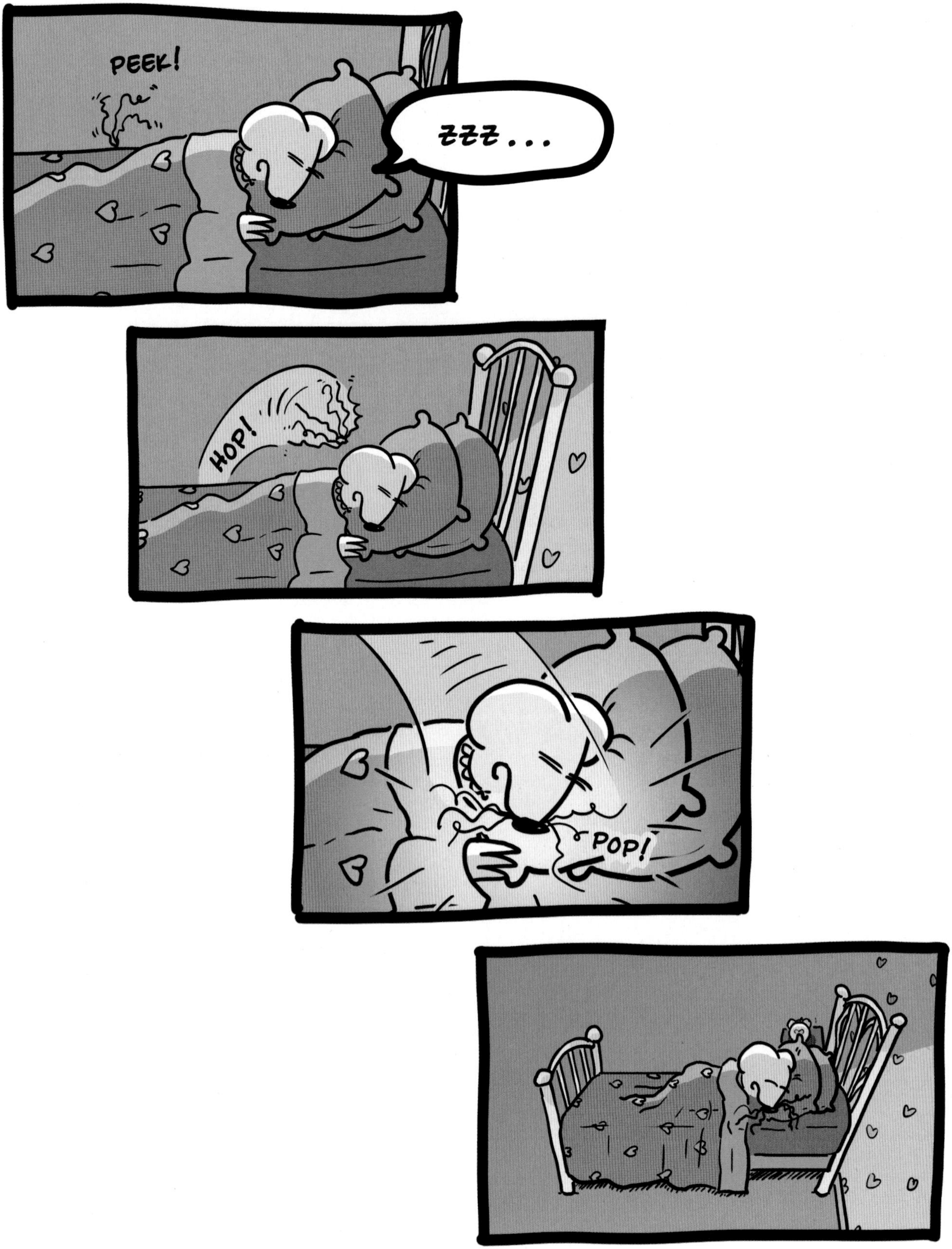
PEEK!
ZZZ...
HOP!
POP!

PART THREE

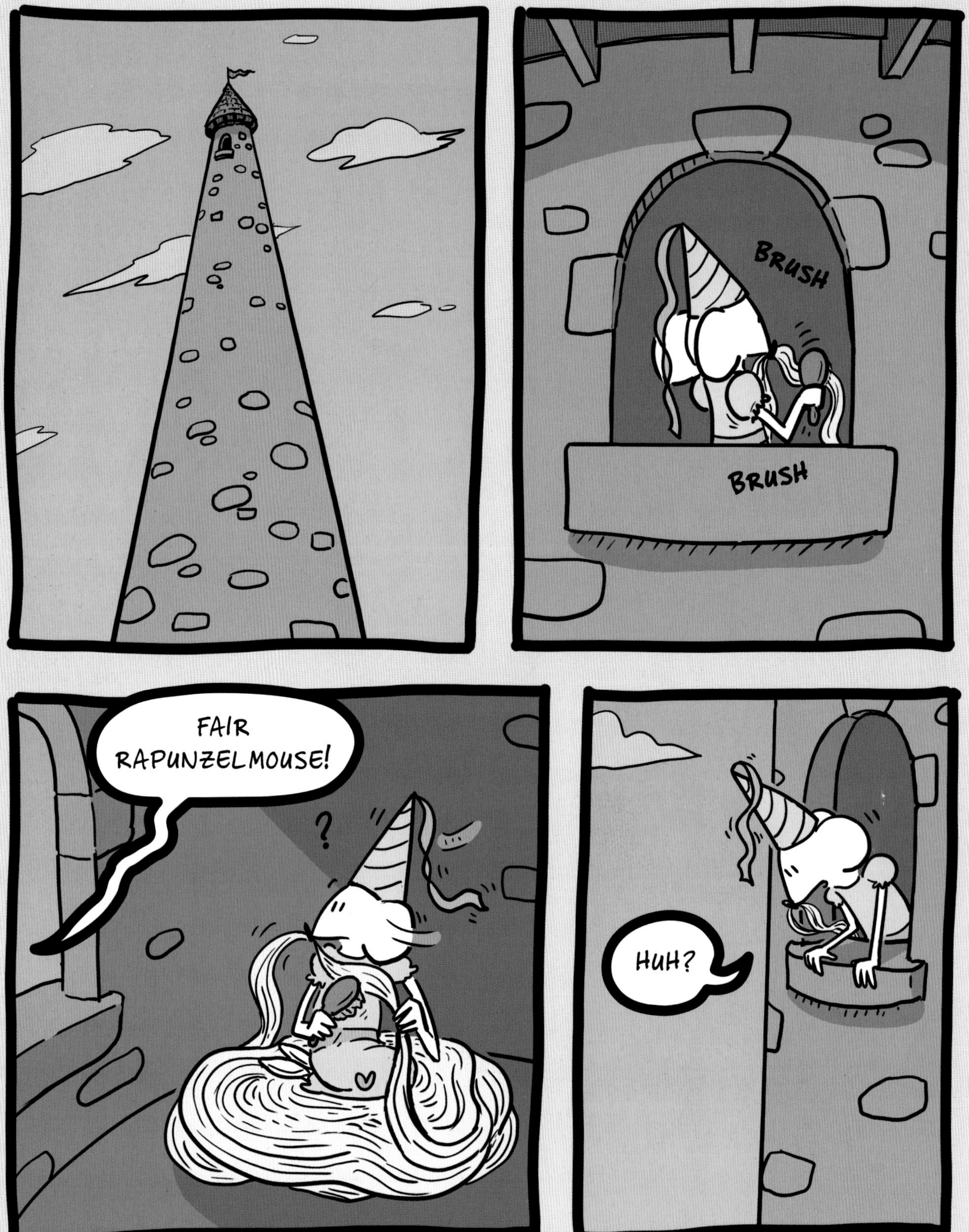
BRUSH
BRUSH
FAIR RAPUNZELMOUSE!
?
HUH?

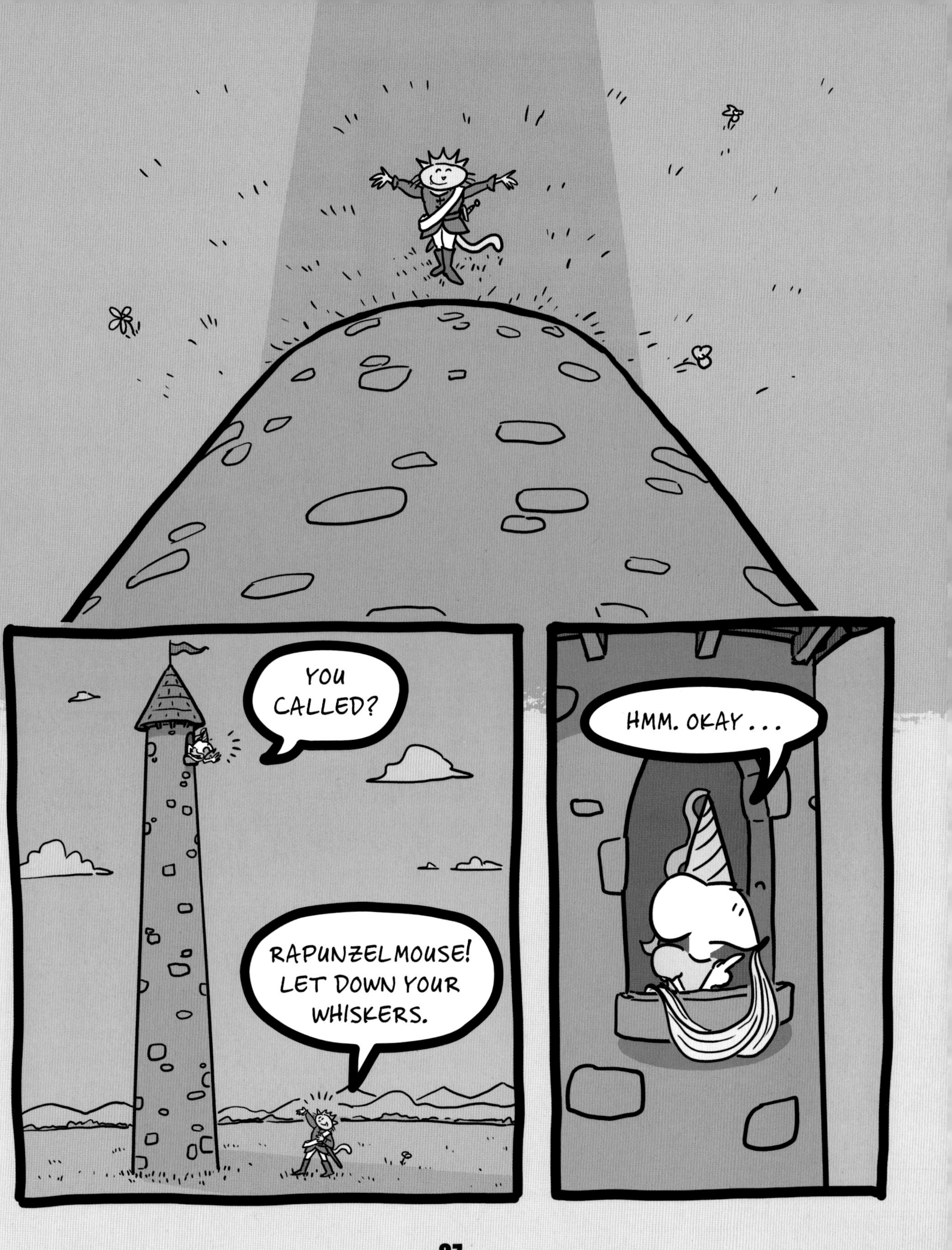
YOU CALLED?
RAPUNZELMOUSE! LET DOWN YOUR WHISKERS.
HMM. OKAY . . .

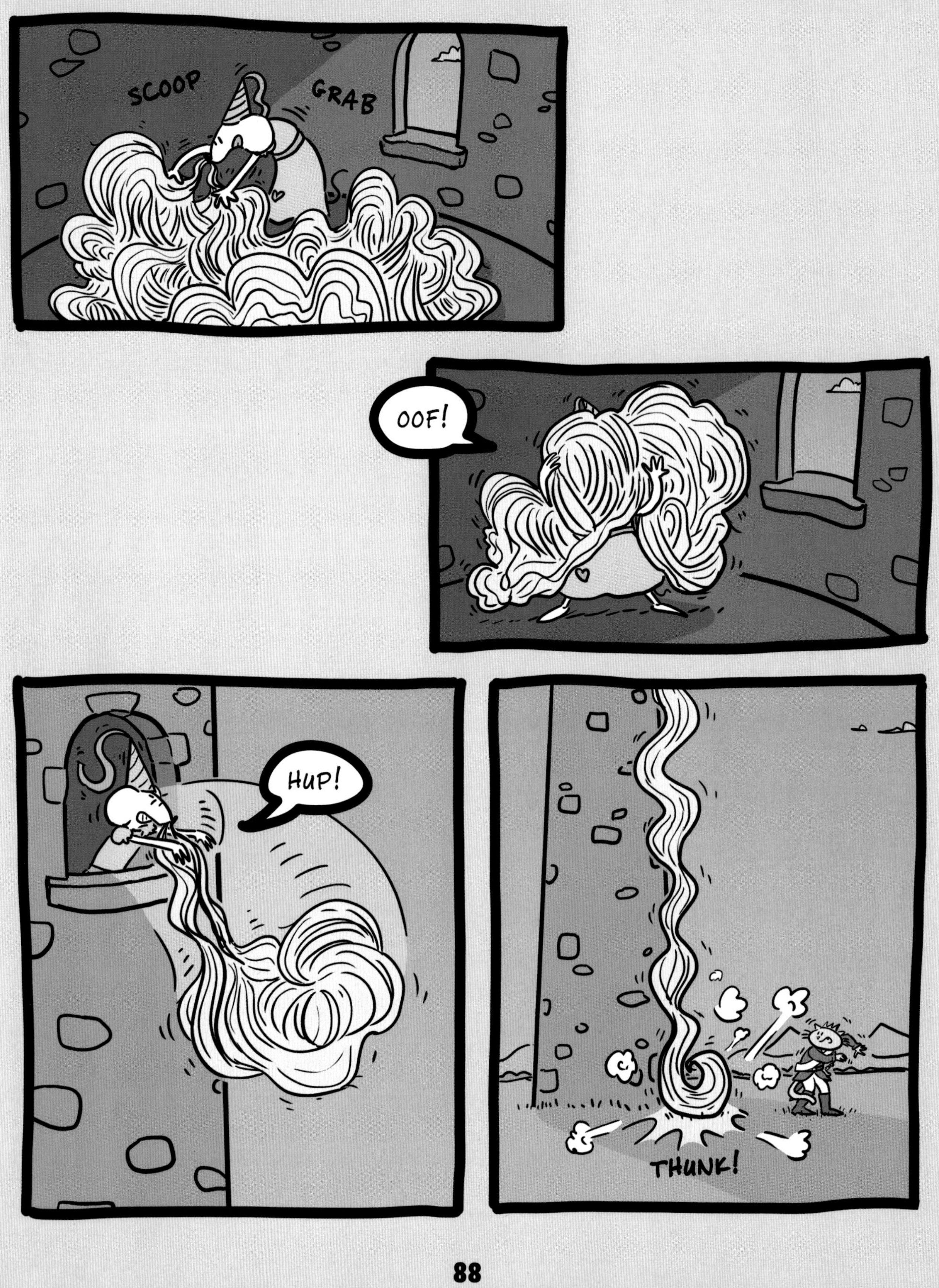
SCOOP
GRAB
OOF!
HUP!
THUNK!

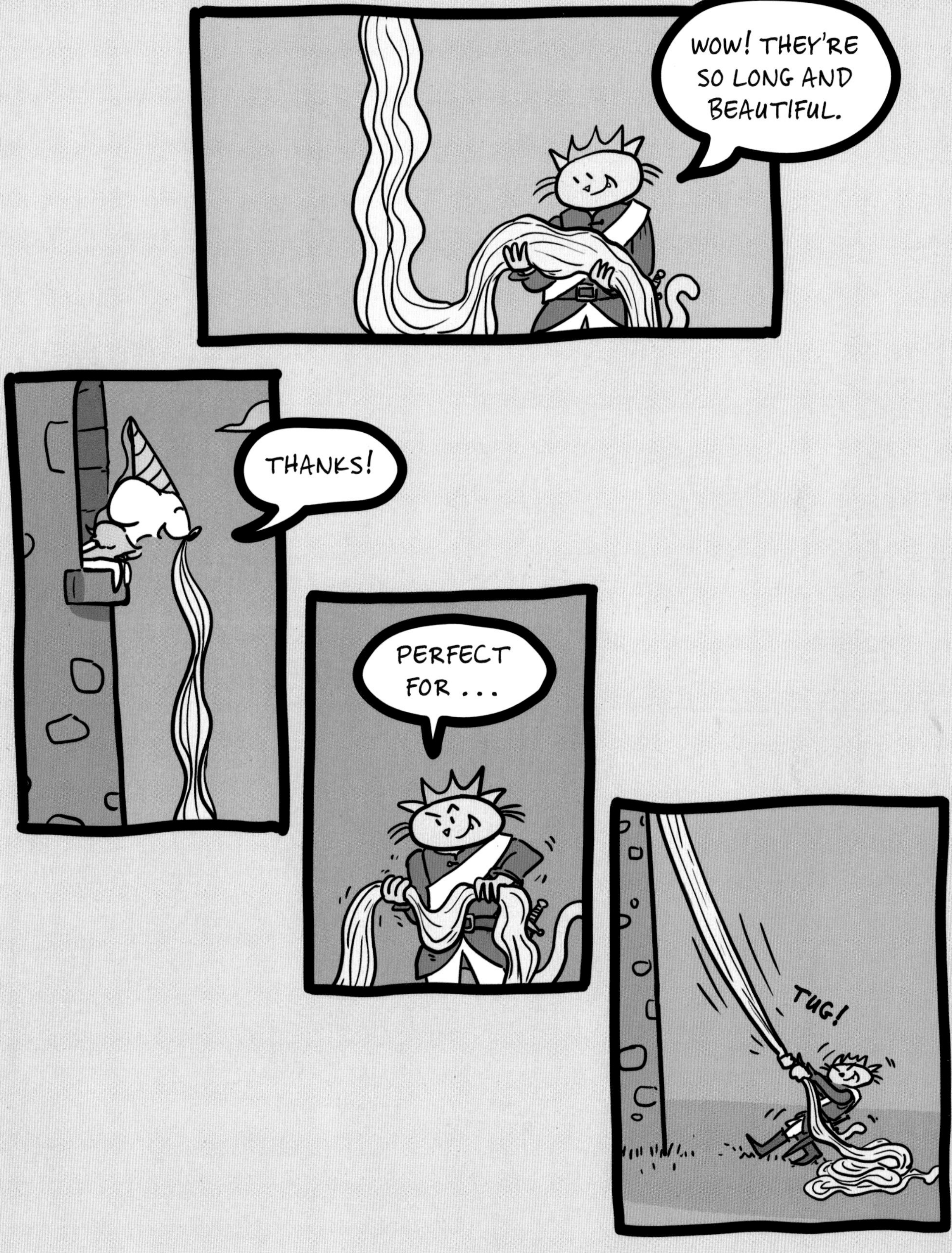
WOW! THEY'RE SO LONG AND BEAUTIFUL.
THANKS!
PERFECT FOR . . .
TUG!

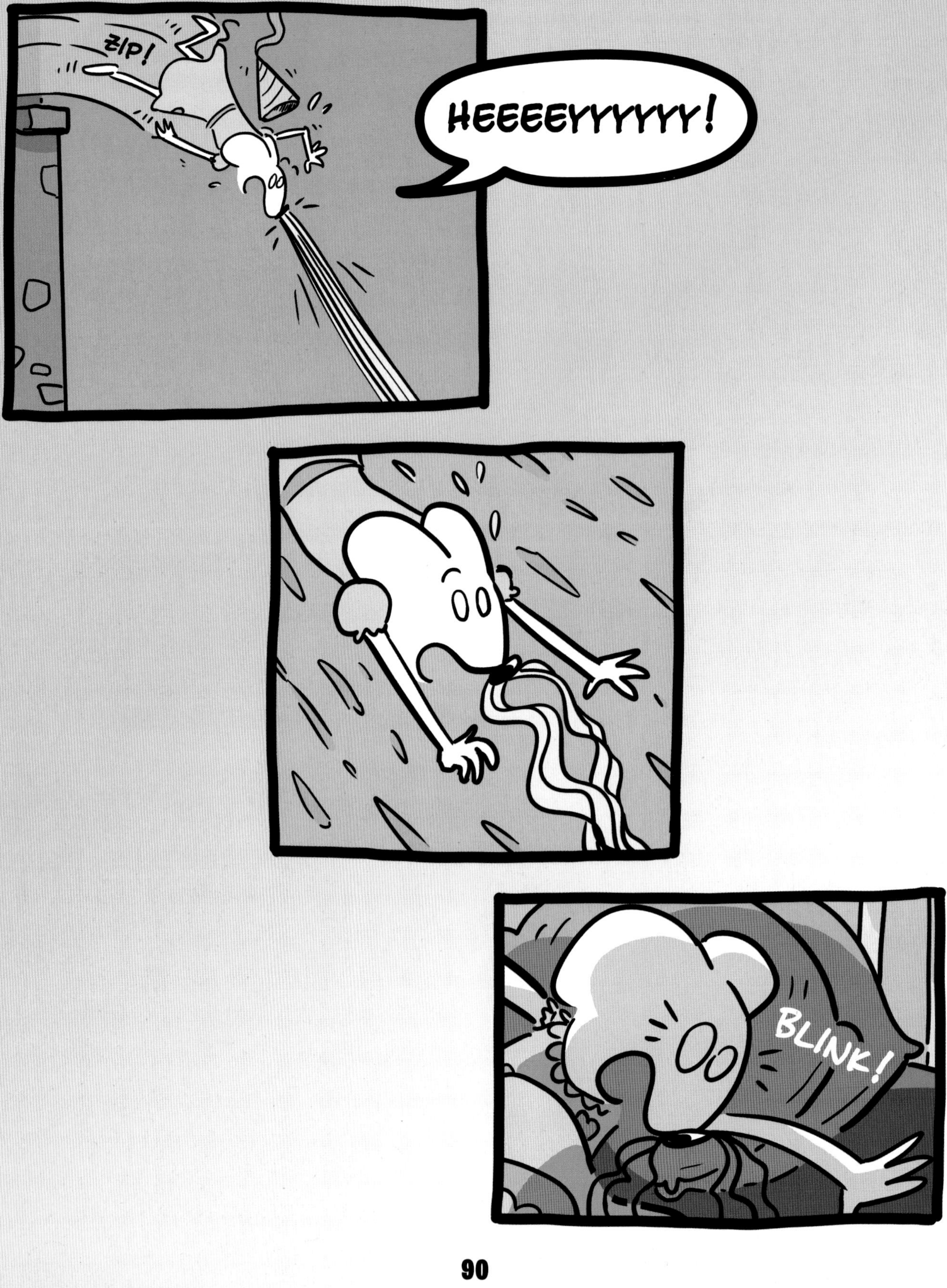
zip!
HEEEEYYYYYY!
BLINK!

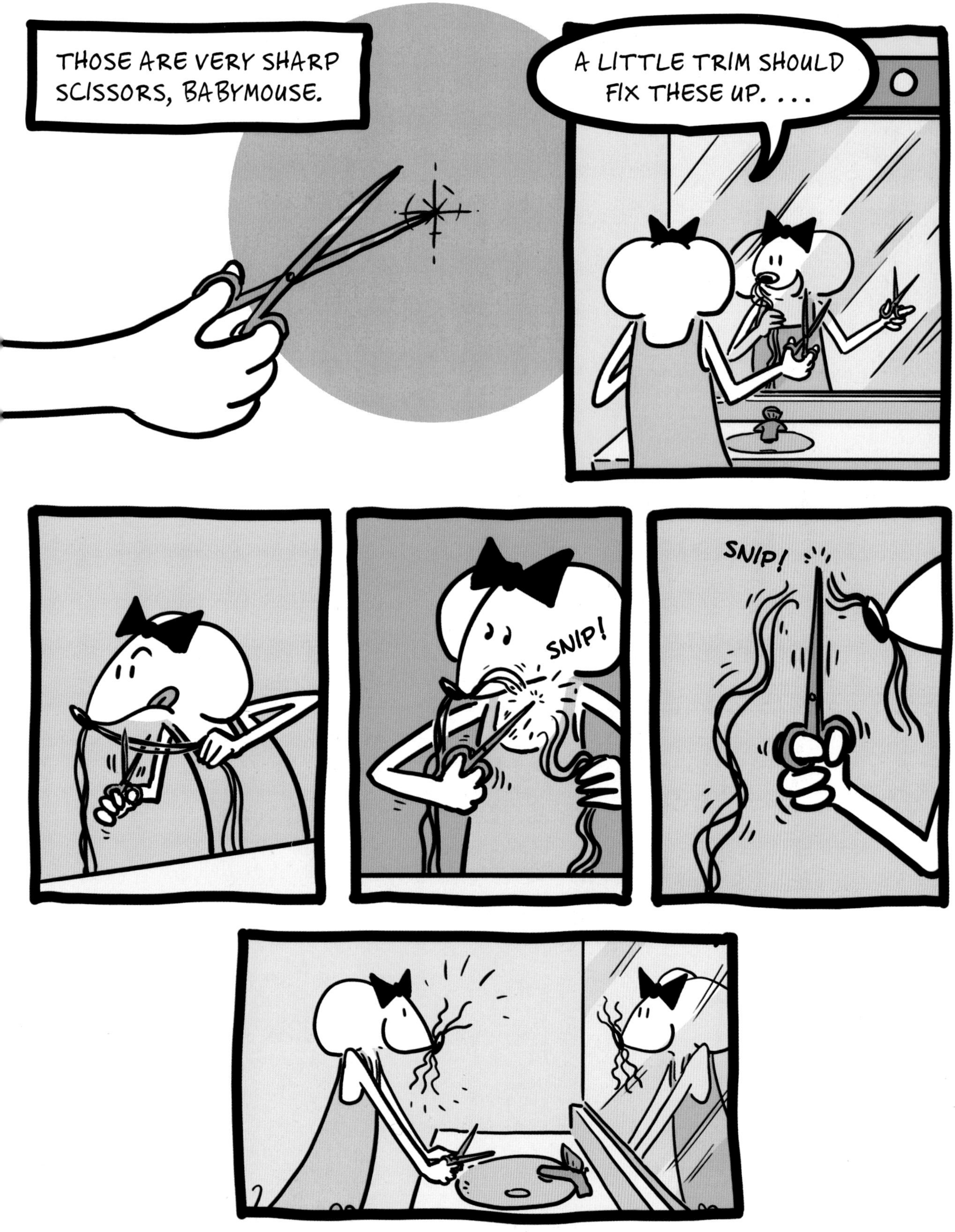
THOSE ARE VERY SHARP SCISSORS, BABYMOUSE.
A LITTLE TRIM SHOULD FIX THESE UP. . . .
SNIP!
SNIP!

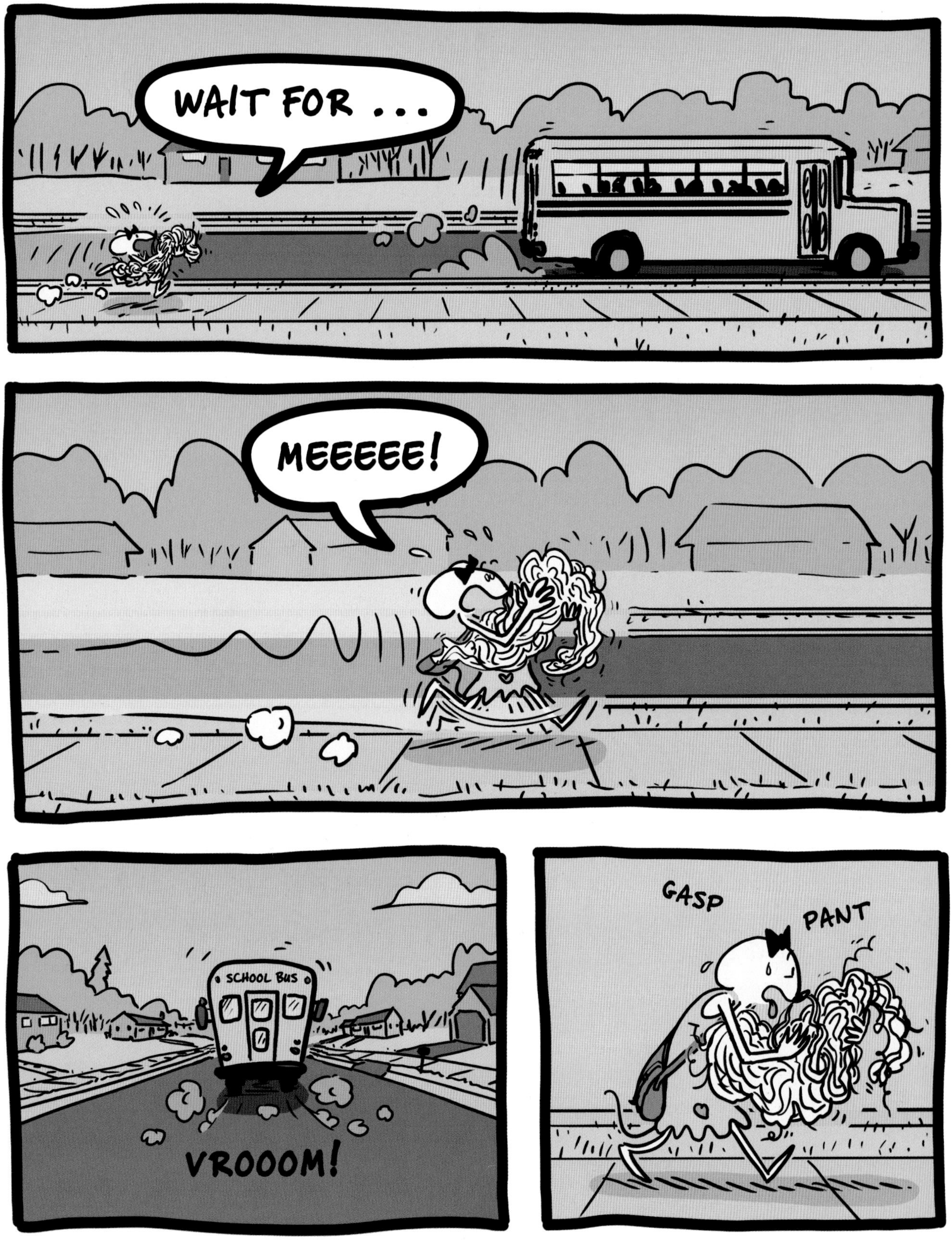
WAIT FOR ...
MEEEEE!
SCHOOL BUS
VROOOM!
GASP
PANT

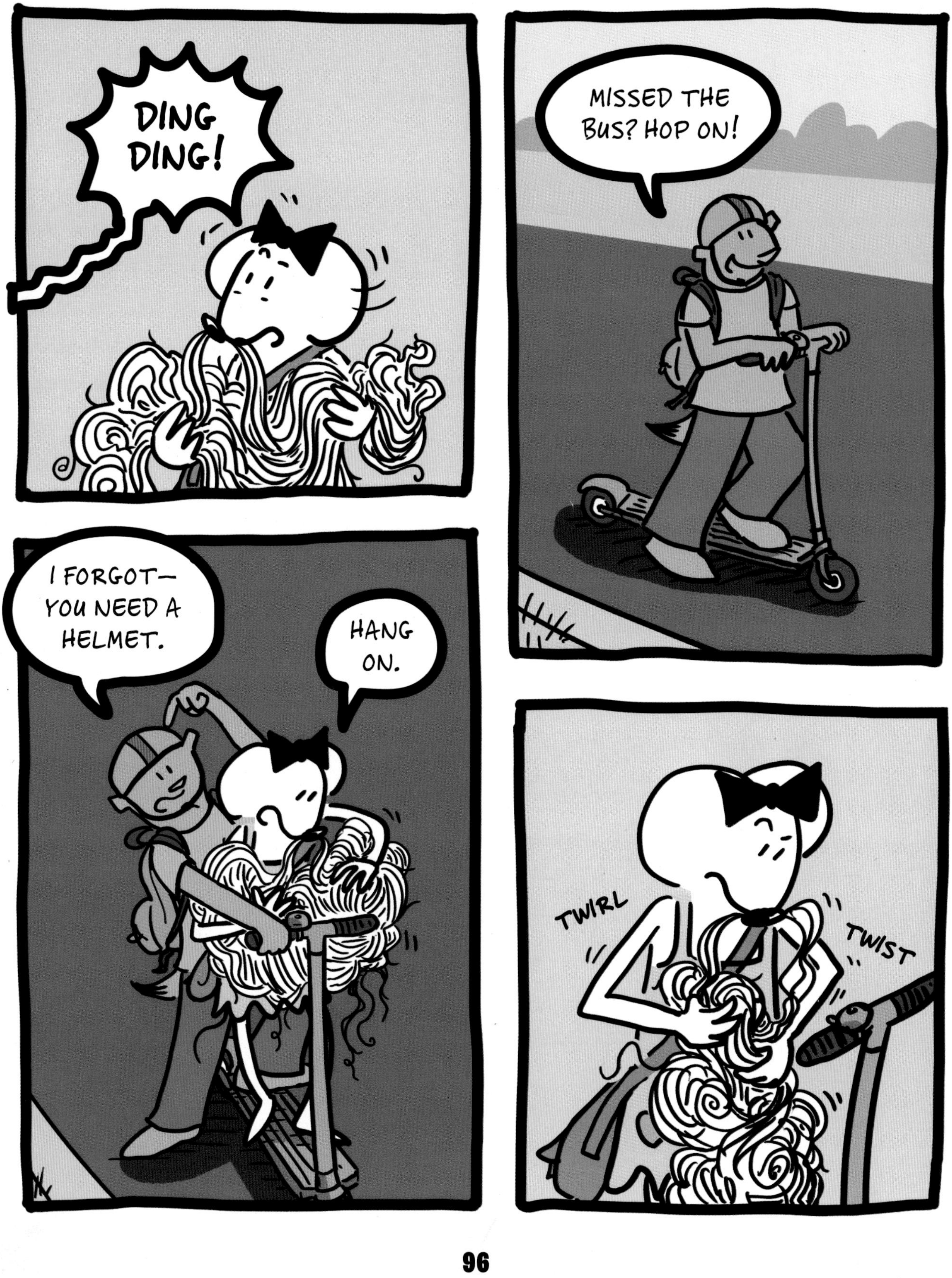
DING DING!
MISSED THE BUS? HOP ON!
I FORGOT— YOU NEED A HELMET.
HANG ON.
TWIRL
TWIST

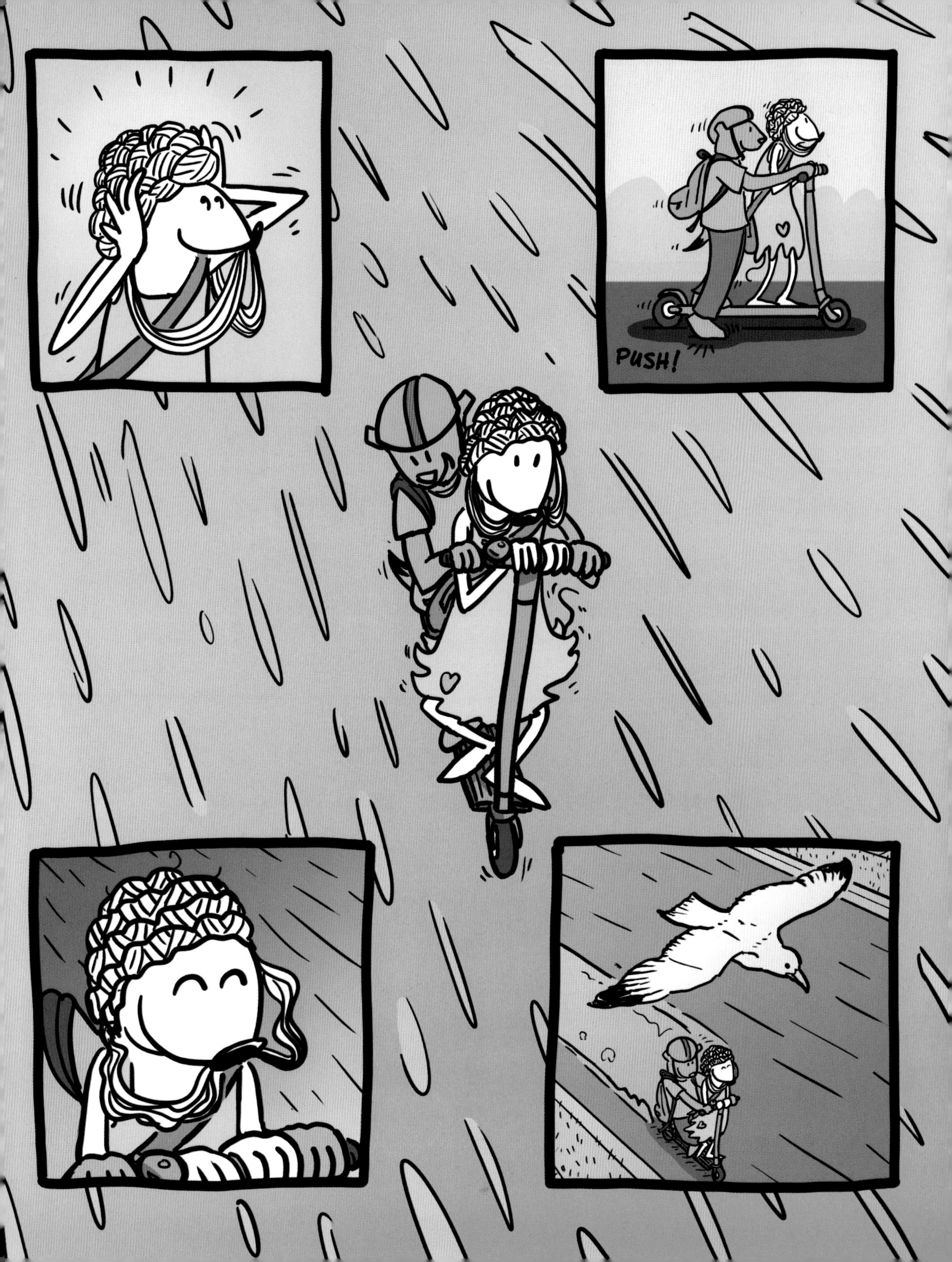
PUSH!

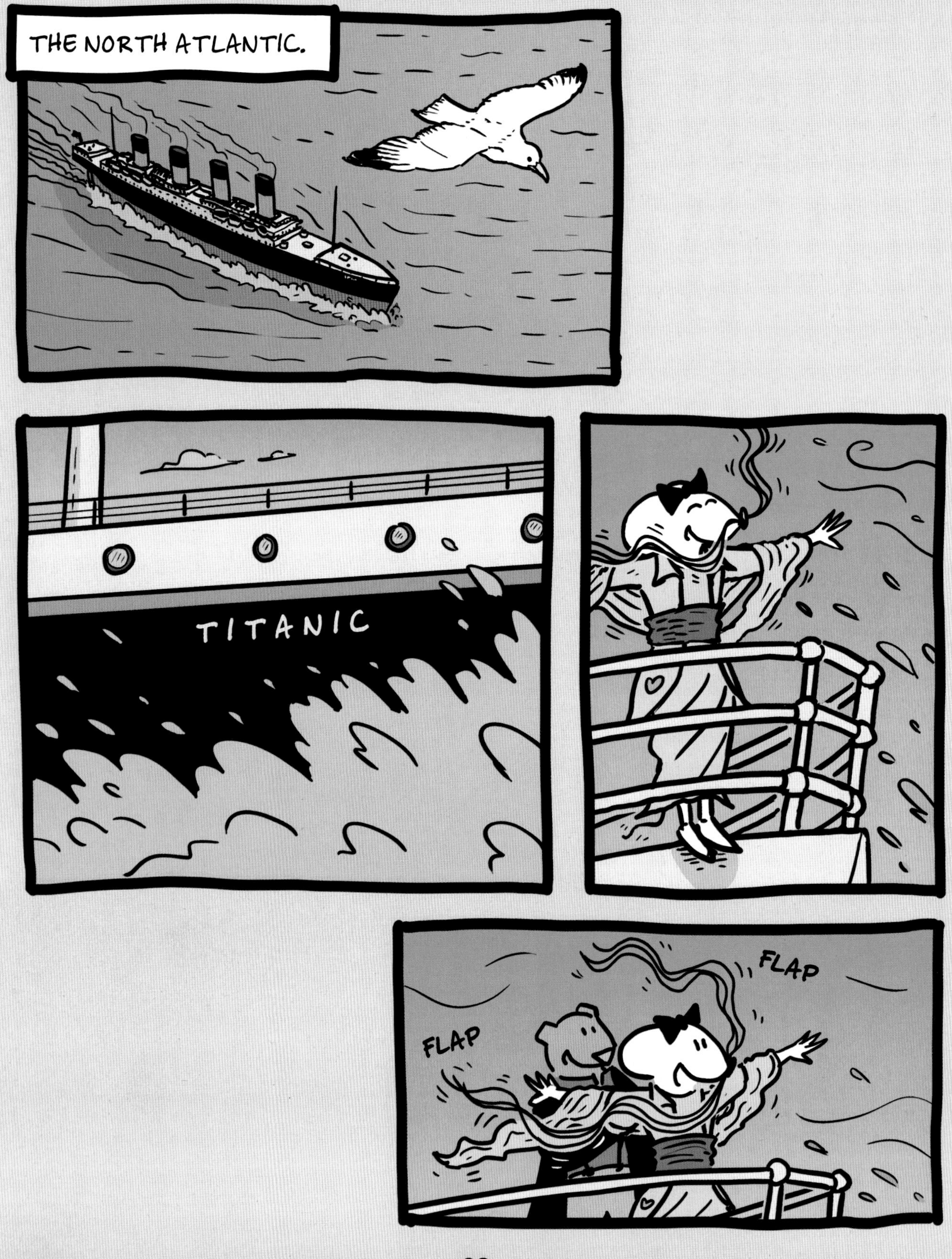
THE NORTH ATLANTIC.
TITANIC
FLAP
FLAP

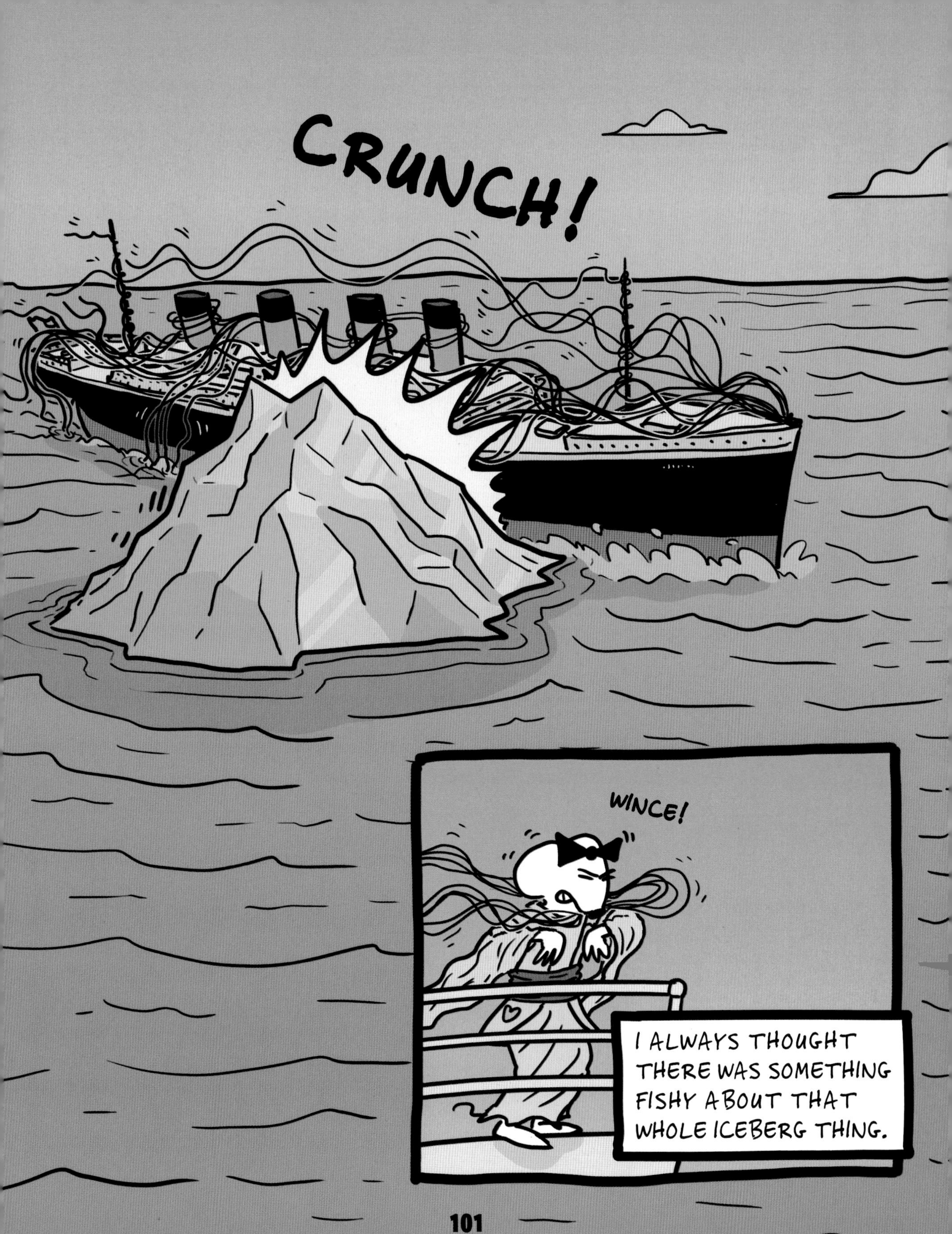
CRUNCH!
WINCE!
I ALWAYS THOUGHT THERE WAS SOMETHING FISHY ABOUT THAT WHOLE ICEBERG THING.

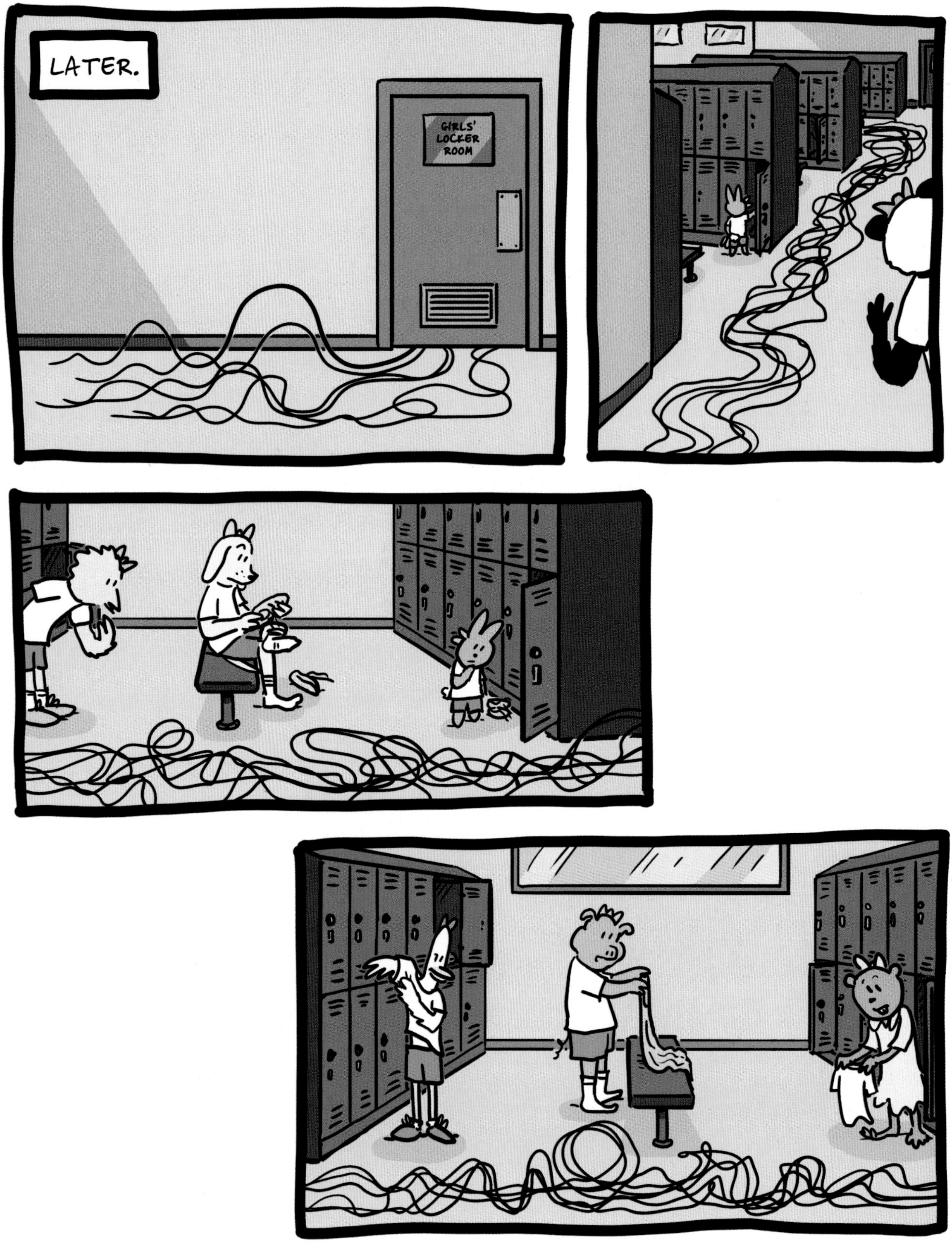
LATER.
GIRLS' LOCKER ROOM

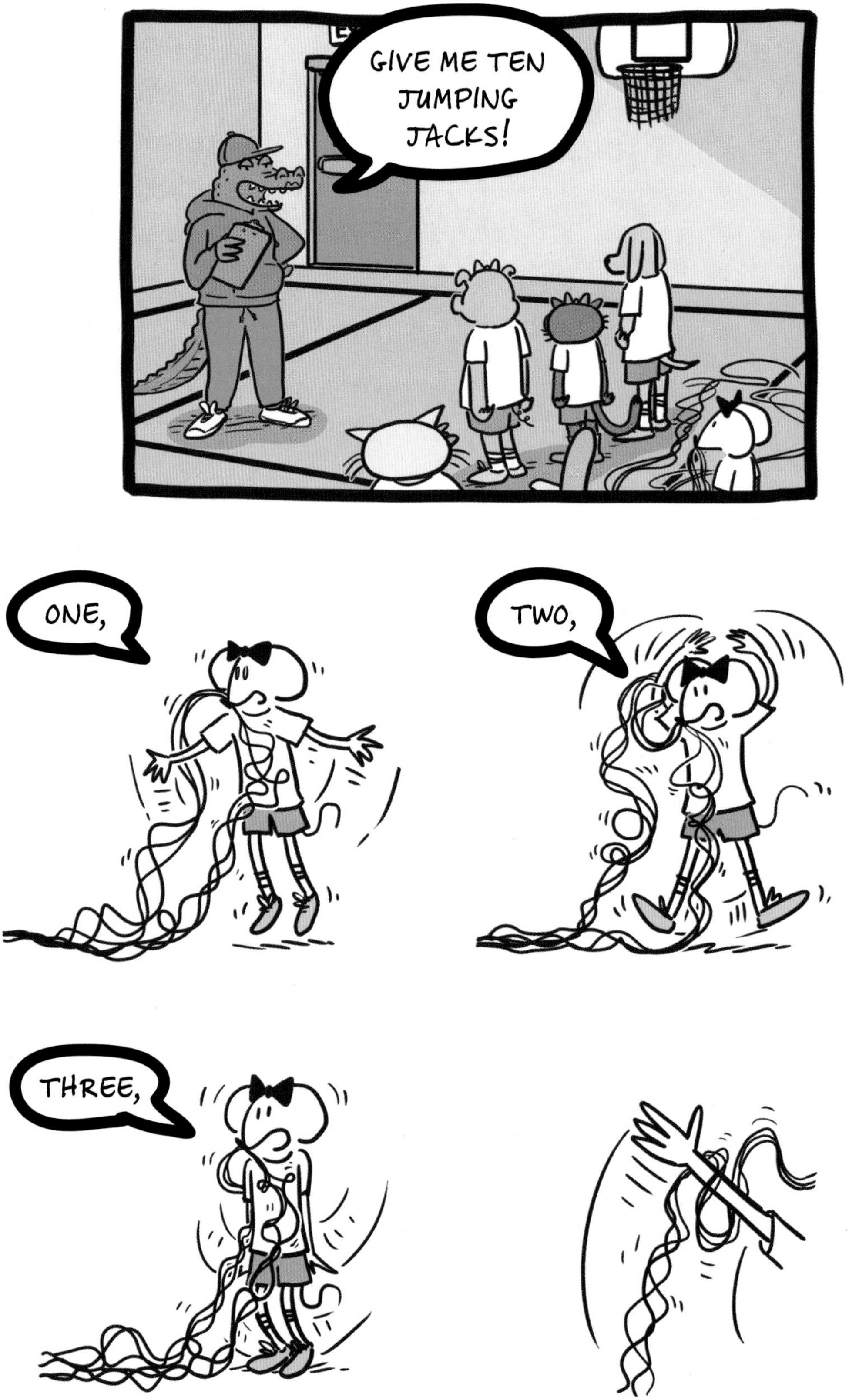
GIVE ME TEN JUMPING JACKS!
ONE,
TWO,
THREE,

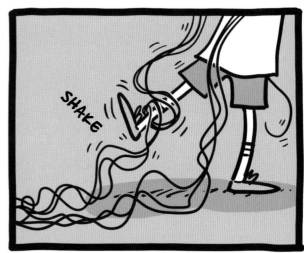

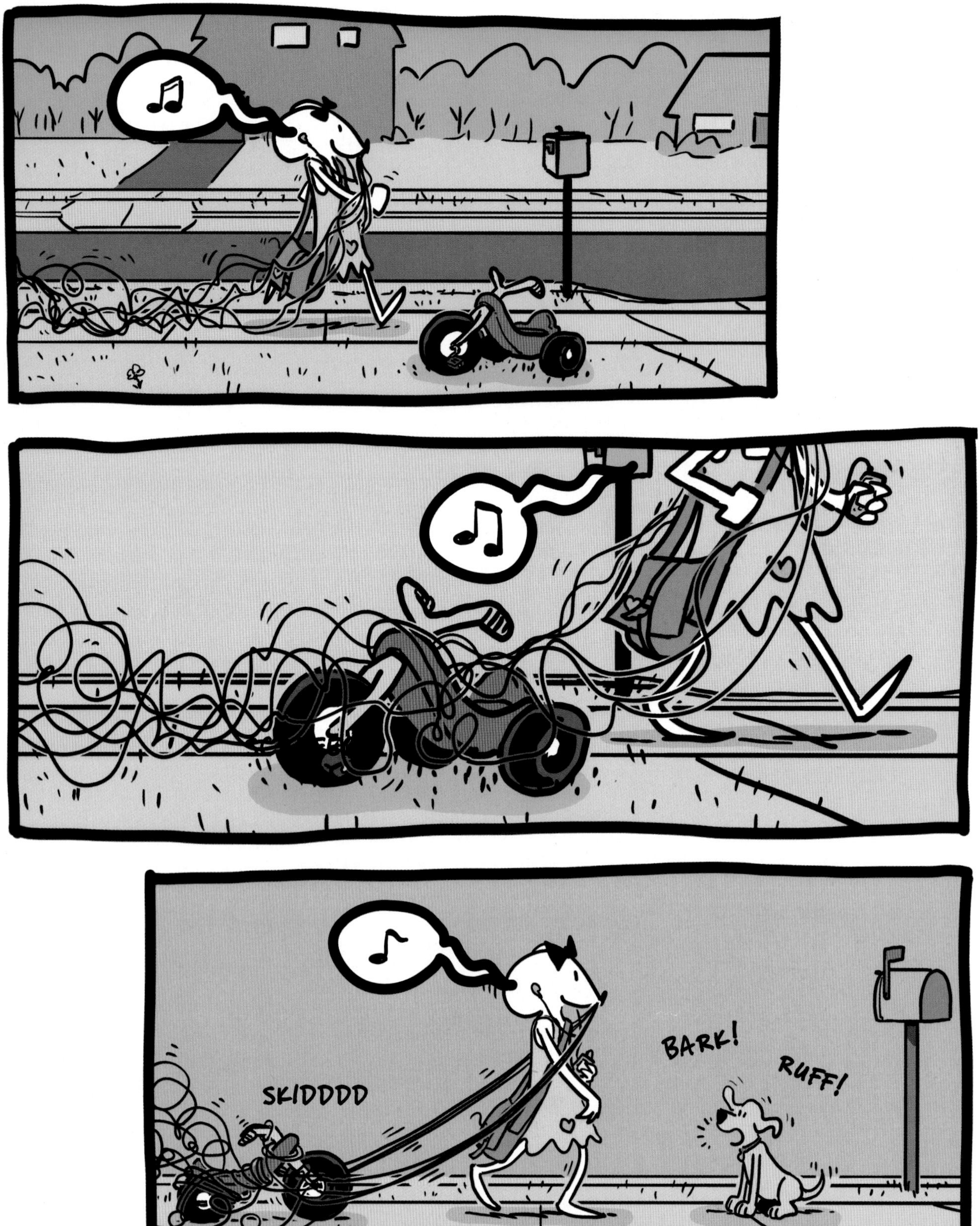
SKIDDDD
BARK!
RUFF!

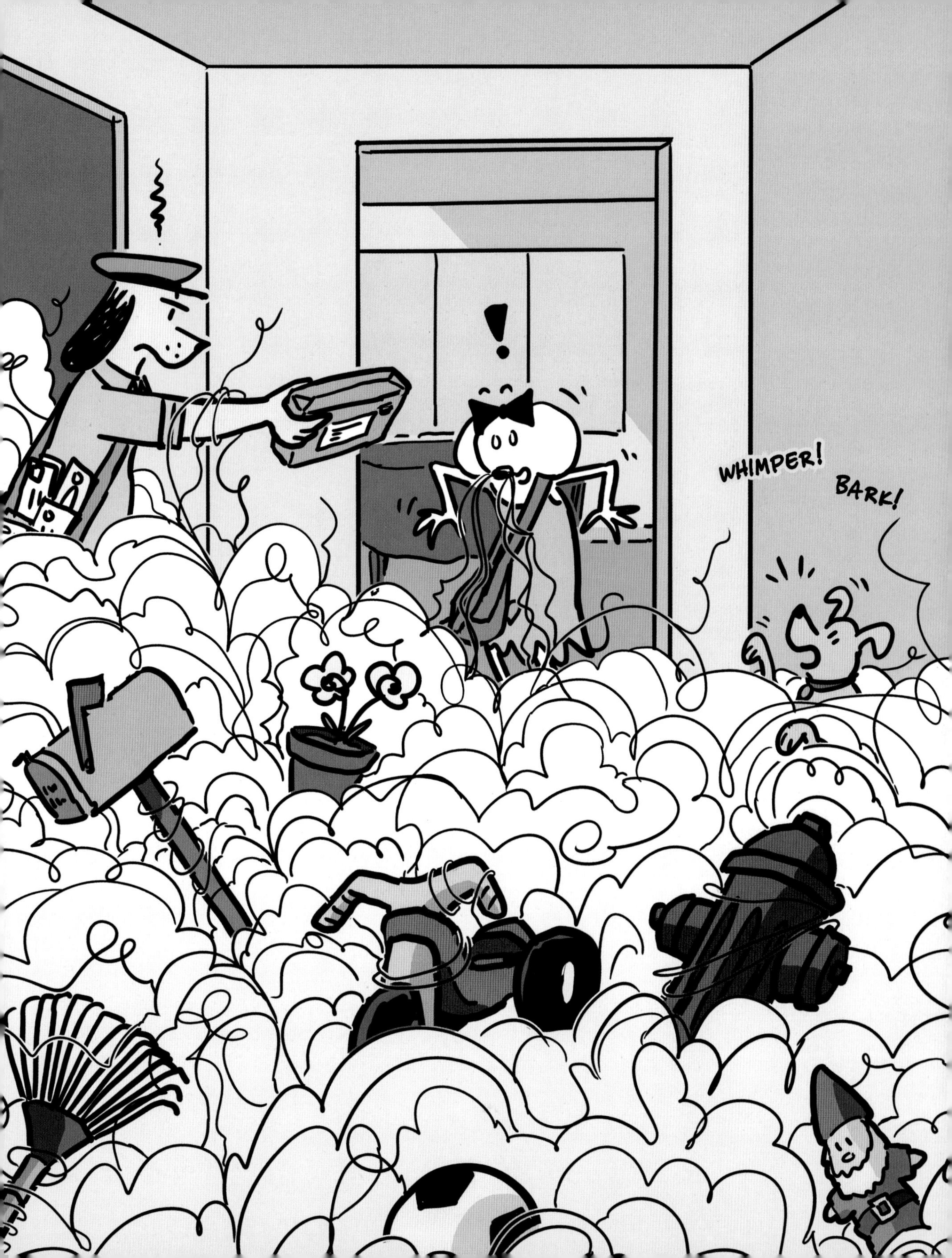
WHIMPER!
BARK!

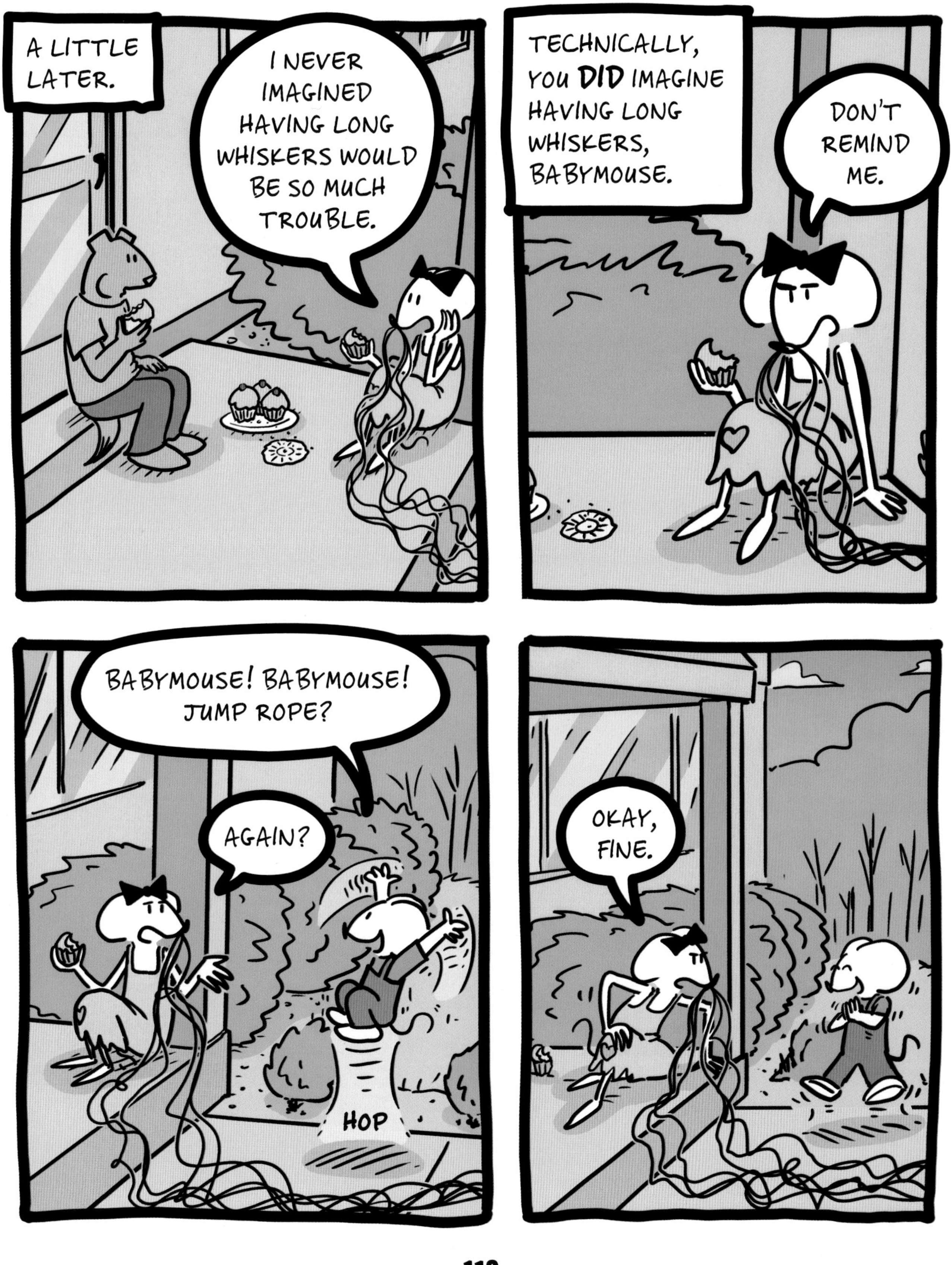
A LITTLE LATER.
I NEVER IMAGINED HAVING LONG WHISKERS WOULD BE SO MUCH TROUBLE.
TECHNICALLY, YOU **DID** IMAGINE HAVING LONG WHISKERS, BABYMOUSE.
DON'T REMIND ME.
BABYMOUSE! BABYMOUSE! JUMP ROPE?
AGAIN?
HOP
OKAY, FINE.

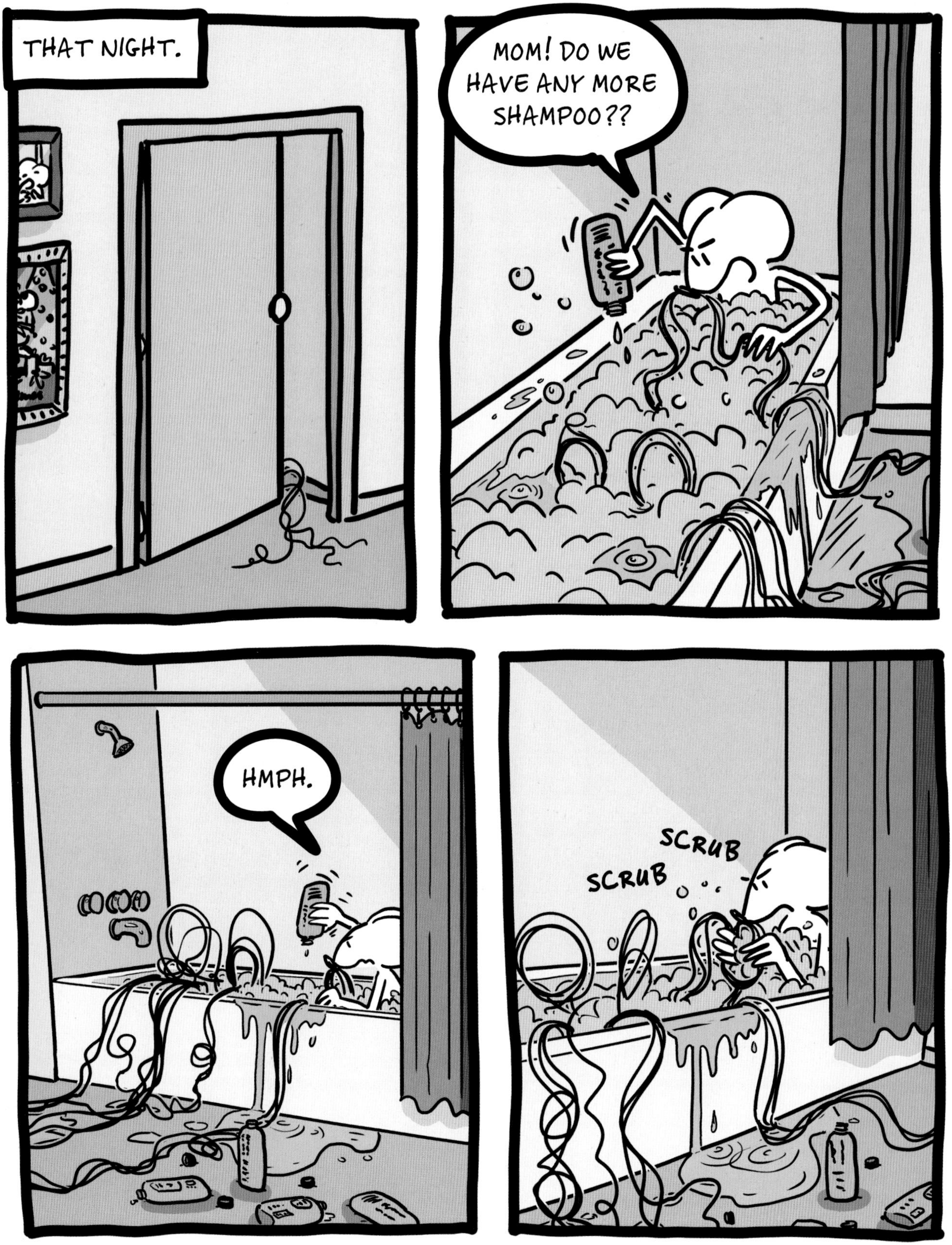
THAT NIGHT.
MOM! DO WE HAVE ANY MORE SHAMPOO??
HMPH.
SCRUB
SCRUB

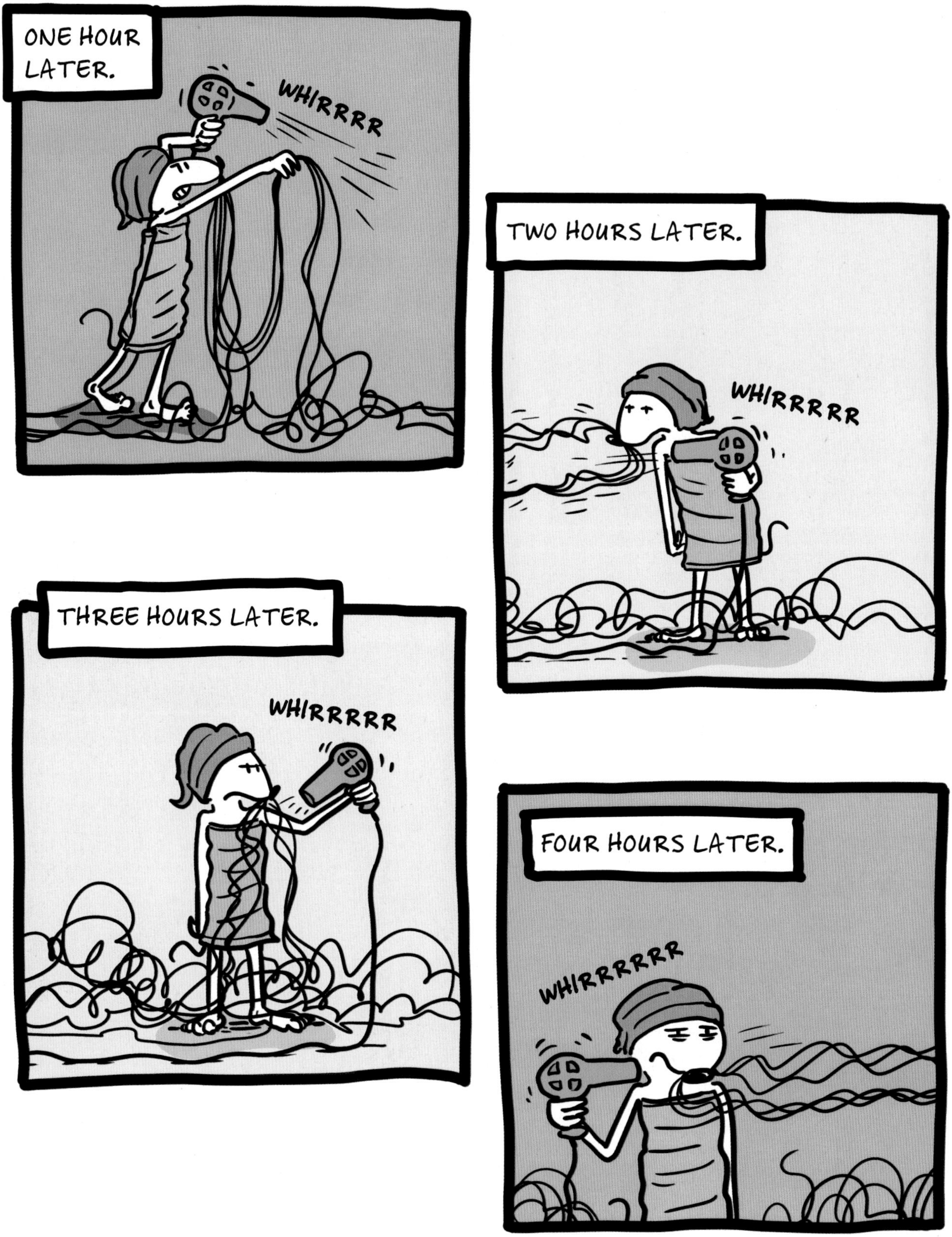
ONE HOUR LATER.
WHIRRRR
TWO HOURS LATER.
WHIRRRRR
THREE HOURS LATER.
WHIRRRRR
FOUR HOURS LATER.
WHIRRRRRR

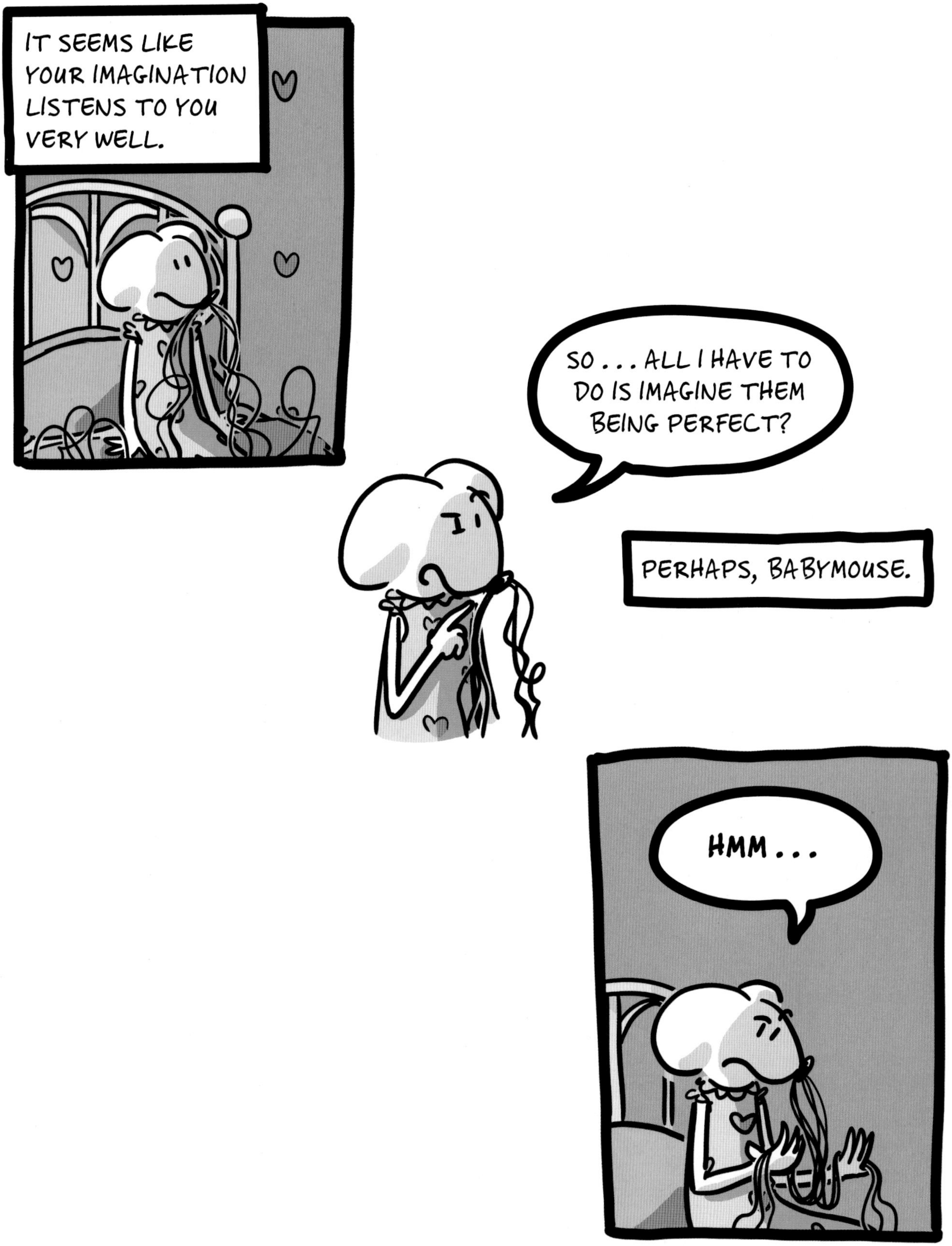
IT SEEMS LIKE YOUR IMAGINATION LISTENS TO YOU VERY WELL.
SO . . . ALL I HAVE TO DO IS IMAGINE THEM BEING PERFECT?
PERHAPS, BABYMOUSE.
HMM . . .

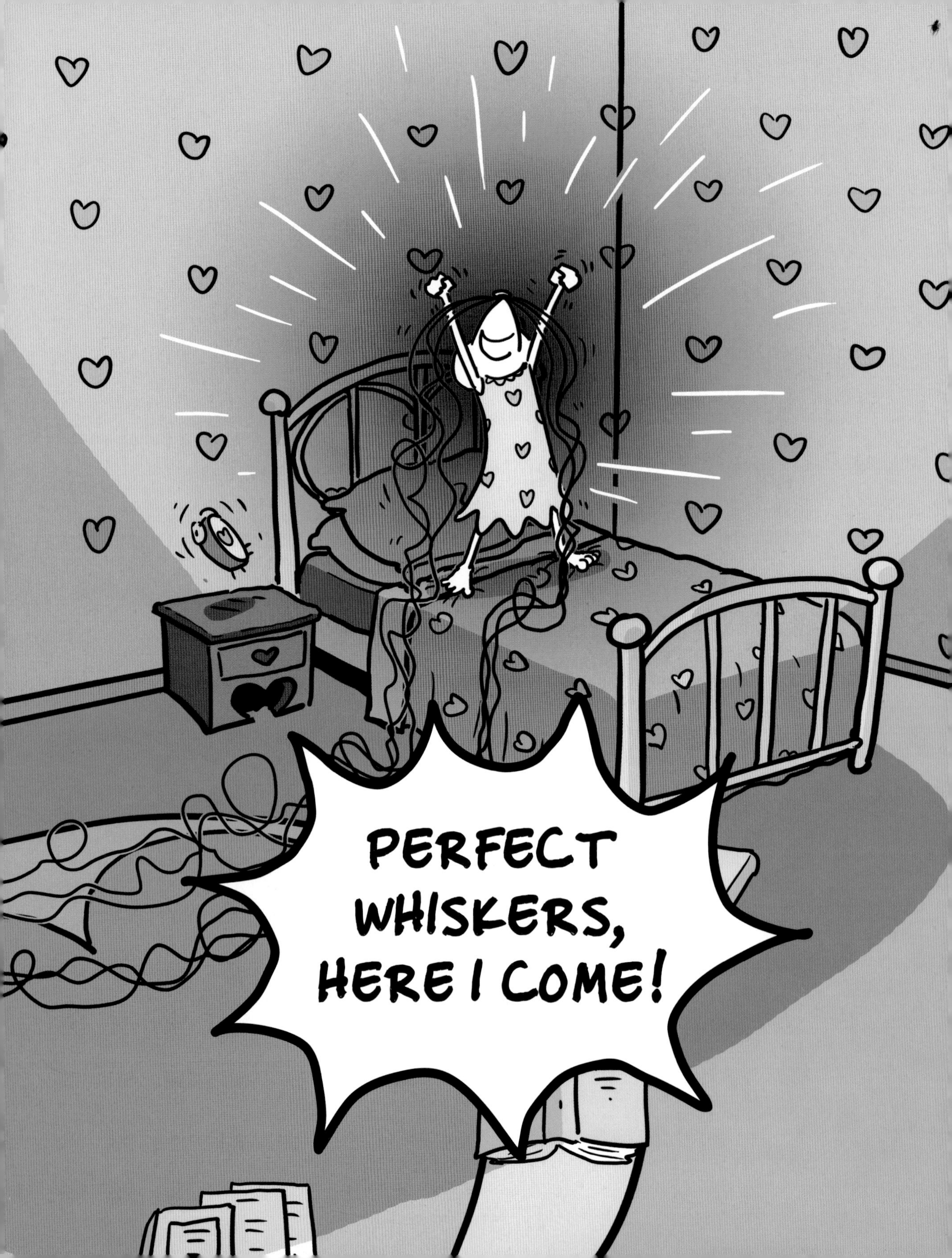
PERFECT WHISKERS, HERE I COME!

PART FOUR

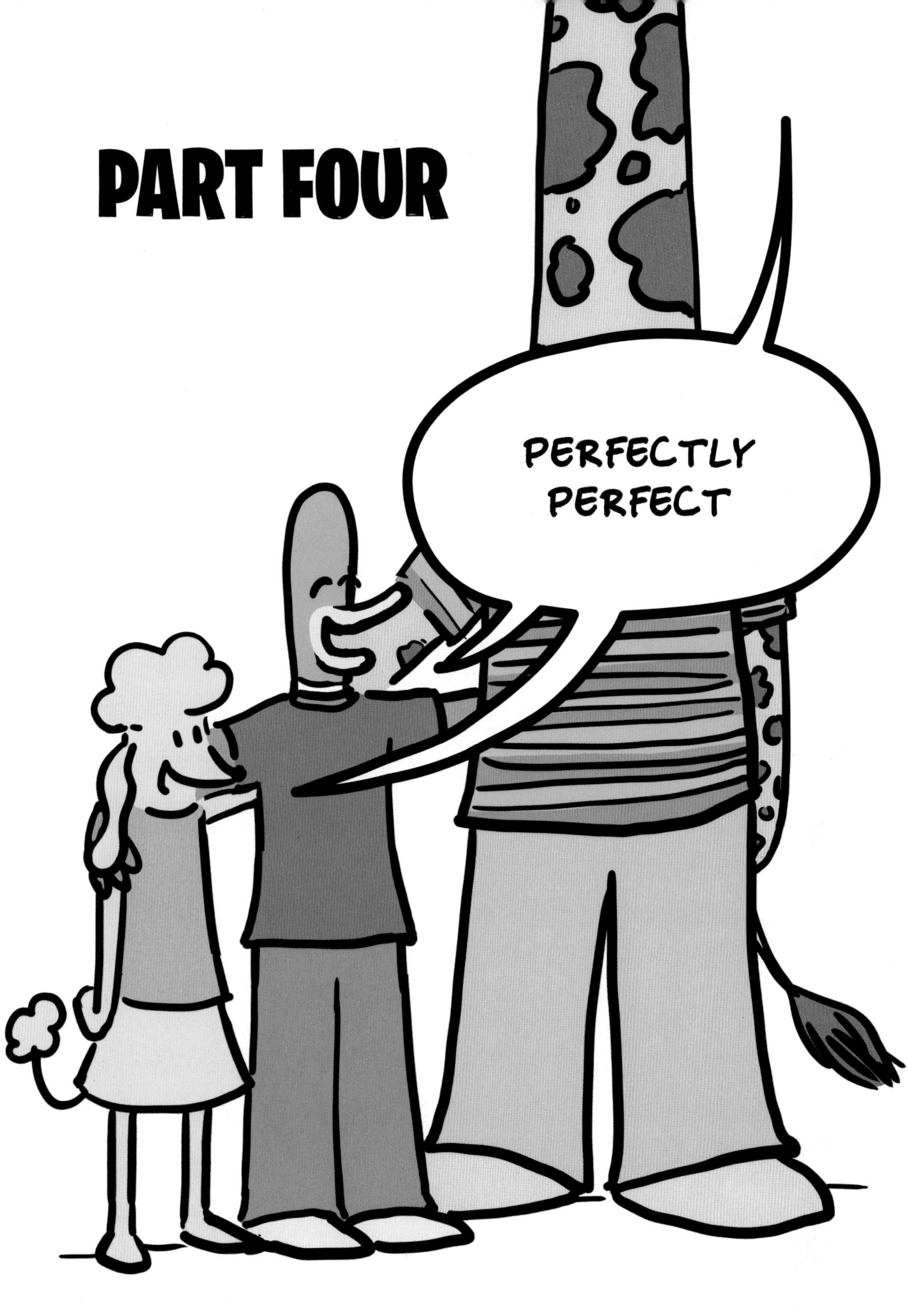
PERFECTLY PERFECT

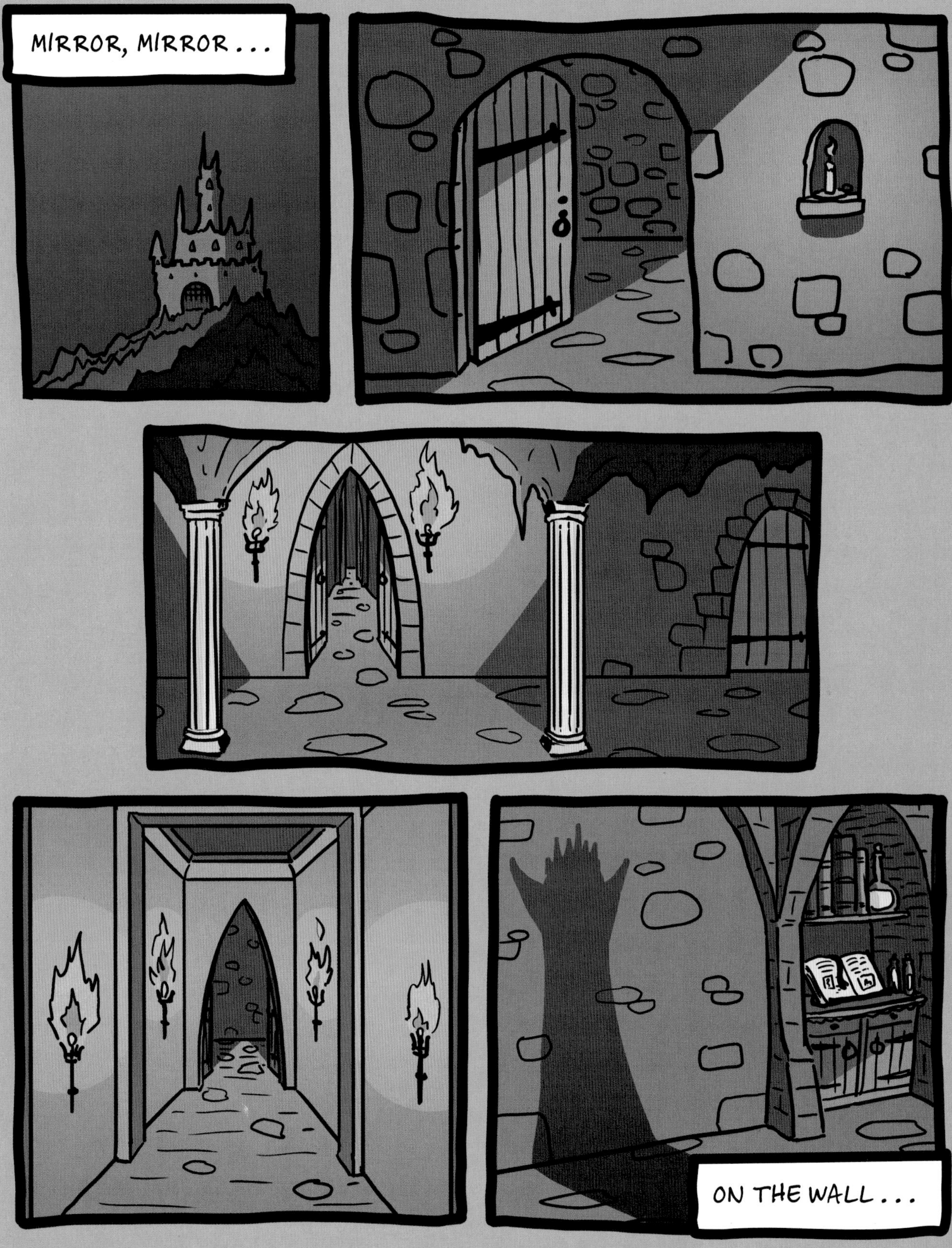
MIRROR, MIRROR . . .
ON THE WALL . . .

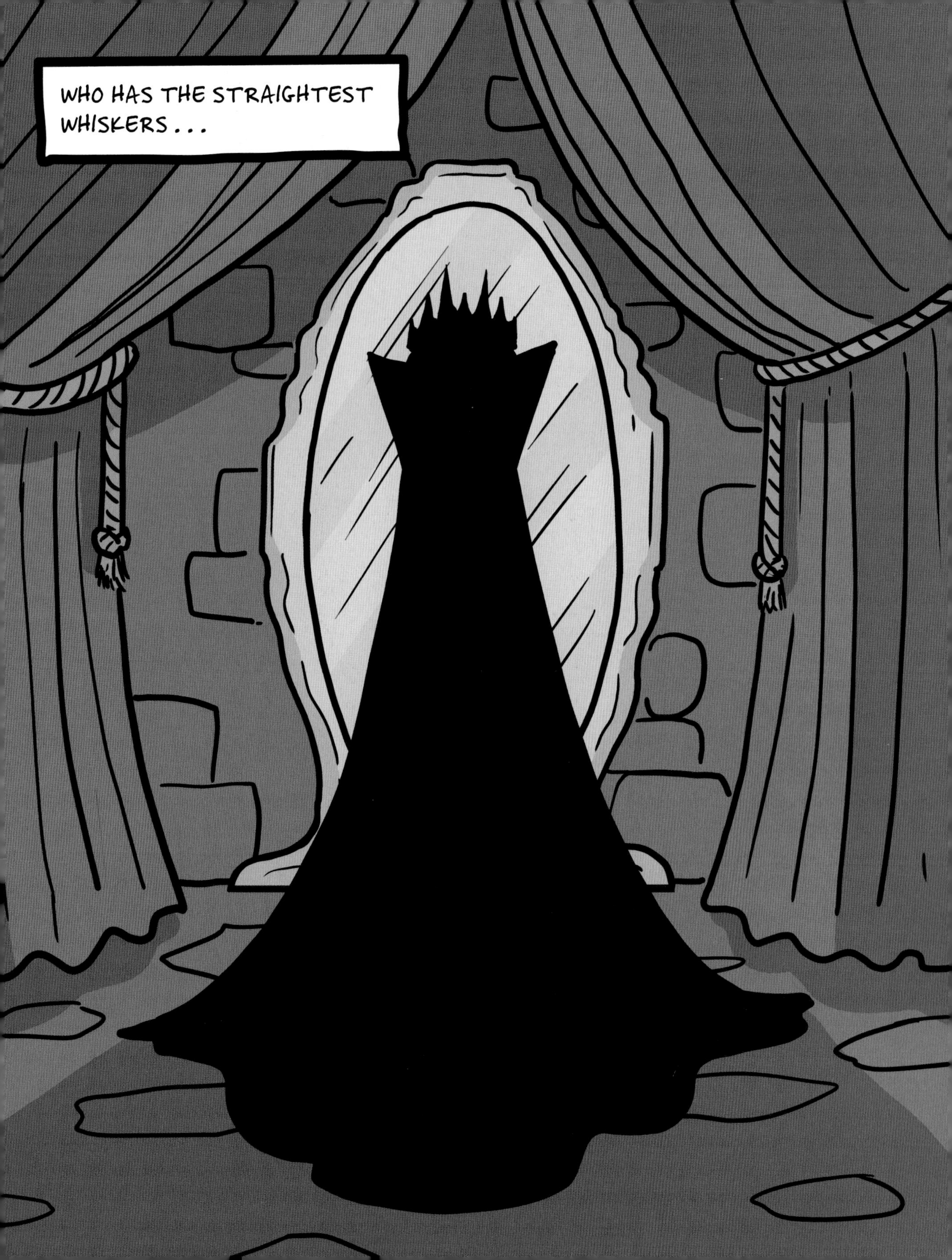
WHO HAS THE STRAIGHTEST WHISKERS . . .

127

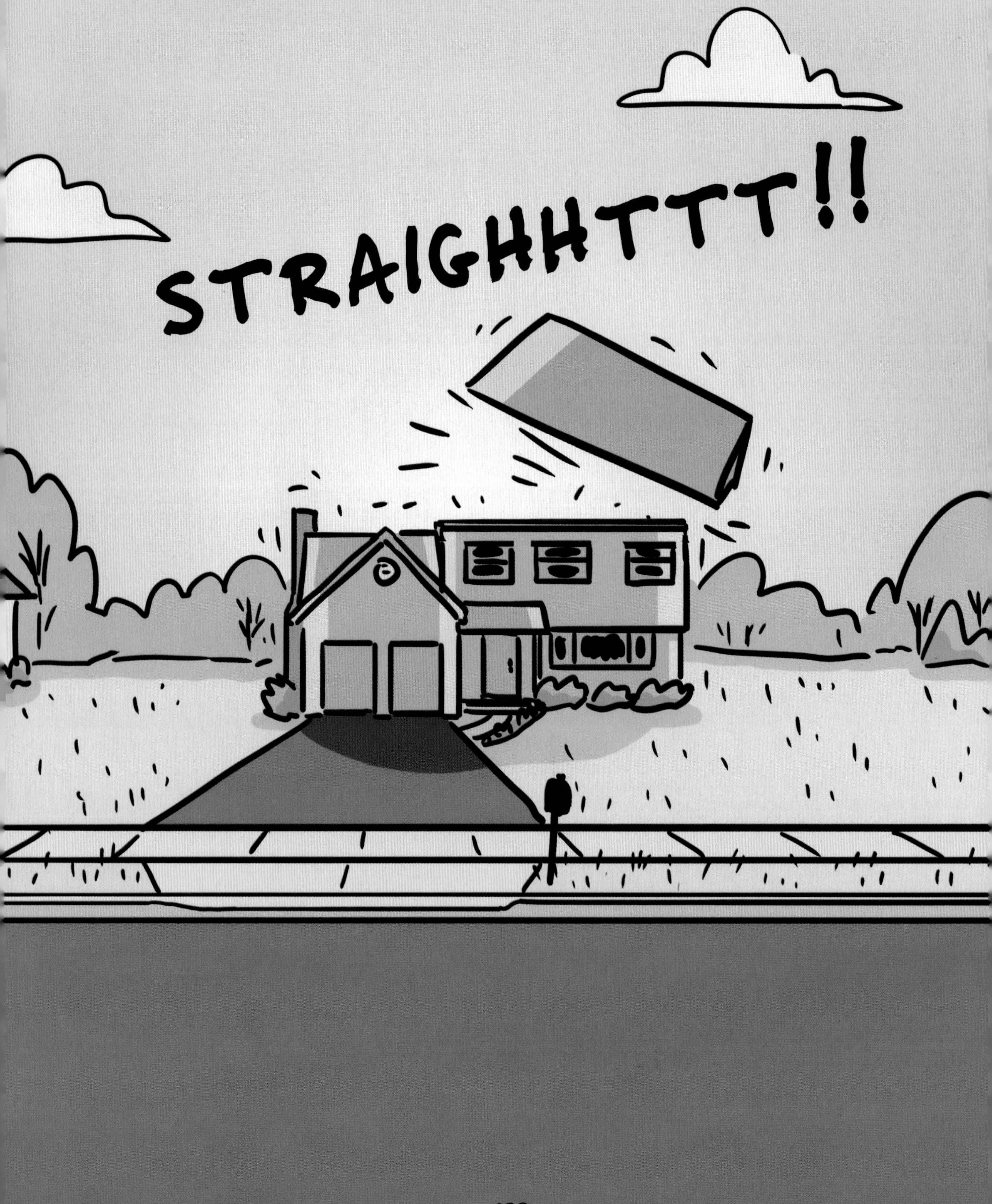
STRAIGHHTTTT!!

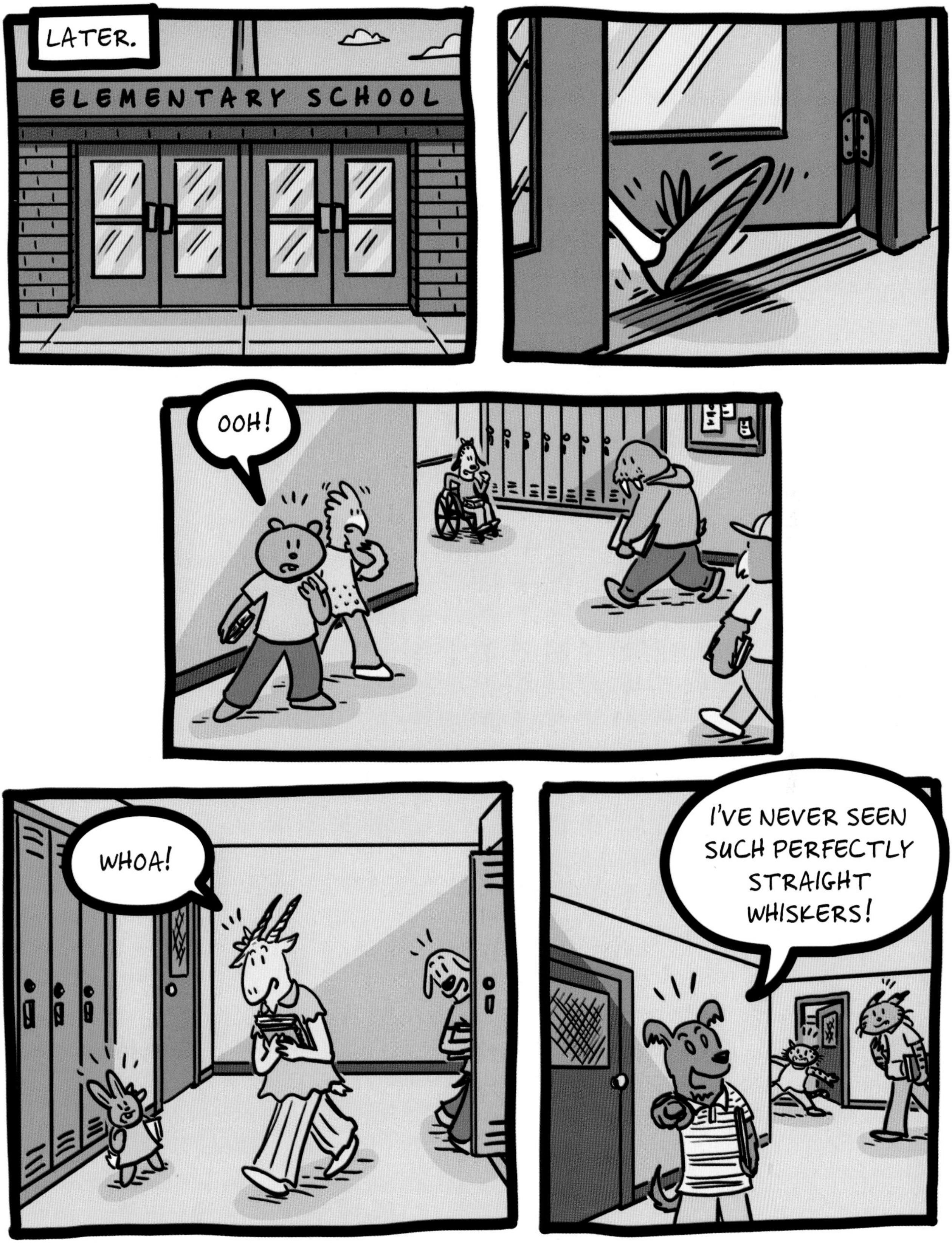
LATER.
ELEMENTARY SCHOOL
OOH!
WHOA!
I'VE NEVER SEEN SUCH PERFECTLY STRAIGHT WHISKERS!

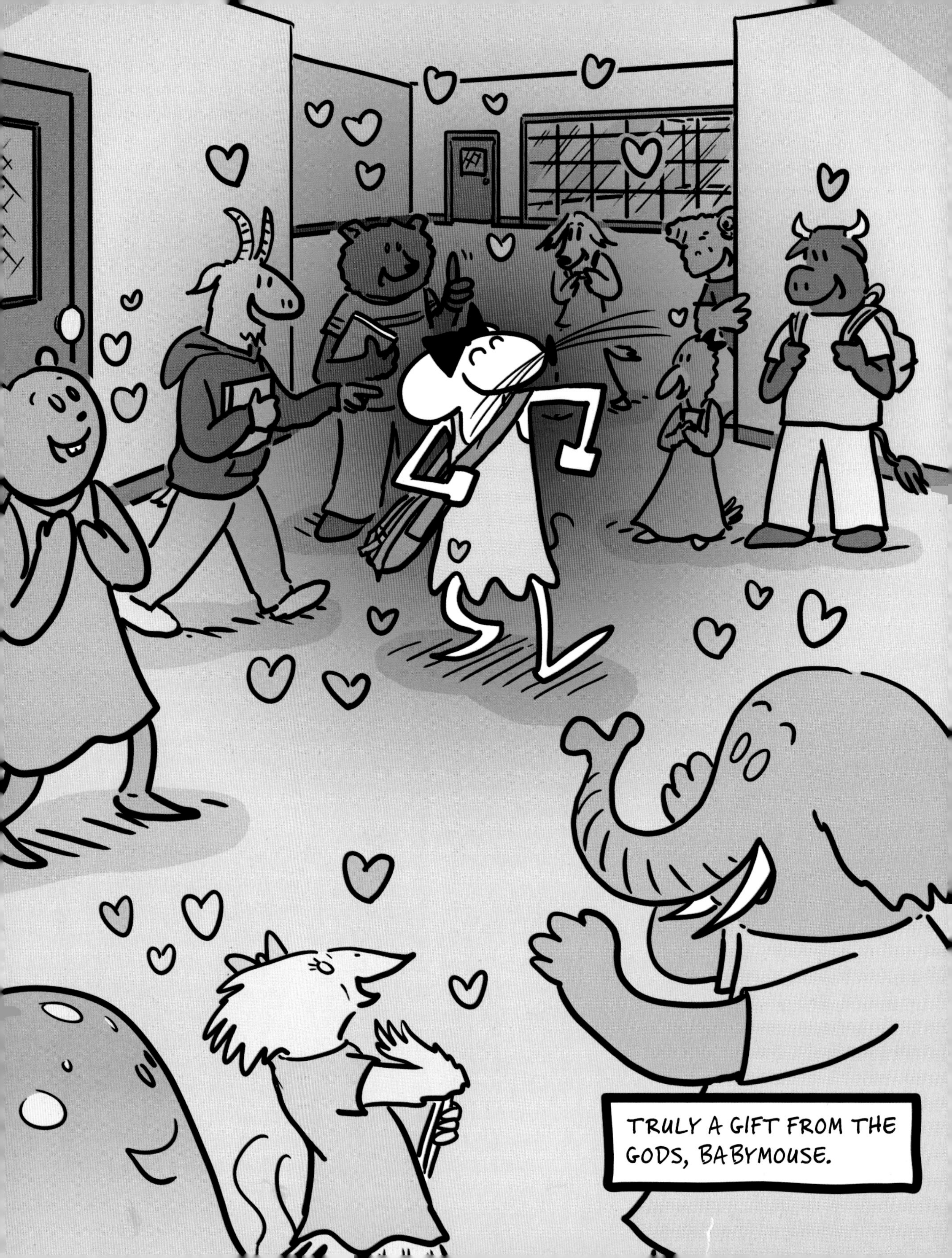
TRULY A GIFT FROM THE GODS, BABYMOUSE.

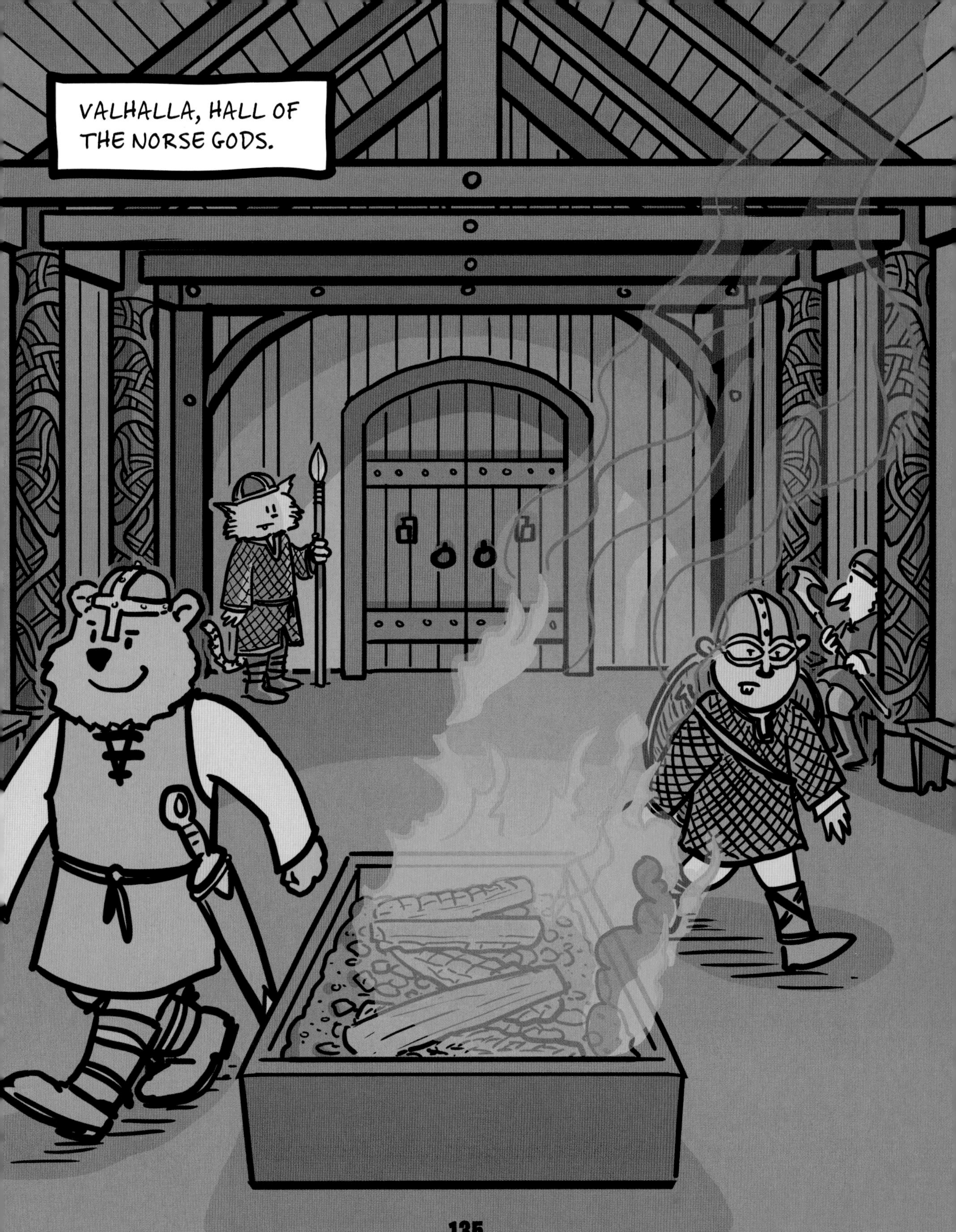
VALHALLA, HALL OF THE NORSE GODS.

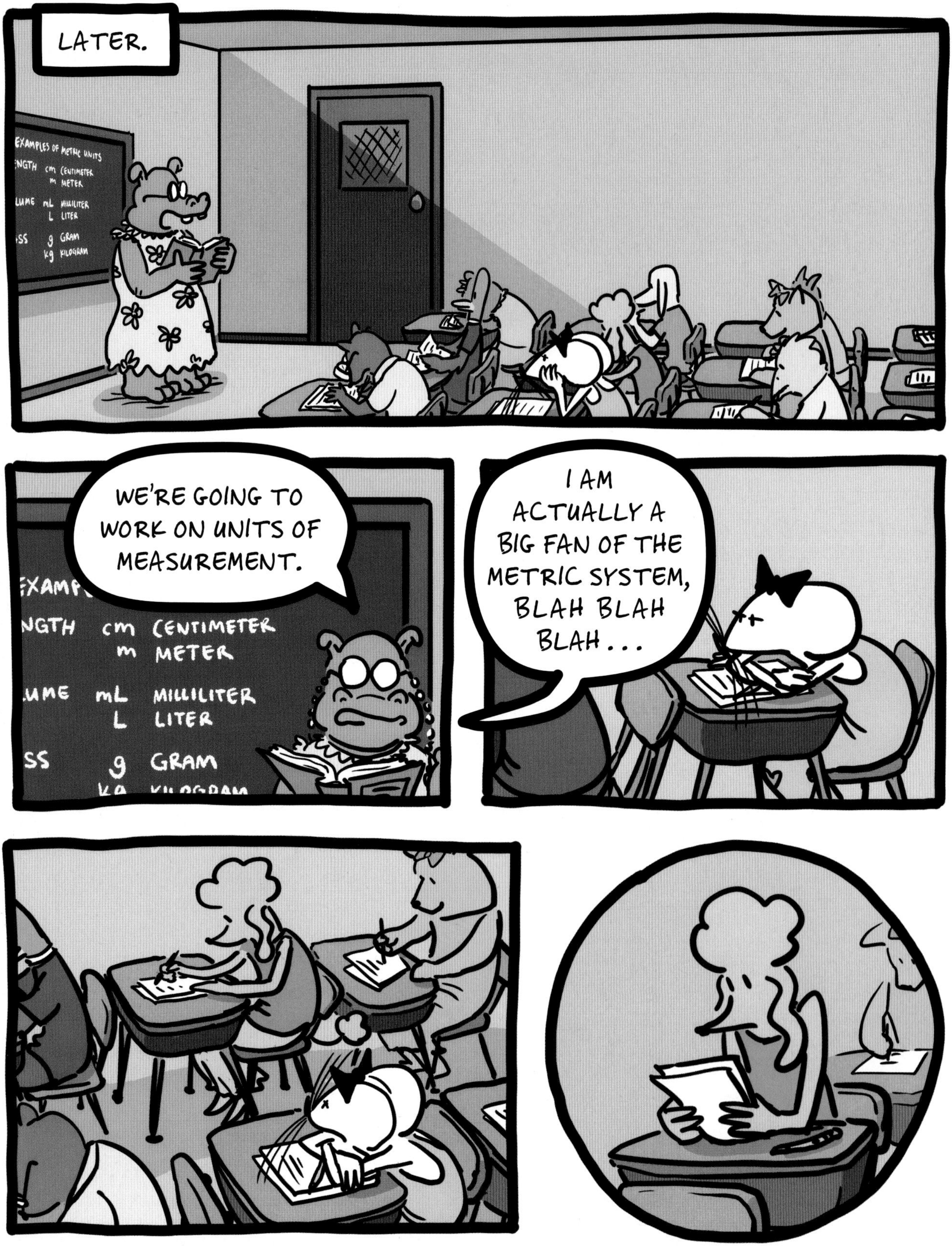
LATER.
cm CENTIMETER
m METER
mL MILLILITER
L LITER
g GRAM
WE'RE GOING TO WORK ON UNITS OF MEASUREMENT.
I AM ACTUALLY A BIG FAN OF THE METRIC SYSTEM, BLAH BLAH BLAH . . .

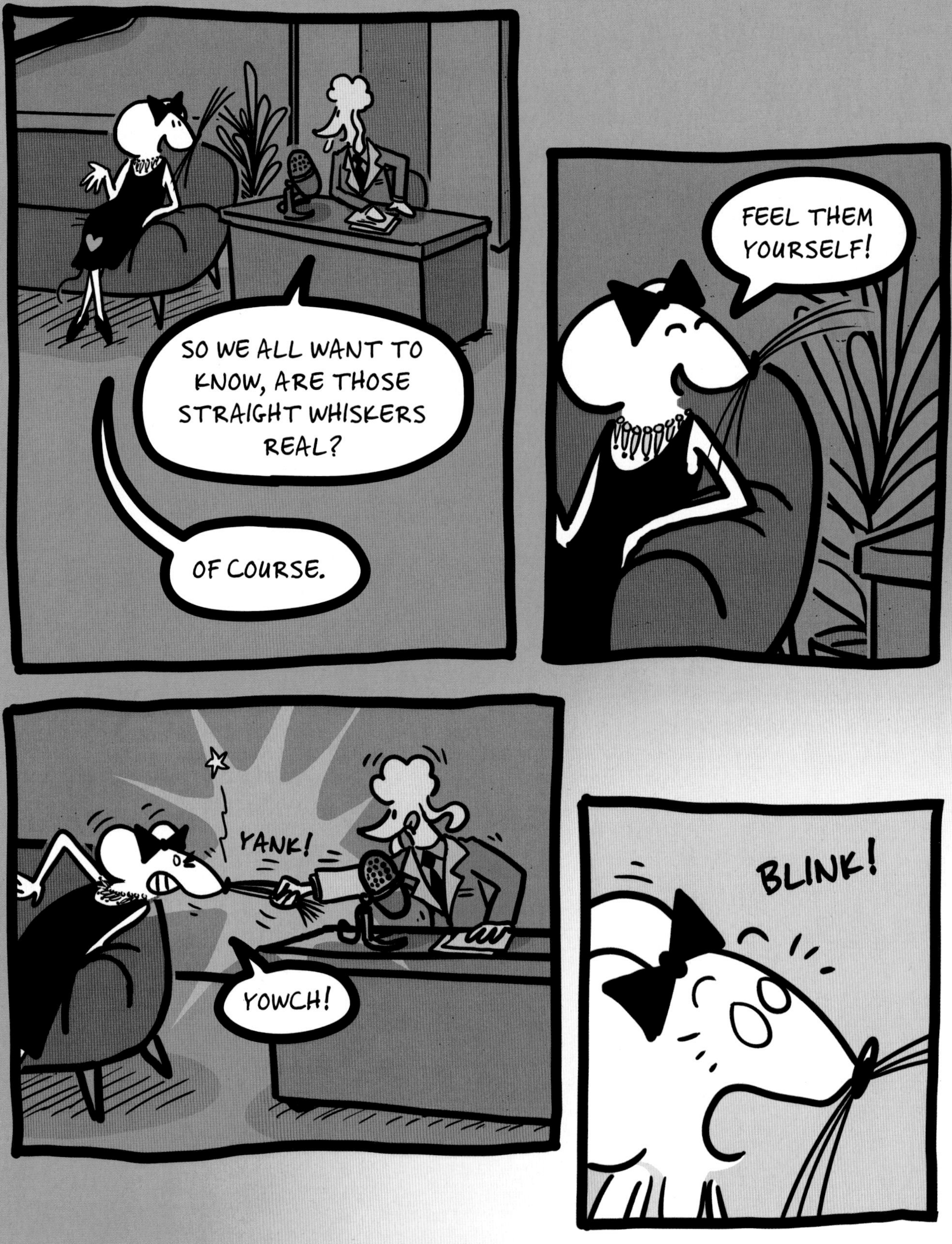
SO WE ALL WANT TO KNOW, ARE THOSE STRAIGHT WHISKERS REAL?
OF COURSE.
FEEL THEM YOURSELF!
YANK!
YOWCH!
BLINK!

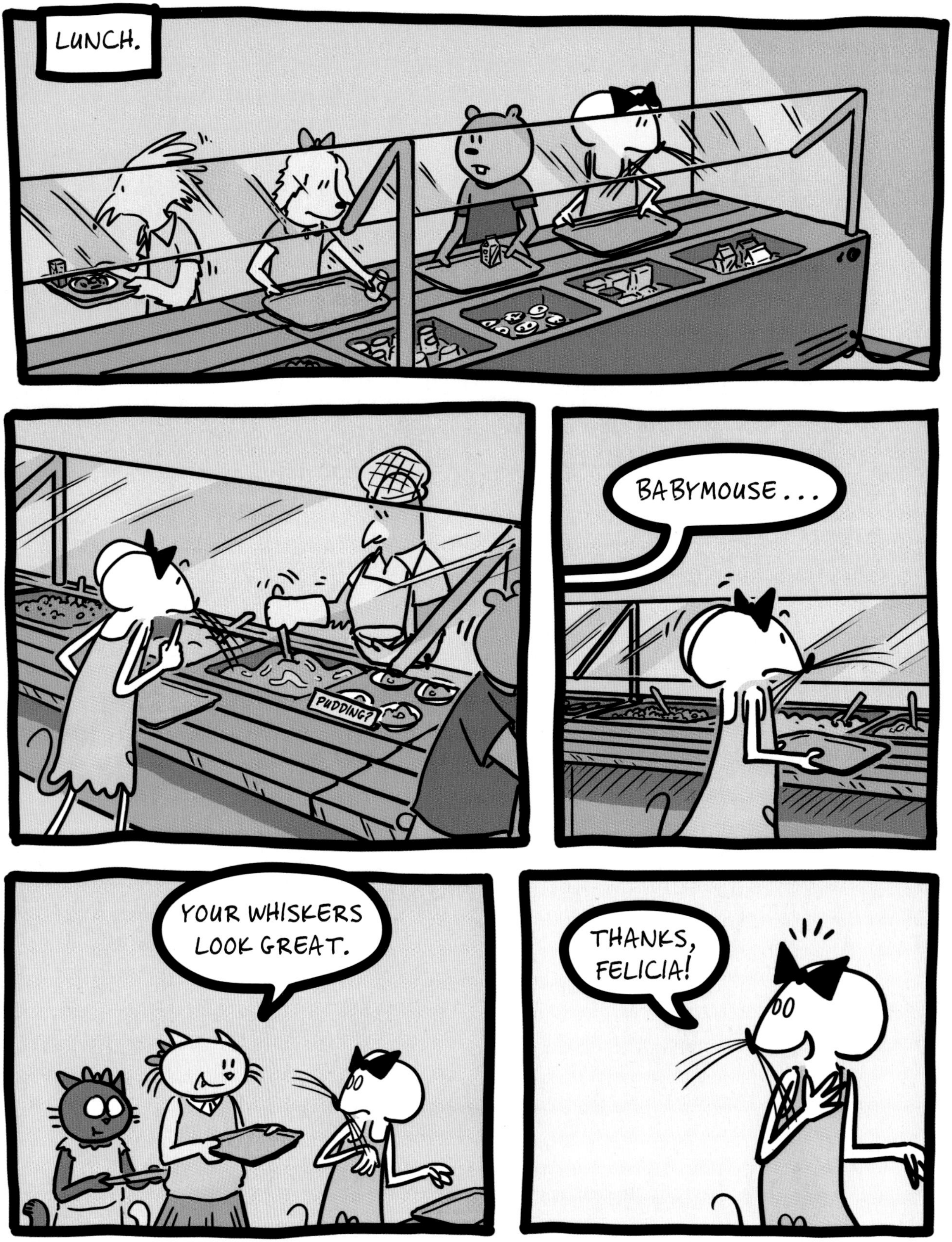
LUNCH.
PUDDING?
BABYMOUSE...
YOUR WHISKERS LOOK GREAT.
THANKS, FELICIA!

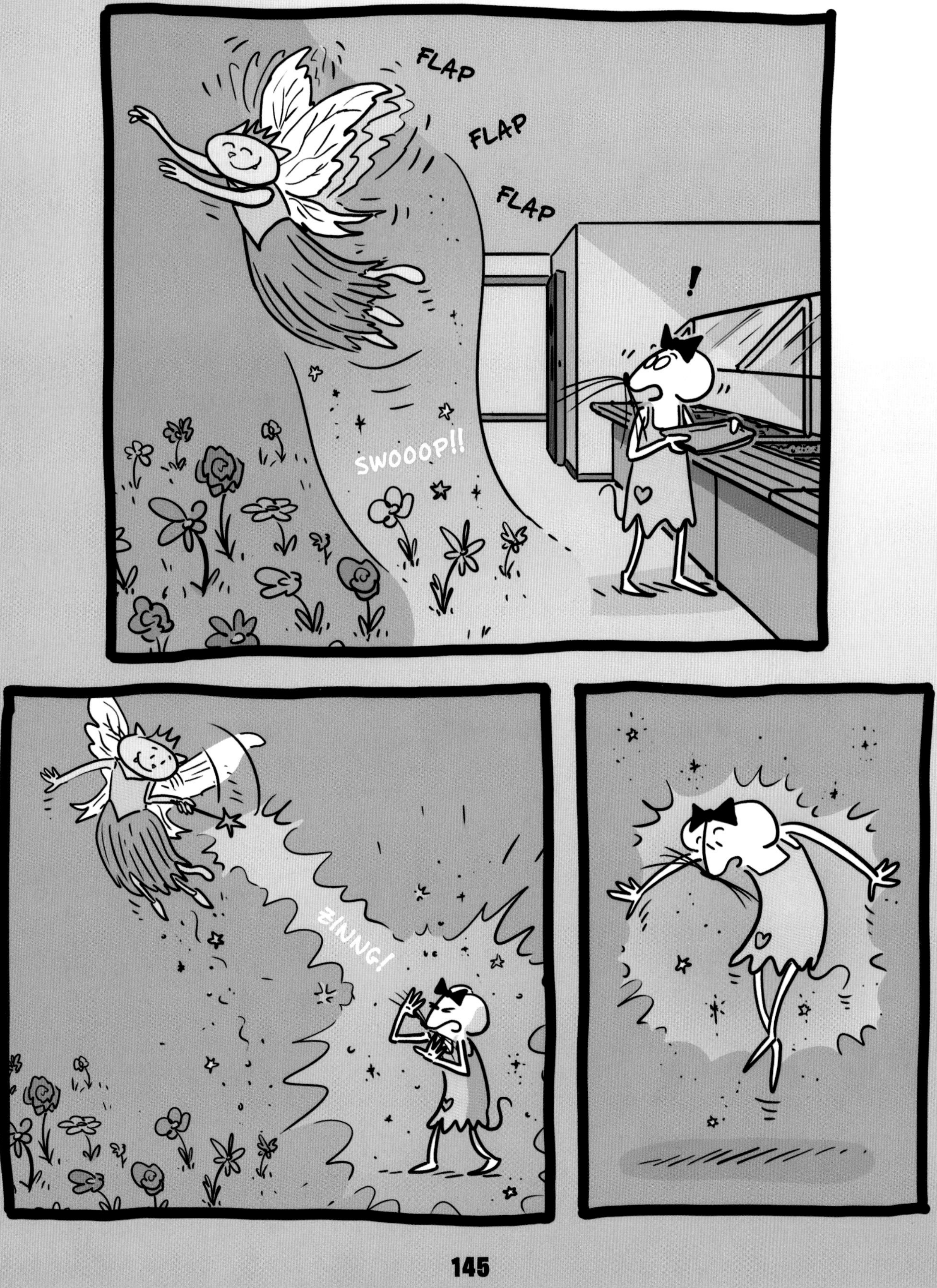
FLAP
FLAP
FLAP
!
SWOOOP!!
ZINNG!

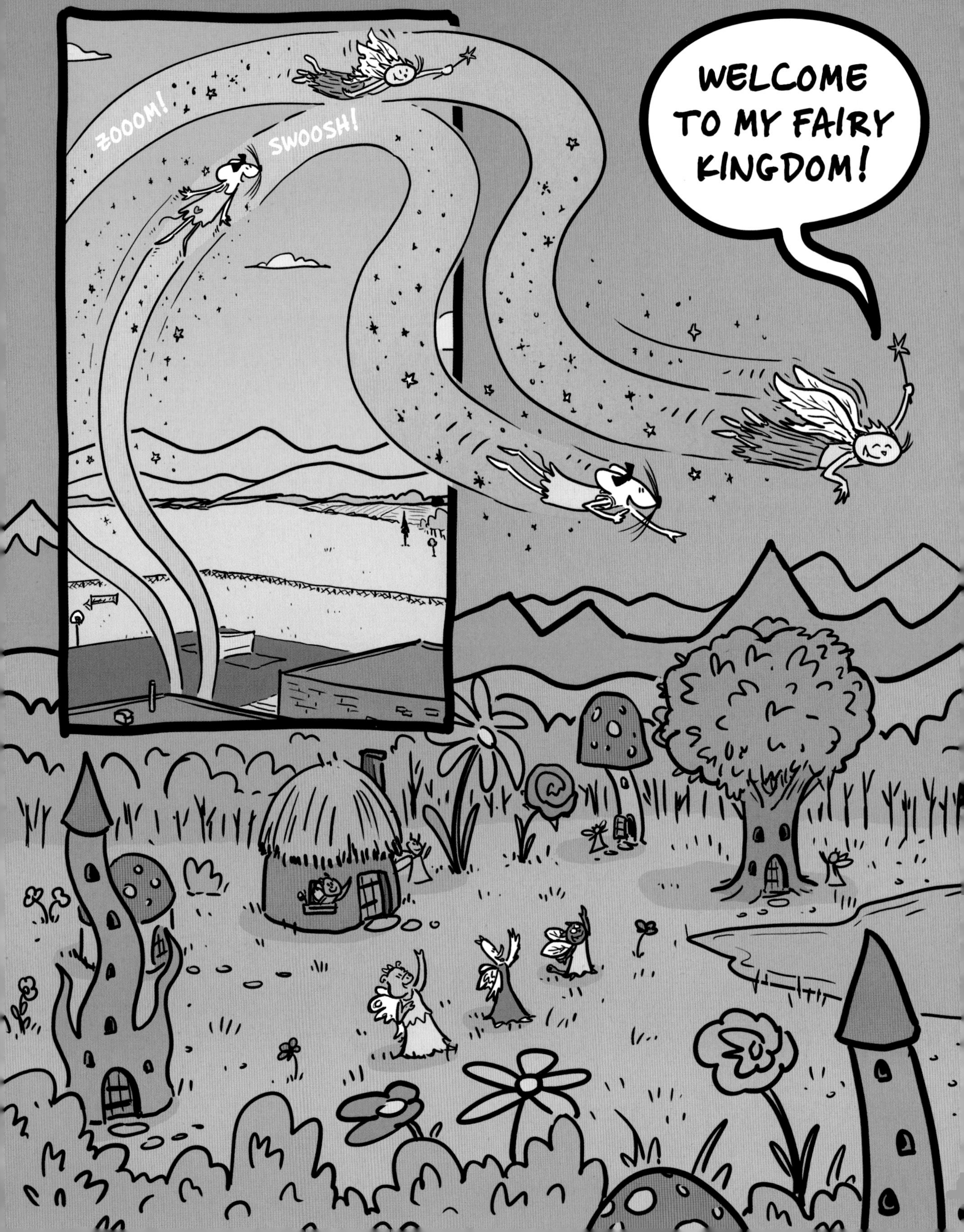
ZOOOM!
SWOOSH!
WELCOME TO MY FAIRY KINGDOM!

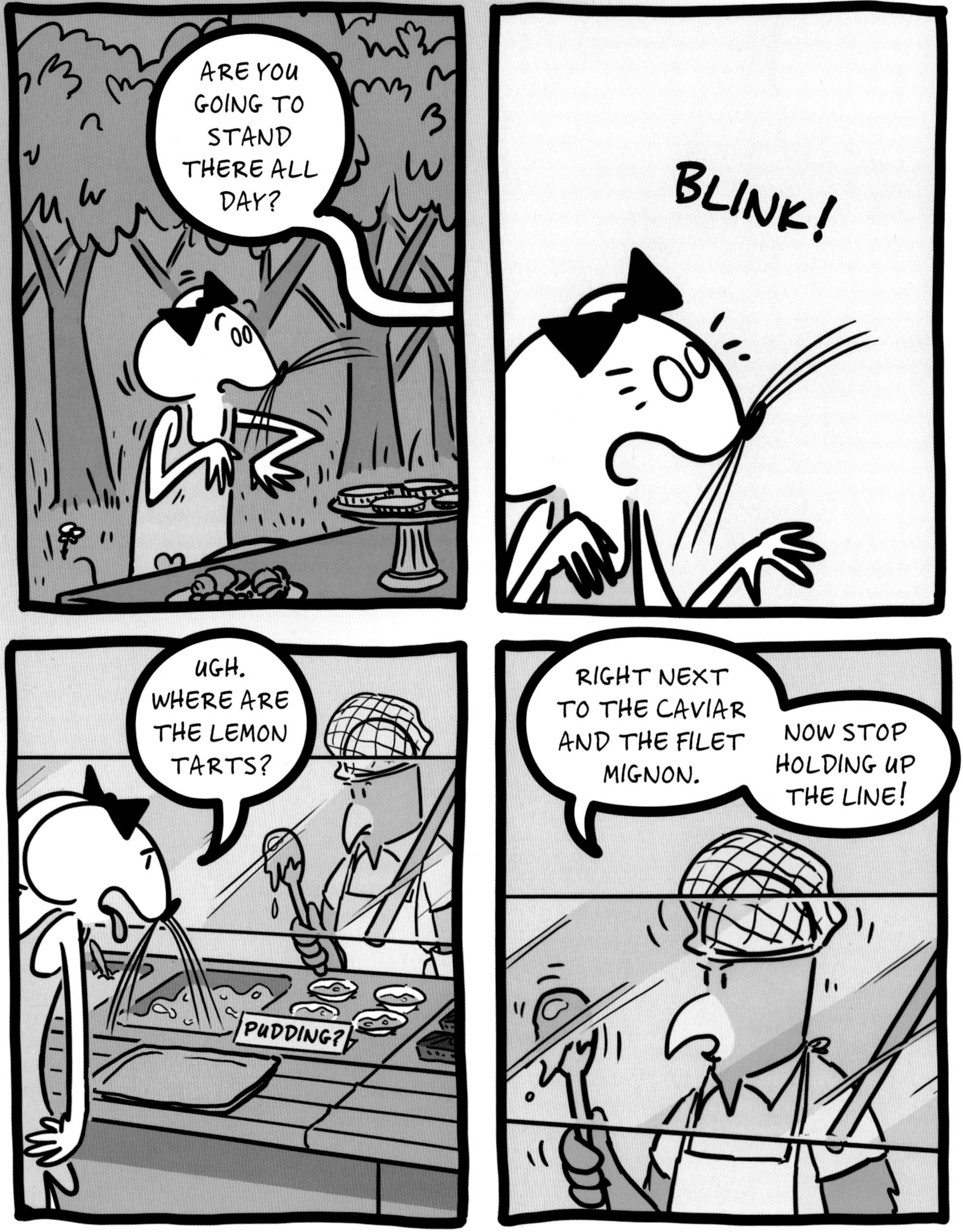
ARE YOU GOING TO STAND THERE ALL DAY?
BLINK!
UGH. WHERE ARE THE LEMON TARTS?
PUDDING?
RIGHT NEXT TO THE CAVIAR AND THE FILET MIGNON.
NOW STOP HOLDING UP THE LINE!

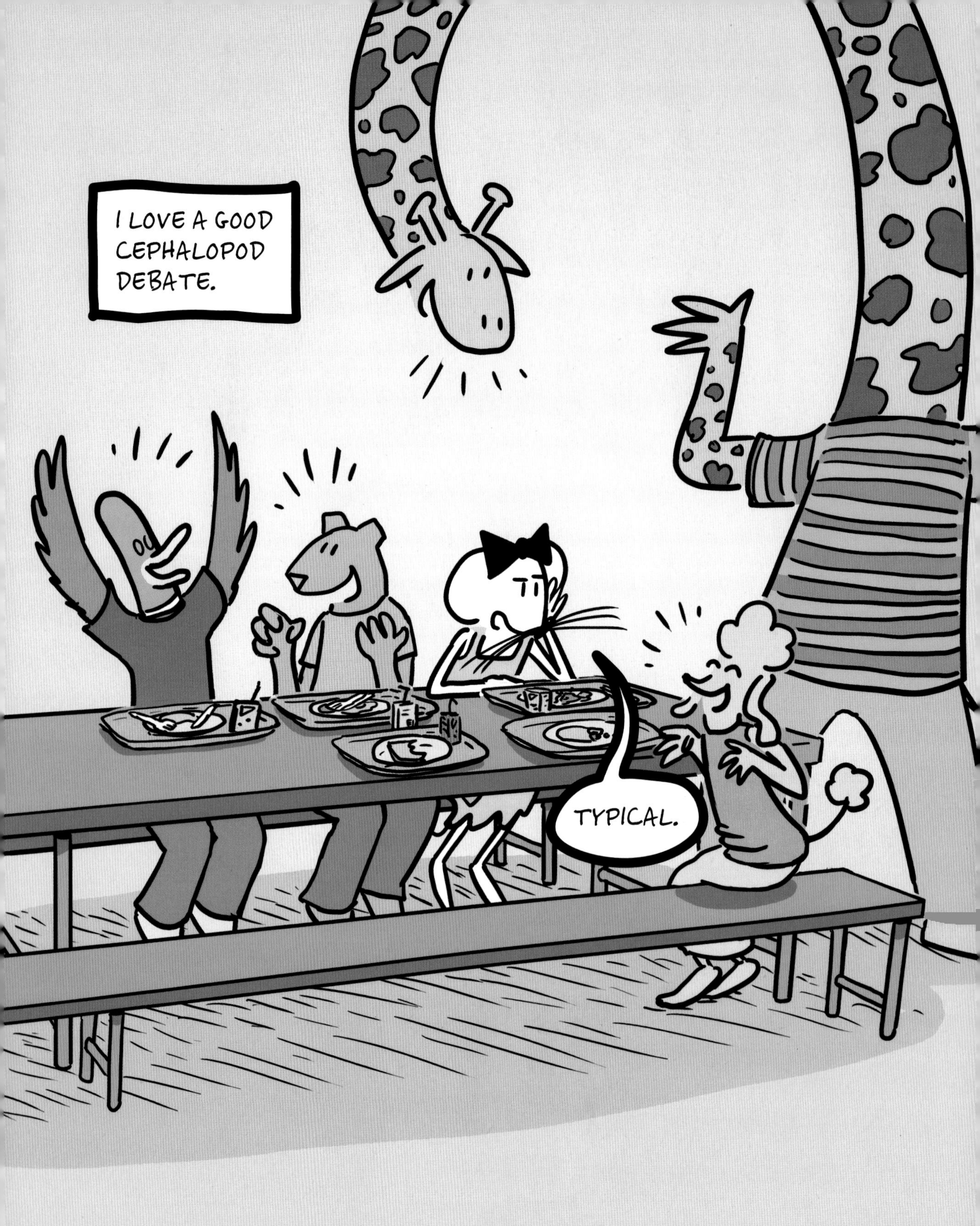
I LOVE A GOOD CEPHALOPOD DEBATE.
TYPICAL.

THAT NIGHT.

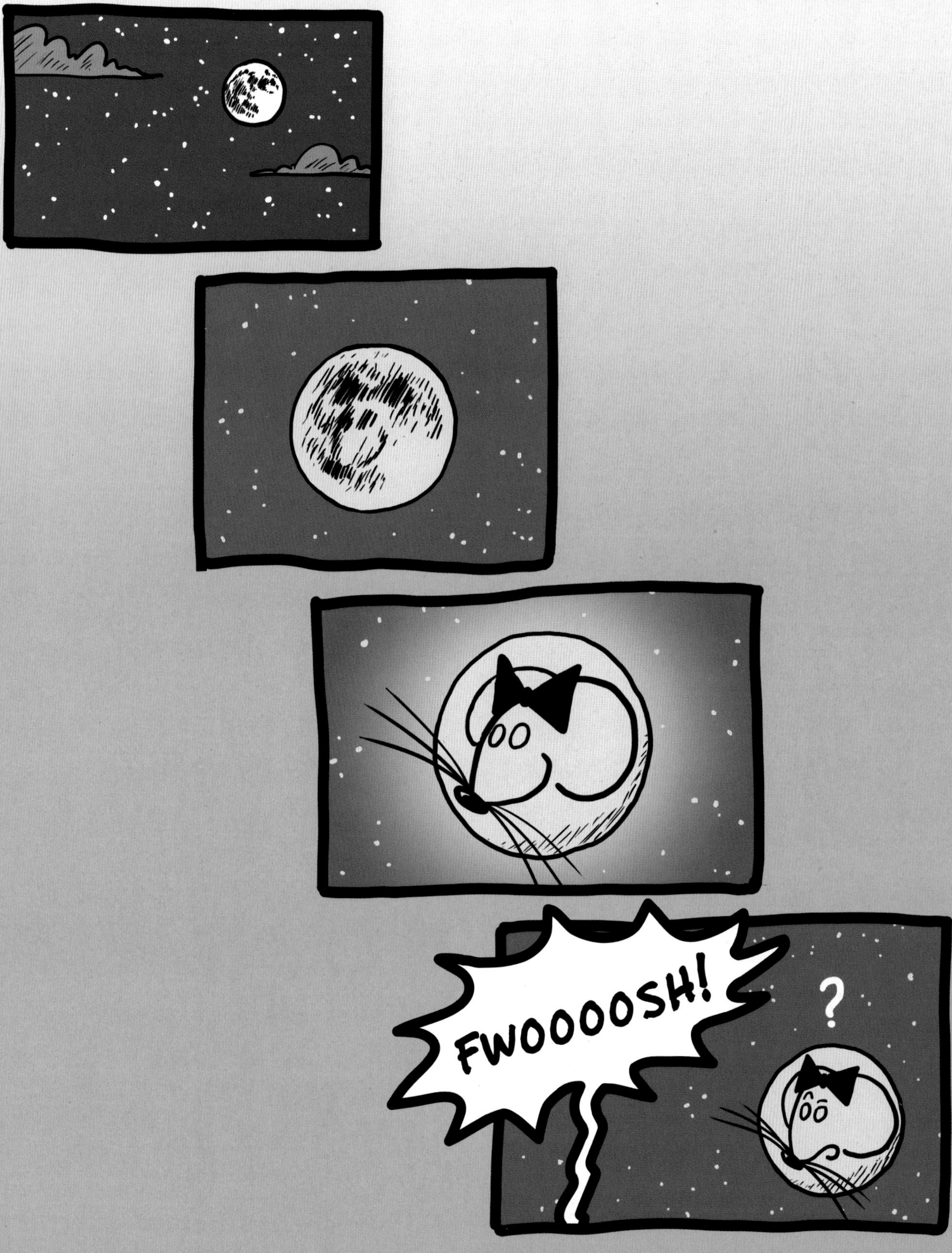
FWOOOOSH!
?

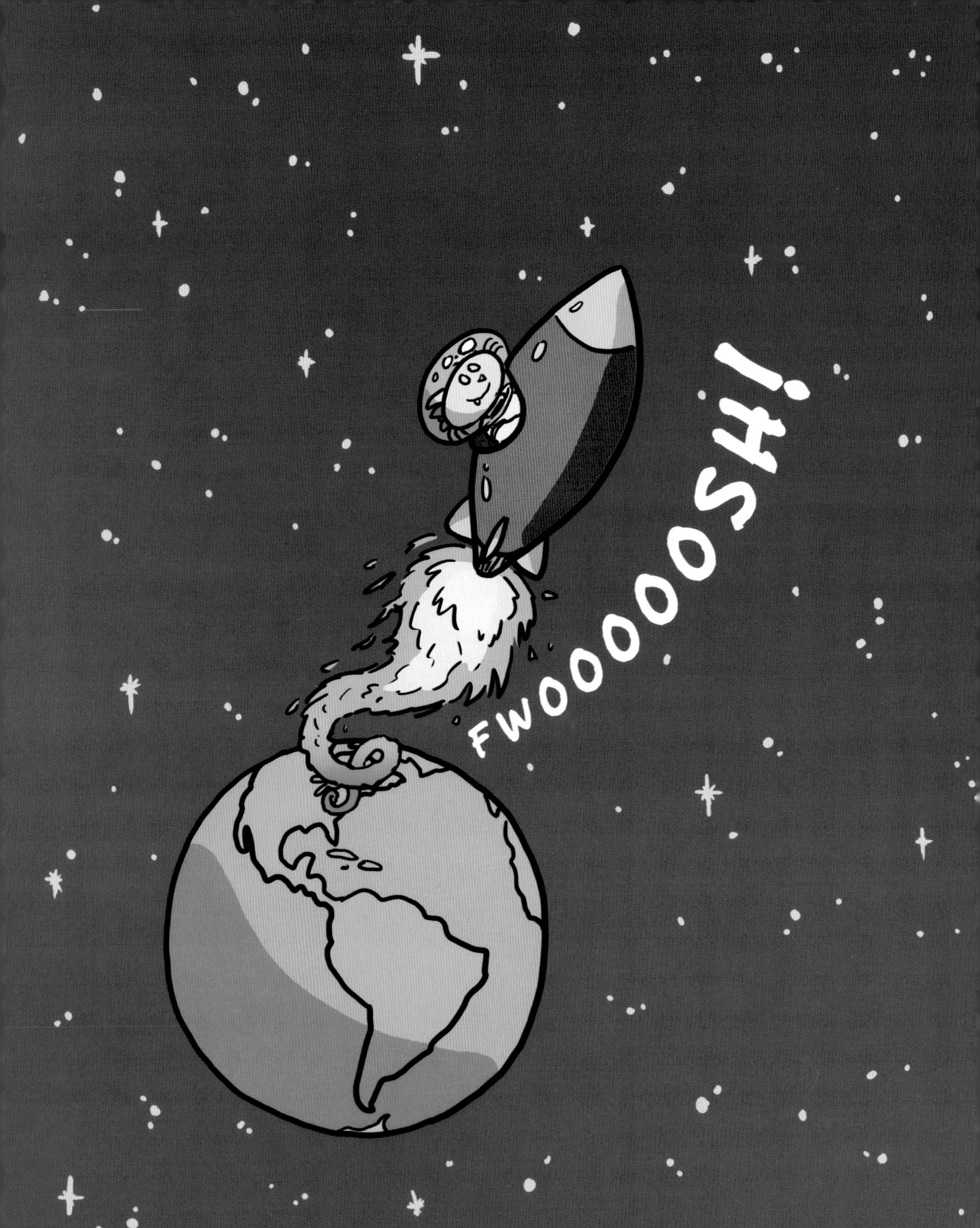
FWOOOOOSH!

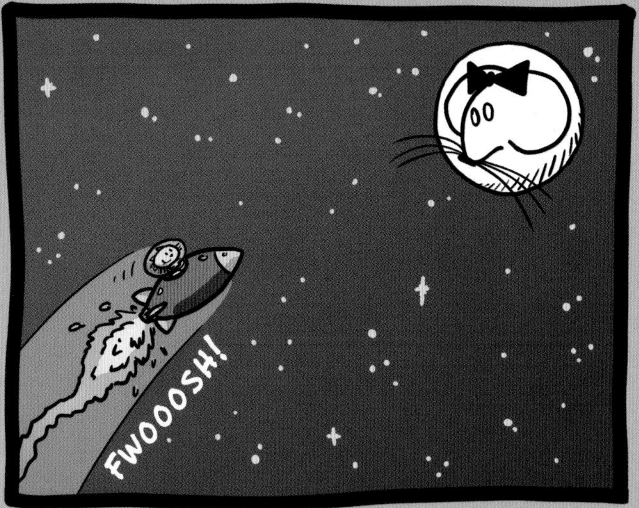
FWOOOSH!

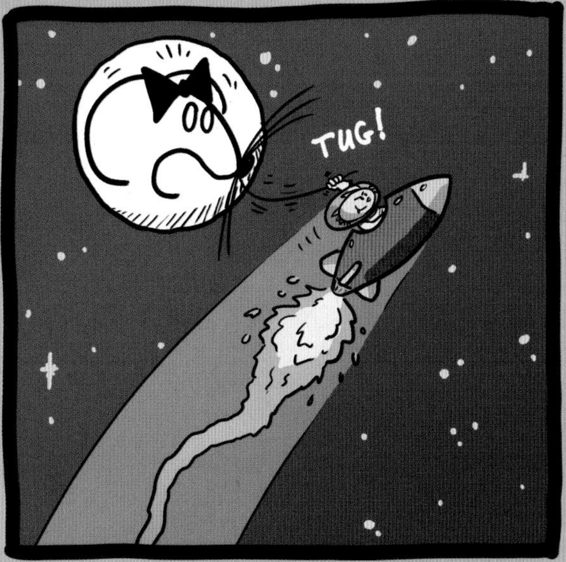
TUG!

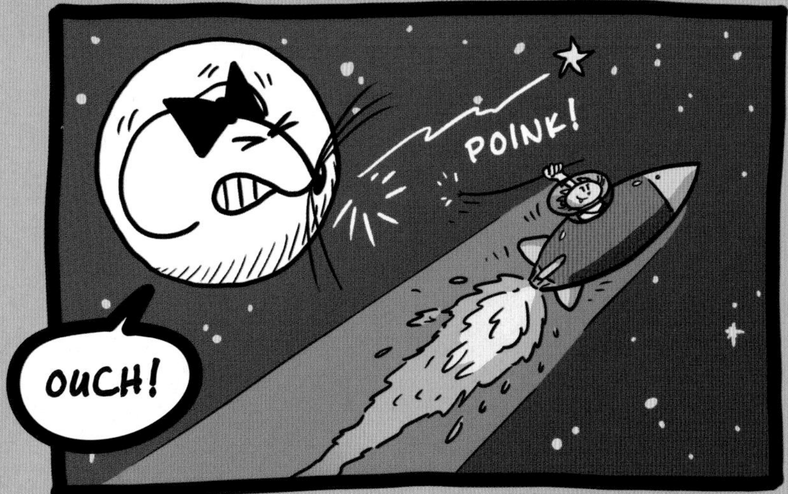
POINK!
OUCH!

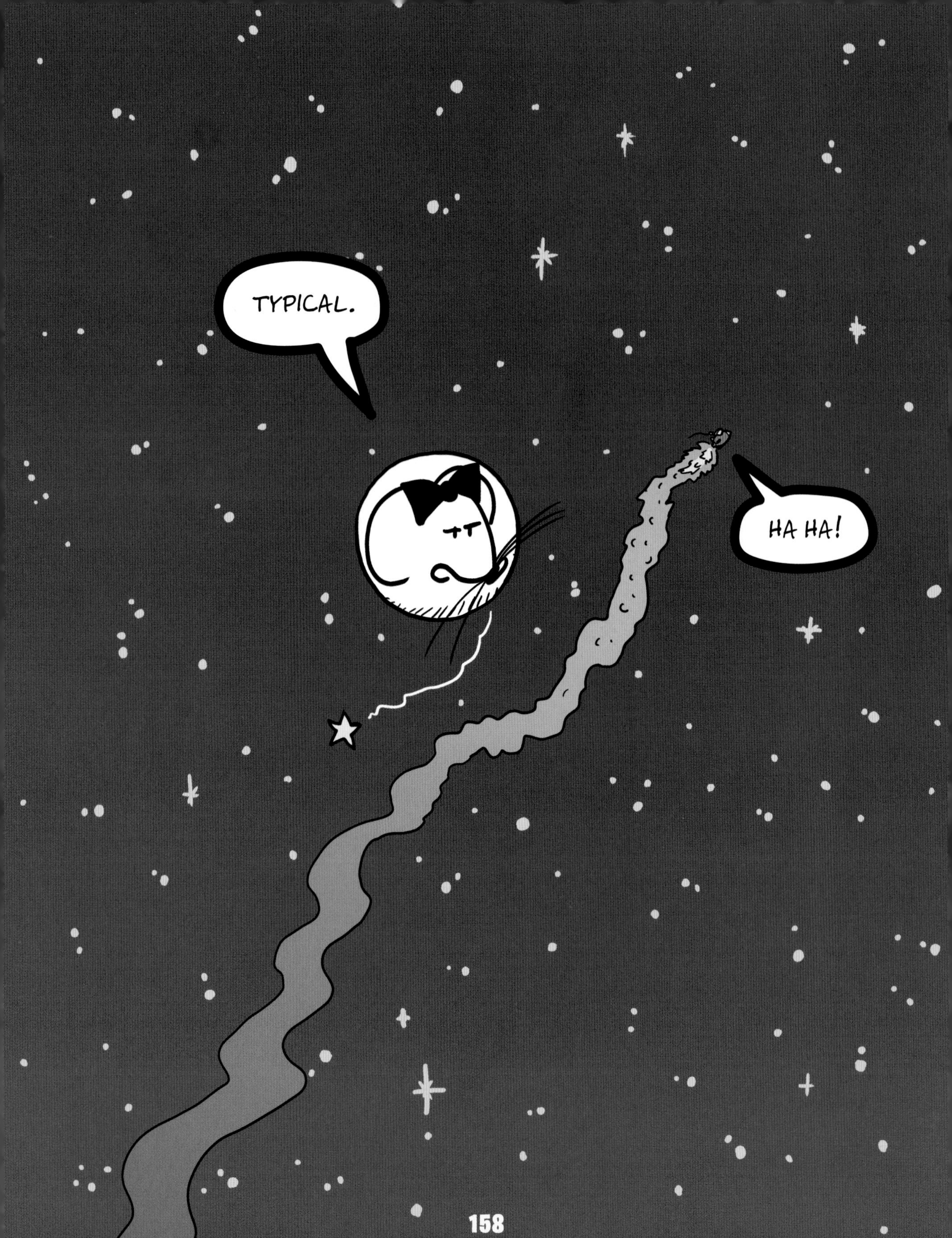
TYPICAL.
HA HA!

PART FIVE

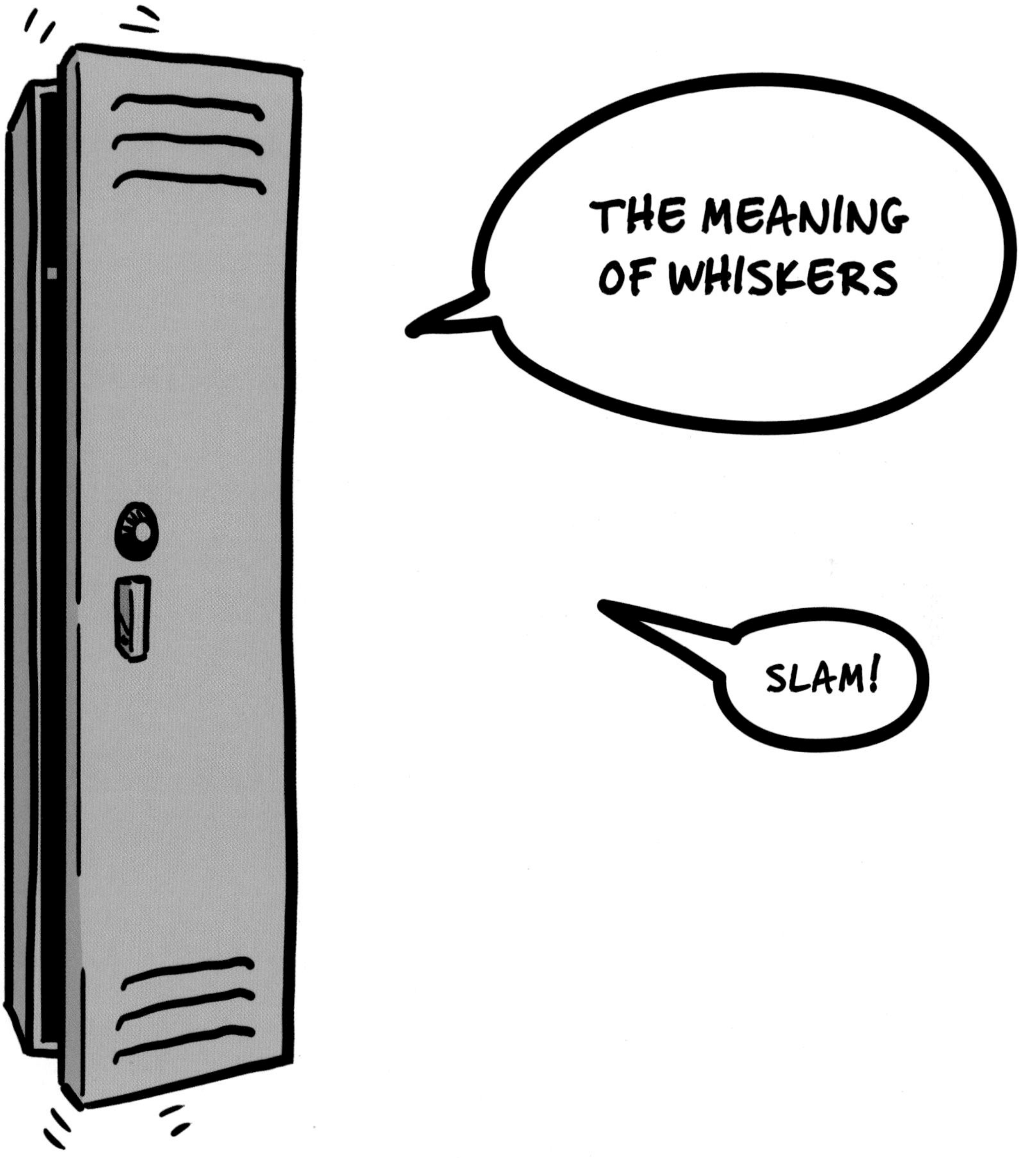
THE MEANING OF WHISKERS
SLAM!

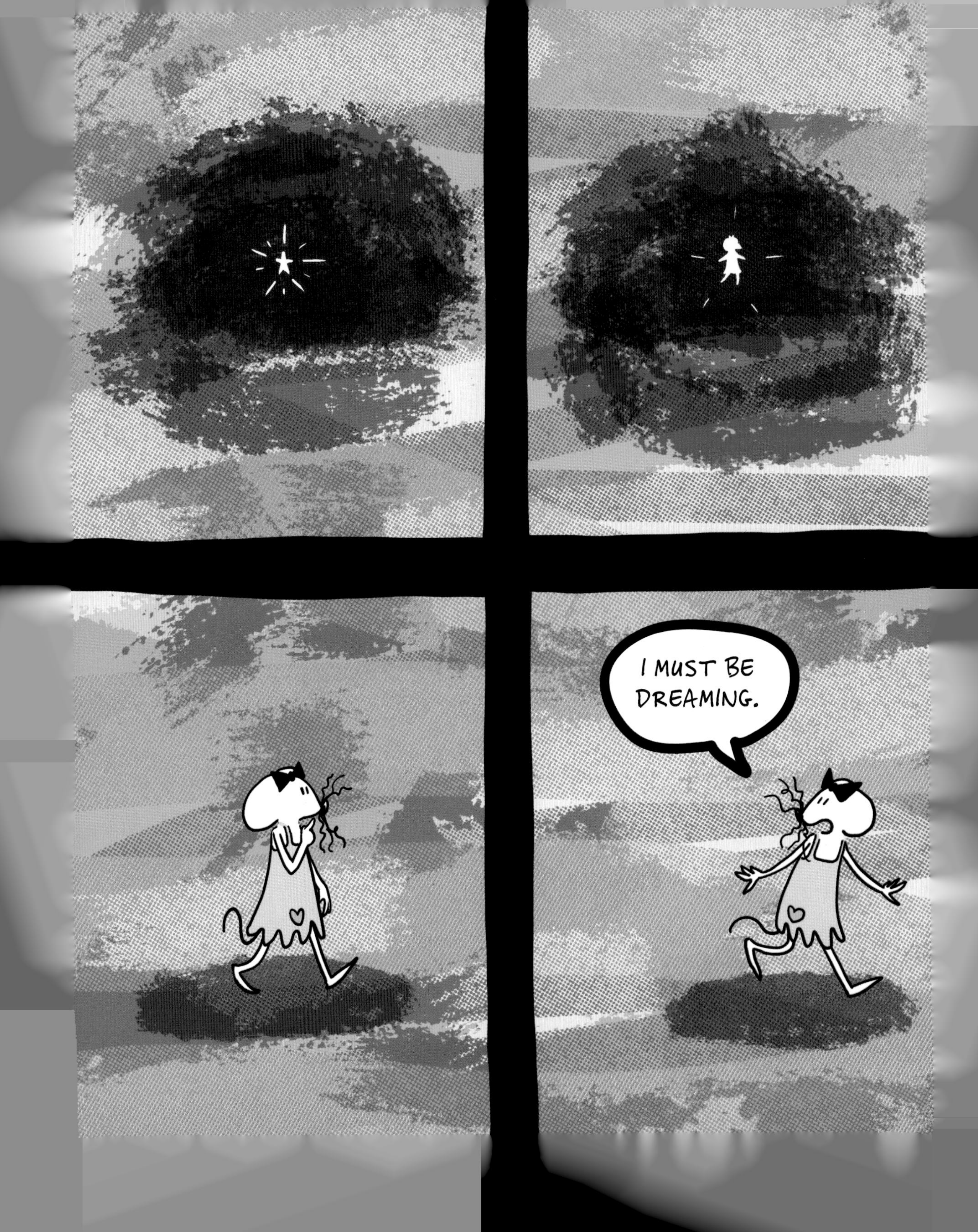
I MUST BE DREAMING.

WOULD IT STILL BE A TREE IF IT LOST ITS LEAVES?

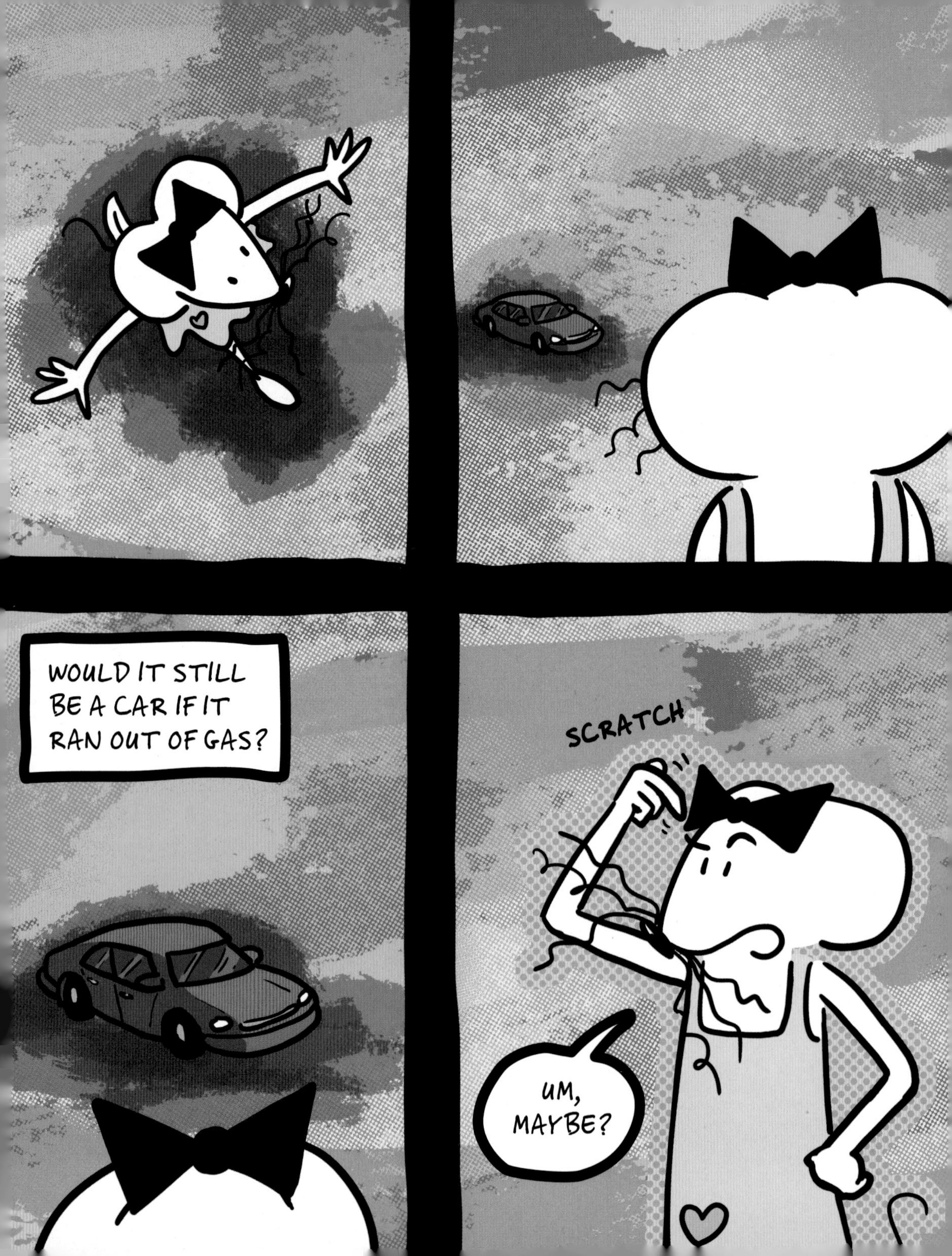
WOULD IT STILL BE A CAR IF IT RAN OUT OF GAS?
SCRATCH
UM, MAYBE?

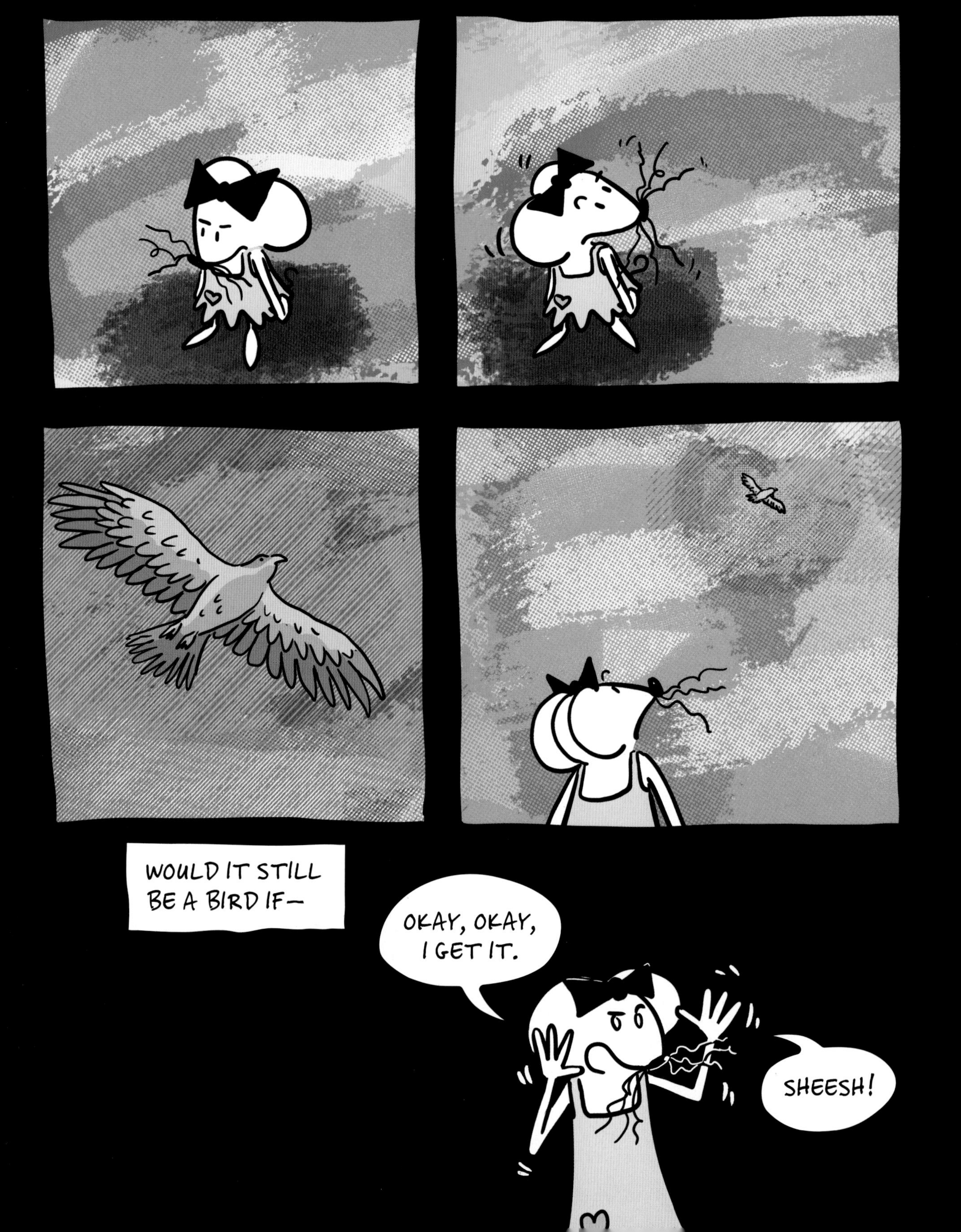
WOULD IT STILL BE A BIRD IF—
OKAY, OKAY, I GET IT.
SHEESH!

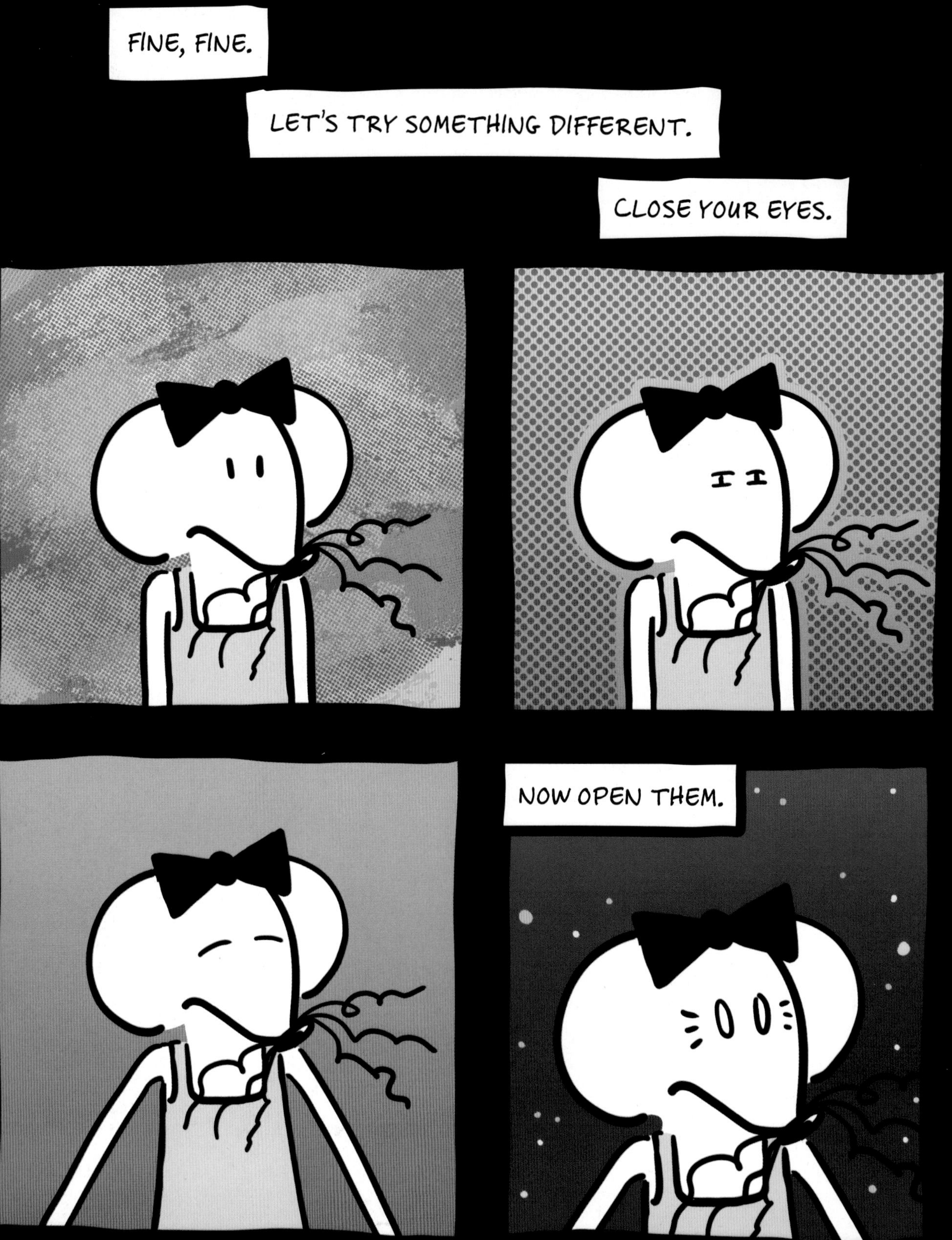
FINE, FINE.
LET'S TRY SOMETHING DIFFERENT.
CLOSE YOUR EYES.
NOW OPEN THEM.

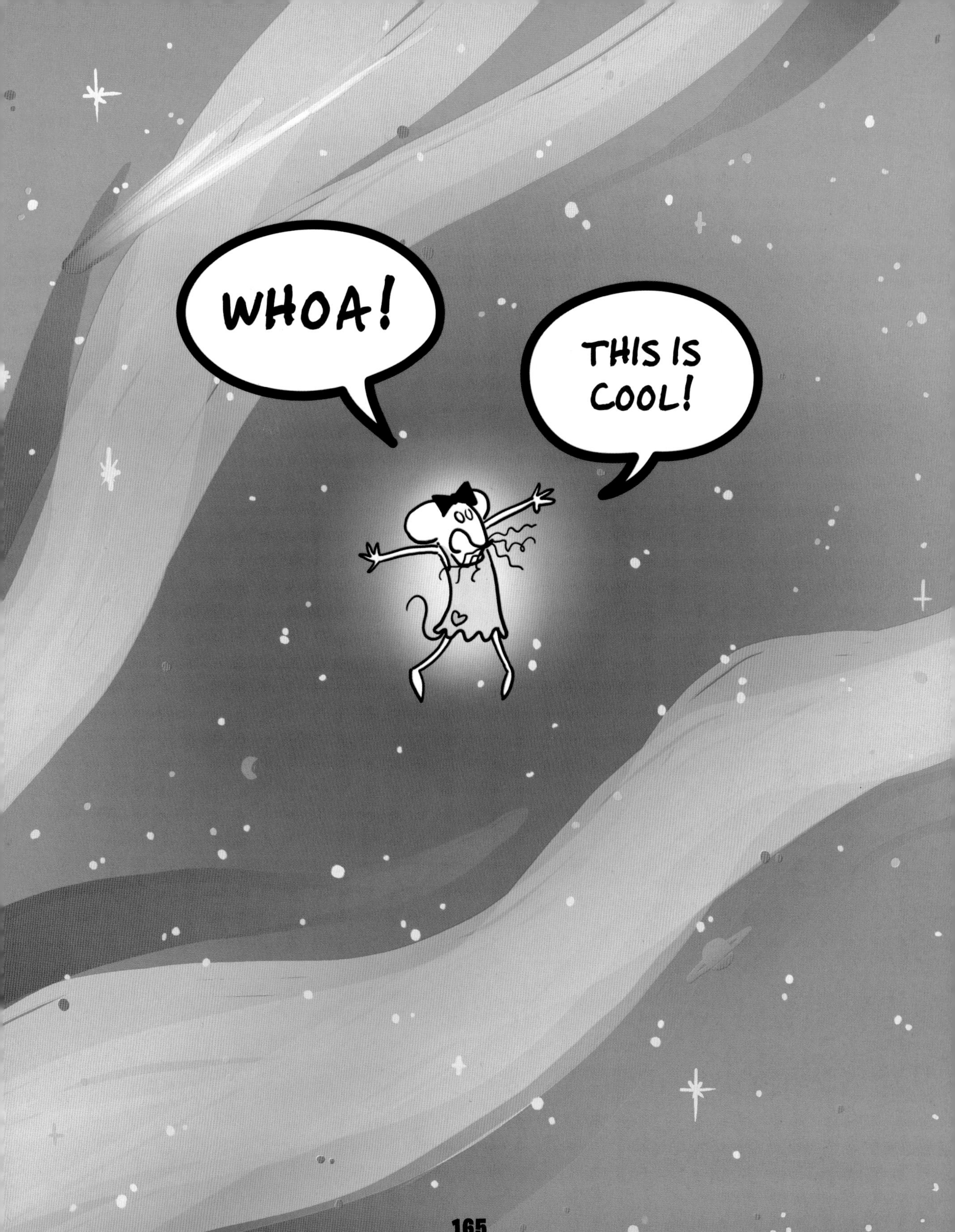
WHOA!
THIS IS COOL!

DEEP THOUGHTS ON
WHISKERS
WHAT DO WHISKERS MEAN? ARE YOU A GOOD PERSON WITHOUT WHISKERS? WHAT IS THE POINT OF WHISKERS ANYWAY? IS IT HARD TO SNEEZE WITHOUT WHISKERS?

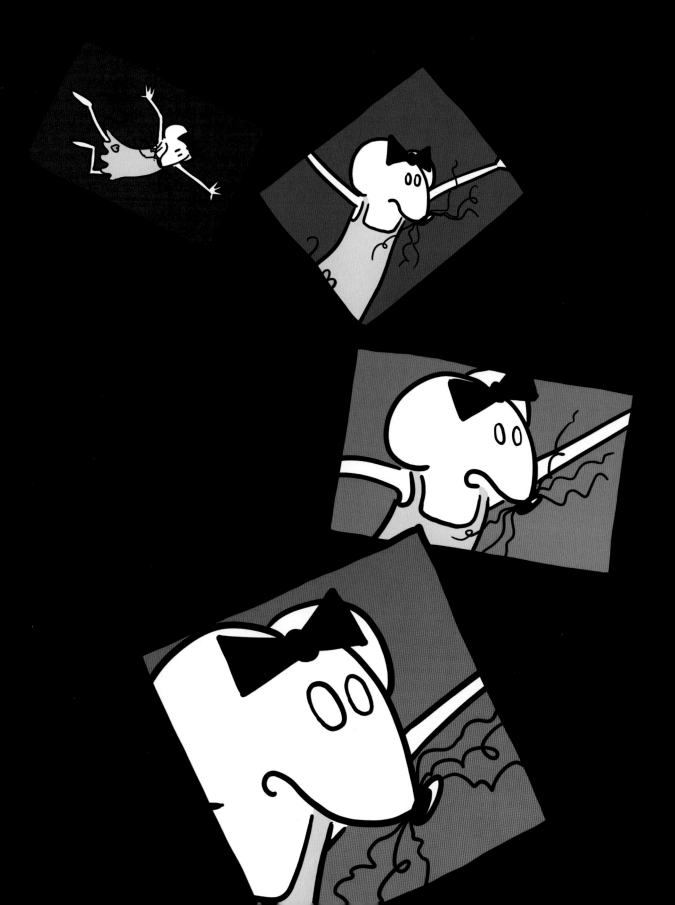

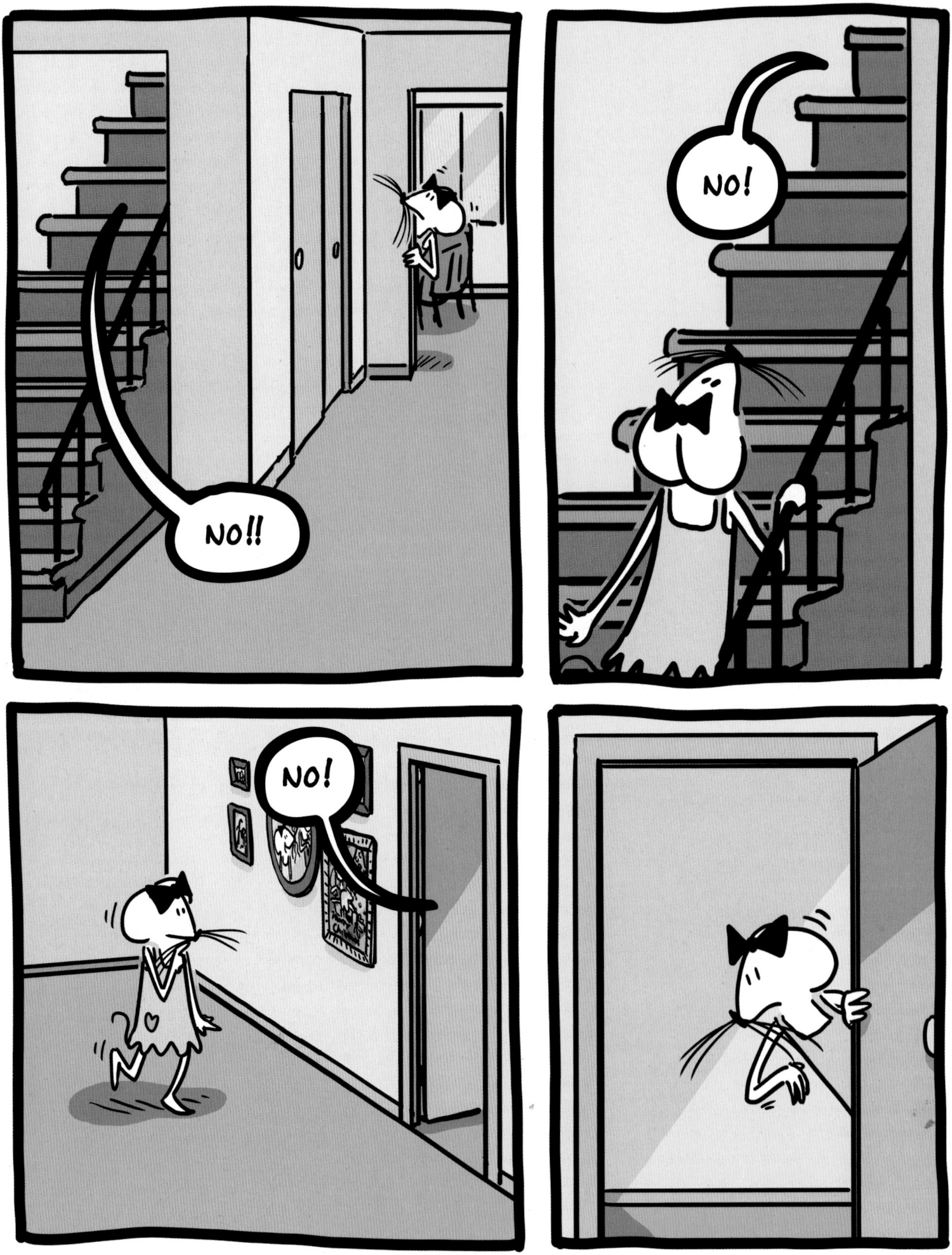
NO!!
NO!
NO!

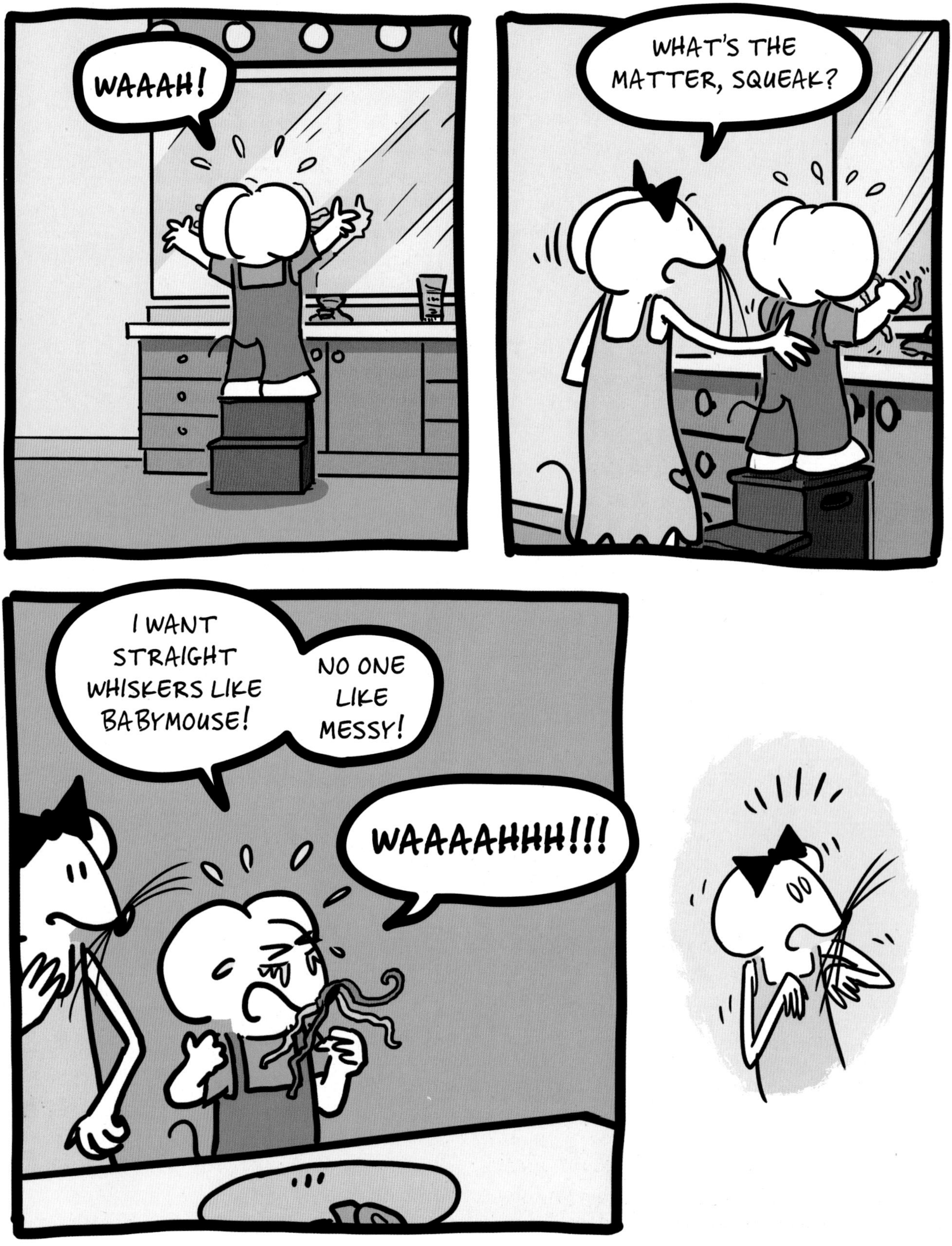
WAAAH!
WHAT'S THE MATTER, SQUEAK?
I WANT STRAIGHT WHISKERS LIKE BABYMOUSE!
NO ONE LIKE MESSY!
WAAAAHHH!!!

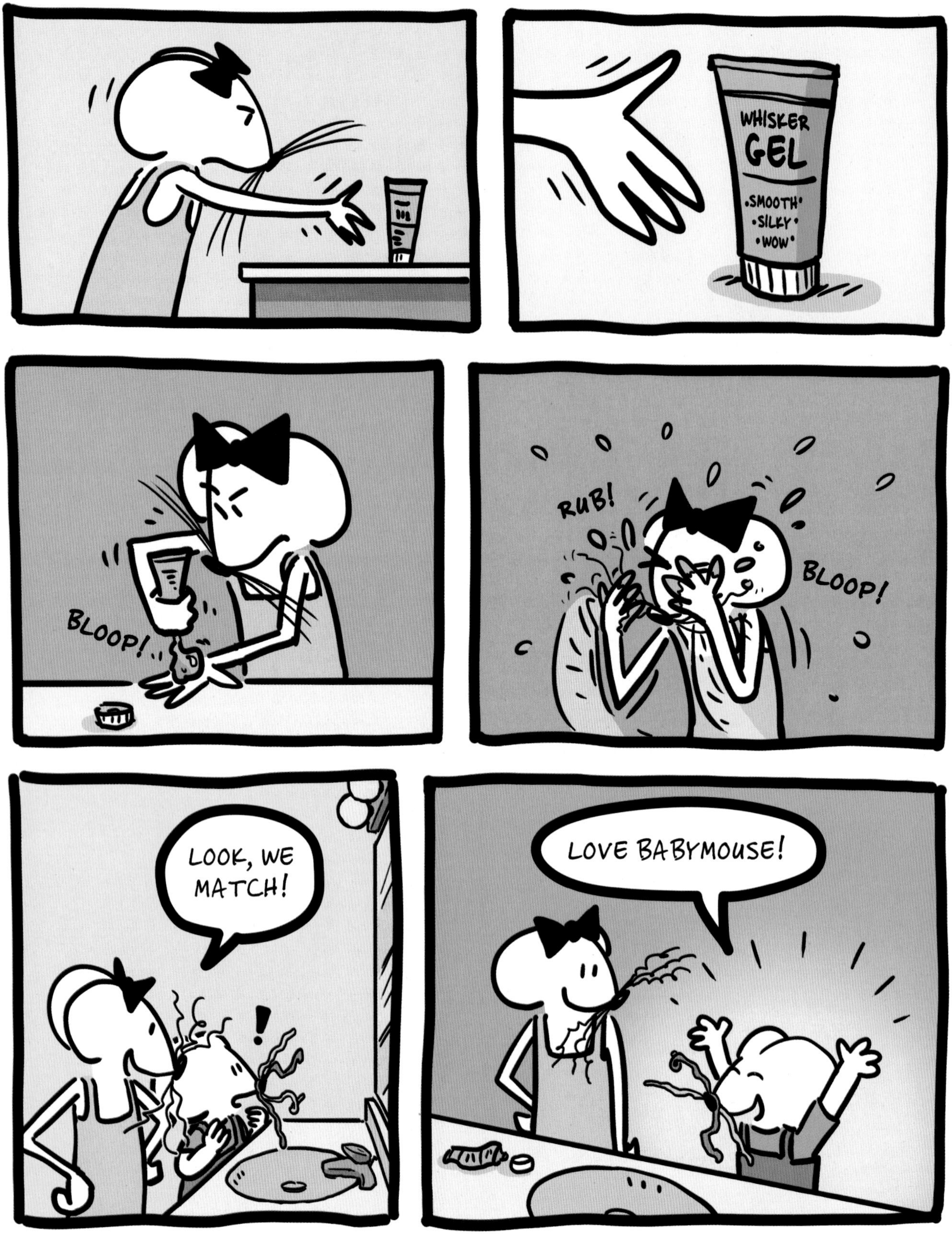
WHISKER
GEL
•SMOOTH•
•SILKY•
•WOW•
BLOOP!
RUB!
BLOOP!
LOOK, WE MATCH!
LOVE BABYMOUSE!

MY HEART JUST MELTED A LITTLE, BABYMOUSE.

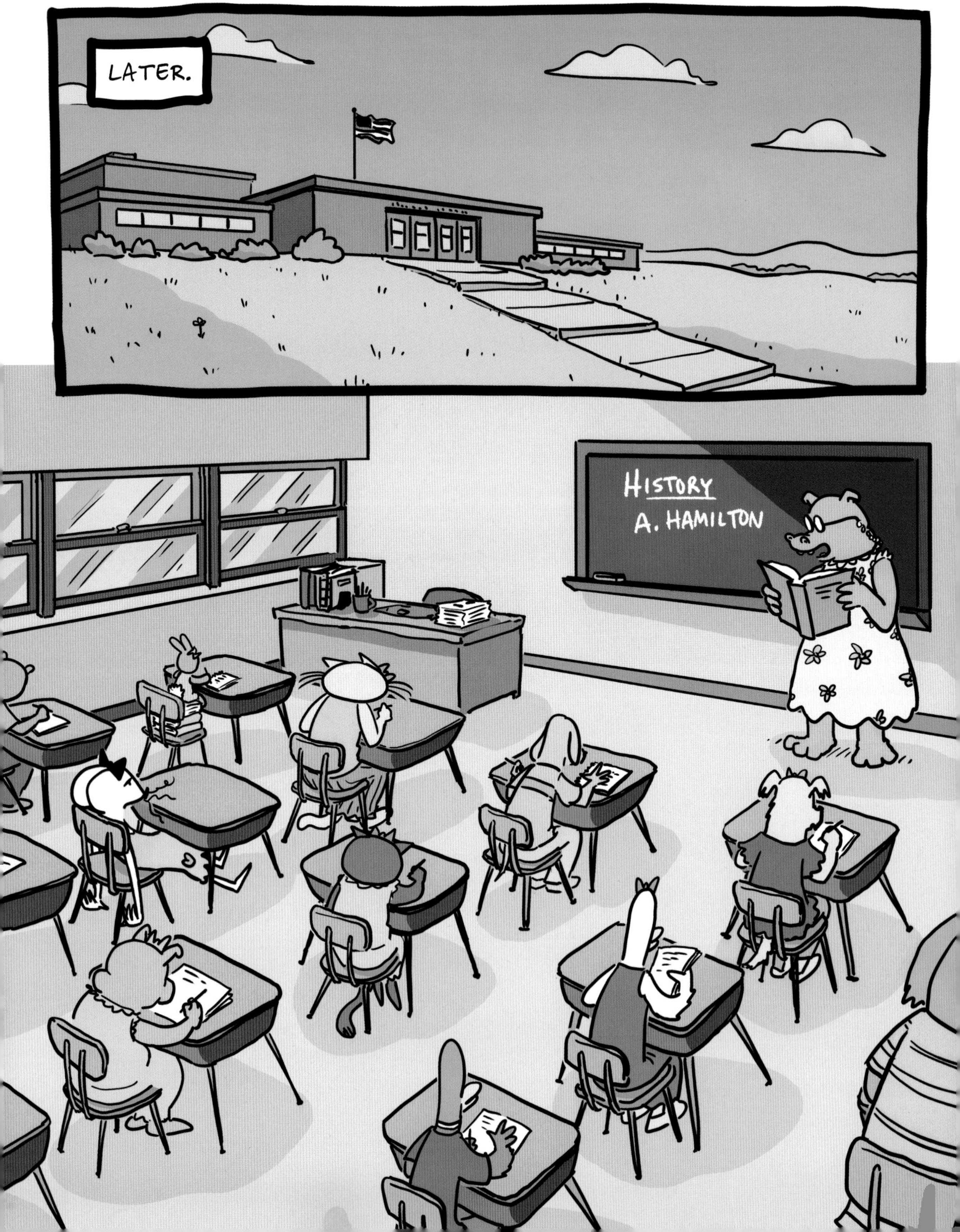
LATER.
HISTORY
A. HAMILTON

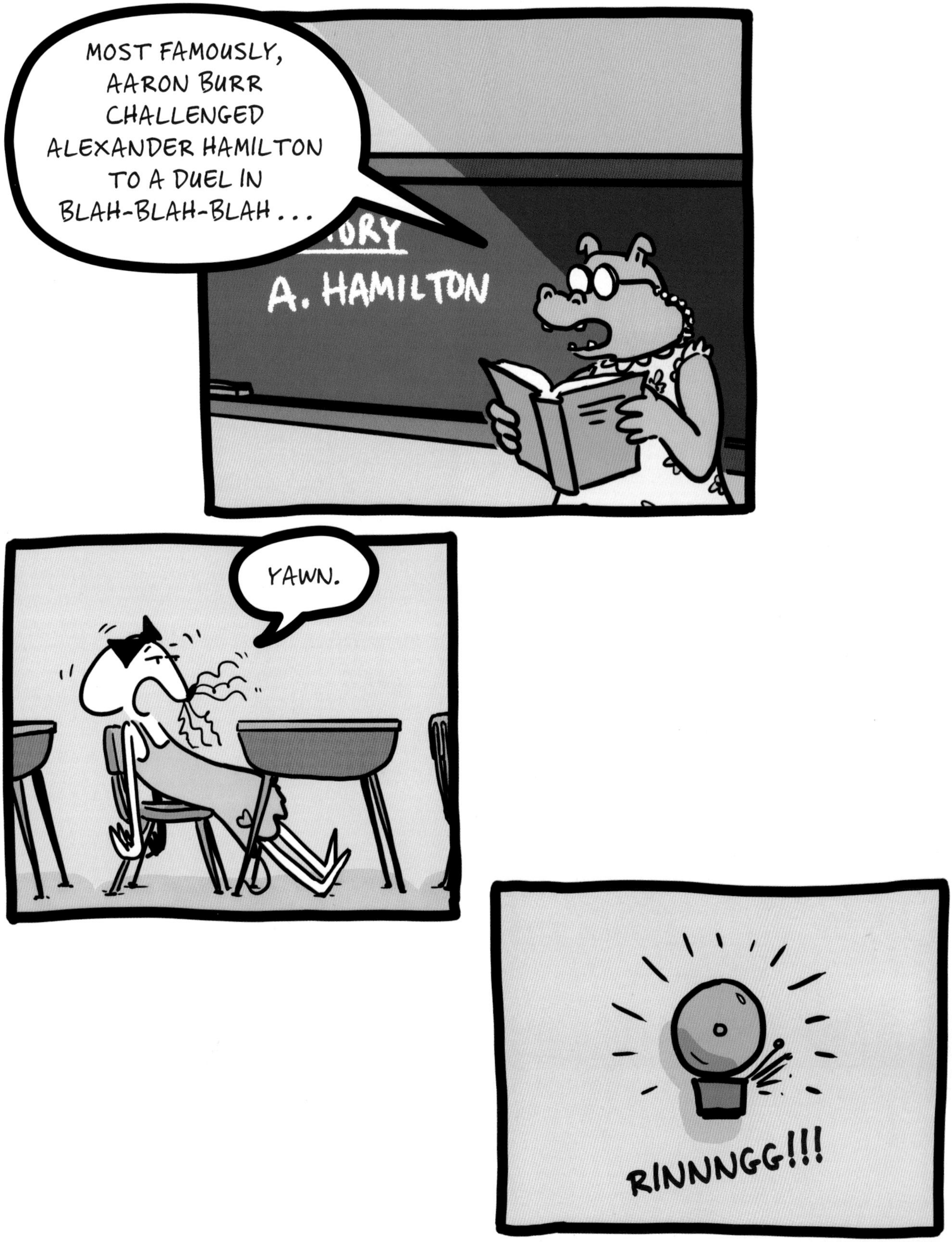
MOST FAMOUSLY, AARON BURR CHALLENGED ALEXANDER HAMILTON TO A DUEL IN BLAH-BLAH-BLAH . . .
A. HAMILTON
YAWN.
RINNNGG!!!

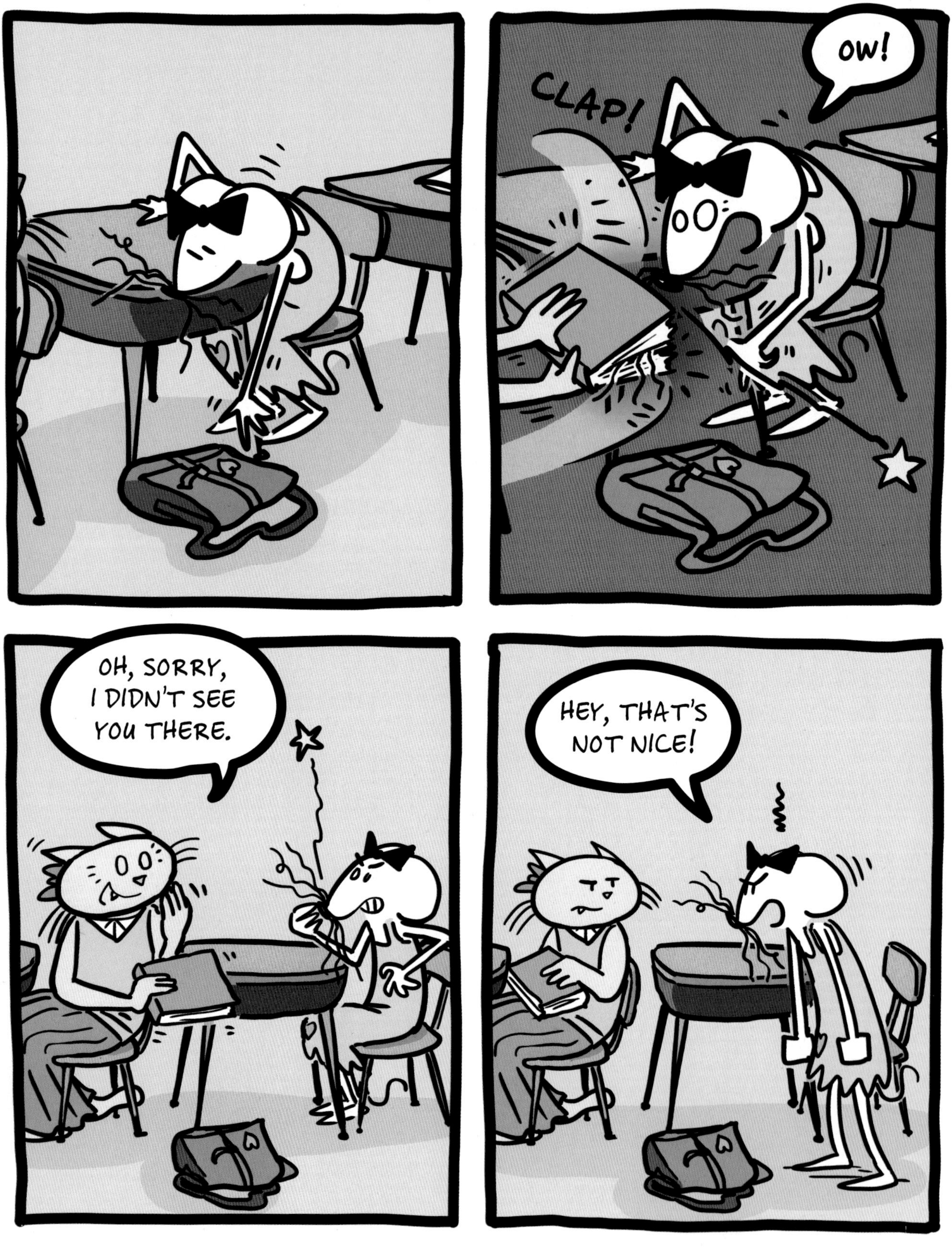
CLAP!
OW!
OH, SORRY, I DIDN'T SEE YOU THERE.
HEY, THAT'S NOT NICE!

LUNCH.

YOU CHALLENGED FELICIA FURRYPAWS TO A DUEL?

MY WHISKERS, I MEAN, MY HONOR IS AT STAKE!

BUT FELICIA IS THE BEST HANDBALL PLAYER IN THE SCHOOL!

SLUMP

YEAH, I KINDA FORGOT ABOUT THAT. HOW WILL I SURVIVE?

YOU HAVE TO BE LIKE YOUR WHISKERS, BABYMOUSE.

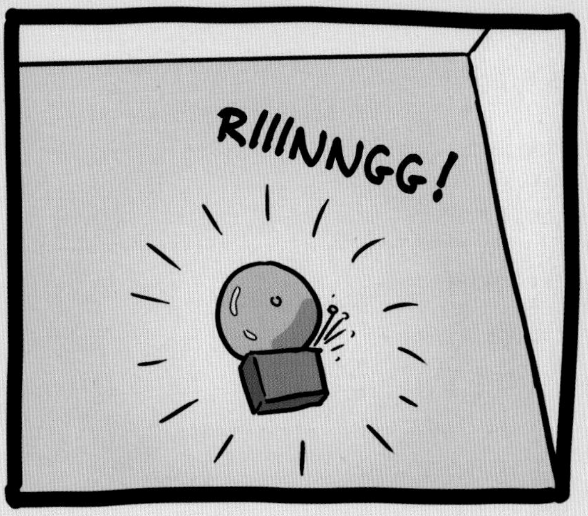
RIIINNGG!

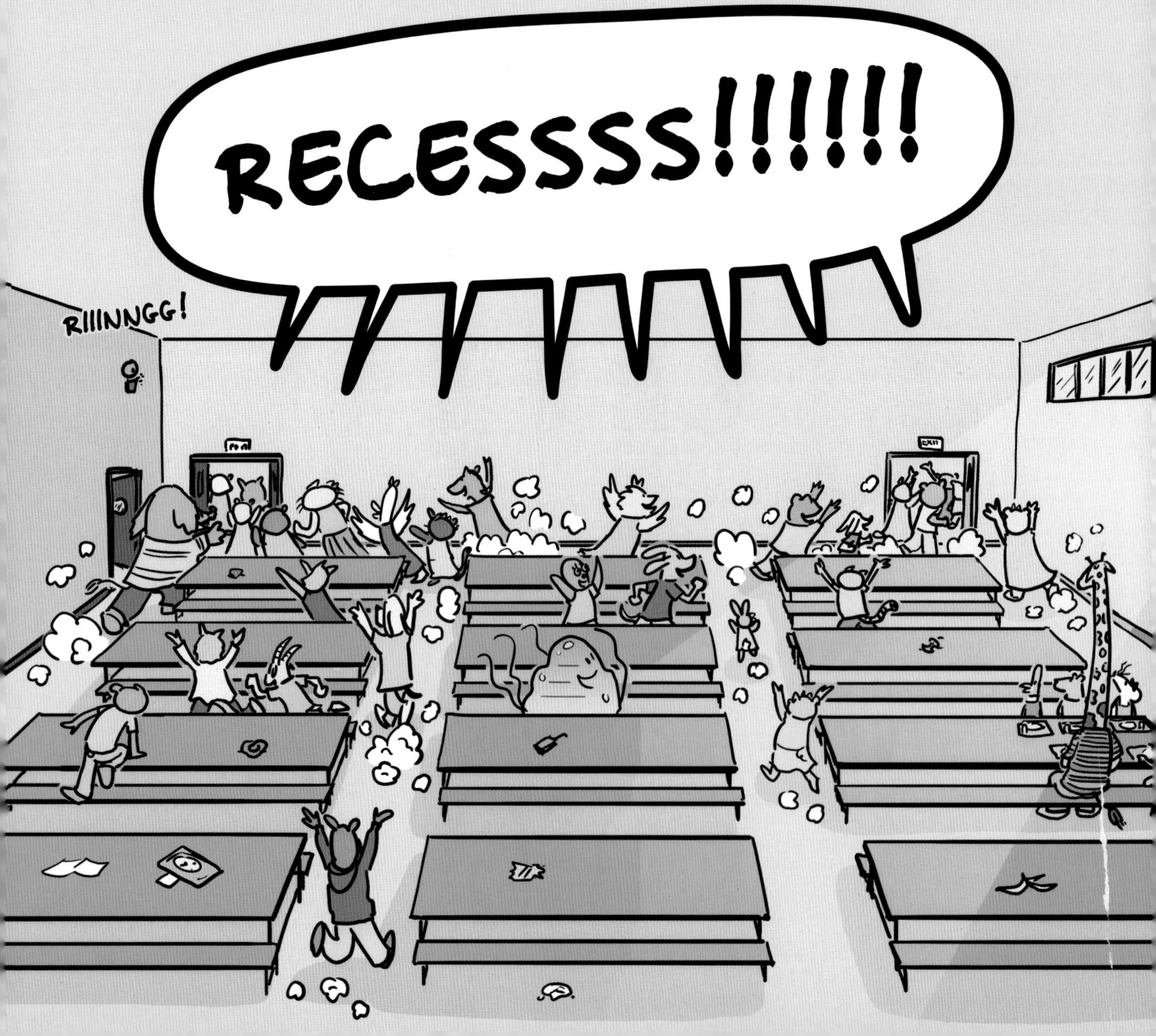
RECESSSS!!!!!!
RIIINNGG!

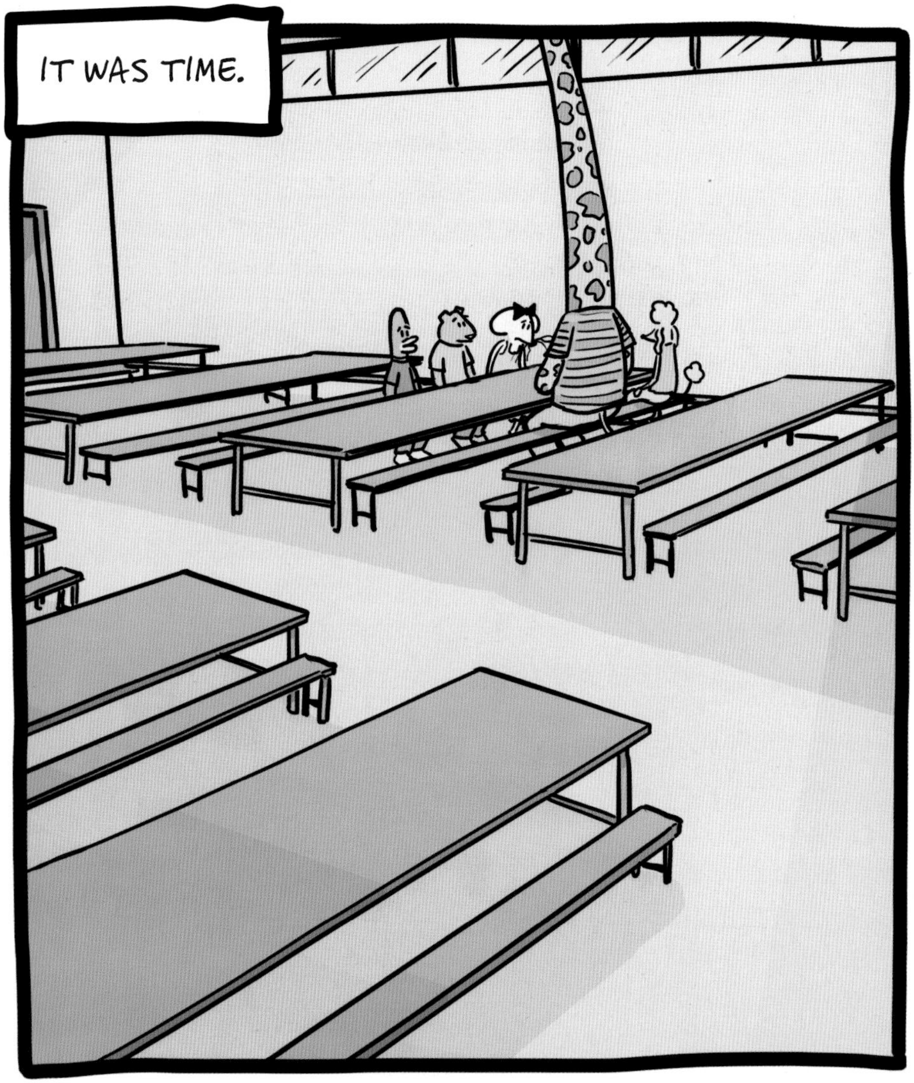
IT WAS TIME.

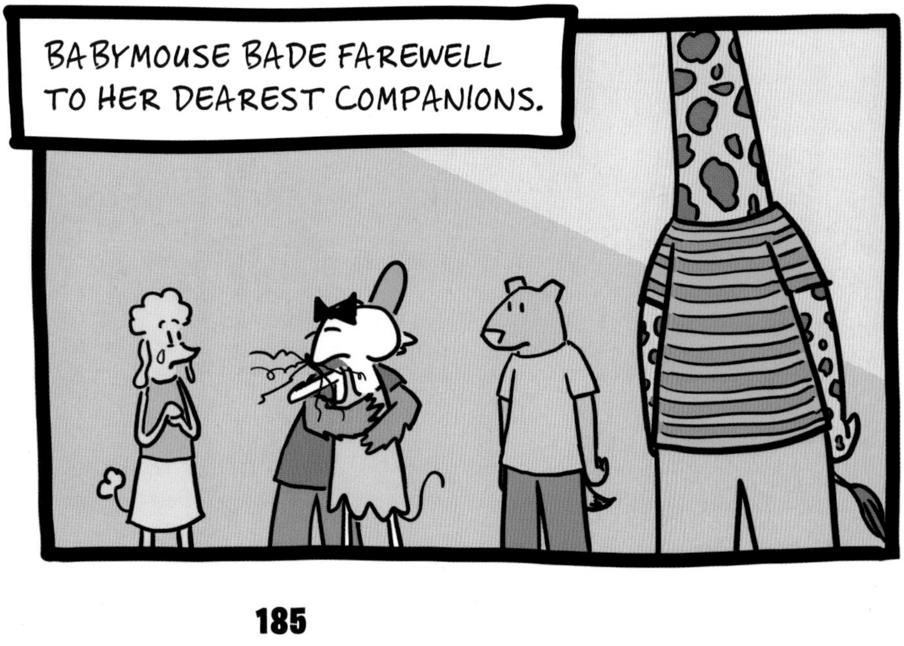
BABYMOUSE BADE FAREWELL TO HER DEAREST COMPANIONS.

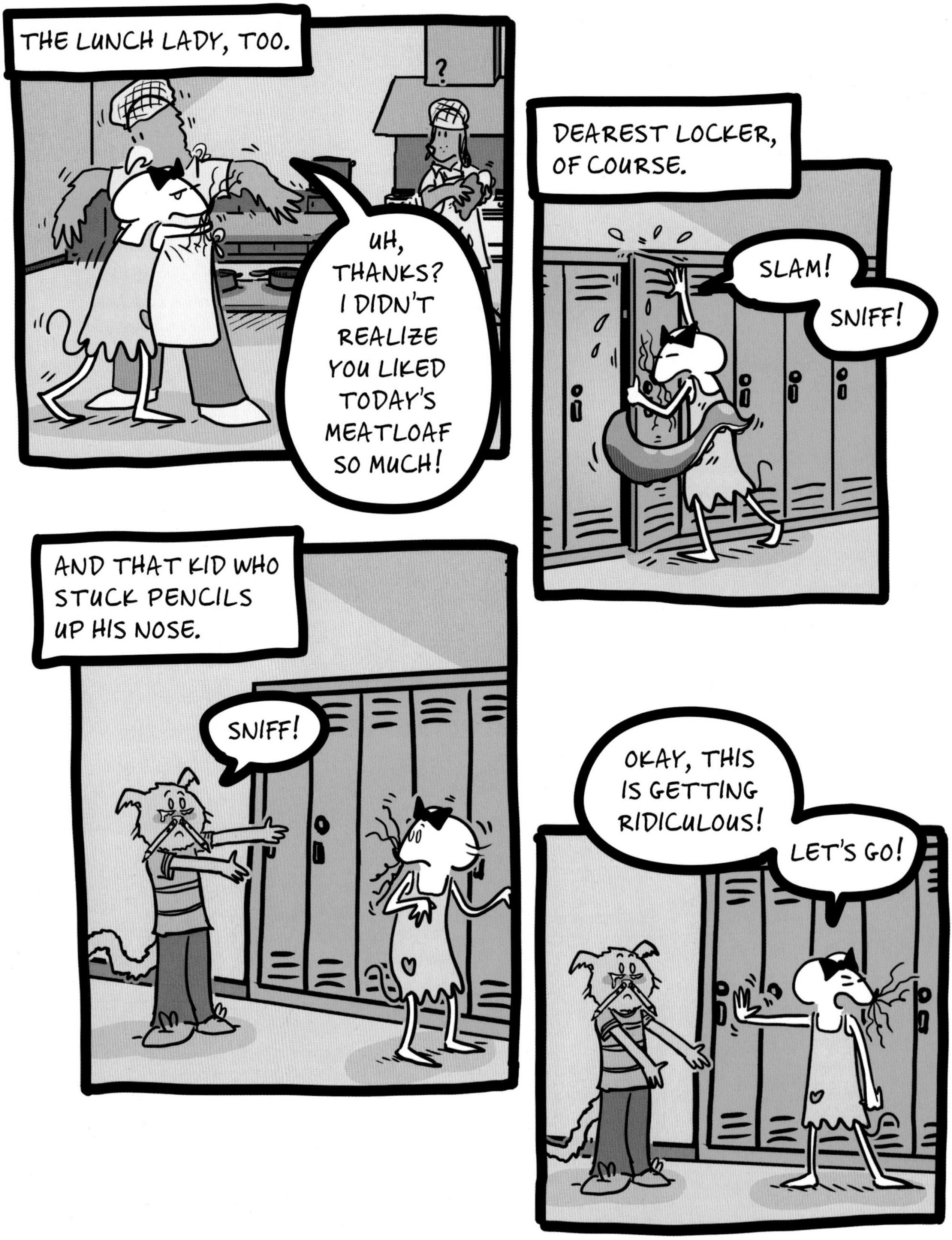
THE LUNCH LADY, TOO.
?
UH, THANKS? I DIDN'T REALIZE YOU LIKED TODAY'S MEATLOAF SO MUCH!
DEAREST LOCKER, OF COURSE.
SLAM!
SNIFF!
AND THAT KID WHO STUCK PENCILS UP HIS NOSE.
SNIFF!
OKAY, THIS IS GETTING RIDICULOUS!
LET'S GO!

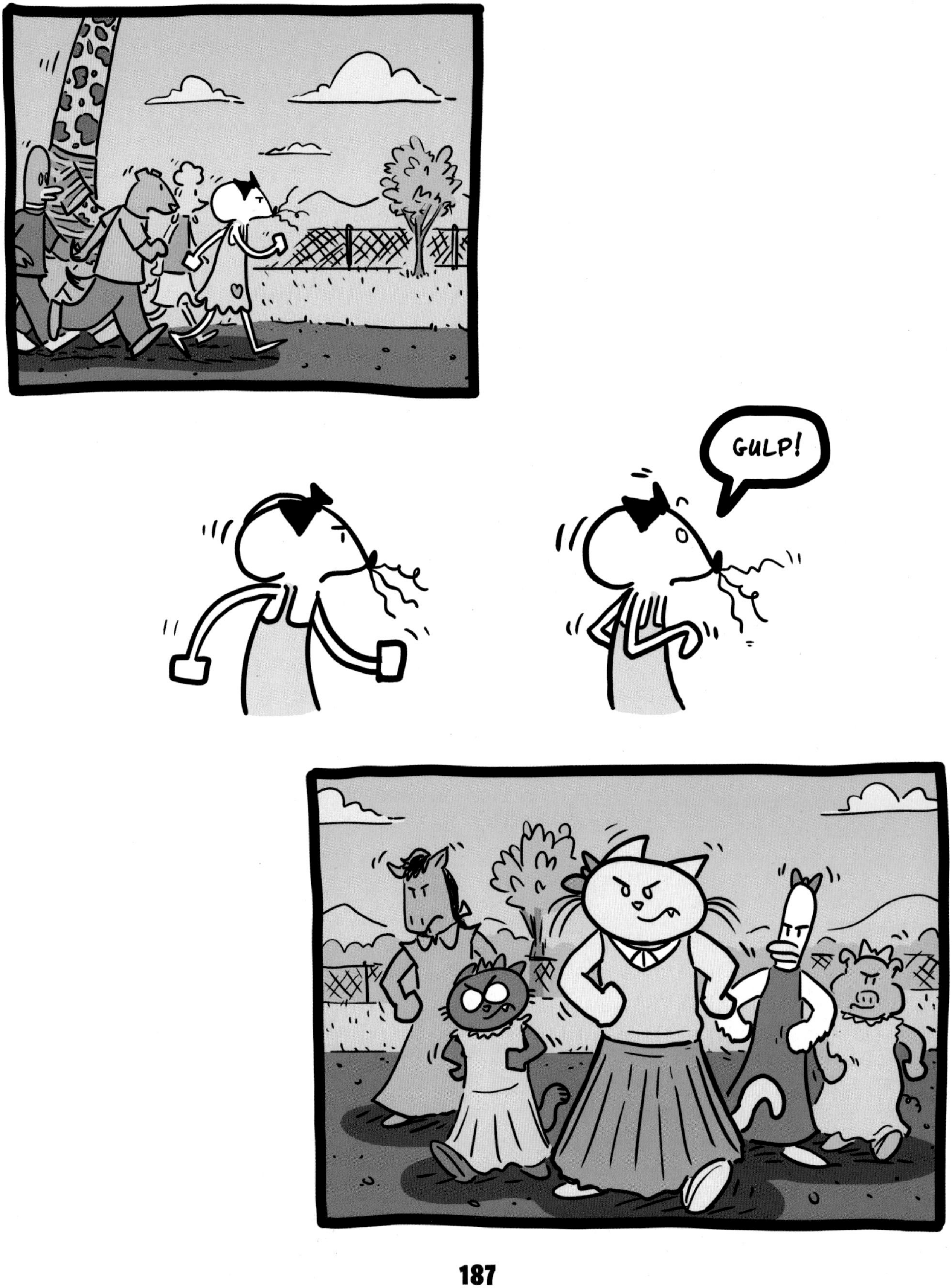
GULP!

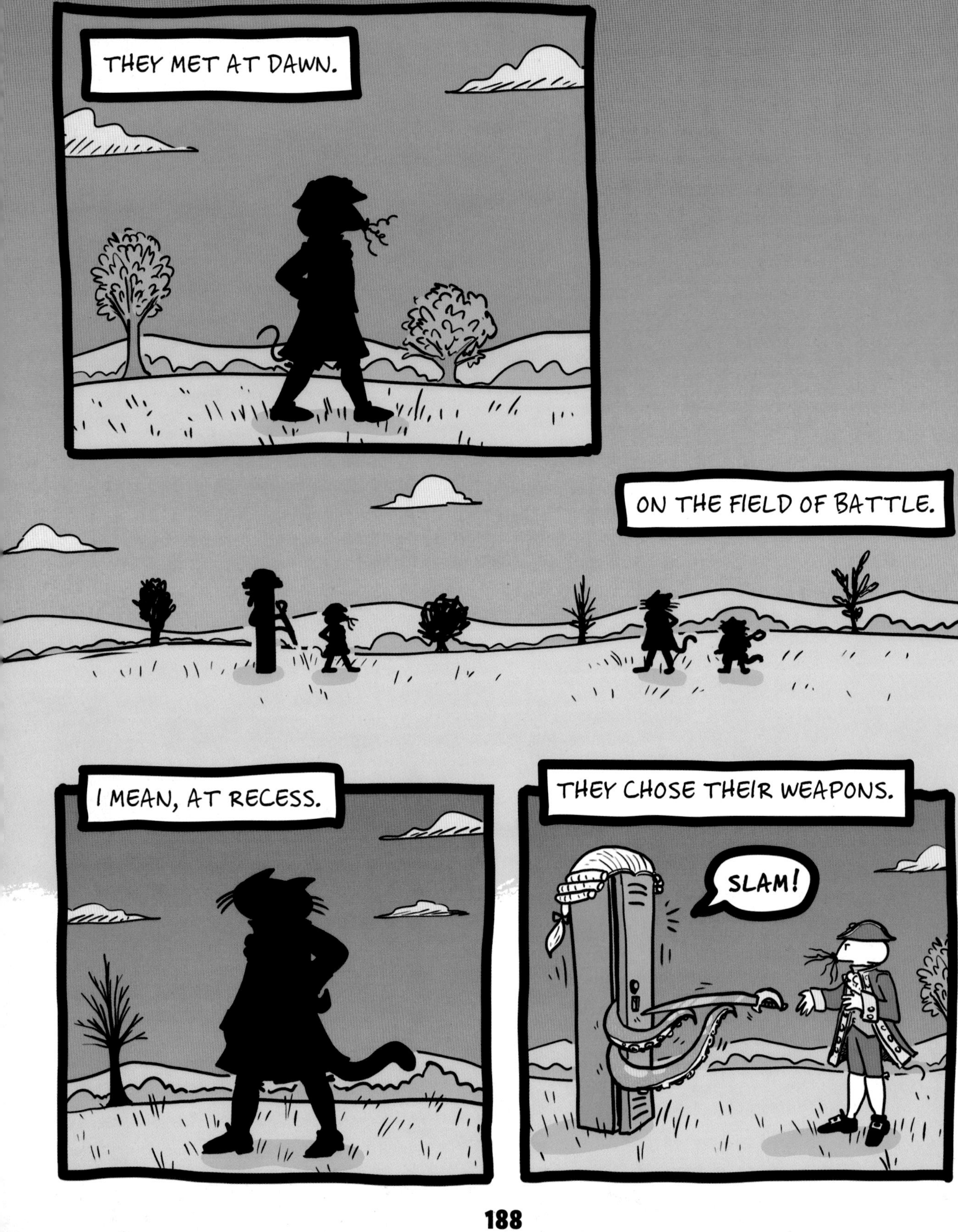
THEY MET AT DAWN.
ON THE FIELD OF BATTLE.
I MEAN, AT RECESS.
THEY CHOSE THEIR WEAPONS.
SLAM!

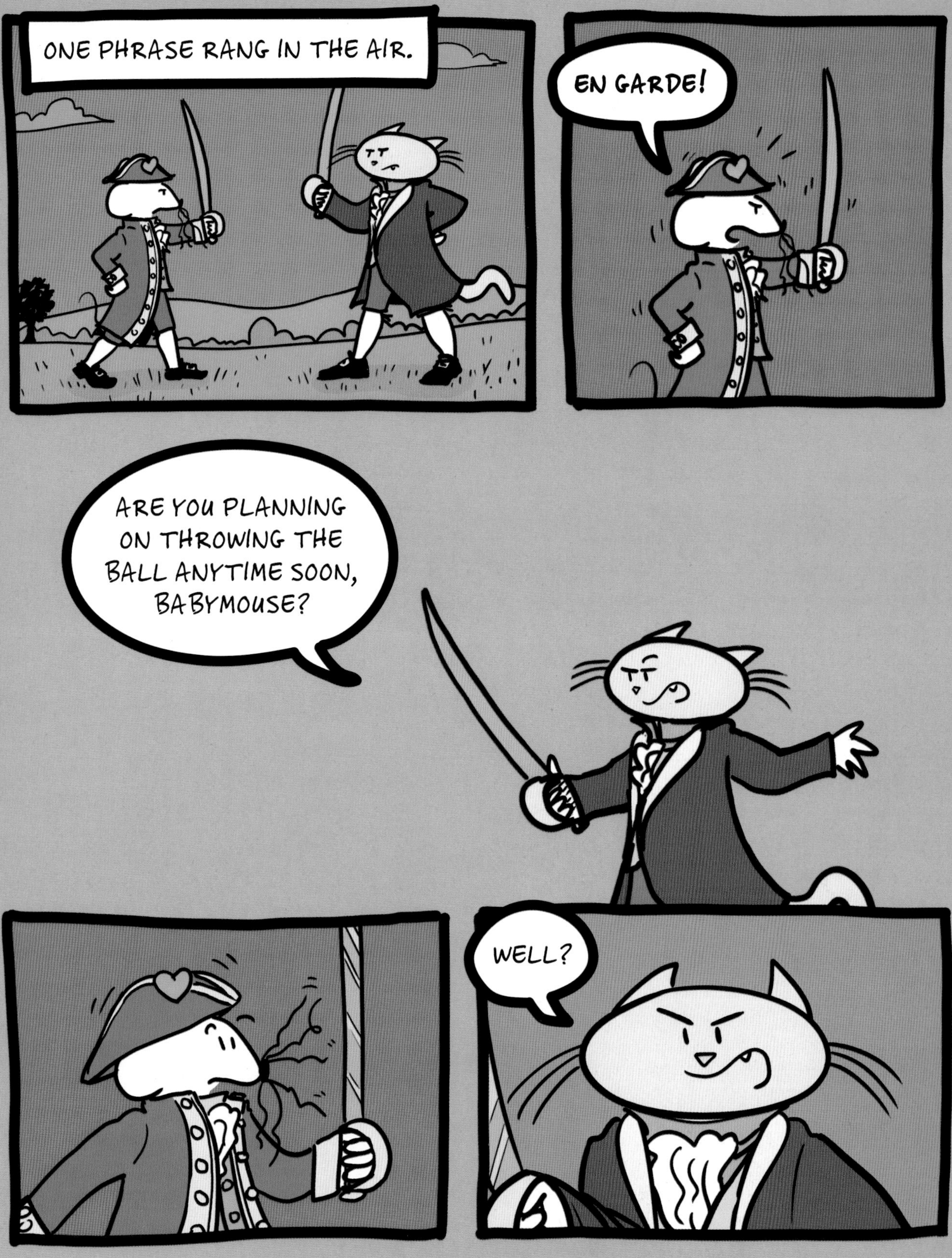
ONE PHRASE RANG IN THE AIR.
EN GARDE!
ARE YOU PLANNING ON THROWING THE BALL ANYTIME SOON, BABYMOUSE?
WELL?

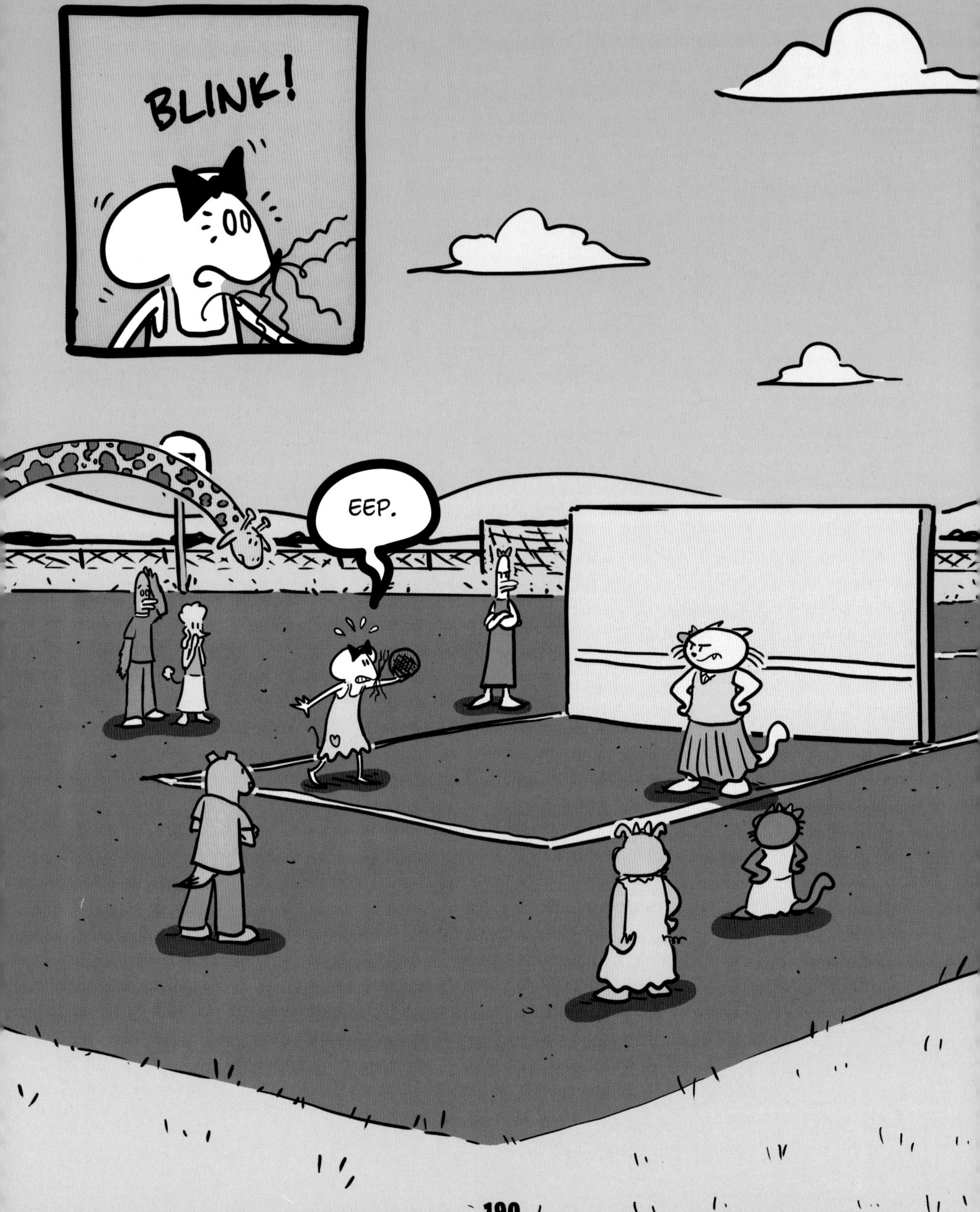
BLINK!
EEP.

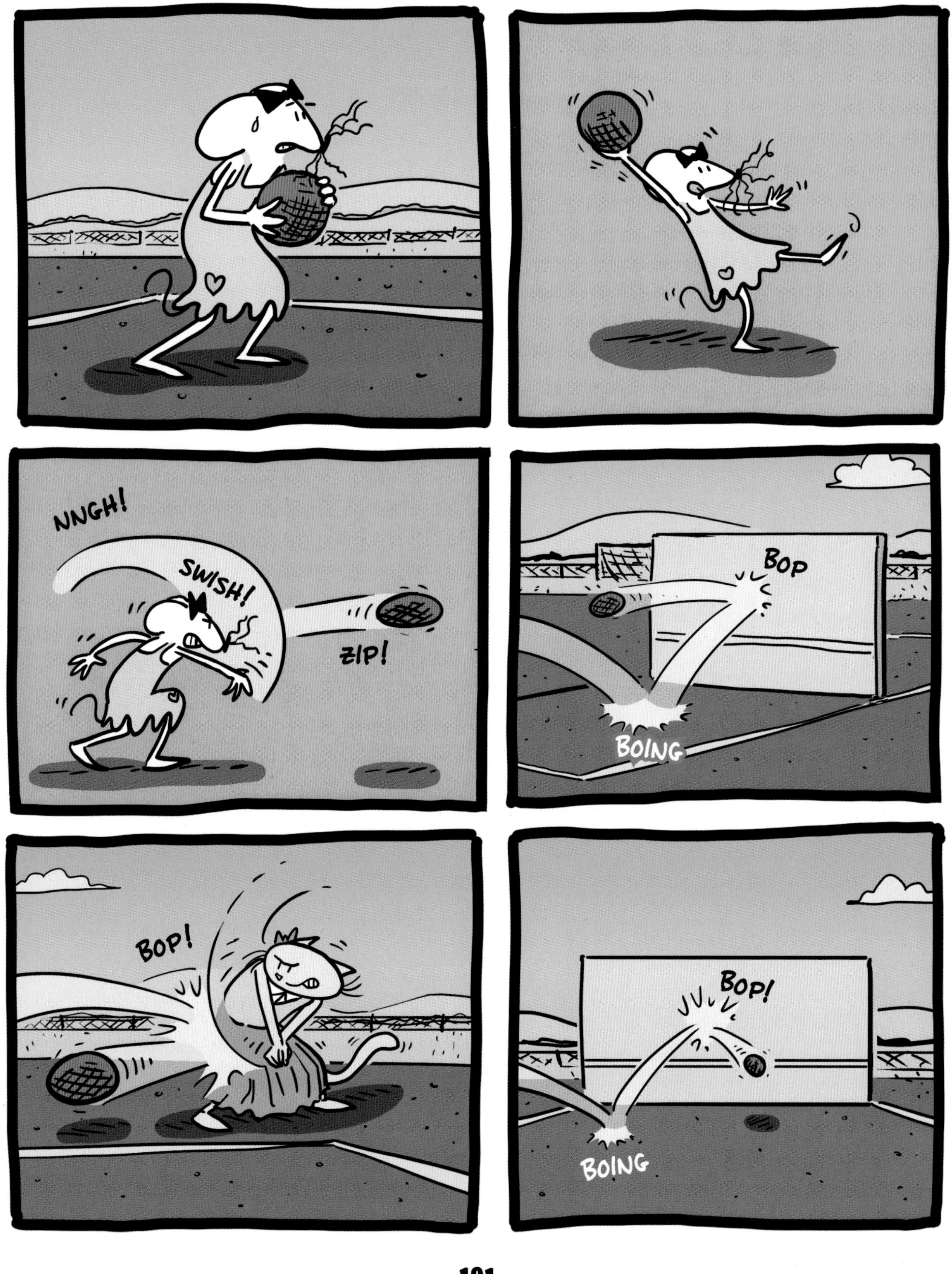
NNGH!
SWISH!
ZIP!
BOP
BOING
BOP!
BOP!
BOING

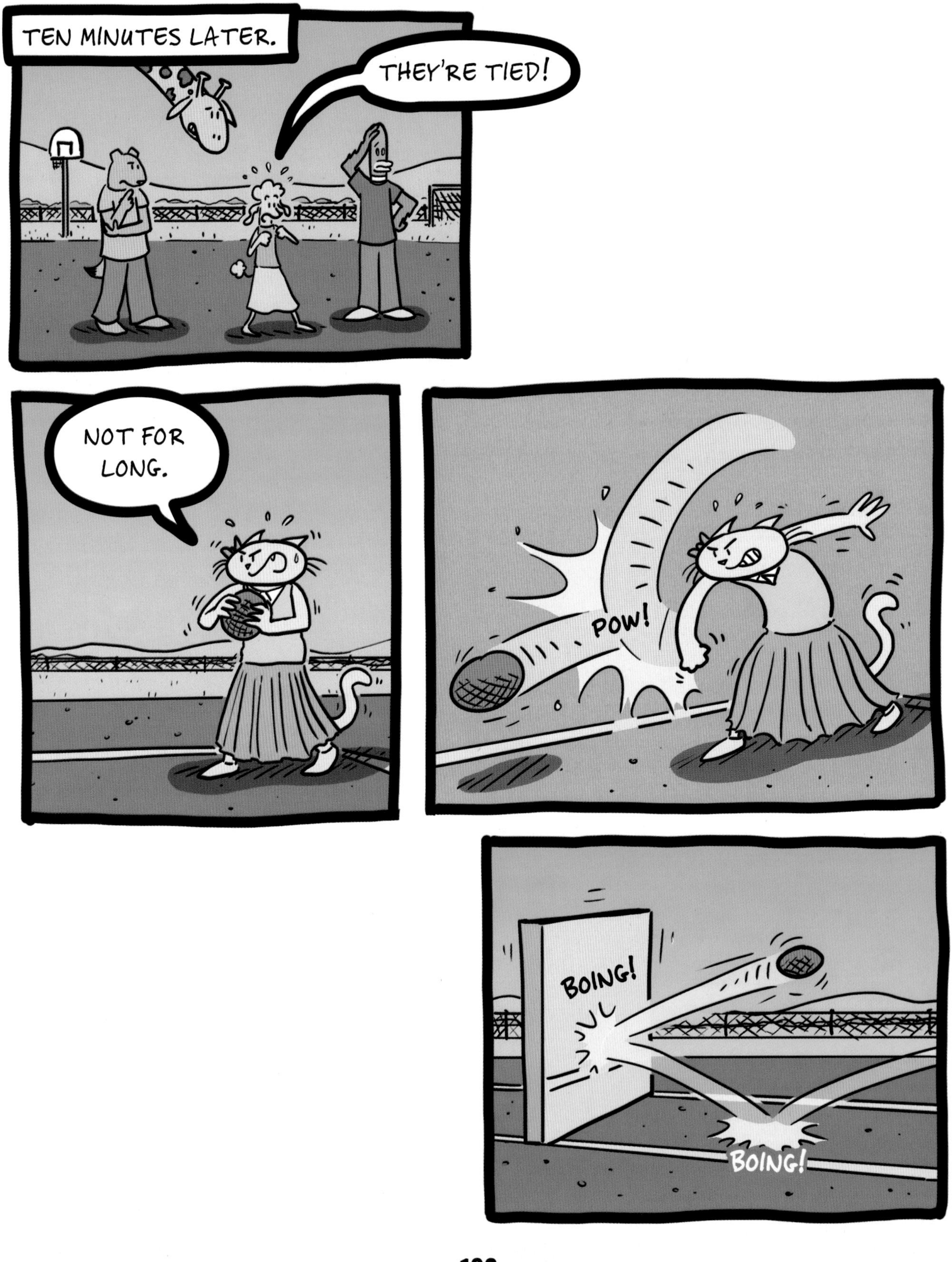
TEN MINUTES LATER.
THEY'RE TIED!
NOT FOR LONG.
POW!
BOING!
BOING!

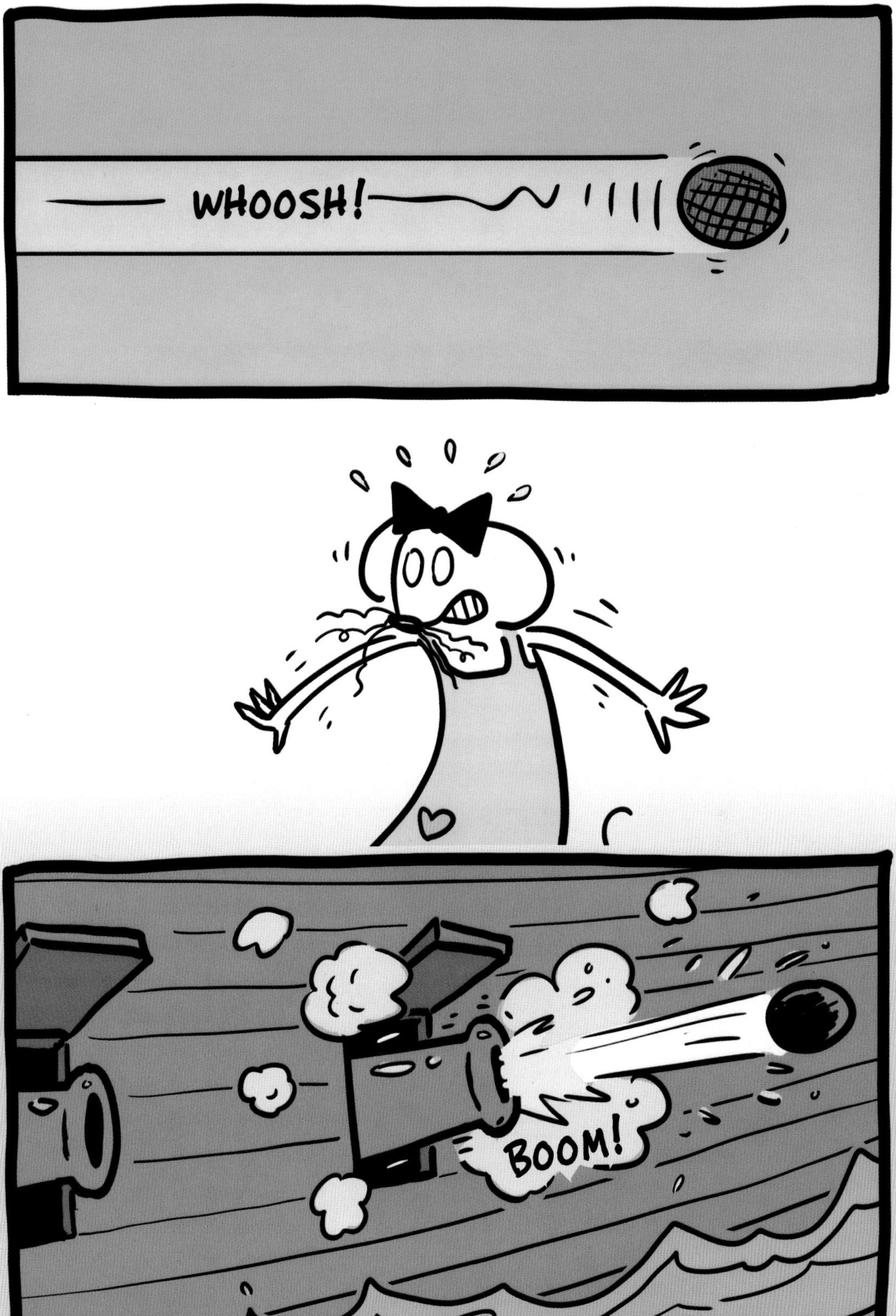
WHOOSH!
BOOM!

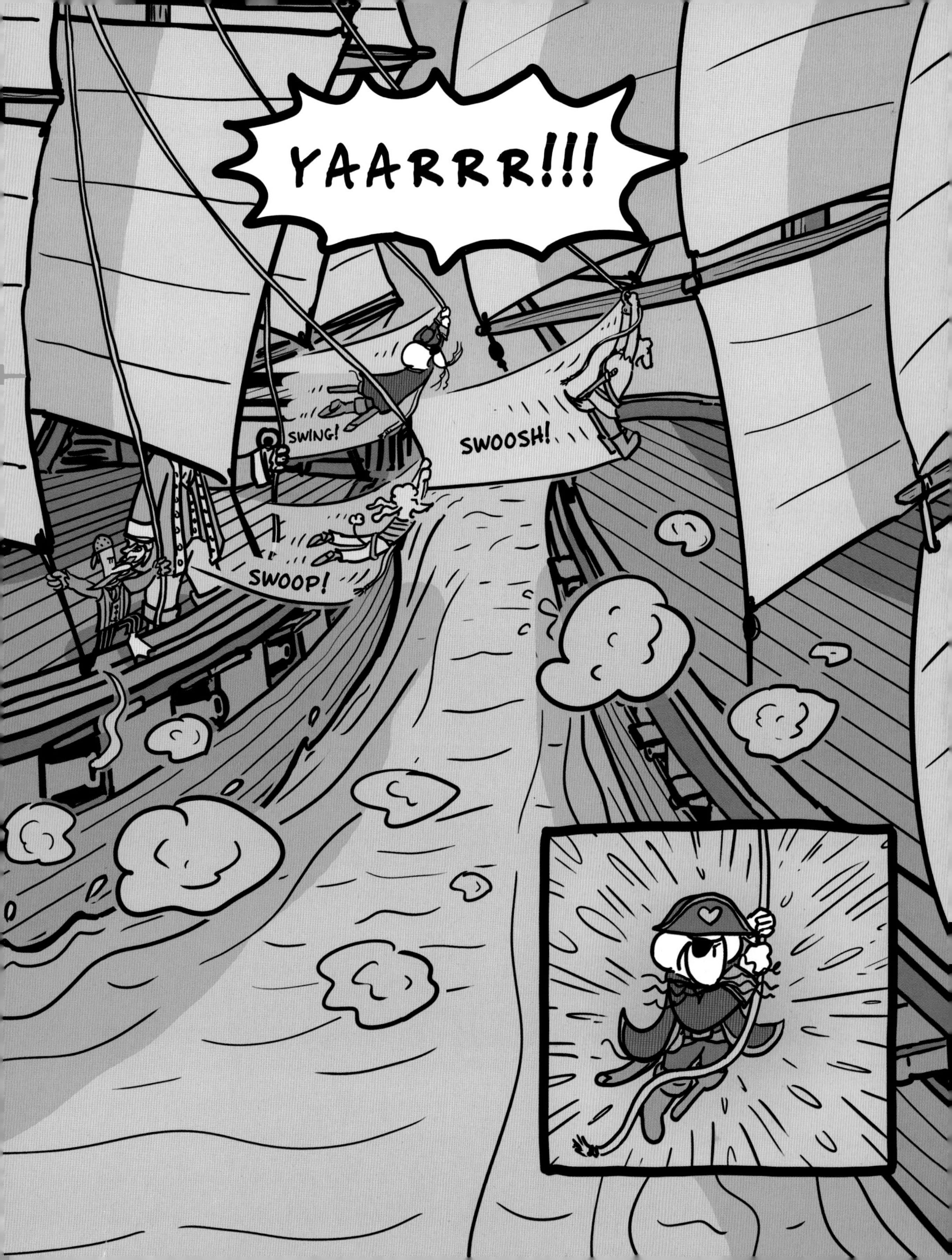
YAARRRR!!!
SWING!
SWOOSH!
SWOOP!

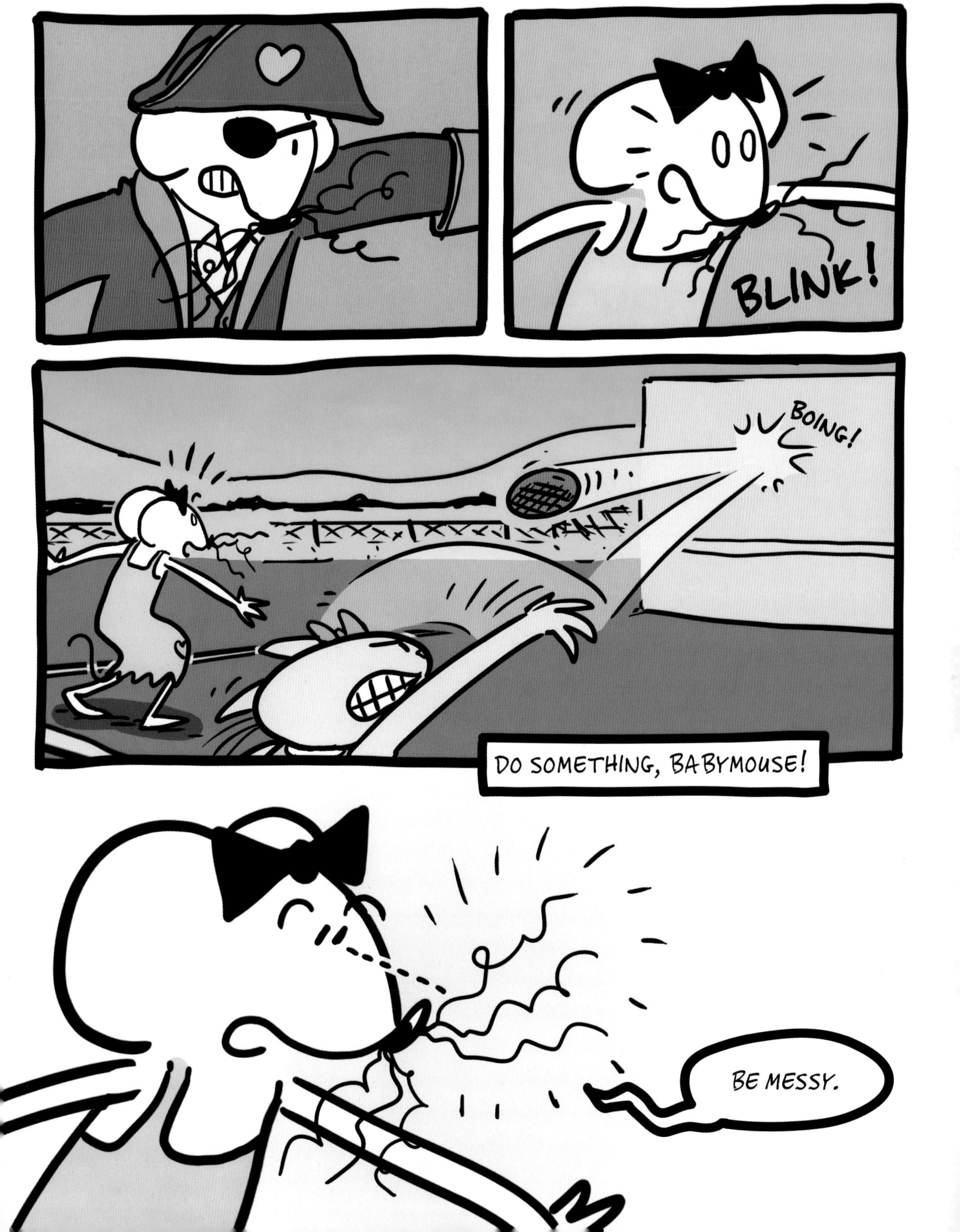
BLINK!
BOING!
DO SOMETHING, BABYMOUSE!
BE MESSY.

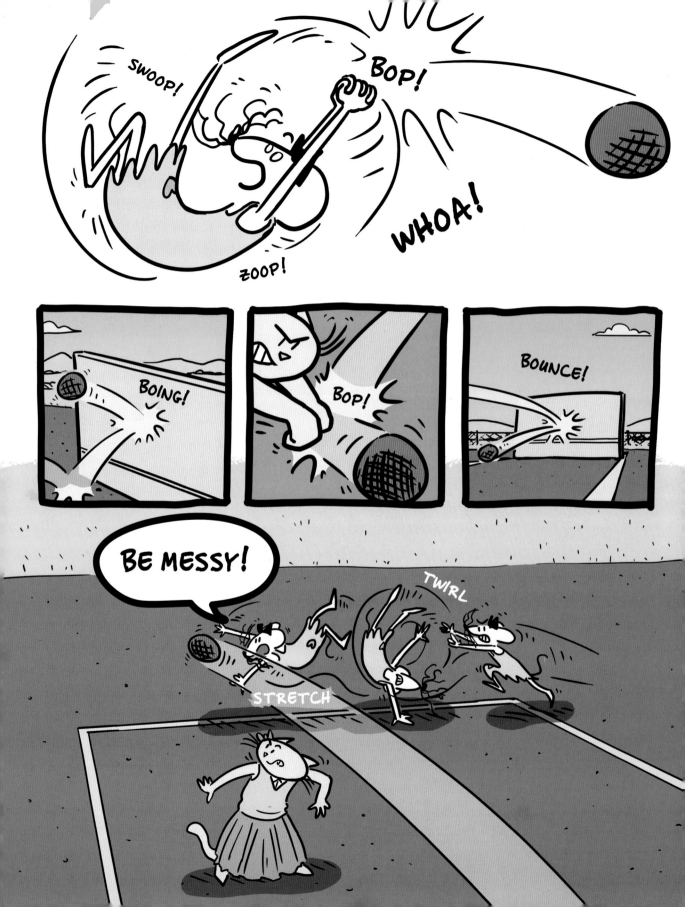

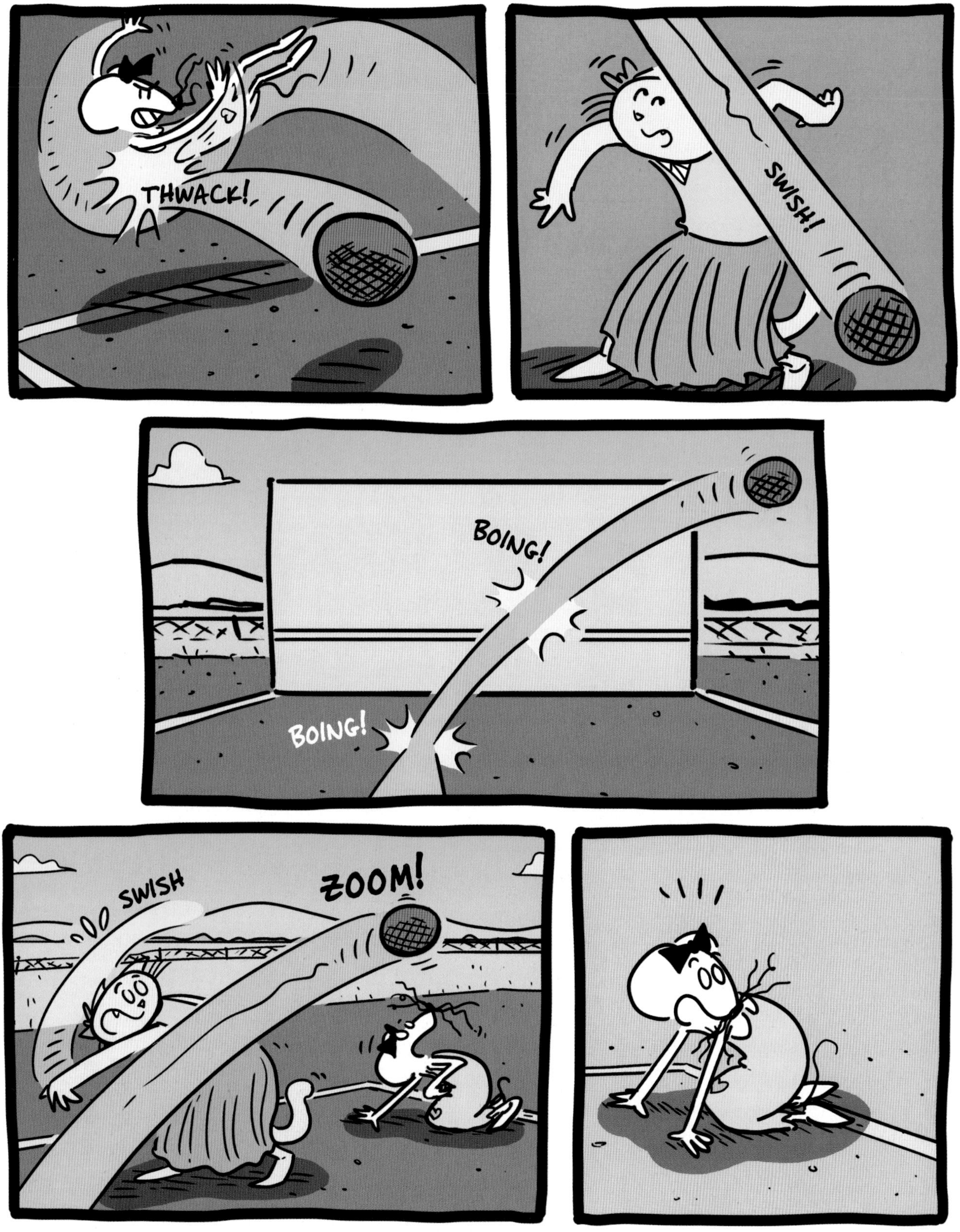
THWACK!
SWISH!
BOING!
BOING!
SWISH
ZOOM!

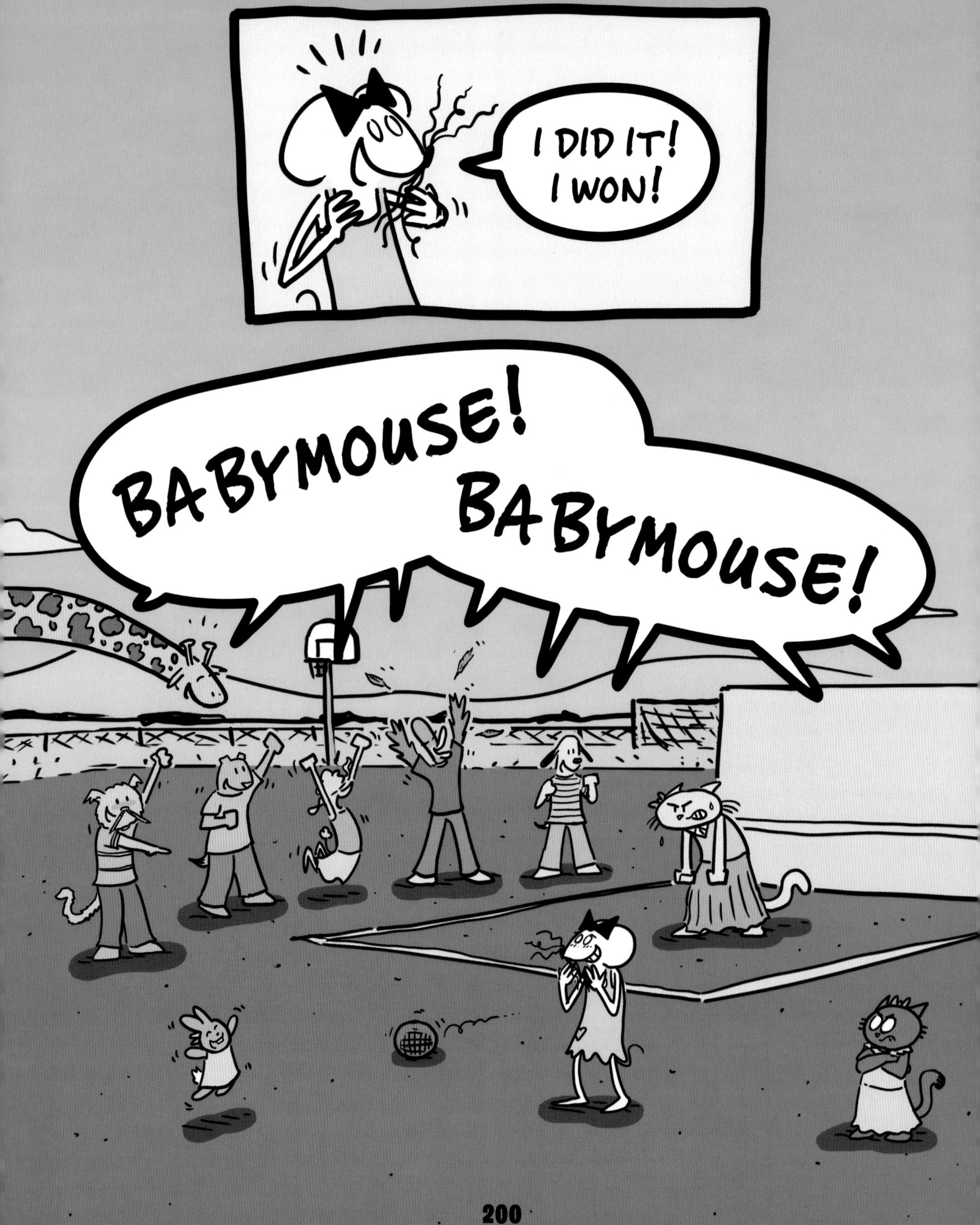
I DID IT! I WON!
BABYMOUSE! BABYMOUSE!

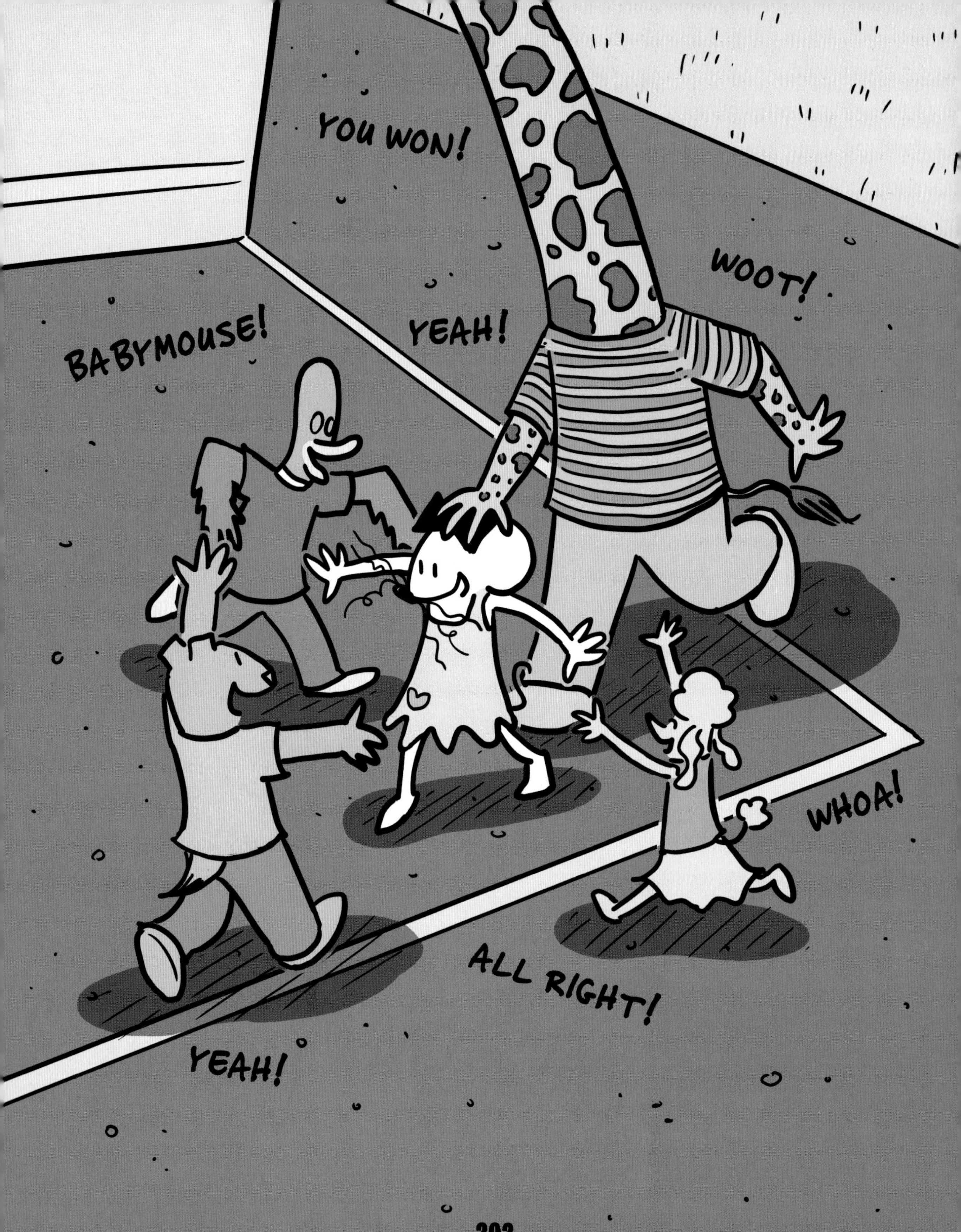
YOU WON!
WOOT!
YEAH!
BABYMOUSE!
WHOA!
ALL RIGHT!
YEAH!

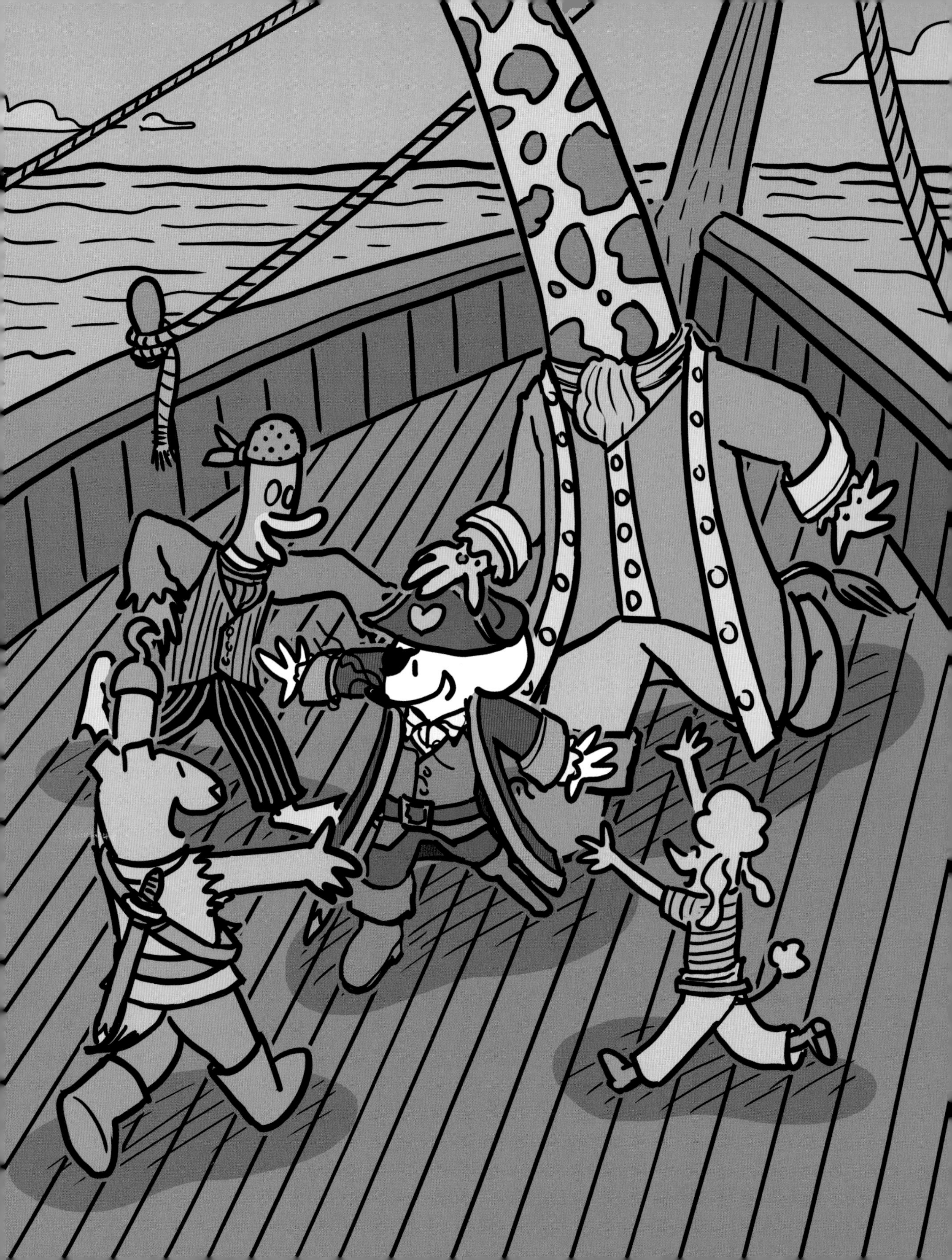

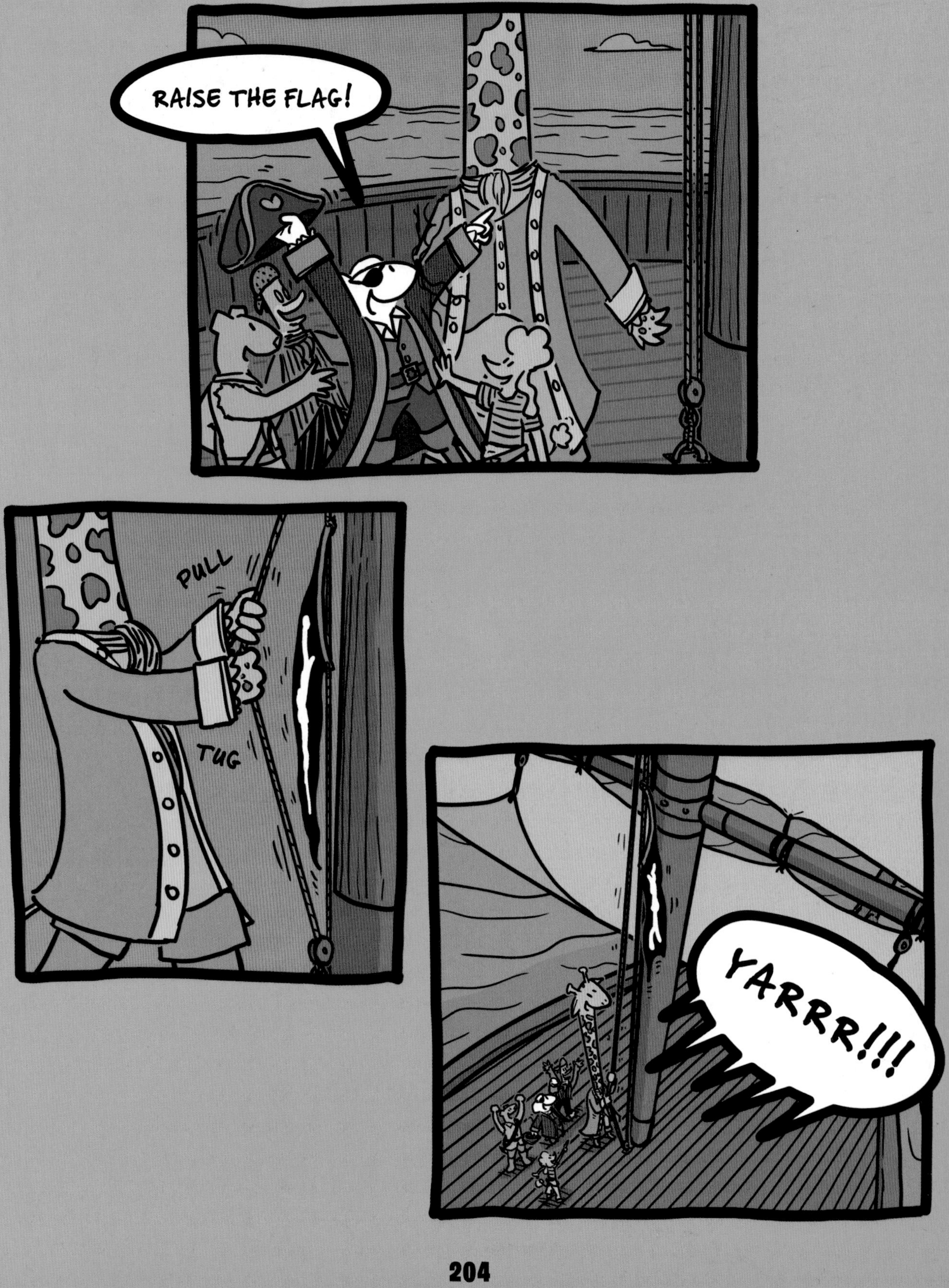
RAISE THE FLAG!
PULL
TUG
YARRR!!!

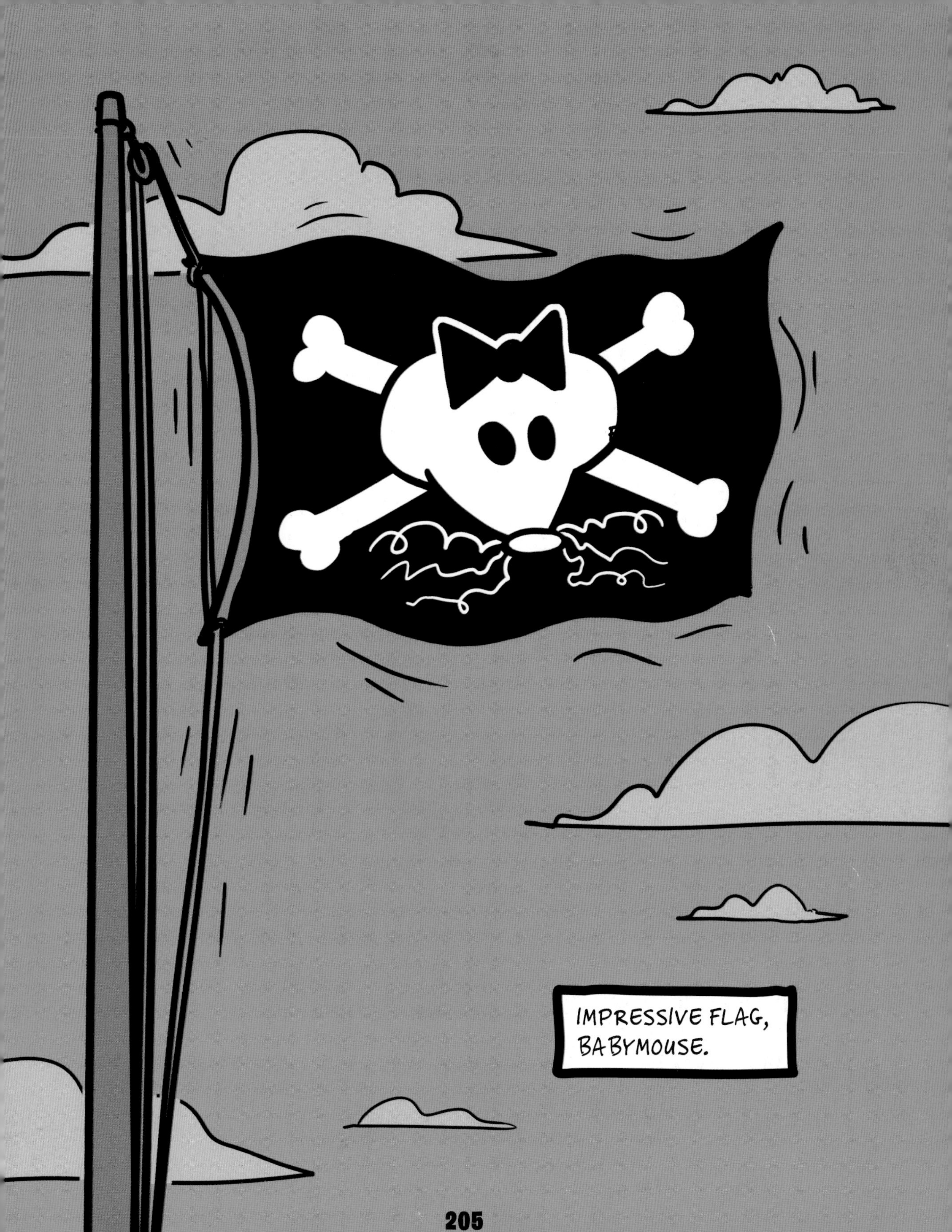
IMPRESSIVE FLAG,
BABYMOUSE.

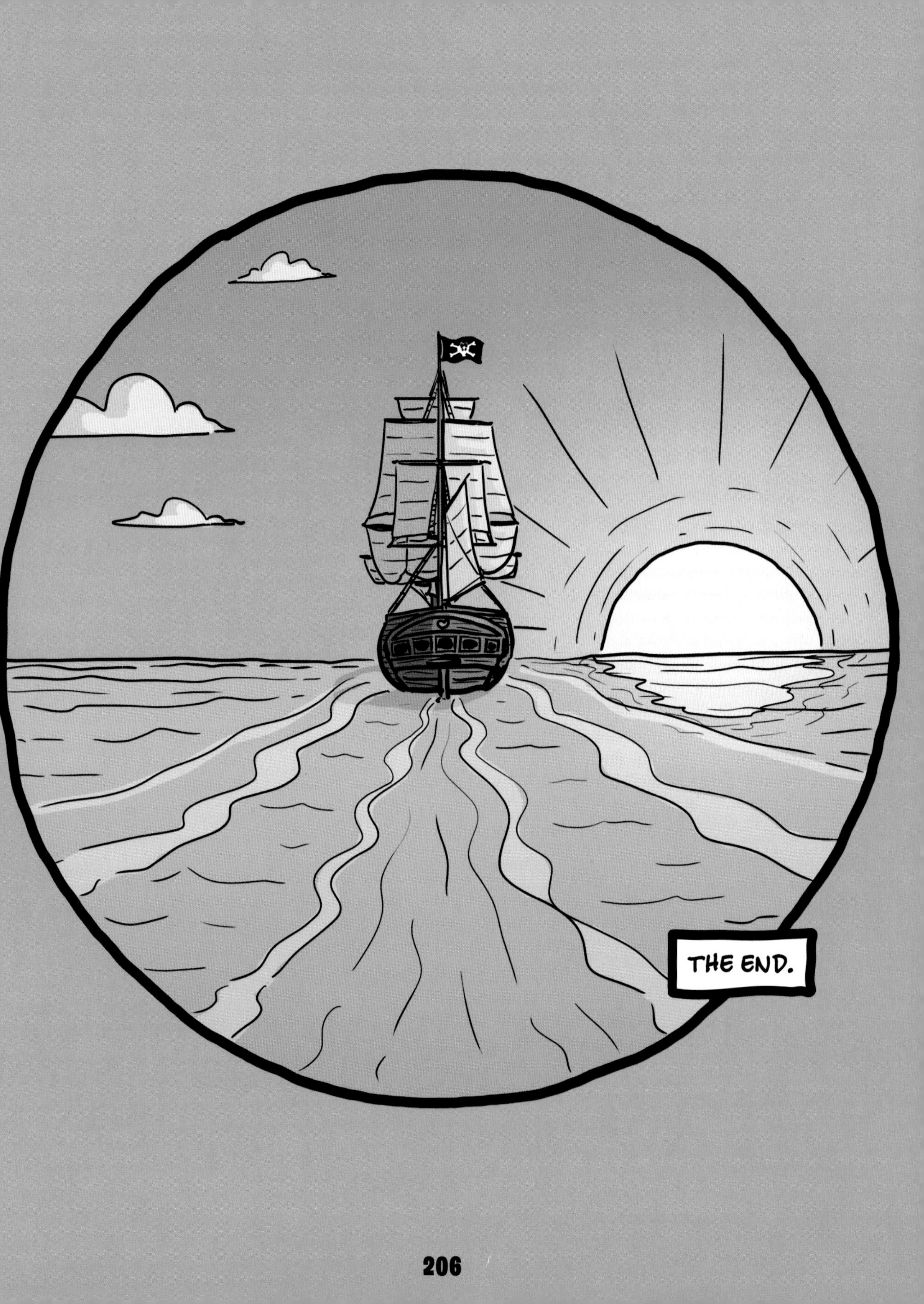
THE END.

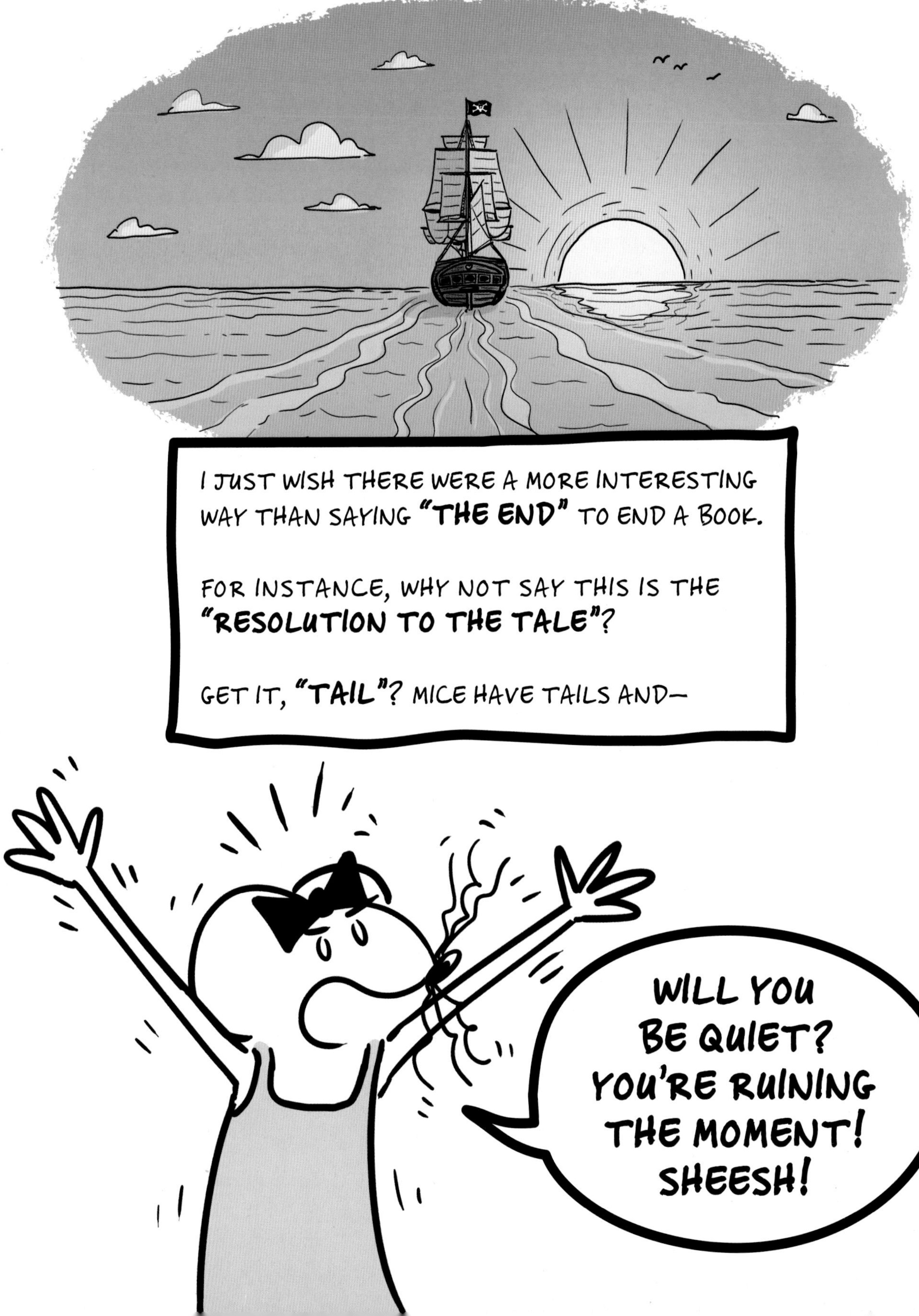
I JUST WISH THERE WERE A MORE INTERESTING WAY THAN SAYING "THE END" TO END A BOOK.
FOR INSTANCE, WHY NOT SAY THIS IS THE "RESOLUTION TO THE TALE"?
GET IT, "TAIL"? MICE HAVE TAILS AND—
WILL YOU BE QUIET? YOU'RE RUINING THE MOMENT! SHEESH!

AND NOW A WORD FROM
BABYMOUSE'S WHISKERS

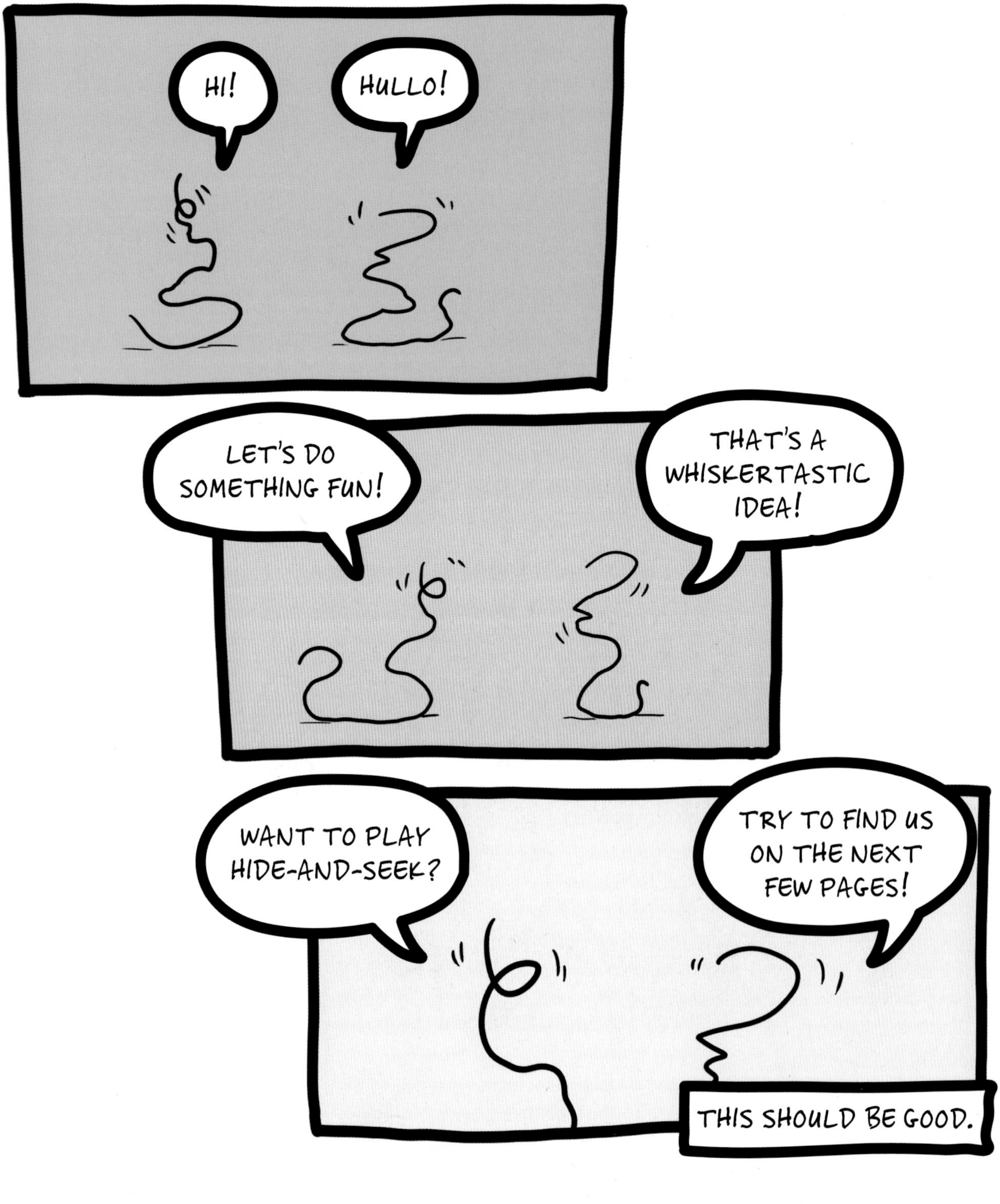
HI!
HULLO!
LET'S DO SOMETHING FUN!
THAT'S A WHISKERTASTIC IDEA!
WANT TO PLAY HIDE-AND-SEEK?
TRY TO FIND US ON THE NEXT FEW PAGES!
THIS SHOULD BE GOOD.

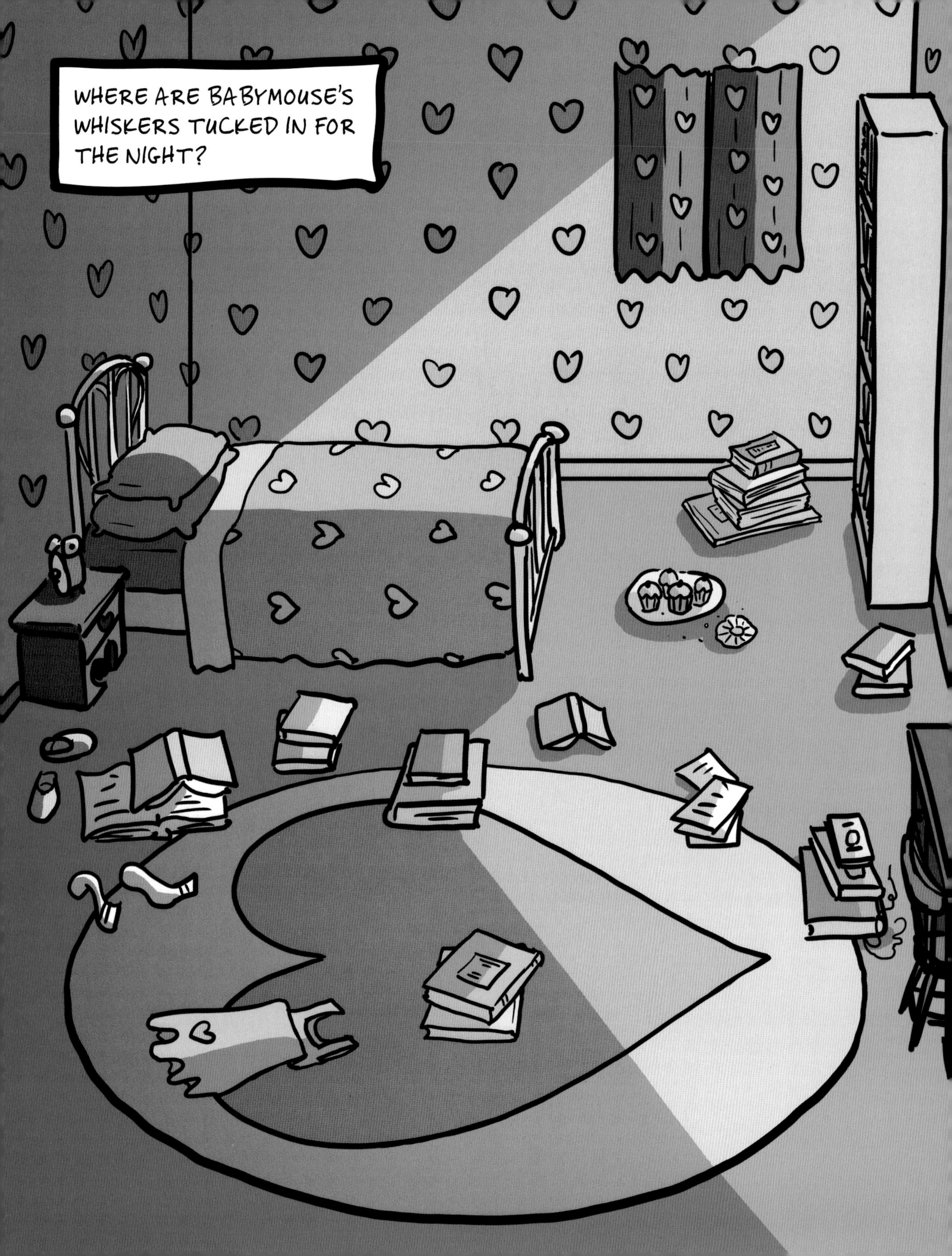
WHERE ARE BABYMOUSE'S WHISKERS TUCKED IN FOR THE NIGHT?

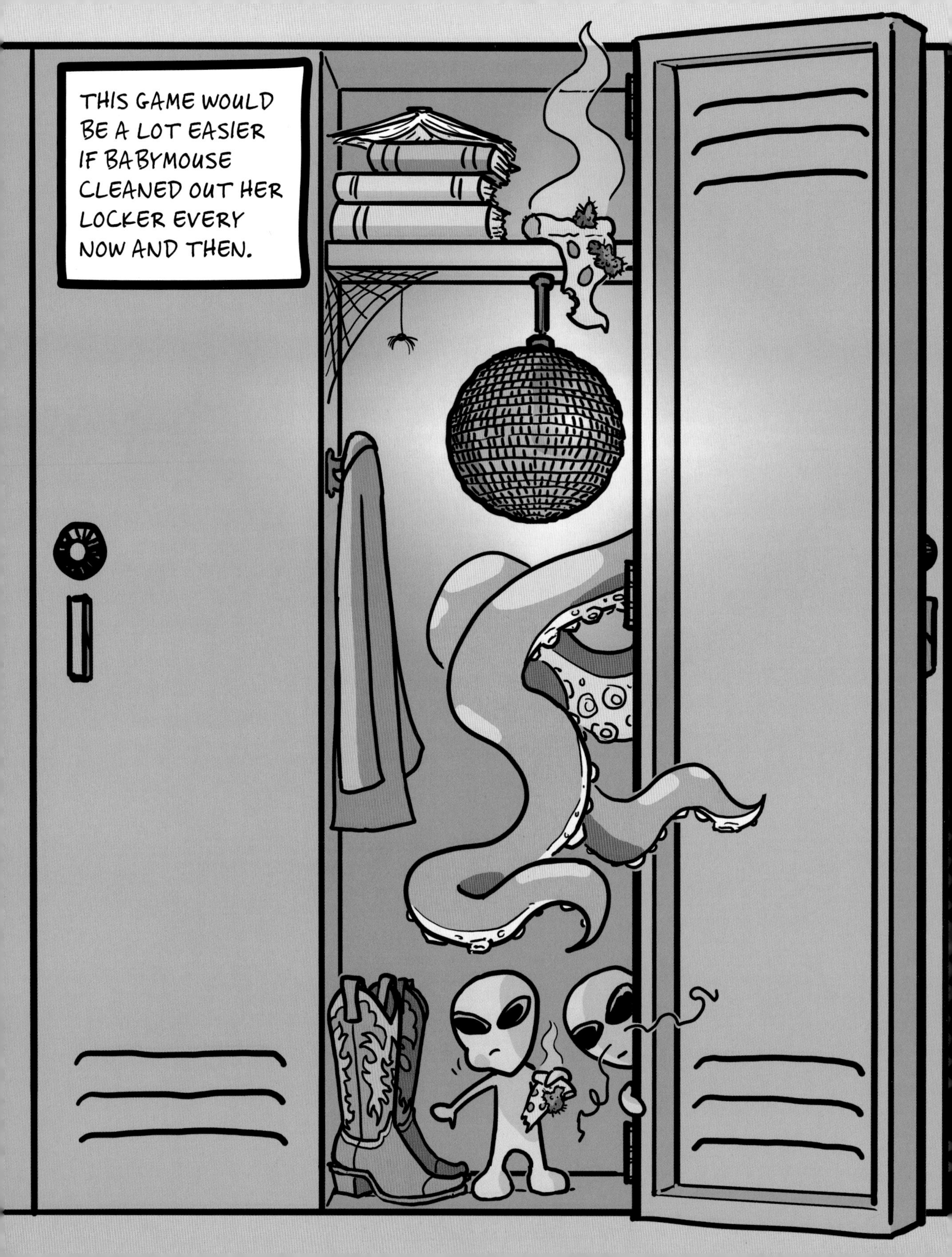
THIS GAME WOULD BE A LOT EASIER IF BABYMOUSE CLEANED OUT HER LOCKER EVERY NOW AND THEN.

Be sure to read ALL the  books:

NO ONE CAN READ JUST ONE!

 QUEEN OF THE WORLD!

OUR HERO

 BEACH BABE

ROCK STAR

HEARTBREAKER

CAMP BABYMOUSE

SKATER GIRL

PUPPY LOVE

MONSTER MASH!

THE MUSICAL

Dragonslayer

BURNS RUBBER

CUPCAKE TYCOON

MAD SCIENTIST

A VERY BABYMOUSE CHRISTMAS

FOR PRESIDENT

EXTREME BABYMOUSE

HAPPY BIRTHDAY BABYMOUSE

BAD BABYSITTER

GOES FOR THE GOLD

BABYMOUSE
TALES FROM THE LOCKER

Watch out, middle school! Here comes Babymouse.

New York Times bestselling authors of Sunny Side Up
JENNIFER L. HOLM & MATTHEW HOLM
BABYMOUSE
TALES FROM THE LOCKER
Lights, Camera, Middle School!

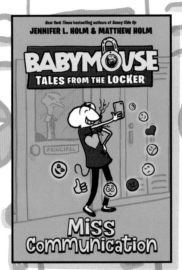

New York Times bestselling authors of Sunny Side Up
JENNIFER L. HOLM & MATTHEW HOLM
BABYMOUSE
TALES FROM THE LOCKER
PRINCIPAL
Miss Communication

New York Times bestselling authors of Sunny Side Up
JENNIFER L. HOLM & MATTHEW HOLM
BABYMOUSE
TALES FROM THE LOCKER
School-Tripped

New York Times bestselling authors of Sunny Side Up
JENNIFER L. HOLM & MATTHEW HOLM
BABYMOUSE
TALES FROM THE LOCKER
Curtain Call

New York Times bestselling authors of Sunny Side Up
JENNIFER L. HOLM & MATTHEW HOLM
BABYMOUSE
TALES FROM THE LOCKER
Whisker Wizard

IT'S GREEN....
IT'S BLOBBY....
IT'S GROSS....

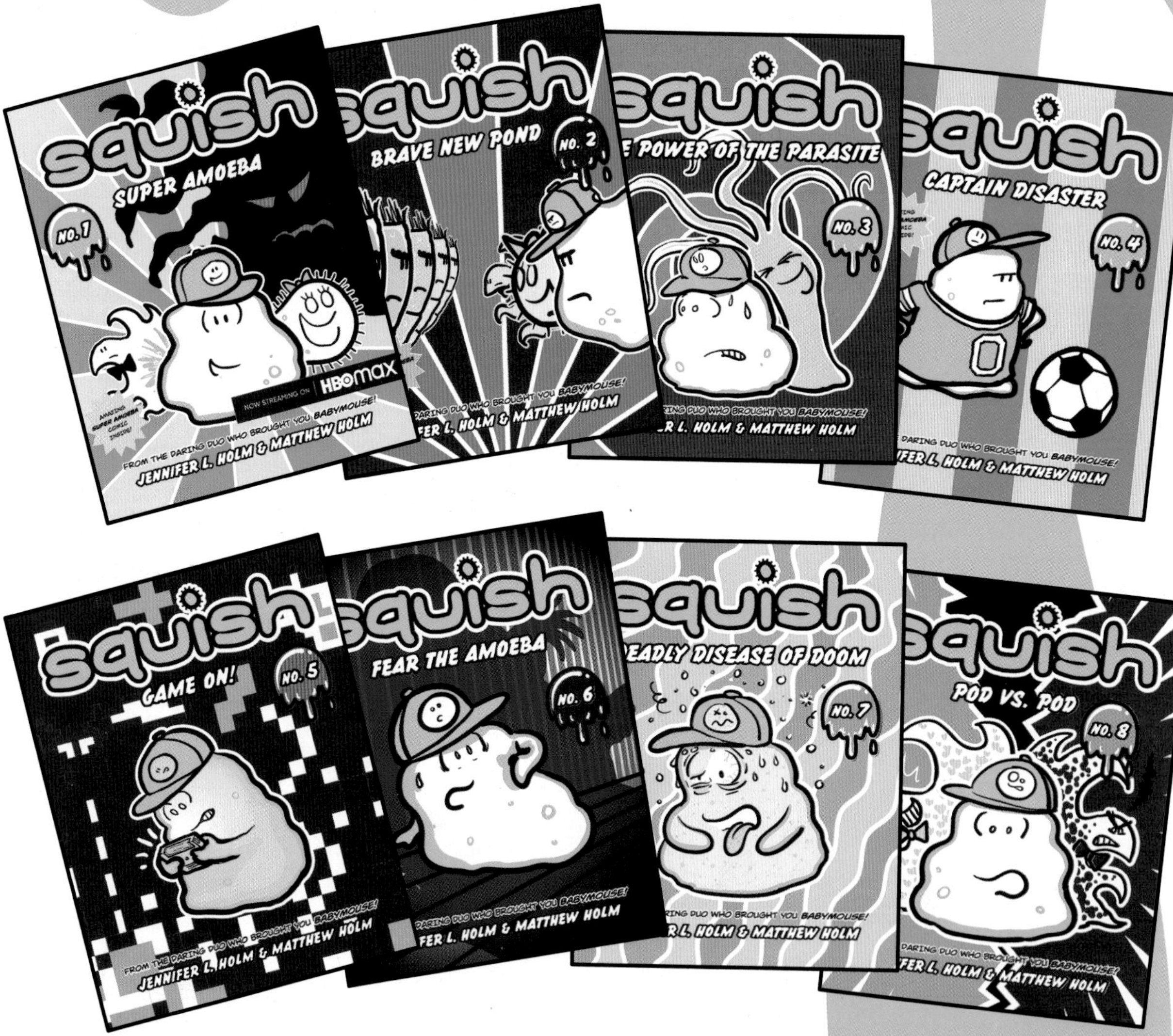
squish
SUPER AMOEBA
NO. 1
NOW STREAMING ON HBO max
FROM THE DARING DUO WHO BROUGHT YOU BABYMOUSE!
JENNIFER L. HOLM & MATTHEW HOLM
squish
BRAVE NEW POND
NO. 2
squish
POWER OF THE PARASITE
NO. 3
squish
CAPTAIN DISASTER
NO. 4
squish
GAME ON!
NO. 5
FROM THE DARING DUO WHO BROUGHT YOU BABYMOUSE!
squish
FEAR THE AMOEBA
NO. 6
squish
DEADLY DISEASE OF DOOM
NO. 7
squish
POD VS. POD
NO. 8

IT'S squish!